BLOOD KISS

Julian, who had let himself into her room while she was showering, watched Amanda. She made little noises in her sleep and twitched fitfully with nightmares. Finally, toward dawn, she settled into a deeper sleep and he stepped from the shadowed corner.

She sighed in her sleep and shivered. Julian reached down and pulled the folded bedspread up to cover her better. He thought about the first taste of blood he had taken from her before. It was different from any other, with a magic of its own. Now he would administer another bite. It would take the second of the three bites to change her. The first time may have left her a little tired, hardly enough to notice. After the second bite, she would feel tired and avoid sunlight, but revive with the coming of dusk.

After the third, she would be his creation.

Julian brushed Amanda's hair from her neck and watched the pulse of blood beneath her skin. In one fluid movement, he lowered his mouth to her neck, sensed the arterial flow, and made the bite. Hot blood, spicy-sweet, flowed into his mouth, exciting him in a way he had not experienced for five hundred years. . . .

Books by Tamara Thorne

HAUNTED

MOONFALL

ETERNITY

CANDLE BAY

BAD THINGS

THE FORGOTTEN

THUNDER ROAD

The Sorority Trilogy

EVE

MERILYNN

SAMANTHA

Published by Kensington Publishing Corporation

CANDLE BAY

TAMARA THORNE

ZEBRA BOOKS
KENSINGTON PUBLISHING CORP.
http://www.kensingtonbooks.com

ZEBRA BOOKS are published by

Kensington Publishing Corp.
119 West 40th Street
New York, NY 10018

All Kensington titles, imprints and distributed lines are available at special quantity discounts for bulk purchases for sales promotion, premiums, fund-raising, educational, or institutional use.

Special book excerpts or customized printings can also be created to fit specific needs. For details, write or phone the office of the Kensington Special Sales Manager: Kensington Publishing Corp., 119 West 40th Street, New York, NY 10018. Attn. Special Sales Department. Phone: 1-800-221-2647.

Zebra and the Z logo Reg. U.S. Pat. & TM Off.

ISBN-13: 978-1-4201-2966-0
ISBN-10: 1-4201-2966-1

First Zebra Books Mass-Market Paperback Printing: September 2012
First Pinnacle Books Mass-Market Paperback Printing: August 2001

10 9 8 7 6 5 4 3 2

Printed in the United States of America

For Chelsea Quinn Yarbro,
the very essence of a friend.

ACKNOWLEDGMENTS

Thanks to Bill Gagliani for help of an Italian nature.
To John Scognamiglio, who knows what it is.
To my darling Damien, who knows how to use it.
And to the boys for keeping me warm at night.

To die will be an awfully big adventure.

—James M. Barrie, *Peter Pan*

Prologue

Julian Valentyn watched the vampire behind the heavy iron bars. It was a male, human-born. This one belonged to the Dante family and was known as Leo. He approached the bars, and Julian took advantage of his nearness, flicking another few drops of the ancient elixir—bloodberry juice and several other things only he knew about—on the creature. Even through clothing, Leo reacted immediately, his eyes bulging, his mouth salivating, his fangs unsheathed.

The amount of potion he had absorbed over the last few weeks was enough to turn him utterly mad, and Julian had enjoyed watching the process. Now, he pushed further, out of simple curiosity. At this point, vampires reacted in various ways, but one thing was true: Given enough, half-breeds were always undone by the potion in the end.

Julian, on the other hand, thrived on it. There were only a few trueborn vampires like him left on earth, and of all of them, except one, he was the most powerful. Thanks to the elixir, he could walk by daylight if he wanted. It did other things to humans; a drop would heal a wound with amazing speed, a quarter of a teaspoon taken orally or absorbed by the skin could turn the sexual urge into an unquenchable drive. But the potion had its most dramatic effect on human-born vampires. He studied Leo Dante. The effect was cumulative; a drop a day soon allowed them to withstand more sunlight and made them less dim-witted in the daylight hours. Their human urges, always present, rarely and poorly sated, were fed because the potion allowed them to eat food and have more satisfying sex in the human fashion. It seemed to improve their senses, but it didn't; it just gave them a false sense of invincibility. Primarily it turned them more human, more primitively human, prone to acting on impulse, to overfeed, to kill unnecessarily. It removed caution and brought out the basest animal in them, but they never even knew it, such was the effect of the drug.

"Leo," Valentyn said. "Leo!"

The vampire, all drool and grunts, turned to him, confusion on his brutal face.

"I have something for you, Leo."

So saying, Julian walked to a dark corner of his sub-cellar and unlocked the manacles holding a half-dead woman off the ground. She was a redhead with lovely skin and formerly flashing green eyes. Her white skin was even paler now that he'd drunk his fill. She had put up a fight, this one, but she wouldn't be hard to handle now. He dragged her, stumbling, toward the cell built into the stone. Arriving, he used a simple glamour to frighten Leo away from the bars, making his own eyes appear to grow until that was all Leo could see, glowing, red-reflecting eyes. As soon as the vampire retreated, he unbolted the door and pushed the woman inside. She took a few staggering steps, then fell.

Leo attacked immediately, throwing himself on the woman instead of lifting her up. Gracelessly, he tore at her breast, raking his teeth up to her neck, leaving a trail of bloody gashed skin as she screamed and attempted to fight him. She was weak and he was strong. He drained her quickly, then began trying to mount her lifeless body like a canine on a human leg.

Let him have his fun. Nose wrinkled in distaste, Julian double-checked the lock, then made his way upstairs. The vampire would never see the dark of night again. As for the woman, he would put her body through the wood chipper later. As imperfect as humans were, they made excellent fertilizer.

PART ONE

Because I could not stop for Death,
He kindly stopped for me—
The Carriage held but just Ourselves
And Immortality.

—Emily Dickinson

1

They sat in armchairs of Empire styling, with swirling scrolled wooden arms, carved animal feet, and dark leather upholstery. The rest of the furniture echoed the chairs, including a graceful Grecian couch and matching curule chairs with lyre backs. An antique world globe rested on a gleaming desk. Cut crystal vases full of flowers, some winter blooms from the gardens and many more from Julian Valentyn's favorite florist, graced several small tables. Flames danced in the marble-edged fireplace. The room itself was high-ceilinged and octagonal, painted a delicate eggshell. On the walls were paintings, mostly florals, some rare, a few of which had disappeared from other collections over the years. One wall opened, via mullioned glass doors, upon a graceful terrace overlooking the estate's winter gardens.

The vampires themselves were opposite sorts, Julian winter blond and slender, dressed in a blue smoking jacket and trousers, the other, heavyset and balding, in an elegantly tailored Armani suit. A third man stood behind the heavy one, younger, tall, and imposing in a similar dark suit.

"I'm offering you something you would be foolish to refuse," said Julian as he handed the heavier man a small, ornate bottle. Valentyn's eyes, blue cracked ice beneath white-blond brows, narrowed briefly. "And my price, I believe you will agree, is small."

"That is where my concern lies." Orion moved his heavy-lidded gaze from Valentyn to the vial of amber liquid. "If this is what you say it is, it would be invaluable to our family. Isn't that right, Ivor?" He glanced back at his tall, brooding nephew.

"Yes, Uncle." Ivor was a man of few words.

Ori nodded. "But such a mixture is mythic. What you have to offer may be something else entirely."

"Perhaps it is not precisely what our legends claim, but I can prove its efficacy, my friend." Valentyn snatched up a small silver bell and rang it once, sharply. A moment later, his servant appeared, an oily, nimble sort whose rodent eyes revealed a feral intelligence.

The man sidled up to his master, his foxy gaze on Orion and Ivor. "Yes, sir?"

Valentyn took a small folding knife from his jacket pocket and flicked it open. The sharp blade gleamed. "Your wrist please, Jinxy."

The spark of fear in the man's eyes left as quickly as it arrived. He extended his arm, wrist upward. It was obvious to Ori that he had done this before.

Valentyn held Jinxy's arm steady in his left hand and put the blade to his servant's wrist, at the juncture of the palm. A drop of red blood sprung up at the knifepoint, but Jinxy didn't flinch. The knife flashed as Valentyn slid the blade several inches up the arm, laying it open. Blood gushed. Jinxy paled but remained motionless.

"Don't get your blood on my guests." Valentyn took the bottle from Ori and uncorked it. "Hold your arm over the tile, Jinxy. Don't let it spill on the rug. There now, keep still."

Jinxy's face remained tight but emotionless as he followed his master's orders. Behind Ori, Ivor shifted on his feet. Ori looked at the raw flesh and saw a flash of white bone. The blood was rich and red as it pumped rapidly out of the arm. He knew the man would faint shortly.

Valentyn dribbled some of the amber potion down the length of the wound. Immediately, amazingly, the bleeding slowed. It stopped completely in another minute.

"This is a very large, very deep wound. It's much more blood than you have to deal with ordinarily, is it not?"

Ori nodded, never taking his eyes from Jinxy's arm. *Fascinating*. The wound had begun to fill in, to heal, as he watched. The bone was already out of view and the flesh was pulling together. It truly was miraculous. *It really might be the elixir of legend.*

Valentyn, a legend himself, cleared his throat. "It will take an hour or two for such a deep injury to heal completely." He turned to his man. "Clean up this mess." He gestured at the blood.

"Yes, master." Jinxy looked at Orion again and slowly licked his lips.

Ori gazed back, still fascinated by the healing wound. So much blood. Ivor had moved closer, his massive body protectively near his uncle's.

"For your purposes," Valentyn told Ori, "a drop of the potion would heal a bite wound in moments. It might take a quarter of an hour for the scars to completely disappear. Come, Orion, let's leave Jinxy to his work."

Ori stood and accompanied Valentyn onto the terrace. Ivor followed, lingering just outside the

door, watching, always watching. Lights illuminated
the flowers, relatively sparse in winter, but what
were there were beautiful. Ori thought he smelled
jasmine, faintly, late-blooming this warmish Novem-
ber night, then picked up a whiff of musky sweetness. "I grew gardenias once, a very long time ago,"
he said fondly.

"So lush, so fragrant," Valentyn said. "Their tex-
ture is like a woman's smooth skin. I developed this
strain to bloom into December. Occasionally, Janu-
ary."

"Who tends your property?"

"I have a regular gardener in once a week, but
Jinxy sees to the flowers himself. He'll be pleased
that you approve."

Ori smiled. It amused him to think of a man like
that taking care of flowers, tending delicate dahlias
and violets and daylilies. Appearances deceived.
"Why do you want to trade all this for a suite in the
hotel?" That was Valentyn's offer: the potion for lodg-
ing. "You have a charming home here."

"It's too large." He paused. "I'm bored." Again.
"I want an extended vacation." Once more. "I want
someone else to worry about maintenance for a
change." He glanced at Ori. "You must admit it's
a good offer."

"It appears to be." He paused. "You do realize
that Candle Bay is very isolated?" He gestured beyond the garden to the lights of San Francisco.
"There's little entertainment there. Nothing like
this."

"But I would be blessed with your family's company. I would be among peers."

Ori eyed the tall pale man. Despite his slender
frame, he possessed the regal bearing of a lion. The
long silken hair, waving loosely around his shoul-

ders, only added to the effect. "We are not your peers, Julian."

Valentyn shrugged. "Most of them are gone now, and I would enjoy your company."

"There is more to it than that. Am I correct?"

Valentyn's eyebrows lifted as he smiled. "Yes, a bit more. I feel the need of your family's protection. I'm weary of constantly watching out for my own safety. Jinxy alone isn't an adequate guard at this time." He paused. "Others are after the potion. You know of the Dantes?"

"The Dantes," Ori repeated with distaste. "We've had a few run-ins recently. What would they want with a healing mixture? They aren't in the public eye as we are."

"They want the potion to sell it, I imagine. Or it may be that they want it to give their lives more subtlety, the same as you. Or perhaps they believe the Inca legends and think it does more than it really does."

"Does it?" Ori asked smoothly.

"I wish it did, but no. Yet it's invaluable just as it is."

"Your mixture in exchange for protection, room, and board. Is there anything else you want?"

"Just an adjacent room for Jinxy. Nothing fancy."

"Anything else?"

"No. Nothing else. Is this acceptable to you?"

"I'll have to discuss it with my family, of course, but I think we can make suitable arrangements."

"Good. Now, a little pleasure. Would you care to join me for a drink? I have something nice in the cellar. A sixteen-year-old Scot, I believe." Valentyn smiled for the first time. "Or perhaps he's Irish."

2

"This is Coastal Eddie on KNDL AM and FM, coming to you from Candle Bay, on the cool California coast. News flash, friends and neighbors. The Weather Bureau advises that the spring fog is going to be extra thick tonight. She's still out on the ocean, but she'll be rolling in soon. If you're a local, you know all about her, but if you're new to Candle Bay, beware! She'll hold you deep within the circle of her white, white arms and smother you against her breast. She'll blind you with her beauty, then go in for the kill. Listeners, heed my warning. Be careful on the roads tonight, lest you succumb to the lady's charms."

Amanda Pearce walked farther out on the pier, away from the fisherman with the radio. Soon, all she could hear was the low, rhythmic crash of waves far behind her and, closer, the liquid lapping of seawater against the old pier's wooden legs. A gull cried in the distance as Amanda caught the odors of the ocean, of brine and fish and creaking, ancient wood. The scent of coffee wafted through the air, then was gone, like a ghost on the wind.

As she reached the end of the pier, the breeze felt like fresh water against her skin. It blew her hair away from her face. The sun was close to the horizon now, bathed in long, ragged clouds turned salmon and lavender and apricot. It was beautiful, but the disk jockey had been right about the fog. It lay in a low blanket out to sea, waiting to fade the sunset. *It's coming closer.*

Turning, she began the walk back to her car. She had been in town for nearly twenty-four hours. Having arrived a day before she was expected at the Candle Bay Hotel and Spa, where her new career awaited her, she had chosen, out of a sense of adventure, to spend the night at a run-down motel where she slept in a tiny room full of mildew and damp. The water tasted like sulphur and the walls were so thin that she'd overheard the frantic lovemaking of the woman in the next room throughout the night. She was conducting a brisk business. Cars came and went, and sometimes in between, Amanda found fitful sleep, but it was full of nightmares about running, lost, along long hotel corridors that telescoped more with each step, that twisted and turned like a mad hatter's path. Once, twice, three times during the night she'd risen from the lumpy bed to look out the window, only to see the fog. It had rolled in at sunset and stayed to shroud the town until morning; then it slowly, so slowly, burned off to reveal a dank, gray sky, which hadn't cleared until an hour ago.

Unlocking her red Civic, she slid into the seat and peered out to sea. The seascape was punctuated with buildings and vehicles and a sprinkling of pines. The fog had sneaked up on her and now the low rolling blanket, wadded dirty cotton, seeped around the edges of the buildings, smothering them. She started the car and backed out of the slot. If she was stuck racing the fog to the hotel, then she'd do her best to win.

Behind her, the fog crept across the beach road, ready to caress downtown Candle Bay, swallowing cars and people and buildings. She could see the tops of tall conifers above the foggy mantle as she drove east, toward the low rolling hills where the Candle Bay Hotel and Spa awaited.

Despite the fog, she had spent the day in town, trying to get to know her new home. The town wasn't as repulsive as the motel she'd slept in. Nor was it a tourist attraction, though it tried to be in its own peculiar fashion. You could walk an old boardwalk along the beach, seeing nothing but vague outlines of small buildings, concession stands, and game shacks, all of them closed on weekdays. Fragile bones of a roller coaster and Octopus ride loomed in the mist, and the Tilt-a-Whirl cars looked like humped mushrooms in the dank grayness.

The town itself had several nice, newer neighborhoods, but older streets were lined with drab, monotonously square clapboard houses sheathed in faded paint, peeling and blistered from dampness. The business blocks were comprised primarily of equally simple wood or stucco buildings, many two-storied, some vacant, most dismal and vaguely ominous. She wondered why. Perhaps it was because everything was weirdly neat and well-swept for a town that appeared to be half-deserted. A brochure she had picked up at the chamber of commerce called Candle Bay the "New England Village of the West Coast." Truth in advertising was not one of the town's assets, unless they were referring to a village created by H.P. Lovecraft.

The sun was almost down as she drove up the curving road into the hills outside of town. She couldn't see the hotel yet—it was nestled low in the hills—but farther up, in the last of the sunlight, she saw hills dotted with gravestones, boneyard after boneyard. Mortuaries and mausoleums hulked here and there. Candle Bay made a good income taking in the dead from as far away as San Luis Obispo to the south and Monterey to the north. She felt the chill of the fog, grayish-dank, as it began to engulf her car from behind, and she turned on the radio, not wanting to be alone and blind.

"The fog has come to call, ladies and gents, and she's especially affectionate tonight," Coastal Eddie crooned. "Her name is Medusa, and she's looking for love, so be warned, my friends. Lock your doors and windows, lest you find yourself entwined in those long, deadly tendrils."

"Christ," Amanda said as the disc jockey's words faded into John Carpenter's theme from *The Fog*. She turned off the radio and slowed to a crawl. She could still see a few yards ahead of her, though she doubted that would last long. At least she was close to the hotel. *Probably.*

The hotel. The Candle Bay Hotel and Spa. She had saved it for last. A treat. She had only seen pictures of it before today, but she had loved it since she was a child. The pictures of the graceful Spanish-style building affected her in a strange way, and now the photographs of the maze of the theme gardens—not many years old but large and lush— drew her as well. She was from Seattle and had never even been in Candle Bay before, but she felt like she belonged here. *You're drawn to it.* Or maybe, she thought, the fog was just familiar, maybe that was all it was. But since the first time she'd seen the photo of the hotel in a travel magazine, she had been fascinated by it, perhaps in love with it.

*So why did you spend the night in that fleabag motel?
Who knows.* A whim, something to make her really
appreciate the luxurious Candle Bay Hotel when
she finally saw it.

She gasped as something tall moved on the road
ahead of her. Slamming on the brakes, she waited
for a sickening thud, but none came. *It must have
run out of the way.* It had been a person, she was
sure. Unless, she thought as she started moving
again, it was just a quirk of the fog, a shadow mis-
understood.

It happened again a moment later, upsetting her
so much that if she'd been able to see the side of
the road, she would have pulled over. Her hands
trembled on the wheel and she prayed she wouldn't
hit anything or be hit. She was as invisible as the
specters she imagined.

The third time, it happened so quickly that she
thought she saw a dark grayish form right at the
driver's side window. It peered in at her, a suggestion
of a face, a cruel face, leering. *It's your imagination!
Shadows and fog.* Instead of slowing, she sped up the
tiniest bit, and checked to make sure her door was
locked. A bird's screech sounded like a scream.

She rounded a curve and saw the hotel, a gleaming jewel. Magnificent, it grew out of the fog, a
shimmering peach ghost near the top of a hill. Fog
eddied and swirled below it, full of dancing phan-
toms, full of secrets.

An elegant Spanish citadel, the aging hotel had
seen its heyday decades ago. She knew it had been
recently restored, but even from the outside, it carried an atmosphere of fading opulence.

The private road was just visible to her right. She
turned, seeing twelve-foot wrought-iron gates to
either side. A rectangular shadow, whiter than the

fog, loomed on the left; then she made out dull
yellow light in the windows. A figure—absolutely
real this time—came out of the building. Relieved,
she stopped and rolled down her window.

Nails clicked against the door as a pair of hands
came to rest on her windowsill. Masculine hands,
large and square, with longish, thick nails. There was
dirt under them. The face that followed was middle-
aged, long, with rubbery smiling lips. The man's eyes
twinkled, reflecting the smile, making it real.

"Good evening, miss. Welcome to the Candle Bay
Hotel and Spa." He glanced up, then held her
gaze. "Looks like you made it just in time."

"Hi," she said, slightly jarred by the man's frank
stare. "I'm Amanda Pearce. I'm—"

"You're expected. Come to help us run the hotel,
did you?"

"Well, I wouldn't put it that way. I'm just supposed to assist the concierge."

"Heard all about you. Been to college and everything."

"Well, yes, but—"

"I'm Eliot Lucre. Night watchman. Just came on
duty." He extended his hand. The flesh was as cool
and damp as the evening air. "Welcome to our little
family." He held her hand an instant too long.

"Thank you, Mr. Lu—"

"Eliot. We're informal around here, Amanda."

After parking, Amanda entered the hotel through
the main entrance and stood, captivated, in the im-
mense lobby. A classical guitar played softly in the
background, and she realized the music wasn't
canned, but came from a musician sitting near a
baby grand. *Nice.*

A Spanish-tiled fountain graced the center of the massive room, and from it flowed a tiered stream, water bubbling over cobalt-blue tiles edged with ornate multicolored tiles. It ended in a koi pond only a few feet from where Amanda stood, near the grand entrance. Little bridges allowed people to traverse the bubbling water.

She thought she caught a faint hint of mildew in the air, but it was gone in an instant, lost in the fresh smell of lush tropical plants, luxuriant beneath arched skylights of stained glass. Rubber trees, succulents, and ferns cast their shadows across the terra-cotta floors. Large patterned area rugs took their color cues from the terra-cotta and cobalt tiles as well as the subtle yellow and red detailing of the tile's edging. Amanda felt dwarfed and out of place in the luxurious room.

The furniture—sofas, chairs, and assorted tables—was an eclectic mix of Arts and Crafts, Mission, and Art Nouveau styles. The predominantly dark furniture in the high-ceilinged, airy room held an air of aging elegance, making her think of the opulence of the 1920s. She could imagine men and women in evening wear, tuxedos and long clinging dresses. There would be cummerbunds and carnations, and tiny sequined handbags, as well as trumpet-sleeved evening coats with fur-trimmed collars. The women would have sleekly waved hair, seal-like, trimmed with combs shaped like butterflies or conch shells. Pearls. There would be lots of pearls.

Oh, snap out of it, Amanda. Chiding herself, she walked in the general direction of the walnut registration counter that ran half the width of the lobby. Around her were people, standing, sitting, talking, silent, laughing, holding hands. On the walls, just out of reach, were black sconces bearing blue candles, interspersed with arched, stained-glass windows, simple and darkish, and paintings, most of them of the sea, a few of Candle Bay, or the hotel itself. A bellman pushing an empty luggage rack smiled at her. She smiled back, then veered toward the concierge's desk, located under one of the colorful arched windows. The young man at the desk was helping a casually dressed couple with dinner reservations. He wore a tasteful dark suit and his face was handsome, with chiseled features that gave way to dimples when he smiled. His lips were full and red and his eyes, they were blue and dancing. *Stop staring. He might be your boss.*

She felt herself blush as the couple moved away, leaving her face-to-face with him.

He smiled at her. "May I help you?"

"I'm Amanda Pearce. Is the manager available?"

"I'm Tyler Shane." His smile broadened, showing straight white teeth. "You're my new right-hand woman."

"Yes." She blushed more furiously than before. "Yes, I think I am."

The young man stood and came around the desk, extending his hand. His shake was cool, firm, and dry. "I'm the head concierge from five to midnight. Those will be your hours too, at least while you're in training. Natasha or Stephen—our managers— should show up soon. Meanwhile, let me show you around. Just a moment." He walked over to the registration counter and spoke briefly with a pretty young woman with long blond hair.

She followed him over, smiling at Amanda as she took the seat at the desk. "I'm Carol Anne. Registration and reservations."

"Nice to meet you. I'm Amanda."

"I steal Carol Anne frequently," Tyler said. He

turned to the woman, a girl really. "We won't be too long. Thanks for covering."

Tyler guided Amanda toward the fountain. "The hotel was built in 1917. This has been here from the beginning. The stream and pond too."

"It's beautiful."

"Originally, a monastery stood in this spot. According to legend, there are tunnels leading from here to the top of the hills. The monks used them to escape Indian and pirate attacks."

"Pirates?" she asked in surprise. "Here?"

"Oh, yes. Red Cay, down the coast a little ways, got the worst of it, but there were rumors that the monks protected a huge fortune within the monastery. Pirates raided regularly. But if there was a fortune, the monks took it with them into the tunnels and no one's ever found an entrance. When Joshua Case, the newspaper magnate, had the monastery torn down to build this hotel, it's rumored that he found at least one tunnel entrance and incorporated it into the design of the hotel."

"How exciting!"

Tyler smiled. "No one's ever found anything, though."

"Why did he build here? Was the town more lively back then? Is this fog unusual?"

Tyler chuckled. "Not much more lively and the fog comes nearly every day. He built here to take advantage of the natural hot springs. He thought it would make a great retreat for the wealthy. Some people came just to relax. Others took cures, exercised, ate whatever was considered health food at the time."

"It must have been magnificent. I've seen pictures, but it's so much more. It's haunted by the past." *Stop gushing! God, you sound like a bad movie on Lifetime.*

Tyler nodded. "The lobby and the spas are very much as they were in 1917. The pool area has been restored to its original look as well. Do you know much about the hotel?"

"Not enough," Amanda said, accompanying Tyler up a curving flight of stairs to a mezzanine overlooking the lobby. At the far end was a bar with small round tables set up near the railing. "Would you care for something to drink?" he asked.

"No, thanks." She leaned against the railing and he did the same.

"The hotel's gone through a lot of changes over the years. It's hosted the famous and infamous. Its heyday was in the twenties and thirties, when its spas were renowned worldwide. There were parties every night, even during Prohibition, when the hotel was rumored to have the finest gin in California." He smiled. "After Joshua Case died, things quieted down. In the forties and fifties the hotel was popular with wealthy polio victims. Also, there was a lot of business with people traveling between Los Angeles and San Francisco, that is, until everyone got in a hurry and started taking the Interstate."

Shaking his head, he continued. "Business never was the same without Case at the helm. There were beautiful resorts in nicer—and sunnier—coastal towns and the hotel started falling into disrepair. By the early sixties, the Candle Bay Hotel and Spa was just too isolated to attract the type of clientele such a luxurious place required to earn its keep. The place went up for sale and was empty for a few years, but in the late sixties, it was reopened under new management and it attracted a lot of people in the rock-and-roll community. They built a small amphitheater just over the hill and lots of people came for a while. Management was smart enough to intersperse rock with classical music, attracting a much bigger clientele than with rock only. The hotel contributed to fixing up the boardwalk at the beach to attract more people, but with the fog, it never did too well. It's only open on weekends during spring and summer now. It doesn't make any money, but the town likes to keep up appearances."

"The inhabitants don't seem the type to encourage tourism," Amanda said. "I could hardly get two words out of most of them."

Tyler nodded. "That's part of the problem." He chuckled. "Maybe that's a good thing since half of them are either morticians or work for one."

"I noticed the cemeteries," she said. "So what happened to the hotel?"

"It started losing money. Its reputation as a rock-and-roll haven backfired after a weekend concert got out of hand. The clientele, including the bands, were tough on the place, and although they still made money letting film crews use the building, management began discouraging the rockers. There was too much vandalism and a number of murders occurred in those years. There was vandalism in the cemeteries too. Cultists, drunken bums, all of that. This stuff happened in earlier years too, but with Case in charge, everything was swept under the rug. It was easy to do when there was plenty of money."

"The hotel is beautiful now."

"Yes." Pride swept over Tyler's face. "After the boardwalk closed in the seventies, the hotel closed again, this time for twenty years. The place began to decay and they boarded it up. That didn't keep anybody out, though. Teenagers threw parties and used it as a make-out spot. A few more people were killed and it got a reputation as being haunted. There was some drug traffic and drifters still broke in and slept there, but not much else.

"Finally, in 1992, your new employer, Moonlight, Inc., bought the hotel. It's a family-owned business. Did you meet Eliot at the gate?"

"Yes, I did."

"He's a cousin of the Darlings. That's the family name." Tyler smiled. "Anyway, they sent him here to guard the place while it was being restored. He still lives in the gardener's cottage, in fact, just like when he first came here. Renovation took several years, and then we had the grand reopening."

"You were there?"

"I was fresh out of school. I started as an accountant, but I couldn't stand it, keeping company with numbers all day. I like people. Now I'm working my way into a management position. Anyway, to make a long story short, the Darlings have updated things and found ways to cut costs so that our prices aren't any higher than those of other nice hotels along the central coast. We have separate charges for using the spa, the gym, things like that, instead of including it all in one price, as it had been in the past. We attract a lot more clientele this way. We're sort of a Club Med for people who can't quite afford the real thing. We have the spas, the indoor pool, a gym, game rooms, one for kids and one for adults, several restaurants, even a small theater. We have tennis courts and there's talk of a golf course, though we're a little worried about the view of the cemeteries."

"But the fog."

"It's often sunny in the hills. The fog lays low."

"How often is often?"

He grinned. "About half the time. When it's sunny it's beautiful. The boardwalk's still closed most of the time, but we use the amphitheater for classical concerts—we have weekends of Bach, Mozart, Beethoven, you know?"

"That sounds nice. I'm a secret Mozart fan."

"Me too," he said, gazing at her. "Let's go back downstairs and I'll show you the kitchen, the spas and pool, and I think I can take you into some of the theme rooms. Carol Anne will know which ones aren't booked. You'll want to see the public rest rooms too, though we'll have to wait till the wee hours to sneak you into the men's room. It's amazing."

Information overload! "Theme rooms?"

"They're very popular. The Darlings designed them. There's Arabian Nights, the Princess's Turret Room, the Desert Island, the Renaissance Room, the Cave, Dracula's Castle, things like that." His eyes twinkled. "We have several dungeon rooms. Very popular. We don't advertise those, but word gets around. We also have a number of other rooms devoted to romance of various kinds. They're usually booked a year in advance. We have several suites for guests, including one honeymoon. There are more suites, but the Darlings live in them."

"I had no idea," Amanda said as they walked toward the kitchen. "Um, I understood that I'd have a room here?"

"Yes. Not a theme room, but the Darlings encourage single employees to live here. Free room and board in exchange for a slightly lower salary. It's well worth it."

"Do you live here?" she asked, wondering if he was single.

"Yes. You'll be a few doors away from me. The rooms are very nice. I think you'll be pleased."

"I'm pleased I don't have to find a place in town. This is much nicer."

3

"Is that the new girl?" Ivy Darling asked her sister Lucy as they watched Tyler Shane escort the young woman into the pool area. The girls stood in the shadows of an arch in the hallway.

"Must be," said her twin, twirling a long lock of dark hair around her finger. "Tyler's such a good boy, you know. Won't leave his desk unless it's business."

"You're just mad because you couldn't seduce him," Ivy observed.

"I had him anyway."

"Slut."

"Look who's talking."

"You're not supposed to mess with the help," Ivy said. "Natasha will have your head if I tell her you've been at them again."

"But you won't tell." Lucy touched her twin's cheek gently, trailing her finger down to her lips.

Ivy moved back, out of reach. "What makes you think that?"

"You've done it too. I could tell on *you*."

"Only once," countered Ivy. "That chef. He was just too adorable to resist. And he smelled good.

Like lamb and mint. You've fucked lots of employ-ees."

"Ivy, is this true?"

She jumped at her older brother's voice. "Stephen!" she said as he joined them. "You shouldn't spy on us."

"You two should speak more softly," he said, frowning. "Anyone, including guests, could have heard you."

Ivy stared at her brother, all innocence, while Lucy tried to grind her foot into the floor. "She did it too," she said at last.

"Only once," Ivy said haughtily. "And it was a long time ago. She's the slut, Stevie, not me."

Stephen rounded on them, his dark eyes flashing. "Don't do it again. Either of you. We don't need more trouble. Where's Ivor?"

Ivor was another brother, one who watched out for the vampires and the human one who kept the guests. "He's with Uncle Ori," Ivy said.

Stephen nodded. "I see. Since it's all just hearsay, I'm not going to speak to Natasha. But if either of you does anything, anything at all, she's going to hear about it. Is that understood?"

"Yes, Stephen," Lucy said sweetly. "We promise."

"Well, I do anyway," Ivy said.

Her sister elbowed her in the ribs. "Bitch."

"Slut."

They giggled together as Stephen turned and walked away.

"Tyler?"

They turned at the deep, rich voice that came from behind as they waited for the elevator.

"Hello, Stephen," Tyler said. "Stephen's our assistant manager. Stephen, this is Amanda Pearce, our new assistant concierge."

Stephen extended his hand. "It's good to meet you, Amanda."

"You too," Amanda managed as they shook hands. His touch was electrifying. It had to be her imagination, but the thrill traveled all the way to her toes. Candle Bay might not be much to look at, but judging by Tyler Shane and Stephen Darling, the men were exceptional. Especially Stephen. He looked to be in his mid-twenties, but his piercing gaze made him seem much older. His eyes were nearly as black as his hair, and they melted her on the spot. He wore a suit even nicer than Tyler's, and it fit his broad-shouldered physique perfectly.

"We were just going upstairs to see a few of the rooms," said Tyler.

"Tyler, go ahead back to your desk. I'll finish the tour and introduce Amanda to Natasha."

"Sure. See you later, Amanda."

"Bye."

"What has Tyler shown you?"

Stephen's voice was riveting, and she turned to look at his face. He was mesmerizing. *Your hormones are out of control!* "Quite a bit," she told him. "The whole first floor, I think. We were going up to see a few of the theme rooms."

"Those will wait, I think. You need to meet Natasha while she's available. Come with me."

They walked up to the mezzanine and Stephen led her to the right, away from the bar. There were several heavy, carved doors along the back wall, all shut, with a camera mounted from the ceiling that covered all of them. There were intercom switches at each door. Two bore tasteful "No Admittance" placards, and a third was marked "Administration" in small gold lettering.

"Where do those two doors lead?" Amanda asked as Stephen took a key card from his pocket and swiped in the administration door's lock.

"Family quarters," he said, opening the door on a long corridor. "We occupy several suites through-out the hotel. The first door leads to a small private wing and the second to areas behind and above the lobby. They shouldn't concern you. You may use the intercom if you ever need to contact us when we're off duty. It's unlikely you will, however. Come this way."

She accompanied him down the dark carpeted hallway, passing doors with labels like "accounting" and "housekeeping manager." "You'll have a card key like mine for this area, but you'll have to be buzzed in here," he said as they arrived at a set of double doors at the end of the corridor, where an-other camera oversaw everything. "These are our private offices."

He used a regular key on the dead-bolt lock and opened one of the doors. "After you."

She stepped into a small lobby where soft classical music, Mozart, filled the air. An Oriental rug, rich with purples, reds, and deep blues, covered the floor. There were two art-deco-flavored chairs and a matching loveseat in the room, plus a sleek black lacquer coffee table that held several un-dog-eared magazines. A small black enamel reception desk sat in a corner, but no one manned it. Three doors presumably led to offices, though they were un-marked.

Stephen pointed to the left-hand door. "That's my office." He indicated the right one. "Several of our family members' offices are behind that door. And this"—he gestured straight ahead—"is the manager's office, where we should find my sister, Natasha." He rapped on the door once, twice. He tried the intercom.

"She must have already gone out. We'll have to try again later." He moved to the right-hand door and knocked. Amanda heard the buzz of the camera as it shifted position. Then the intercom came to life. "Come in, Stephen," said a gravelly voice. The door clicked and Stephen pushed it open to reveal three more doors, one a double set. He escorted her to the double doors. There was an electronic noise, then they opened.

The office was huge and opulent, its walls lined with dark bookshelves, another Oriental carpet on the floor. There was a small desk across from the doors, a leather couch before them, and two matching leather chairs. A huge desk hulked at the far end of the room, crossways between draped windows on two walls. Beautiful, sad music played in the background, something Amanda almost recognized. The lighting was dim, and a ghost of cigar smoke wafted by, mixing with the scent of a bouquet of yellow roses on a bookstand that stood out brightly despite the gloom. Behind the massive desk facing the door from deep in the room, a stocky figure moved. A dimmer switch was turned and filtered golden light bloomed in the room.

"This is my uncle," Stephen said. "Orion Darling. Uncle, I'd like to introduce you to Amanda Pearce. She'll be learning about being a concierge."

"Miss Pearce. Delighted to meet you. You may call me Ori when guests aren't present." He neared, putting his black-gloved hand out to shake hers, and she nearly jumped. Stephen's uncle

looked like a slightly balding Robert DeNiro with a
potbelly, and suddenly she realized that the music
was the theme from *The Godfather.* It was creepy—he
was creepy—but she took his hand and smiled. "It's
a pleasure," he said. "Allow me to introduce Ivor,
another of my nephews."

At that, another man came out of the shadowed
corner and turned toward them. Taller and broader
than Stephen, he stepped into the light. He had
the same coloring as Stephen and Orion, dark hair
and eyes, light skin. Handsome in a slightly Nean-
derthal way, he made the perfect goon. *Am I working
for the mob? Don't be an ass,* she told herself. *It's just
the music.* Rather than offer his hand, he nodded,
a bare hint of a smile on his lips.

"Ivor is head of security," Stephen said.

Amanda believed it.

"He also keeps an eye on my troublemaking twin
sisters, whom you haven't yet met," Stephen added.

"Prepare her for those two," Orion said, laughing.
He looked at Amanda. "My nieces are sixteen. It's a
bad age and they love to make the most of it."

"Uncle, we were looking for Natasha," Stephen
said. "Any idea where she's off to?"

Orion nodded. "She said she was going out for
a bite." His smile was devilish.

It was too early for dinner, but she was absolutely
starving. Natasha Darling, forever twenty-nine, studied her snack. He was a businessman, perhaps
thirty-five, handsome, with brown hair and eyes and
excellent taste in clothes. She had spotted him a
little while before in the hotel's main restaurant,
Satyrelli, where he ate an early dinner, a filet of
sole baked with lemon and oil, and broccoli Flor-

entine. He'd gone to his room immediately after. His was one of the rooms with cameras, and by the time Natasha returned to her office to check on him, he lay on his bed in a T-shirt and shorts.

Now, Natasha bent carefully over him, fighting her urge to gulp him down. Instead, she held her own hair back and bent over him, gently inserting her teeth in his femoral artery—she preferred oxygenated blood over venous. She took a half pint, warm and vital, then forced herself to withdraw despite her voracious appetite. That would have to hold her until a more reasonable dining hour. Then she would have another half pint. A pint per person, that was the rule, and she didn't need more than a pint a day— that was why she had created the rule in the first place. And if she didn't obey her own rules, how could she expect her family to do so?

She dabbed the wound with the medicine Ori had procured. The wound immediately began fading. It was wonderful not to have to worry about leaving marks anymore.

She watched the man as he slept. The price—allowing Julian Valentyn to live at the hotel—still bothered her. Although Julian tried to hide it, he was an elitist, merely patronizing her family of human-born vampires. Valentyn was a trueborn, one of the pure vampiric race, born, not made. Pure. To him, Natasha and her kin were half-breeds, and that rankled her. It always had. She was, after all, powerful in her own right, as were her siblings. But Julian was as far beyond her as she was beyond humans.

Oh well, she thought, slipping back into the hallway, *life goes on. And on.*

4

"It's eleven-thirty-five in the p.m. here on KNDL AM and FM," Coastal Eddie announced, "and I want you to ask yourselves this: do you know where your Congressman is right now?"

Amanda wanted to stay up later, to get used to her new working hours, but tonight she was just too tired. Even *Dracula*, the version with Frank Langella playing on cable, couldn't keep her awake tonight, and she'd finally given up and turned off the television.

After showing her around a little more—she never did see a theme room or Natasha Darling—Stephen had taken her to eat in the most elegant restaurant in the hotel, Satyrelli. He encouraged her to order a full meal, which she gladly did, but all he ordered for himself was a cup of coffee and a small plate of fragrant fruit—orange slices, pineapple chunks, cantaloupe wedges. He sipped the coffee, but seemed to get more satisfaction from breathing in its aroma, and he toyed with his fruit, eating a little, but mostly spearing it and holding it near his mouth. She could see him sniff with such a look of pleasure on his face that it lent a whole new meaning to "inhaling your food."

"It's the wee hours here in Candle Bay," Coastal Eddie said as Amanda put on tailored pajamas, navy blue and satiny. "Close your curtains, my friends," Eddie crooned. "Stay warm and safe. Don't venture outdoors tonight. Trust me, children, heed my warning. The fog is waiting, lurking, and it will kill you if it can. It's Crawling Eye fog, and maybe that big old eyeball is out there watching you. And there are worse things waiting for you. Things that read your thoughts, your dreams. They know your darkest secrets and drink of your soul. Here's a little music to ponder that by."

"Idiot," Amanda said as the theme from *Play Misty for Me* filled the room. "Crawling Eye fog and ocean fog are *not* the same thing." She turned off the radio, slid between clean white sheets, and was asleep within a few minutes.

An hour passed, perhaps more. Amanda dreamed of mountain peaks and starry nights filled with the sound of chanting. Then came screams and visions of blood, sheets of it flowing over smooth white stone. It was an old dream, a familiar nightmare, but tonight it seemed absolutely real, more than it ever had before.

She awoke, galvanized, heart racing, breathing quickly, lightly. The visions faded, and suddenly she was certain someone was in the room with her. She lay under her covers, unaccountably cold, trying not to tremble as she strained her ears for the sound of footsteps, of breathing. Opening her eyes on darkness, she saw nothing but the suggestion of a full moon behind the fog crowding the balcony glass. No shadows moved, no one breathed.

You must have been dreaming. She turned on her

bedside lamp and got up. She was a little dizzy. The chill of the fog had invaded the room, and she slipped on her robe before checking the thermostat. It read sixty-eight degrees, but that had to be wrong. It felt more like fifty. Turning the heat up, she heard the furnace click on. Then, still anxious, she crossed to the door—*why doesn't it have a peephole?*—and put her ear to it. Hearing nothing, she finally opened it. Wall lamps cast a dim glow, just enough to show the hallway runner, with its tight, geometric patterns assaulting her eyes. A wave of dizziness passed through her.

The end of the hall was only two doors down, and there was nothing there except a small table holding a vase full of flowers. She turned and peered down the long length of corridor, and caught a glimpse of a figure in dark clothing just as it turned the corner into the main hallway. All she saw was black clothing and a suggestion of long white hair, a bright contrast to the dark maroon walls. *This place doesn't shut down at night,* she reminded herself. Then, *Thank God my room is painted white.* The maroon above the wooden wainscoting of the corridor looked ominous. She tucked back into the room, shut and locked the door.

Hoping the dreams were done for the night, she lay back down and watched a wisp of fog ooze in the balcony doors, like a twisting, snaky wraith.

Natasha studied the bank of camera images on the wall of her interior office, the one never seen by anyone but a few members of her family. Not even the twins were allowed here; only Stephen, Ori, and Ivor.

There were over seventy-five small images being

screened. A third of the cameras, which also sent their images to the security room, were in public places, the grounds, the pool and spa, the restaurants, and every hallway in the hotel. The rest were hidden in guest rooms, those designated as feeding rooms for the family and certain employees. Only healthy adults were rented these rooms, and Natasha was careful not to abuse the cameras. She only used them to inform her family where food might safely be found. It was a rule that no one entered any of the unwatched rooms. It was just too dangerous. They did now and then—or rather the twins did, along with her little brother David, who had fortunately left on an extended trip, visiting friends. Troublemakers, all three, especially in recent weeks. Creating a vampire that hadn't reached adulthood was a bad idea all the way around. They grew older mentally, yes, but somehow the youthful body still exerted its influence; hormones still disrupted the system. She wished Ori had never taken those three, or had at least waited for them to mature. But he'd wanted a big family and he was too self-absorbed to think about the consequences. Still, she loved him, stinky cigars, gangster movies, and all.

Now her concern lay with Julian Valentyn. He was poaching again. She had glanced at the bank of screens just as Julian exited a room in an off-limits area—the staff quarters in the right wing of the third floor. She watched him move rapidly down the hall. Behind him, the door opened and someone looked out.

She turned to Stephen. "He's going to ruin us," she spat. "He thinks our rules don't apply to him. We've got to do something about him."

Stephen nodded. "He is a problem."

"A problem?" Natasha snapped. "He's a threat to our way of life."

"Calm down. He's better at hypnosis than the rest of us. If he gets caught—and that's almost impossible—he can diffuse the situation, you know that."

"Oh, Stevie! Don't make excuses for him."

"I'm not. I just don't know what to do about him. Ori's given his word that he can remain here and he won't go back on that. And if he did . . . what might Julian do to us? He has more power than we do. Who knows how much?"

"Does it matter? Tell me, what if he walks in on a couple? Is he going to hypnotize two people at once? Maybe he can; but more likely it would be a problem. He's not checking first, he's just going in. You've heard him brag about his powers of 'invisibility.' Ever since we opened our first inn, we've always made sure the guests we drink from are alone and asleep." Her eyes flashed. "That's why most of us still survive."

"Julian's a trueborn. His senses are keen, 'Tasha. He probably knows exactly what he's walking into. But I agree, he shouldn't feed off the employees and he should live by our rules when it comes to the hotel. Let's talk to Ori."

"We've already talked to Ori," Natasha said. "What has it gotten us? Our uncle doesn't live in the real world. He spends his time smoking cigars and listening to Sinatra."

"He does more than that, 'Tasha, and you know it. He does his share of business work."

"Especially if it involves 'whacking,' as he calls it. Stevie, he's got Ivor completely brainwashed. The two of them are a joke. I don't like our guests to catch sight of them, especially when they're together. The Godfather and his goombah," she added with distaste.

"He's eccentric, but he'll get over it. He's only been on the gangster jag since 1972. Remember before that? Everything was Paris-this and Paris-that. The City of Lights."

"The city of dog droppings," Natasha countered. "What a relief when we finally returned to America."

"The Paris infatuation lasted only twenty-five years. The point is, he does his work and he's our vampiric father. We have to respect him."

"He'd love hearing that, Stevie. But he still doesn't take things much more seriously than Julian."

"He doesn't poach. He's serious enough," Stephen said. "Let me talk to him alone."

"You mean play into his chauvinistic attitudes?"

Stephen smiled. "Exactly. I'll go see him after dinner." He peered at the cameras. "Who's good on the menu tonight?"

"Room 209," Natasha suggested, looking at a curvaceous young woman whose fair hair haloed around her pillow as she slept. "She looks like your type." She wouldn't tease him about choosing beautiful women for his meals. After all, she chose the most beautiful men—and the occasional woman—for herself. "Go ahead. I'll give dinner assignments to the others. Have your supper and talk to Ori."

5

Julian Valentyn's living room at the hotel was a mix of the trueborn's graceful Empire furniture and the hotel's Spanish styling. The ceiling had decorative open beams and the floor was covered with hunter-green carpet. Vases of spring flowers and primitive South American artifacts ornamented the room, the centerpiece a golden Inca mask displayed above the fireplace. It was an odd room, but interesting, Orion Darling thought. He'd never seen Julian's bedroom, and he wondered what it was like. The bedroom of a vampire was always telling.

Julian sat on a Grecian sofa across from Ori's chair, sipping from a crystal wine goblet matching the one he'd given Ori. The blood was heady, excellent, and Ori sipped with pleasure, wondering at the source of such excellent vintage. It was nearly as good as fresh blood pumping from a living human.

"Well, what do you think of it?" Julian's long narrow fingers spidered over his goblet.

"It's quite rare," Ori ventured as he swirled the blood and inhaled. "A fine nose. The bouquet is carnivorous yet understated." He sipped from the glass, then looked back at Julian. "An AB positive, if I'm not mistaken. Young, yet mature at an early age."

"You are a true connoisseur." Julian held his own glass up and they toasted, then drank.

"That means a good deal, coming from you. I thank you."

They finished their drinks in silence, then Ori reluctantly cleared his throat. "I've been asked to talk with you about a potential problem."

"What sort of problem?"

"Poaching."

Julian gave him his thin-lipped crystalline smile. "Hunting is not in season?"

Ori chuckled politely and uncomfortably. "We have rules our family has followed for centuries, and we would ask you to abide by them as well. For your safety as well as ours."

"Yes, I remember your rules. Which are you referring to specifically?" Julian's eyes gleamed with amusement.

"You were seen exiting an employee's room last night. Employees are off-limits, as are rooms without a camera. As you know."

"Jinxy?" Julian called.

The tall, rodenty man appeared almost immediately. "Yes, sir?"

"Two more glasses, please."

They waited in silence while Jinxy refilled their goblets. After he left the room, Julian smiled and spread his long hands. "Who can resist a little fresh blood now and again?" He picked up his glass and began to sip delicately. "My powers allow me to know the state of the food's consciousness. And if they awaken, they don't even know I'm there."

"True." Ill at ease, Ori drank deeply. He'd never dared speak so strongly to the trueborn.

Finally, Julian gave him a patrician smile. "Your niece made all this quite clear, and I realize you haven't been hoteliers this long without abiding by certain rules. Assure her I'll consult her before my meals, as she asked."

"Thank you." Filled with relief, Ori finished off his blood. He should be past his limit, but he felt fine. His thirst had increased greatly in the last few weeks.

They talked on, Julian asking for stories of the hotel's tunnels and the rumors of the Treasure allegedly hidden in the catacombs, Ori turning the conversation each time, asking about some of the apocryphal trueborn lore. There were myths attached to the trueborns that pertain to what might lie beneath the hotel, but Julian avoided his questions as studiously as Ori had avoided his.

"Tell me something, Orion," Julian finally said, motioning Jinxy to refill the glasses. "How do you handle your human employees?"

"The vast majority know nothing and we're careful to keep it that way. The ones who do are our most trusted and oldest employees and we take very good care of them."

"Is that all you do?"

Ori smiled. "We, ah, put the bite on them. And use a little hypnosis. Just enough to maintain their loyalty. We don't feed on them, however."

"How commendable of you. How successful is your hypnosis?"

"We call it 'turning on the charm.' A handy euphemism. We've only had one failure since we opened here. That person eventually met with an unfortunate accident." Ori paused. "Our powers of suggestion are not as strong as yours, but generally they work well."

"With practice you can become quite strong."

"We do practice. I don't as much as I should, but Natasha, Stephen, and Ivor are on top of things. As for the twins, we don't encourage them."

"I understand." Julian smiled, barely.

"You're pure. You're trueborn. You can do anything. I realize you rarely talk about your more arcane powers, but I also know you possess them."

Julian's eyebrow raised. "I have some powers, but mainly they are simply powers that you have, but stronger. I am not all-powerful."

"Over the years, I've heard many times that trueborns are shape-changers."

"It's not shape-changing, merely appearing to change. Your own power allows you to pass among humans unnoticed, at least if you practice the art."

"Practice, practice, practice. You'd think creatures of the night wouldn't have to try so hard."

"No one ever said it was easy being undead." He sat forward. "Now, Ori, you've evaded my every attempt to talk about what lies below the hotel. I'd love to hear the tale."

"And I would love to hear more of yours, but I'm afraid it must wait until another time." Ori stood and moved quickly to the door. Jinxy swept in and opened it for him. "I have some hotel business to attend to."

"Very well. Another time."

Julian's icy smile burned into the back of Ori's head as he hurried down the hallway.

After Orion left, Julian finished his drink, and wondered what was on his host's mind. And what he actually knew. Although he had plied Ori with double the amount of blood the vampire was accustomed to, he hadn't been able to draw him into a discussion of the tunnels and the entrances. Ori had repeatedly turned the conversation back to Julian, asking his own questions about trueborn vampires and, though he didn't seem to realize it, about the Treasure. Julian wondered if Ori even knew what it really was, what it really meant. It was unlikely. The stories of the Father had been corrupted by time, and mixed with other mythologies until it was barely recognizable. The Darlings showed no signs of knowing that the time for the ascension drew near. They seemed merely curious.

After a while, Ori's eyes were bloodshot from too much drink and his voice slurred a little, but he still wouldn't crack. Instead, he began asking questions about the elixir. Julian stuck with his story that it did nothing but heal human wounds, and Ori seemed to accept that. *Seemed.* Julian wondered again about what, if anything, the vampire knew, and realized he himself was indulging in a very human trait: paranoia. But a little paranoia helped keep one safe. *Particularly now.*

He needed to know how to get into the tunnels; he had to find the Treasure, if it remained below. He doubted any other trueborns could have found it over the years. He and his human vampires had hidden it deeply. Now, he had to find it and attempt to destroy it. Barring that, he had to renew the wards and perhaps remove it to a safer place, one that would serve as prison and tomb.

His thoughts turned to the girl he had silently visited the previous night. Almost certainly, she had been drawn here by the Treasure, just as he had.

The difference was, she didn't know it. And he intended to keep it that way. *You cannot have her.*

He conjured her image, and it stirred the old sensations in him, sensations buried half a millennia. *You don't even know if it's really her. But surely, blood that sweet, that rare . . . She is the real treasure.* And his soul knew she was the one, if not his intellect.

Time was running short. He had to find the Father soon and keep the prophecies from coming true. He'd spent the winter season searching for an opening into the tunnels on his own, to no avail. The Darlings resisted his attempts to climb into their minds, to know their secrets. He had first concentrated his efforts on Orion Darling, but now he knew the twins might be the weakest link.

Taking a small vial from his pocket, he opened it, let a drop fall on his tongue, and put it away again. The Inca priests who first gave him the potion knew some of the properties of the bloodberry concoction, but Julian discovered many more as the years passed, and likely, there were still more to uncover.

He had kept the elixir's secrets even from the handful of other trueborns left on earth, and that would soon make him the most powerful vampire in the world. *The time is coming.*

Human vampires like the Dantes only suspected the potion existed, and he was taking a chance in giving it to the Darlings, in bringing it to light, as it were, but it was necessary if he wanted to lure the Dantes into helping him throw the Darlings off track so he could more easily find the tunnels.

The potion's worth was beyond measure. The Darlings only knew that it healed wounds, which was all they needed to know. But it also let Julian take direct sunlight (though by no means did he enjoy it), and in vampires like the Darlings, if a tiny amount was ingested, they could withstand some light—though nothing like he could—and be able to better function during daylight hours. It had other humanizing effects as well. Unlike Julian, human-born vampires often craved things other than blood. Many were voluptuaries. They loved food and drink, but could ingest very little. With the potion, food digestion became possible. If a human vampire were to ingest a drop a night—this could be done orally or by rubbing it on the skin—he would gradually become more and more humanized. It was happening to the Darlings and they didn't even know it; they took in a small amount each night from applying the elixir to bite wounds.

But there was a price. The potion inflamed the human animal from which the vampire was created. It brought emotions that destroyed common sense, it brought sexual appetites that could easily destroy them, again because it affected common sense, as well as the hormones. Hormones fascinated him. They stayed in the vampires, affecting behavior the same way they had when they were human. They retained their personalities, senses, and their appearance.

As an experiment, he was giving Lucy and Ivy an extra drop here and there, to see how the hormonally challenged pair would react. They had been borderline to begin with, and it probably wouldn't take much more to send either of them over the edge. It ought to happen any time. And, of course, he could speed things up for them if they didn't reveal the information he sought soon.

However, he had to keep the other Darlings on their toes. After all, they were his protectors. Or so they thought.

6

"He's back," Carol Anne sang softly.

"Who's back?" Amanda asked the little blond clerk. It was an hour before she was due to go on duty, but already dressed in her dark suit, she was spending time behind the counter with Carol Anne, picking up some pointers on registration procedures. She wanted to learn everything she could about the business.

"You're about to meet one of our regular guests. Douglas Harper."

The man heading their way had a thick head of hair, expensive clothes, and if he didn't have a rolled-up tube sock in his pants, he was hung like a horse. She forced her eyes upward, but could tell by his coy look that he knew she'd noticed.

When he paused to talk to the bellman who was following him with his luggage, Amanda whispered, "Is it real?"

Carol Anne blushed. "I don't know."

The pair held back giggles as Harper approached the desk. "Hello, ladies," he said, his voice a rich tenor. He pushed a platinum Visa toward Carol Anne.

"It's nice to see you again, Mr. Harper," Carol Anne said as she ran things through the computer.

"This is our new assistant concierge, Amanda Pearce."

Amanda nodded, feeling like she was twelve years old again. "I hear you're one of our favorite customers. Just let me know if I can help you in any way." Double meanings drenched her brain, but she kept her outward calm. Except for the heated cheeks.

"Thank you, Amanda."

His eyes danced and her cheeks grew hotter.

Carol Anne came to the rescue, sliding a key card to Harper. "You're booked for ten nights in the Mirror Room."

"I need time to reflect," Harper said, taking the key. He grinned broadly as Carol Anne motioned for the bellman and grinned back.

Harper and the bellman walked toward the elevators left of the registration area. "He always says that," Carol Anne said.

"The Mirror Room?"

"We really have two of them, they're so popular," explained the clerk. "Especially with women."

"That man was no woman," Amanda said with a snicker, still wondering what made Harper so humongous.

"The rooms are for either sex. But the Dracula rooms . . . I think women have a real thing for Dracula. Couples too. I think they role-play. We not only keep bathrobes in the closets, but black capes as well in the Dracula rooms. And you know what? They get used so much that we have to replace them every couple of months."

"Really?"

"Really. By the way, I think I know who Mr. Harper likes."

"Who?"

"Natasha."

"The manager?"

Carol Anne nodded. "I've seen them together, talking in the halls. Once they had dinner together at Satyrelli."

"That doesn't mean anything. Stephen and I did that last night."

Carol Anne shook her head. "The way Natasha looks at him, I think his package is for real."

"Then he must split women in two."

Carol Anne giggled. "I saw you and Stephen. He didn't take *me* to dinner when I started here." She giggled again. "But Tyler did." Another giggle. "Which one do you like best?"

"Oh, stop it. I hardly know them."

"They're both cute. So's Ivor, if you like them big." She cracked herself up. "Do you? Like them big?"

"Cut it out," Amanda said, barely in control. She felt a little hysterical. "Ivor's not my type."

"Then who is? Tyler or Stephen?"

"I don't know." Then she blurted, "Stephen."

"I knew it. I knew it. I like Tyler."

"Does he know?"

"Well, I'm not sure. I have to know if he likes me first. Maybe you could find out for me?"

"Excuse me, miss?"

"Oh, I'm sorry. May I help you?"

It was a delivery guy. He held a foot-long, narrow box. "I have something here for Orion and Natasha Darling. I need a signature."

"Will mine do?" asked Carol Anne. "The Darlings won't be available for another hour or so."

"You can sign."

After she did so and the delivery man was gone, she examined the package, with Amanda looking over her shoulder. There was no return address. Carol Anne put the package on a shelf beneath the counter.

"Shouldn't we get it to them right away?"

"Absolutely not," replied the clerk. "They aren't supposed to be disturbed this early short of the hotel catching on fire. Or flooding. Maybe an earthquake, if it's strong enough."

"Why?"

The girl shrugged. "I don't know. They're just weird about that. Now, about Tyler."

"I can't just ask him if he likes you. I haven't even started working here officially yet. Not for another hour."

"Well, do it as soon as you can."

"I can't promise anything," Amanda said. She liked Carol Anne, but decided she had to keep some distance from her, at least in public places. The girl brought out the adolescent in her.

"It's time for my dinner break," the blonde announced. "Have you eaten?"

Amanda hesitated. "In a restaurant?"

"No, silly. In the employees' dining room. The food's the same as the food in the coffee shop. Don't worry, it's really good."

Amanda was famished and they weren't going to be in public, so it would be okay to stick with Carol Anne. "Let's go."

The meal had started with crostini and a crisp green salad, but it was Satyrelli's veal-stuffed cannelloni Gabe Leoni lived for. Tonight the chef had outdone himself, producing a dish fit for the gods. Leoni put a heavenly forkful in his mouth, savoring the tomato tang and the mellowness of the béchamel that topped it. And the veal. The veal was to die for.

Leoni had been a wise guy in search of a family when he was tapped by the Dantes. Though a personable fellow, he'd never quite fit in with his own extended "family" since he was so accident-prone, but that didn't matter to the Dantes. They paid him well to spy on the Darlings, specifically the charming Orion Darling, who was completely into the mobster thing. Ori didn't have any real mob connections—at least the Dantes had assured him he didn't. Who knew if it was really true?

The Dantes hired him because they wanted to know how the Darlings operated, their habits, their likes and dislikes. And they wanted him to find the tunnels that supposedly ran from the hotel to the hills. He wasn't sure why, though he'd heard the stories about monks' treasure and he thought that was probably what they were after even though Ori had never mentioned treasure or tunnels.

The thing was, Gabe liked Orion Darling (who never called him "Fredo," unlike *some* people), and he liked Orion's family a hell of a lot more than the Dantes. The Darlings had class. Well, most of them did. Lucy and Ivy were sluts. He'd been coming here for three months, and in the last few weeks they had cornered him several times and demanded a good fucking. The twins were hot and he'd been with them a couple of times. But they liked to bite, and they scared him when they stared at him and licked their lips. Scared him and excited him both. He avoided them now, but they were the sandwich bread in his fantasies, and he was the meat.

He swallowed his burgundy, a big gulp. They had nothing to do with the reason he had made a very important decision concerning the Darlings and

Dantes. Nervously, he wiped his mouth with a dark crimson napkin. It was a decision that might kill him.

Amanda had a cheeseburger and fries for dinner, and rarely had anything ever tasted so good. She'd been nervous all day, and had only eaten granola bars and an apple she'd had in her suitcase. That was because she'd had a sudden attack of shyness this morning and hadn't wanted to barge uninvited into employee areas. Plus she wasn't sure when she'd get her first paycheck, so she skipped the restaurants too. The cheapest sandwich in the coffee shop was $5.95.

But now everything was fine. Carol Anne introduced her to at least twenty employees, many of whom were eating before their shifts. Tyler Shane was among them, and after they finished, the three walked back to the lobby together.

Amanda accompanied Tyler to the concierge area, where a second chair now sat behind the desk. In the next hour, they helped guests, and in between, Tyler taught her some of the hotel procedures. Soon, Carol Anne brought over the long, narrow box delivered earlier.

"This is for Ori and Natasha," she said, handing it to Tyler. "It came a couple hours ago."

"Thanks." He took the box, and after Carol Anne was gone, asked Amanda, "How would you like to deliver this?"

"Really?"

"Somebody has to and you haven't met Natasha yet. I'll tell her you're on your way."

"It goes to Natasha then, not Mr. Dar—"

"First names only around here, except in front

of guests. There are too many Darlings to do otherwise. Orion likes everyone to call him Ori."

Five minutes later, Amanda used her new key card to enter the administration door on the mezzanine. She walked past the long row of outer offices, hearing voices behind some of the doors, a phone ringing behind one, the whir of a printer behind another. Reaching the far door, she was immediately buzzed into the private reception room, and to her surprise, she found a thin dark man already there. He was well-dressed but definitely not a Darling, not with his olive complexion. A shopping bag sat at his feet. He looked nervous.

Despite that, she was keenly aware of his eyes crawling over her body. Amanda nodded a greeting and crossed to Natasha's door. The door clicked open before she had raised her hand to the intercom.

"They always know," said the man in the suit. He sounded nervous too.

Without looking back, Amanda entered the office. It was large, with a conversation area with a sofa and chairs around a gleaming black marble coffee table near the door. Exquisite art, some outdoor scenes in the fashion of Monet, some portraits, decorated the walls, and bouquets of flowers rested on tables, cabinets, and bookcases. Both of the latter lined the far portion of the room, where, in the middle of it all, a woman sat behind a sleek desk. Red carnations beside her gave off a rich, spicy scent.

"Hello, Amanda."

Her voice was as sultry as her looks. She rose, revealing a voluptuous figure enhanced by a black, form-fitting skirted suit.

The touch of her hand was electric, like

Stephen's. With Stephen, Amanda had assumed it was a sexual reaction, and to react the same way to Natasha wasn't in her nature. She tried not to show her confusion. Natasha only smiled and retreated back to her desk chair. Amanda handed her the package.

"Sit down," Natasha said.

"Thank you." She sat in the chair facing the desk and held her hands firmly in her lap to keep from fidgeting.

"I'll be with you in just a moment," Natasha said as she began opening the package. "How do you like our hotel?"

"It's beautiful. Tyler and your brother showed me around and I took a walk on the grounds today. Your patios and flower gardens are breathtaking."

Natasha removed the outer box to reveal a more elegant one within. "Thank you. Many of our cut flowers come from our gardens. Our family is very proud of them. Gardening is in our blood." She smiled, then began to lift the dark green cover from the inner box. "Let's see what we—" She cut off her words. "When did this arrive?"

"About two hours ago. I—"

"No." Natasha's pale face seemed to blanch even whiter as she let the cover drop on her desk. "Excuse me, Amanda," she said in a low voice. "We'll talk later." She set the box on the desk as if it were hot.

"Of course." Amanda rose and caught sight of the contents of the box. It was a foot-long stake. A wooden stake. Quickly she brought her eyes up, and was caught in Natasha's black gaze. She couldn't look away. A wave of dizziness washed over her.

"You will say nothing of this," Natasha said. "It is our secret."

"Yes." The dizziness passed and Amanda realized the lid was back on the box.

Outside the office, she paused to steady herself. She couldn't understand what had happened. *A stake?* The door to Ori's office opened and the olive-complected man stepped out, without his shopping bag. Sweat sheened his face, and she could see dampness around the collar of his pale almond shirt. His hand shook as he let go of the door, but he still managed to give her the eye. "How ya doin'?"

"Fine," she said. She loitered while he left, and waited another half a minute so she wouldn't run into him in the hall of outer offices.

Just as she put her hand on the door to exit herself, she heard two doors unlock. Stephen came out of his office. She started to say hello to him, but he barely looked at her as he moved quickly to Ori's door and pushed his way in. As Natasha's door opened, Amanda scooted out into the outer office hallway. She hurried toward the door to the mezzanine. Straightening the cuffs of her suit, she had only one thing on her mind: not running into any more Darlings.

7

Juicy Lucy stood in the shadows of a lobby arch and watched the people coming and going from Satyrelli. She could smell the food, the tomatoes, the garlic, the spices, the people, their blood. Though she always had trouble with her appetites, tonight her hunger was fierce, gnawing, and she knew she couldn't wait until midnight or beyond to have a meal. She inhaled deeply, her eyes closed.

A pair of hands touched her shoulders, then moved gently down her arms to her wrists. "Hello, Ivy." Lucy turned to look at her sister. "Are you hungry?"

"Starving." Ivy, like Lucy, was dressed in black jeans and a clingy scoop-necked top. Lucy's was red, Ivy's black, and she had a short black leather jacket on over it. Ivy's hair was pulled back, while Lucy's waved and curled over her shoulders. Some nights they dressed alike, mainly because it confused people, but usually they liked a little difference between them. "Do you have any bottles in your room?"

"No, not a drop." Lucy watched a tall trim woman wearing shorts over a bathing suit walk past, and felt her fangs twinge. "She looks good enough to eat."

"Yes."

"Let's follow her."

"Lucy, not after Stephen heard us talking last night."

"They're all in a meeting." As she spoke, she began moving toward the elevators, where the athletic-looking woman, her blond hair still wet and dark from the pool, waited.

"No," said Ivy, walking beside her. "Besides, she's awake and probably will be for hours."

Lucy grinned. "We'll do a little of that voodoo we do so well!" The pair had been practicing their hypnotic skills, and were becoming quite proficient at it, something they hid from their uncle and siblings. If they knew about it, Ivor would be permanently attached to them, and that was the last thing they wanted. It was bad enough already.

"We've never done it for real, Luce. Not to get blood."

"Yes, but when we've tried it on humans, it works."

"Usually."

"Well, if it doesn't work, we won't bite her," Lucy said. "Do you have your potion with you?"

"Yes."

"Good. Let's find out her room number. Chances are she'll go directly into the shower."

Ivy studied her briefly, then a slow smile stole across her face. "You're bad."

"Yeah," Lucy said. "Isn't it nice?"

"The package is postmarked San Luis Obispo," Natasha said as the stake was passed among Ivor,

Stephen, and Orion. "It has to be from the Dantes."

"I agree," Stephen said.

Ivor merely nodded, but Ori's eyes lit up. To him, Natasha knew, the stake was the equivalent of a horse head in a bed. He sensed an adventure, even if he denied it. She saw it in another light, one that fostered hatred and a little dread. They didn't need trouble. They didn't need the bother. "So, the question is, why?"

"As I told you some time ago, Julian thought they might try to steal his potion."

"*Our* potion," Stephen said quietly.

"Yes," Ivor said. "And there's the Treasure. That could also be attracting them."

Natasha nodded. "They came after that once before." She chuckled.

"A fool's errand," Ori agreed. "I have some news."

"What?" Natasha and Stephen said simultaneously.

"You're aware of my friend. Gabe Leoni."

"The little gangster," Natasha said distastefully. "I noticed him come in earlier. What was in the shopping bag?"

"A DVD player. Right off the truck."

"I wish you wouldn't—never mind."

"Don't be concerned, but he was on the Dantes' payroll. *Was.*"

"What?" Stephen asked, pushing forward. "Don't be concerned? What are we supposed to be? Pleased?"

Natasha stared at her uncle. "I told you, you shouldn't—"

"It's all right," Ori soothed.

"How can it be all right?" Natasha tried hard to

keep her anger from overflowing. Her uncle and his idiotic binges. Gangsters. *Christ, when will he get sick of them?* Unbidden, her fangs began to unsheathe, and her surprise instantly helped her calm down. They receded. "Please explain," she managed, aware that they were all staring at her. No matter how angry she became, she could always retain control of her vampiric functions. What had happened? *You're just under too much stress!* "What does he know?"

Ori took out a cigar, caught Natasha's glare, and put it back in his pocket. "He knows nothing. Do you think I'm fool enough to reveal our secrets?"

"You've said too much at times in the past," Stephen said. "I remember a time in 1976 when we had to kill a member of a prominent crime family to keep our secret from getting out."

"And in 1982—" Natasha began.

"I'm aware of my mistakes. That's why I haven't made one this time. Gabe knows nothing about us."

"What does he know about the Dantes? Does he know they're vampires?"

"No. He thinks they're a crime family. He says they took him in as one of their own, but treat him with no respect."

"And?"

"And? I treat him with respect, so he admitted the connection and changed his loyalties." Ori smiled grimly. "I suppose he now considers himself part of the Darling family. I've given him a job: find out everything he can about the Dantes. I don't know how long he'll survive, but the information could be very useful."

"A mole's mole," Stephen said dryly. "What did they send him here for in the first place?"

"To find the tunnels. He's to go back to them

and tell them how to get in. He doesn't know what they're looking for."

"You believe him?" asked Stephen.

"Yes. Gabe is really a simple sort. He wants to be a wise guy, but he doesn't have the heart for it. He's not cold enough; he's prey to his emotions."

There's a lot of that going around. "What's to stop him from going back to the Dantes and playing triple agent?" Natasha asked.

"His emotions, as I said. I make him feel he's my friend, that he can trust me. The Dantes give him nothing but a little money up front and more when he delivers. That's not what he really needs."

"Everyone needs money," Natasha said.

"I'm paying him better than the Dantes. He'll still collect from them, of course, so this is a sweet deal for him. You see, Natasha, he took a huge chance coming to me as he did. He knew I was likely to kill him for such a thing."

"Maybe you should," Natasha said. "We can mail the Dantes his body. That would make an effective statement."

Ori smiled wryly. "If he deviates from the behavior I expect to see, that will happen. Rest assured, my dear."

"So do you really believe it's the potion they're after, not the Treasure?" Stephen asked.

"Probably." Ori steepled his fingers thoughtfully. "Of course they'd like to get their hands on the Treasure, but the potion is the main thing. They know it's real now, and they naturally assume we keep it in the catacombs." He smiled. "After what we did to their goons when they attempted to break in last time, they're not going to do anything lightly, or for a mere rumor. Julian said a vampire tried to talk him into sharing the potion shortly before com-

ing here. He killed the vampire. It was a blood
Dante, one of the three brothers."

Natasha nodded impatiently. "So what do we do
about all this? How do we deal with the stake?" Left
up to her, she would deal harshly with every problem they had discussed, but she knew the men were
softer on such things. And often, they were right.
That was something she'd learned the hard way.

"We wait and watch," Ori said.

Sparks in his flinty eyes, Ivor finally spoke. "I will
kill them with their own stake if they come here."

"I'll speak to Julian and see if he has any sugges-
tions on handling things," Ori said.

"You will NOT!" Natasha's" explosion surprised
everyone, including herself. Her teeth twinged, but
stayed hidden this time through sheer willpower. "I
don't trust him and he has no business in our family
business."

"He's wise," Ori began.

"He looks out only for himself," Natasha countered.

"I agree with Natasha," Stephen said. "He's not
one of us and he does things that endanger us.
Poaching, for example. Uncle, have you spoken to
him about that yet?"

"I have done so." Ori looked at Ivor. "What is your
opinion on Julian?"

Ivor looked uncomfortable. "Speaking as chief of
security, I must agree with Stephen and Natasha.
He's too big a risk."

"Very well. I'll abide by the majority." Ori rose.
"Now if you'll excuse me."

Natasha nodded and waited while Ori and Ivor
left the office. She looked at her brother and asked
quietly, "Stevie, have you been yourself lately?"

"What do you mean?"

"Have you felt more hunger pangs than usual?"

He considered. "Yes, I believe I have." He studied her. "I want to overindulge and I want my dinner earlier in the evening. I've also felt rather emotional. I had to fight the urge to flirt with that new employee when I took her to dinner last night."

Natasha raised her eyebrows. Stephen was usually cool as ice. "Amanda Pearce. She brought the package to me. And she saw the stake."

"Any problem?"

"I told her it was a secret between the two of us, but didn't give her any explanations. We'll see if she keeps her mouth shut."

"I hope she does. I enjoy looking at her."

"It was her room that Julian came out of last night."

Stephen's nostrils flared and his eyes turned flinty. "That son of a bitch."

"Stephen, why are you so upset? Don't let it bother you. We'll see that he doesn't do it again."

"I'm sorry." Stephen calmed himself. "I assume from your outburst that your emotions have increased too?"

"You noticed?"

"Everybody noticed. I felt the same way."

"You've always been the one with all the self-control."

He grinned, then became serious. "We should keep this to ourselves."

"I agree. That's why I waited until Ori and Ivor were gone. I was afraid Ori would want to consult the oracle."

"Julian?"

"Yes." She nodded. "Julian didn't bother me so much at first, but your suspicions have rubbed off on me. This poaching business . . ."

Stephen's eyes flashed, and Natasha was amazed at the fury she sensed within him. Certainly Amanda Pearce was attractive, but his reaction was completely out of character.

"Don't let emotions get in the way of common sense, Stevie." She put her hand over his and they twined their fingers together.

"I won't, 'Tasha. But we must stop the poaching."

Poaching. It wasn't so different from her early evening snack. Both broke the rules. She pulled her hand back. "Keep your eyes on all of the family, especially the twins. If they're feeling hungrier than usual, well, they're not terribly trustworthy to begin with."

"What about Ivor? Shall we warn him to keep a more vigilant watch on them?"

Natasha curled a dark tress around her finger. "No. He'll have more to do now, watching out for Dantes. Something could get back to Ori, and then what? We only have his word that he hasn't told that Leoni creature anything important."

"Ori's always been trustworthy," Stephen said, then added reluctantly, "Except for his slipups."

"At least they're infrequent." Natasha drummed her fingers on the desk.

"We should keep a close eye on our adopted family too," Stephen pointed out. He was referring to the vampires they had hired or created to work with them. Three held management positions, and the others were divided between housekeeping and Ivor's security team. Some things couldn't be left to unsuspecting human employees.

"Yes, of course. I don't really think it's anything to worry about. Probably a tidal influence, something like that. It will pass." Natasha allowed herself to sigh. "The Dantes, and Julian, they're our real problems."

It was a hot, steamy shower. Lucy and Ivy had used a pass key to slip into the room, and now both stood in the bathroom, hidden in foggy steam as water beat fast and hard on the woman in the enclosure. Lucy smiled at Ivy and her fangs showed, just a little. She resumed whispering, her voice blending with the water sounds, fading into them like a spirit. Without making eye contact, she wasn't sure the hypnotic trance would come over the woman; then she heard her begin humming a melody the twins had been concentrating on, "Strangers in the Night," one of Uncle Ori's favorites. That was the sign they needed; it proved they'd gotten into her mind.

The shower was turned off, but the humming continued. The door slid open and the woman stepped onto the bath mat, water dripping from her body, her breasts firm but voluptuous. She saw the twins and didn't react. They were in her mind. Ivy handed her a towel, and she took it with a small smile. Lucy began humming along with her.

"What's your name?" Ivy asked softly.

"Jennifer."

"Come with us, Jennifer," Lucy said, taking the towel and dropping it to the floor.

"Come with us," her sister echoed.

They led her out of the bath, to the bed. The room was not a theme room, but it almost seemed to be. It was Spanish in style, with arched doorways and heavy dark furniture. Willingly, Jennifer lay down after Ivy turned back the rich patterned bedspread. She was still humming, almost purring with contentment as she stretched out on the bed like a cat. Sliding onto her side a moment, she revealed a tiny careful tattoo on her hip. It said "Jennifer" in graceful letters. Lucy climbed onto the bed next to her, and Ivy followed on the other side. Jennifer's hair was short, and her neck and shoulders gleamed in the faint light. Ivy leaned across her body and whispered to Lucy, "Just a little, remember. We don't want anyone to notice. Especially that bitch Natasha."

Lucy nodded and watched, trembling with hunger, as Ivy bent to the woman's neck and put her mouth over the carotid artery. After a few seconds she could stand it no longer. She considered biting the breast, but she was too hungry, so she bent to the white, clean skin on Jennifer's inner thigh and bit into the femoral artery.

8

So far, Amanda's first official evening of work had gone well. It was a quiet night, offering little to do but answer a few guests' questions, make some reservations, and order flowers for a couple celebrating an anniversary. She and Tyler talked, mostly about hotel procedure, but he had a warm smile and she was slightly titillated, despite herself. His manners were impeccable. She had said nothing to him about the stake, just as Natasha had asked. He and Carol Anne had both wondered, not too subtly, what the package contained, and Amanda pretended she didn't know.

Now, she wandered the strategically lit, misty gardens. It was her dinner break, but the meal she ate before starting her shift had been heavy and she wasn't hungry. Fog eddied in little wisps, slowly growing thicker, and the air smelled of the sea and the flowers in the patio gardens that wove in and out along the paths, a maze of gardens. Like the theme rooms, each garden was different. She smelled roses and some other flower, very sweet and heavy in the thick, moist air. It was wonderful, but a little spooky as the fog began to fill the air. She wondered at the scents of flowers that shouldn't be in bloom yet.

Moving farther from the hotel, she found a square patio covered almost entirely by an arbor entwined with a wisteria in full bloom. Its lavender flowers hung like clusters of tears, their fragrance mild in the foggy night. There was an ornate bench of white wrought iron and wood beneath the arbor, and Amanda decided to sit down for a few minutes.

She loved the hotel and the gardens. They were everything she hoped for. She had been drawn to other places and other buildings, and she yearned to travel someday, to see more of the world. She longed to tour the Grecian ruins, to see Italy, and the ruins in South America. But this place . . . This place . . . It wasn't déjà vu, she didn't feel as if she'd been here before. It was something else. Something indefinable. The hotel seemed alive.

The misty fog soon obscured what lay beyond the patio, and Amanda felt as if she was in a little world of her own, cut off from everything and everyone. It was wonderful, romantic, spooky, and mysterious all at once. On the breeze, she heard distant notes played by the guitarist in the lobby, but they floated away as quickly as they had come, leaving her draped in silence. She shivered, wishing she'd brought a sweater.

"The new girl."

The voice came from nowhere, startling her, but before she could stand up, a tall figure appeared in the mist, a shadow man. He didn't move, and she fought down an unjustified panic, scared half to death for no reason. "Hello," she finally said.

"You don't know who I am, do you?"

It was a soft, knowing voice, vaguely familiar, and it made her very nervous. "No, I'm afraid not."

At that, the figure stepped closer. "The gate-keeper, that's who I am. Eliot Lucre, remember?" He extended a hand to her, but she hesitated to shake it. It was filthy.

He realized it and pulled his hand back. "Oh, sorry. I was doing a little gardening."

She looked him up and down. Lucre's jeans were filthy too. "You garden at night?"

"Sometimes." He grinned, showing large white teeth. "I like to get my hands dirty."

Wasn't that the truth? His hands and everything else except his pearly whites needed washing.

"Do you want me to walk you back to the hotel?"

"No, thanks. I'd like to sit here a little while longer."

"It's easy to get turned around in the fog, and it's not a good idea to go wandering away from the hotel."

"I'll follow the path back," she said, wishing he'd leave.

"I think I'd better go with you."

"I'll be fine."

He stared at her with repulsive greenish-yellow eyes. "It's not safe to be alone in the fog."

"Why? Is Jack the Ripper lurking out here some-where?"

"Could be. Come on."

A man cleared his throat. "Eliot, you may go. I'll take care of Miss Pearce." Stephen stepped into the patio.

"Only trying to help, Chief."

"I appreciate it, Eliot. Why don't you go wash up? It's time to relieve your man at the gate."

"Will do." He took a few steps, and was swallowed up by the fog.

Amanda started to rise, then settled back down

as Stephen Darling sat next to her. "How's your shift going?"

"I'm enjoying it. This is a nice place to work."

"And your room? Is it satisfactory?"

"Yes, it's great." That was true. In addition to the bed, there was a small sofa in front of the television, and a little dining table and chairs near the tiny kitchenette, which had a sink, a half-width stove, a mini-refrigerator, and a microwave. The cupboards above the counter came with a few pans, dishes, glasses, and silverware. There was even a pot holder. "I really like it. But I dreamed someone was in my room last night." She laughed lightly.

"You did?" he asked in a concerned voice. "Tell me about it."

"It was just a dream."

"Tell me anyway."

"I woke up, certain there was someone in my room. But there wasn't." She hesitated, then added, "I got up and looked down the hall. Someone was just turning the corner. It was sort of spooky. I'm sure it was just coincidence. May I ask you a question?"

"Of course." He sat close to her, no more than six inches away, and his gaze was mesmerizing.

"Why did Eliot tell me it's not safe to be out here? In the fog?"

"One, it's very easy to lose your sense of direction and end up wandering into a graveyard or falling down a slope. You'd probably be stuck outside all night."

"That's one," Amanda said. "What's two?"

"It's something we don't talk about. We've had several attacks on people who've been out here alone during fogs."

"Attacks? What kind of attacks?"

"Assaults. Nothing serious has happened, at least not yet."

"What kind of assaults?"

After a moment, he said, "Purse-snatching. We believe kids from town are responsible. Our fencing is more decorative than anti-trespassing, and Eliot and our other grounds men can't see everything, especially when it's like this."

"What happens when guests come out here? Do you warn them?"

"They rarely come out in a fog, but if they do, a guard lingers nearby."

"Can you actually keep track of everyone who comes out here?"

"I wish we could. Then there would have been no incidents." Stephen faced her. "I'd like you to promise me that if you come out here when it's foggy, make sure you bring someone with you, or stay close enough to the hotel so that you can hear and be heard. Nothing's ever happened when there are two people present, or when there's no fog." He rose and put his arm out to her. "Shall we go back to the hotel?"

"All right." It gave her a little thrill to take his arm. They began walking, Stephen guiding her lightly by the elbow. His touch was gentle and necessary—now she could barely see the brick path in front of her. "The gardens are beautiful."

"They're Uncle Ori's pride and joy. Recently, we've made quite a few additions, courtesy of Mr. Valentyn."

"Who?"

"You haven't met him?"

"No."

"He's a long-term guest in one of the suites. He's

a friend of Ori's and his interest in horticulture may even surpass my uncle's."

"It's nice they have something in common."

"They have many things in common. We're just passing the water garden now. Hear it? You should visit it in the daytime. It's beautiful."

She wanted to lean against him, but resisted the urge. He was, after all, her employer. "I'll come out tomorrow before my shift begins."

"Yes. We're almost there. Have you met my sisters yet?"

"Natasha?"

"No. The twins."

"No, I haven't."

"They'll find you soon enough. Don't take them too seriously. They're always out to shock people. Here we are." He let go of her elbow and opened one of the double doors that led into the rear of the lobby. "I'll see you later." He walked away.

Amanda missed his touch.

"I drank too much," Lucy said, dabbing potion on their victim's femoral wound.

"Me too." Ivy took the little vial and did the same to her neck. She gazed at Jennifer's pale white face, almost bluish in the faint light. "She doesn't look so good."

"Oh, shit," Lucy exclaimed. "She's not breathing!"

"We killed her?"

"That's what not breathing means, idiot."

"Don't get bitchy," Ivy said. "What are we going to do? My head's spinning. I think I might be sick."

"Then get into the bathroom and don't get

blood all over the place. I don't want to spend all night cleaning up."

Ivy rose and ran. Lucy, stomach roiling, followed her a moment later, and found her hugging the toilet. Lucy vomited in the bathtub. After, the sisters flushed and ran water and washed their faces. They looked at each other, and Lucy said. "We drained her dry."

"Yeah. It's been a long time since we went and did that."

"That musician in Paris."

"We had to grind him up into little musician bits and add him to the sausage." They laughed, then Ivy said, "You're the smart one. What are we going to do this time?"

"The tunnels, stupid. We can stick her down there."

"Won't she stink?"

"We can toss her down the stairs into the catacombs. It won't matter if she stinks."

"Near the Treasure?" Ivy asked. "What if Natasha or Stephen goes to check on it?"

"They won't. They hate going down there."

"Me too."

"It's safe, don't be a pussy. We'll have to get rid of her luggage and cover her tracks so they think she skipped out. We need to check registration to find out about her. You do that."

"Why do I have to—"

"Don't whine, Ivy."

"Fuck you."

"Fuck you too. Are you hungry again?" Lucy wasn't crazy about going near the catacombs either. They were totally creepy. And those stories about the Treasure . . . "We could get something to eat first. We can't move her right now anyway. We'll have to wait until morning."

"Morning. What a bitch," Ivy moaned, then added, "I could eat."

"It's still too early, though. We can't get our room assignments from Natasha yet."

"We'd better not press our luck." Ivy nodded toward the bedroom. "There's still some left in her. It's still warm."

"Okay." Lucy took Ivy's hand and they walked into the bedroom, where the woman lay sprawled on the bed.

"We'd better clean her up and put her under the covers in case somebody comes along before we get rid of her."

"We will. Let's eat first." She climbed onto the bed and went for the unused carotid. It was no fun doing the femoral on a corpse. Lucy looked at her sister, poised over the other side of Jennifer's neck. "I hate how hard it is to get blood out of one of these empties!"

"Sucks, doesn't it?" Ivy grinned, showing fangs, then bent to her meal. Lucy followed suit.

9

It was almost seven in the morning when Natasha finally followed her relatives' example and went to bed. For Lucy and Ivy, the wait had been interminable. Sure, some of it was passed in semi-drunken splendor after they had their assigned meals. That blood, on top of what they'd managed to drain from Jennifer's corpse, was enough to get them tipsy, but not make them sick. It had been great.

But it wasn't so great now. For one thing, it was way too late to be up and the girls were logy with blood and exhausted from their busy night. Juicy Lucy and Poison Ivy had hangovers. Not bad ones, not like they had expected, but they needed to sleep, not try to function during daylight hours, as they needed to now.

The suite they shared only had one large bedroom, so they had to share. It was a pretty good setup, the entire suite decorated almost like a Dracula room, with black leather upholstery, heavy dark wood furniture, and ornamental candle sconces on the red walls. They decorated with old rifles and swords, and even had an antique mace—a real one—hanging over the fireplace. They had black carpeting, and a black satin bedspread on their king-size bed. Sometimes Natasha and Stephen teased them about the decor, but they never went back on their word about letting them do up their suite any way they wanted.

Now, the blinds drawn against the sun, Lucy put the finishing touches on her hair. She had a ponytail and Ivy wore a blond wig. They had used different-colored lipstick than normal, and Lucy had drawn a mole near her mouth. They were dressed in blue and white maids' uniforms, because they didn't want to be recognized as twins if anyone saw them. That would make them too easy to remember.

"Ready?" asked Ivy, her voice a little dull. In daylight, vampires weren't at their best and brightest, and it would only get worse as the minutes passed.

"Ready," Lucy confirmed. They walked into the living room, where a laundry cart waited. They'd brought it in in the dead of night, and it appeared no cameras had caught them since neither Ivor nor anyone else had come to see what they were up to. Lucy stood behind the cart. "Open the door." She added, "I don't feel as stupid and rotten as I thought I would. Usually at this hour, I can hardly walk, let alone talk." She thought her voice did sound a little off, though.

Ivy nodded agreement, then opened the door and, after looking around, signaled Lucy to push the cart out. It was a dead time of day in the guest room areas, but they had to work fast because, by eight, the real maids would be out and about. All they had to worry about now was running into room service personnel delivering breakfasts, but Lucy figured there wouldn't be much of that going on for another half hour, at least. The Candle Bay Hotel didn't inspire getting up early. It was more of a snuggle-up-in-bed kind of place.

Quickly, attempting to look efficient, they headed down to the first floor of rooms, where old dead Jennifer was ensconced. No one was around and they let themselves into the room, just like real maids. Slipping inside, they pushed the tall cart to the bed. Lucy pulled the covers back and surveyed the damage. "Dead bodies are so gross."

Ivy poked the cadaver with her finger. "She feels like rubber. Aren't you glad I thought of curling her up in case she went stiff?" She grinned.

"You look like you're stoned, smart-ass." Lucy smiled. "But it was a really good idea."

"Thanks." Ivy stood up straight and wiped her finger on the bedspread. "Corpse cooties," she observed. Both of them laughed far more than warranted, which wasn't unusual, considering the hour.

Lucy knew Ivy was losing it and she was too, but they didn't stop giggling for several minutes. "Let's get her into the cart."

Noses wrinkled in disgust, they yanked the covers off the bed and pulled the bottom sheet up around the body. Ivy looked at Lucy. "One of us has to come back with fresh linen. And to get the luggage. We have to make the room look like it hasn't been used."

"We can put her luggage in the cart and get rid of everything at once." She paused. "What was I saying?"

"Luggage."

"Oh, yeah. We'll do the cleanup now too. Come over to this side of the bed," Lucy ordered. Ivy joined her; then the sisters hoisted the sheeted corpse up and lowered it into the heavy cloth hamper.

It took them fifteen more minutes to clean up and pack the suitcases in on top of the body. They threw the top sheet and a used towel on top of everything to make it extra-realistic. Ivy peeked out the door. "All clear. Come on."

"Christ! It weighs a ton!" Lucy complained, yanking the cart over the threshold. "Help me."

Together they pushed the cart down the hall and rounded a corner. "How are we going to get the tunnel open?" Lucy asked. "There'll be too many people around now."

"If we have to we can leave it in our suite for a while," Ivy said.

"Gross! Not in a million years."

They'd stopped walking while they were talking, and both realized it at the same time. The sisters began pushing the cart along again, discussing where to put the body. "This way," Lucy said. They took the elevator to three and started down a hall. "Why are we up here?" Ivy asked. "I forget." Her brain was frying fast.

"I—well, where exactly *are* we?"

"I dunno. The third floor."

"I know *that,*" she said, though she really didn't. "I'm having trouble with room numbers. We need to get this hidden right away."

Julian Valentyn emerged from his suite. "Get what hidden, my dears?"

He heard them before he saw them, and when Julian looked out his peephole, he was delighted. The twins were up to no good, and it didn't take any brilliant deductions to know that they'd slipped a little way over the edge. Obviously, they were trying to rid themselves of a body, but they weren't functioning well—better than they would have without the potion in daylight, true, but rather badly nonetheless.

Now they stood together behind the cart, eyes downcast, at a loss for words.

"Have you done something you shouldn't?" Julian stepped forward and lifted the towel and sheet, peered under them. There was luggage and, between two of the bags, a foot—a foot's pink-toenailed toes, to be precise—was visible. "A little accident?" he asked them gently.

"Yes, yes." Lucy jumped on it. "Please don't tell anyone! Please!"

"Your family is rather strict about these things."

"Yes. Please don't tell."

"I won't."

They looked at him in awe. He was their savior.

"Now, come inside and have a drink with me. It will refresh you; you look like you could use refreshing." He held the door open and they walked in. Ivy glanced back at the cart. "Don't worry," he said, "Jinxy will get it in a moment." He shut the door behind him.

Gabe Leoni knew what was going on. Somebody got whacked.

He'd followed the twins—he was pretty sure they were the twins—ever since they'd left their room dressed up like maids. He had been up early, just snooping around, keeping an eye on things for Ori. That's what a goombah did for his boss. Ori was the kind of boss you did things for, not like Christopher and Nicholas Dante, who never appreciated anything, and always wanted more, more, more. Now, Leoni moved silently toward the alcove, where he could see part of the laundry cart. Ori had to know about this right away. He had to tell him, but first, he had to get the cart out of there.

He walked quickly and silently up the hall until he reached the cart. He began pushing, surprised at its heaviness. As soon as he took it around a corner, he peeked under the linens, saw the suitcases and the toes. He returned to pushing, wondering why the girls took the cart to Ori's friend Julian Valentyn in the first place. Maybe he was up to something. Ori wouldn't talk about him.

Gabe didn't trust Valentyn. Not only was he too blond, nearly albino, Gabe could hear something in Ori's voice when he mentioned him. Something like fear, maybe anger, he wasn't sure. All Gabe knew was that he was a friend—so Ori said—who was not to be bothered. Gabe turned another corner and started down a long hall, expecting to find another turn, or hopefully, a dark alcove where he could temporarily park the cart while he consulted with Ori.

He got to the end of the hall, and found there was nothing but a table holding a massive vase full of colorful flowers. In the other direction, where he'd come from, a room door opened and a man dressed in a hotel uniform came out and moved toward the hallway intersection without noticing Gabe. *That was lucky.* Another door opened and Gabe shrank into the corner by the table. Another uniformed employee exited. *A shift must be starting.* He had to get out of there, had to hide the cart. He pushed it three doors forward, then halted when he heard the door he was in front of being unlocked. He left the cart and backed into the corner by the table, scrunching down a little to let the big bouquet help hide him. A young woman dressed in jeans and a white shirt poked her head out, saw the cart, disappeared, and reappeared holding her key card.

His luck held; she didn't look his way. Instead, she started to push the cart away from her door, then stopped and looked inside it, no doubt startled by its heaviness. He heard her gasp; she'd seen the foot. He should have covered it up better. She stood there a moment, then disappeared back into her room.

Gabe moved. Grabbing the cart, he began pushing it back down the corridor. He had to hide it fast.

"Tyler," Amanda said into the phone. "Tyler, meet me in the corridor."

"Why? What's wrong?"

She could tell she had disturbed his sleep, but she didn't bother to apologize. "Just meet me. Now."

"Okay."

Amanda hung up, her hand trembling. She couldn't believe what she'd seen. Was that really a foot in the hamper? *You saw it. Now get back out there!*

Swallowing hard, she took a deep breath and opened her door. Tyler's, across the hall and twenty feet down, opened an instant later.

He stepped out wearing a yellow hotel robe, his legs and feet bare. "What's wrong?"

Amanda looked around. "It's gone!"

"What's gone?" He approached her, keeping his voice down.

"The laundry cart."

He looked baffled. "What—"

"There was a body in it!"

"What?"

"Somebody left it in front of my door. I went to move it and it was heavy, so I looked inside. There were suitcases and a body. A foot, at least. The nails were polished. Pink."

She was shaking, and Tyler put one arm around her. "You've been tricked," he told her. "Initiated. It had to be a fake foot. Welcome to our staff."

"It looked so real!"

"I'm sure it did. It's supposed to look real."

"Who did it?"

"I don't know and you'll probably never find out. The employees cover up for each other. Don't worry. Every new person gets a trick played on them. Okay?" He smiled at her.

"Okay," she said.

"See you later." He turned and went back to his room.

Amanda stood there in the hall a long moment. Tyler had to be right, but she still felt unnerved. It had looked so real.

10

"Master Julian?" Jinxy said, coming in empty-handed from the alcove.

"Yes, Jinxy?"

"There's no cart out there. Nothing around the corners either."

Julian glanced at the twins, draped over one another, just this side of asleep on the Grecian lounge. He had offered to help them because he knew they could lead him to the tunnels. Unfortunately, even he could not read vampiric minds clearly. He could sense their presence and mood, though, which was more than most human-born vampires could do.

"What do you want me to do?" Jinxy asked.

"Come in and shut the door."

He turned his attention back to the twins. The missing cart changed things; he wanted nothing to do with them if it meant his reputation might be questioned. It was bad enough that whoever had taken it had found it outside his door. *Who?*

"Girls," he said, rising. "Girls."

All he got was a low moan from one of them. But there was a way to remedy the situation. He brought a small bottle of the elixir from the safe in his bedroom and carefully unscrewed the lid, drawing out an eyedropper with a few golden drops inside. Taking it to the living room, he held back the girls' heads and opened their mouths. Both were compliant. He shook his head. Human vampires were so vulnerable. He let a drop hit the tongue of each twin in turn, then let their heads loll.

Before more than two minutes passed, both awoke and looked around curiously.

"Do you remember what happened?" Julian prompted. "Regarding the laundry cart?"

Though they still appeared dazed, their eyes opened wider. "Where is it?" Lucy asked.

"Is it here?" echoed Ivy, alarmed.

"We have a small problem. It disappeared from outside my door. Do you have any idea who might have taken it?"

"No," said Lucy, her voice slurred with sleepiness.

"Nobody saw us," Ivy said.

"Maybe a maid took it?"

"That's possible, I suppose, Lucy." Julian paused for effect. "You can't let anyone know you had this little accident. It would be a good idea to find the body. When you do, hide it somewhere until you can dispose of it."

"Will you still help us?" Lucy asked.

"I can't be involved in this, not if someone else knows about it."

"But maybe no one does. I think I'm right—a maid took it."

"Possibly. If you can get the body back and keep it hidden, perhaps I can help you take it under-ground around dawn," he said, taking the direct approach. "Into the tunnels. Would that be amena-ble?"

They looked at each other, then at him. "What tunnels?" Lucy asked, all innocence.

"Girls, I know all about them."

"You do?" Lucy studied him, almost wide awake now. "Who told you?"

"Why, your uncle, of course, though he asked me not to mention it. But it seems to be important to mention it now." He smiled paternally. "Because of your current situation."

"Do you think it's all right to tell?" Ivy asked Lucy.

"We're not supposed to. He's not family."

"Yeah, but Uncle Ori told him already."

Lucy took Ivy's hand and they stood on slightly wobbly legs. "We'll think about it, Mr. Valentyn."

"Julian, please," he said, hiding his annoyance at their hesitance. "But remember, as far as anyone else knows, we never had this conversation, is that understood?"

"If we never talked to you, then how—" Ivy began, obviously not too coherent at this hour, potion or no.

"Ivy, shut up."

"But—"

"We have to go now, Ivy."

Ivy looked doubtful, but nodded.

Julian led them to the door and told them, "If you wish to speak to me, be discreet about it." He held the door for them, and shut it behind them after they left. They would probably be found out by their siblings, but Julian was clean. He had done nothing but invite them in.

Gabe Leoni was worried. He'd ditched the cart in a storage room—he was an accomplished picker of locks—but he didn't know how long it would remain undiscovered. He needed to talk to Ori, but no one would let him. From his room, he tried by phone to talk to him, but wasn't allowed to get through or even leave a message. He tried to get into the inner sanctum of the Darlings' offices, but he wasn't even allowed through the door from the mezzanine. He talked to nearly everyone at the lobby desks, and finally someone called the day manager, who promised to deliver a note to Ori. He gave Leoni a piece of hotel stationery, and Gabe quickly scribbled that he needed to talk to Ori on the double. After sealing it in an envelope, he gave it to the manager.

"I'll get this up to him immediately, sir."

"Good, thanks. I'll wait here for him."

"I don't think you'll receive an answer before five o'clock."

"But this is an emergency."

"May I ask who you are, sir?"

"Gabe Leoni. A special friend of Mr. Darling's. I assure you, he'll want to see me."

"Well, you're certainly free to wait here in the lobby, but I fear it will be a long wait. We can call you in your room as soon as we hear from him."

"Okay. I'll wait here for a while, and if he doesn't call for me soon, I'll be in my room." Leoni glowered at the man. "Don't forget."

"Don't worry, sir. I'll see to it you're notified immediately. If you're not in for any reason, we'll leave a voice-mail message."

Leoni walked away from the manager and sat down in a slat-sided Mission easy chair, feet planted firmly on the ground, arms crossed. He stared at a thirtyish nerd sitting in a matching chair across from him until the man got up and moved to another part of the lobby. That made Gabe feel good. For a small man, he knew, he had a huge presence.

That was why Orion had taken him into the Darling family.

He was a little nervous, true. Happy and relieved to be received by Ori into his family, he hadn't thought much more about dealing with the Dantes. He'd promised Ori he'd find out everything about them, but he wasn't sure how. All he knew about the Dantes was that they wanted him to gain Orion's confidence and find out where the tunnel entrance was located. That was it. He knew nothing about the Dantes themselves except that if they found out he was now spying on them, they'd kill him.

He waited and worried for an hour in the lobby before asking to see the manager again. He questioned him closely about Ori, intimidating him with his steady gaze. It seemed to work until the tic by his left eye started up. Stress. Stress did that to him. He needed Ori, he had to face the Dantes, and there was a dead body in a supply closet that could be discovered at any time. He had every right to be stressed.

Disgusted, he turned his back on the manager and went upstairs, tempted to go to the third floor to check on the body. He didn't, though, because it was too risky. Instead he went to his room, where a bottle of vodka on ice and a bag of barbecued potato chips awaited him. Ah, breakfast. The most important meal of the day.

On the third floor, Rosie Rodriguez, a senior housekeeper of the human kind, opened a large supply closet to get some paper towels and found a laundry cart blocking the way. "Damned girl," she muttered. The cart was heavy, but Rosie was strong. Probably, it was full of wet towels left to rot while Ginny screwed one of the bellboys. "Tramp." She pulled the cart into the corridor, grabbed her paper towels, locked up, and began pushing the cart toward the laundry room.

11

"So, no one is going to 'fess up?" Amanda asked the others at her table in the employee dining room.

"I wish I thought of it," Carol Anne said, smiling. "Especially the painted toenails."

"You will," Tyler assured her.

"It wasn't me," Billy the bellman said.

"Me either," said Jack Inglewood, the hotel caretaker who had just come off the dayshift.

Grady Conner, a valet, shook his head. "Me neither."

"Do you want me to ask the others?" Tyler said, gesturing at the other dining tables, most of which were filled.

"No, no, don't." Amanda blushed. She hadn't really wanted to talk about the prank in the first place, but curiosity had gotten the better of her. "Whoever did it really got me. It was so realistic!" She didn't tell them she was still shaken up by it. Something about the foot had seemed grimly real. Maybe it was the grayish cast of the skin, maybe the gloss of the polish and the little chip on the big toenail.

"I saw you come in from the garden with Stephen Darling last night," Carol Anne said in a voice filled with innuendo. "What were you two doing out there?"

Shut up! Amanda was beginning to dislike Carol Anne and her big mouth. "We weren't doing anything. I was taking a walk and we met up near the door."

Tyler was looking at her funny.

"What?" Amanda asked.

"Nothing. Nothing."

"You know," said Jack. "I was thinking about changing jobs, maybe getting into gardening."

"But, Jack," said Grady. "You've always been the caretaker."

"I know. I'm just feeling a little stir-crazy."

"Time to get to work," Tyler said, looking at his watch. He looked at Jack as he stood. "We'll leave you and Grady to hash that out by yourselves."

"Hurry up!" Lucy told her sister. "We need to find that cart." She sat at her dressing table, applying makeup.

Ivy yawned and stretched serenely across the bed, her nude body gleaming against the black satin sheets. "I'm up, I'm up." She rose and crossed to her dresser, pulling drawers open.

"Wear black. We don't want to be noticed."

Ivy pulled on jeans and a long-sleeved black top with a lacy bodice that stretched tight across her breasts. She stood behind her sister and applied lipstick, bending to look at herself in the mirror.

"Get your boobs off my head! Christ!" As Lucy spoke, she picked up her vial of potion and opened it.

"What are you doing?"

She dabbed a drop on her lips, then rubbed it

in. "See? Look how glossy my lips are now? And soft. There's kind of a slight smell, too. Have you noticed? It's nice. Weird, but nice."

"Oh, I have to try that," Ivy said as she retrieved her own vial. "How long have you been putting it on your lips?"

"Last night was the first time. Hurry up. Let's go."

Ivy finished her makeup and slipped her vial in the watch pocket of her jeans. The fragrance was so mild that she wasn't sure she even smelled it. "What if somebody's already found the body?"

"Then we play totally dumb."

"That'll be easy for you."

"Fuck off," Lucy said amiably.

They prowled the hallways on each floor, using a skeleton key to check inside the storage rooms. Lucy hoped to hell that Natasha wasn't keeping an eye on the monitors. She probably wasn't, Lucy told herself, opening a supply room on the third floor.

"Let's ask Julian if he knows anything," Ivy said as they shut the door. "It disappeared from outside his apartment."

"He said to be discreet. I don't think—"

"There's nobody around right now, so we're being discreet. Maybe he'll give us some blood. I'm starving."

"Me too."

They checked the last storage room on the third floor, with Lucy wondering if the body could have been moved into a guest room. It didn't seem likely. Finally they entered the alcove outside Julian's apartment and before they could knock, the door swung open. Horsey-faced Jinxy, dressed all in gray, stared at them. "The master says to come in."

"The *master?*" laughed Lucy. "You actually call him that?"

Jinxy glared at her. "Come in *now.*"

"Okay, okay." Lucy brushed past him, Ivy following. Jinxy shut the door behind them. "Sit down."

Before they could, Julian appeared in the hall from his bedroom and made a grand entrance. Over his loose black trousers and silk shirt, he wore a flowing capelike satin robe, ruby red trimmed with gold piping. Lucy thought he looked like the foppish host of *Iron Chef.* His white-blond hair was pulled back in a ponytail, accentuating his high cheekbones and prominent forehead. "Good evening, ladies," he said. "Won't you join me in a drink?"

"Yes!" they said simultaneously.

"Jinxy, please open a Type B positive for us, won't you?"

"Yummy," Ivy said.

"This one is a nice domestic. One of the nicest domestics I've ever had the pleasure to imbibe actually. Please sit down." He indicated the Grecian couch, then waited for them to sit before he took his seat in the curvy curule chair across from them. Shortly, Jinxy brought in a tray bearing three goblets and an uncorked bottle. He set the tray on a lamp table next to Julian. "Pour, please," said the master.

Lucy watched with fascination and hunger as Jinxy, who appeared to have cantilevered joints, poured a small amount of the crimson fluid in one glass and handed it to Julian, who first sniffed, then inhaled deeply. "Lovely. This will do nicely."

Jinxy filled the glasses and served. "Jinxy," said Julian. "You may go do what we spoke of earlier. Be sure to act with the utmost caution."

The man nodded and went out the door.

Lucy wanted to ask what he was up to, but didn't dare. She held her wine glass, dying to drink. At last, Julian raised his. "To two beautiful ladies who are doubly enchanting together."

"Once we heard that same toast at a party in Louisiana." Lucy smiled, and as she raised the glass to her lips and forced herself to sip slowly, she saw her sister out of her eye, obviously as hungry as she. She held her glass in both hands, her face hovering over it as she took in the aroma. "It was a debutante ball, just before the War between the States."

"Well, ladies, I wish I had seen you then, in your hoopskirts and corsets. Now tell me, what do you think of the vintage?"

"Delicious," said Ivy.

"Refreshing," added Lucy.

Julian sat back in his chair and his cracked-ice eyes held theirs. "How has your hunt for the missing cart proceeded?"

"We—well, we were too tired to hunt during the day," Lucy admitted. "We went back to our place and slept like the dead."

Julian smiled, Mona Lisa-style. "Understandable. And this evening?"

"We've checked all the supply rooms, but we didn't find anything."

"Perhaps the cart is in the laundry room?" Julian suggested.

"If it is, then the body's probably been found already," Ivy said after finishing off her blood.

"I've had Jinxy keep an ear open. The body remains undiscovered. I think you two should check the laundry room and the spa, and anywhere else laundry carts tend to congregate. Do you have keys to the guest rooms?" He paused, smiling. "That was a silly question. Of course you do. Perhaps your problem is inside one of the rooms. Think. Who would hide a body for you? Or from you?"

"Nobody," Lucy said promptly. "Except you." She smiled flirtatiously, knowing no one would help her and Ivy except, possibly, this man. It would all get back to Natasha otherwise.

"It was dangerous looking in the storage rooms because of Natasha's cameras. It would be really dangerous to check all the rooms," Lucy told him. "She'd see us for sure."

"Yes, I suppose she would. In this case, I think it would be best to leave the guest rooms alone. If the body is found, simply deny all knowledge."

"You mean you'll back us up?"

"No, no. I know absolutely nothing about this, remember? I won't lie and say I haven't seen you. But I will tell them you came to me simply to hear a story or two."

"Stories?" Lucy asked doubtfully. She set her glass on the coffee table, hoping he would notice it was empty. Ivy followed suit. "What kind of stories?"

"Go check the laundry room and spa and later, when you come back to see me, I'll tell you one. I'll give you the same advice I gave my servant. Be cautious. Now, off with you."

12

"A body, Boss. A body in a laundry cart. I nabbed it for you." Gabe Leoni sat forward as he spoke urgently to Ori, who had called him personally in his room only ten minutes before. Buzzed in quickly, he'd found Ori awaiting his arrival impatiently. "I wanted to tell you this morning, but nobody'd let me talk to you. I tried all day." He followed Ori into his office.

"Yes, Gabe, so I heard. Cigar?"

"No, thanks." The smell of smoke was already strong, and mixed badly with the other scents: flowers, leather, and Lemon Pledge. Gabe had sinus problems.

From the stereo came Caruso singing from *Pagliacci*, and as "Vesti La Giubba" crescendoed in the background, Ori prepared and lit a Havana. "I'm rarely available during the day, my friend. I have other business interests to tend to." He inhaled, then let out a puff of smoke.

It made Gabe want to cough, but he managed not to. A wise guy who couldn't take a little cigar smoke wasn't worth shit. He would take it and like it, if it killed him. "I just wish I'd been able to tell you sooner, Boss."

Leoni had spent a frustrating day waiting for a message from Ori. He called in every half hour, but there was nothing. Squat. Shit squat. He had walked past the storage room where he'd hidden the body several times, but he didn't dare open it because there were always people coming and going. He doubted he could have found a busier corridor.

"Do you have any idea who the victim is?" Ori asked, leaning back in his chair.

"No. I only saw the foot. A woman's foot. The toes had polish on them. Who do you think did it?"

Ori looked thoughtful, then asked, "Who do *you* think did it?"

"I dunno, Boss. But it was a whack job for sure. Suitcases were piled on the body, so it must have been a guest that bought it."

"Yes." Ori put the cigar in the ashtray and steepled his fingers. Then he looked Gabe right in the eye. "Maybe another guest did it in a fit of passion. Or maybe it's a setup."

Gabe couldn't look away, not from those eyes. "A setup?"

"The Dantes? Maybe they did it."

"As a warning?"

Ori nodded. "We'll talk more about it later. Let's go see this body of yours." He carefully stubbed his cigar, used a remote to turn off the stereo, and stood while Gabe scrambled to his feet and rushed to the door, to open it for Ori.

They didn't run into any Darlings on the way up to the third floor, and once they were there, Gabe first led him to the room with the alcove entry. "I found the cart here," he said.

"And no one was around?" Ori had a funny look on his face, kind of squinty and thoughtful. He tugged his jacket sleeve and glanced back at the door.

"Nobody, Boss. I think it was ditched there. Do you know who's got this room?"

"No one of consequence," he said quickly. "Let's see the body."

"Okay. Down here." Gabe led the way to the storage closet, and they waited while a young couple walked by. Then Ori unlocked the door.

The cart was gone.

They had gone to the spa first and found one weighty laundry cart, but Lucy and Ivy were disappointed to find nothing but damp towels within. They checked the pool area and found another cart, also heavy with towels. Now, they stood in the laundry room. No one was there, but there were half a dozen carts full of laundry in plain sight. *Please let it be in one of these.* "The attendant's probably on break, Ivy. Start looking."

They went through the six carts in two minutes and found nothing. They headed for the door, eager to leave the humid room. Their hair was getting frizzy from all the moisture.

"Look," Ivy said, stopping in her tracks. She pointed at a darkish corner where two more full carts were waiting, cut off from the rest by some cartons of supplies hastily set down.

Quickly, each girl went to a cart.

"Found it," Lucy chirped.

Ten minutes later they had the cart up to the first floor of guest rooms and were unsure of what to do with it. "Let's put it in an empty room and go tell Julian. He'll help us."

Lucy knocked on the nearest door and waited.

No one answered. She tried again, then went ahead and opened the door.

It was the Arabian Nights room and no one was using it.

Goddamned motherfucking fog. Jinxy, gray like the foggy night, had been stalking a girl on downtown Front Street when it came rolling in. The girl was dressed cheap and her hair hung in clumps, so he knew she was a slut of some sort, maybe a hooker or a runaway. Either way, she was something tasty for his master. But suddenly, she was lost in the fog.

Jinxy had listened carefully, trying to pick up the sound of her footsteps, but the fog muted them. Disgusted, he slowly found his way back to the black 4-Runner he'd driven into town.

It took him nearly an hour to make it back to the hotel. He parked Julian's SUV, then instead of returning in defeat, he walked farther up the hill to the oldest cemetery, St. Simon's. It was loaded with small family mausoleums—and there were always kids there, making out, doing drugs, all that stuff.

Here on higher ground the fog was lighter, hanging in the air like tufts of cotton. Jinxy prowled quietly, invisibly, passing up couples here and there. He heard a pair in one mausoleum, and saw another couple making love on top of an above-ground grave as a stone angel with a chipped wing looked on. Jinxy watched for a few minutes, then moved deeper into the cemetery, where he'd found fresh food for Julian on several other occasions. He was in the drug-users' region, a place of syringes, rubber tourniquets, burnt spoons, and who knew what all else.

He found the junkie in a small mausoleum of

dark gray granite. Its stone pillars were images of the Virgin Mary, head bowed, hands up in prayer, and the name over the wrought-iron door was Johnson. Jinxy stepped quietly inside, his eyes first falling on the pair of concrete sarcophagi and the names above them. One was Mary Johnson, the other, Peter Johnson. They'd died in 1917, probably in the flu epidemic. Behind Peter's sarcophagus, a young man, not too dirty, and possibly handsome if he weren't so thin, cowered. A needle lay beside him. Blood tainted with drugs wasn't Julian's first choice—it didn't affect him, he just didn't like the flavor as well—but it would have to do tonight.

"Hey, I'm not here to hurt you, man," Jinxy re-assured the guy, who was probably in his late teens or early twenties.

The youth just stared up at him, terror in his glazed eyes.

"Could you use some food, man? Maybe a little cash?"

Still no reply.

"Hey, it's okay. I work with the Candle Bay Shelter. We're here to help people with problems, not judge 'em."

The young man looked at him with shadowed eyes. "Place to sleep? A little cash?"

"I think we can do that. Let me help you up."

He couldn't have weighed more than 130, though he should have carried forty pounds more. Together they walked out into the night. "We don't have far to go," Jinxy said. "And don't worry, we'll go in the back door. No one will see us."

"Thanks," said the addict. "I appreciate it. Been having a hard time, you know?"

"I know. We'll take care of all your troubles."

13

Natasha Darling sat at a secluded table for two in Satyrelli. Across from her was her favorite guest, Douglas Harper, the man with the massive member, the penis of the gods. Douglas had the spiedini and she had a bloody-rare steak. They shared a bottle of valpolicella, and what amazed Natasha was the amount of human food and drink she was consuming. Usually, she barely touched food; a bite or two was all she could ingest; she had to content herself with the aroma. But tonight, she'd nibbled through the entire, cool center of her tenderloin. And the wine—normally she barely tasted it, yet she'd had half a glass and she wasn't finished yet.

"What are you thinking about?" Harper asked.

"Nothing important. Just how good the food is."

"But you're just picking at it."

"I have to watch what I eat," she told him. "What about you?" She smiled seductively. "What's on *your* mind tonight?"

"Pleasuring you any way I can."

"You're my guest. I should pleasure you."

"Then we'll pleasure each other." He reached across the table and held her hand briefly. "I've missed you. It's been six weeks since my last visit."

"What kept you?" Natasha studied the handsome man. For a human, he had amazing eyes, green and piercing. His voice was special too, an irresistible clear tenor. Douglas was a romance writer and, typically, he spent a week or ten days of every month at the hotel. He said it was good for his concentration. He spent his days with his laptop, writing in the gardens, and his nights, as often as possible, with Natasha. Her family knew about her human lover, but never objected. How could they? She never let her affair interfere with the family business. "I missed you too."

"I was on Maui for several weeks, researching my new book; then I had to visit my publisher in New York." He rolled his eyes.

"You poor thing," she chided. "Stuck on a tropical island. It must have been terrible."

"I'll probably have to go back for another week's research in a few months. Would you care to join me?"

Natasha felt a pang, but smiled through it. "I wish I could, but I don't think they make a sunscreen powerful enough to protect me."

"You could use a little sun," Douglas told her. "You're almost too pale."

"My skin is overly sensitive, so you'll have to put up with me the way I am."

"I'll be glad to. What do you think of the valpolicella?"

"I never drink—wine." She paused. "Well, almost never, so I can't really compare it to other vintages, but this is delicious."

"What happens when you drink?" He smiled coyly as she took another sip.

"It makes me giddy. It loosens my inhibitions."

"Then why don't you drink? That's what it's for."

"Because of my job. I have to be on my toes at all times." She smiled. "Without inhibitions, I would be too much for you to handle. Trust me."

"I'd like to try."

She wanted him. Right now she wanted to do more to him than just make love. She wanted to bite him, and that scared her. She looked up. "Here comes my uncle."

Ori arrived at the table in an immaculate Armani suit and maroon silk tie. "We have a little problem," he said to Natasha. "I'm sorry for disturbing you, but it needs your attention as soon as possible."

"Douglas, will you excuse me? I'll join you for a nightcap at, say, ten?"

"I wouldn't miss it."

Stephen Darling looked down at Amanda Pearce, who was manning the desk by herself. "How's everything going tonight, Amanda?"

"Fine." She could get lost in those eyes. "I was initiated today." She told him about the foot in the laundry cart.

"And you don't know who did it?" Stephen didn't sound especially amused.

"No one admitted to it. Stephen, it was only a joke. I don't want to get anyone in trouble."

"No, no. Don't worry about it."

Tyler Shane approached them. "Excuse me, Stephen? Natasha wants you for a meeting in her office right away."

"All right." He smiled again at Amanda, held her eyes an instant longer than necessary. "I'll see you later. Here's my number." He handed her a small card. "Call me if you need me."

Amanda, complimented, smiled to herself as Stephen walked toward the mezzanine stairs.

"He likes you," Tyler said, sitting down. "He rarely gives his number to anyone."

"Oh, no, it's nothing," she said, though it seemed like a very big something.

"Have you seen any more strange feet tonight?" Tyler smiled and continued before she could answer. "I have a job for you."

"Oh? What is it?" Getting away from the desk for a while sounded like a great idea.

"See that couple at registration?"

"The redhead and the dark-haired man?"

"Yes. They're the McLeods. Susan and Randy. They're among our best customers."

Amanda nodded.

"This visit, they're staying in the Arabian Nights Room. I'd like you to accompany them and the bellman to the room and point out the features. They've never been in this room before." He smiled. "They usually stay in the baseball room."

"What?"

"A lot of home runs are made in that room."

"Okay," she said slowly. "I'll take your word for it. I've never been in the Arabian room. What are the features?"

"Most of them, you'll see right off. Show them how the tent flaps around the bed pull back, show them how to operate the Jacuzzi. Point out the Arabian silk robes in the closet. Most importantly, point out the massage oils and other luxuries. You'll see them. They're in plain sight. It's room 121. To the right. Let the bellman lead."

"I—" She was still processing information.

"You'll do fine. Don't accept a tip."

"Of course not," she said, rising. She straightened her blazer and smoothed her skirt. "Here I go."

She approached the couple and introduced herself before walking with them to the room. "I'm sure you'll enjoy your visit," she said, following Billy the bellman and the McLeods into the room.

It was breathtaking. A swirl of chiffons and silks decorated the room, from the tufted ceiling to the sheer tent over the bed. She showed them how that worked—thank heaven she had enough common sense to figure it out. Then she showed them the beautiful robes in the closet, and followed that by pointing out the small containers of salves and oils on the dresser. McLeod blushed as his wife patted him on the rear.

"You have a Jacuzzi in the bathroom," Amanda said, leading them into the large luxurious room. She stopped short as her gaze fell on the laundry cart in the corner. "Oh, dear," she exclaimed. "It looks like the maid left something behind." Billy was hanging garment bags, so she manhandled the cart out of the room herself. There were dirty sheets on top and it smelled a little. *Could it be?* After leaving it in the hall, she returned to the room. "Billy, I'll take care of the laundry cart myself."

"You sure?" he asked after thanking the McLeods for his tip.

"Positive," she assured him. Billy nodded and wheeled his luggage rack out of the room.

"Somebody's in trouble," McLeod said, smiling.

"Don't bawl anyone out on our account," said his wife.

"I just want to find out who left it and remind them not to be so forgetful next time," Amanda said. "No one's in trouble." That wasn't the primary reason, though. She wanted to look in the heavy cart. "Please call us if you need anything. Have a nice stay."

She left the room and pushed the cart away from the door, up close to the wall. It seemed heavier than ever and the faint rank smell was distinct. Holding her breath, she lifted the sheets and there, among the suitcases, were the toes, the flesh grayish, the nails cotton candy pink. The disgusting smell wafted into her nose and she let the sheets drop back over the top. Her stomach began to rise.

She ran for the lobby, just making it into the stall of a public rest room before losing her dinner. *Oh, God, that smell.*

She cleaned up and returned to the lobby, only to see that Tyler was busy with someone. Instead of waiting for him, she called Stephen's pager. A moment later, her phone rang.

"This is Stephen. What's wrong?"

"You know the prank I told you about? The foot?"

"Yes?"

"It's not a prank. I found the cart on the first floor. The foot is real."

"I'll be right down. Keep this to yourself."

"We have a body," Stephen said as he stood up. "Amanda Pearce just found it."

"Good," Natasha replied. "Make sure and use your charms on her before she talks about this to anyone. If you can't do it alone, bring her to us." She nodded toward Ori and Ivor, who sat in other chairs fronting her desk. Lucy and Ivy sat behind them.

"Don't worry, I'll get it done." He left the room.

Natasha turned her gaze on the twins. "What do you two have to do with all this?"

"We don't know anything about it," Lucy said.

Ivy looked Natasha in the eye. "We were asleep all day."

"I see," Natasha said, unconvinced. The twins very well could be innocent, but there was no way to tell—they could lie as well as they could tell the truth. In fact, they didn't seem to know the difference. "You two can go for now. Ivor, why don't you accompany them until someone else can chaperone them?"

"Of course." The big man stood and followed the girls out.

When the door shut, she turned to Ori. "We need to talk about some things."

"Gabe Leoni is no problem," Ori said before she could go on. "I've already made sure he doesn't remember anything."

"How can you be so sure it worked?"

"You worry too much, Natasha. I quizzed him. And if my charm doesn't hold completely, he still won't talk because he's loyal to me."

"Only yesterday, he was working for the Dantes."

"Trust me. I added a small suggestion. He now will believe, if any memory comes back, that the Dantes left the body here, which may be true. And Gabe continues to have no clue as to our true nature. We're simply his 'family.' And he's loyal."

"I'll have to see proof before I believe it. How can you put so much trust in a human, especially one who changes loyalties so easily?"

"The Dantes are nothing but animals. It's not too difficult to see why he changed loyalties. They treat him like dirt. They disrespect him."

Natasha felt her stomach gnawing. She tried to

tell herself it was a response to consuming so much human food and drink, but she knew it was blood hunger. She wondered if Ori felt the same thing. Perhaps it was time to talk to him. But not now. Not without Stephen.

"Why don't we continue our conversation in my office?" her uncle asked. "I have a lovely bottle of B negative on hand. I could use a drink. How about you?"

"Yes, that would be nice."

Stephen Darling arrived back at the concierge desk after being stopped by guests and employees four times along the way. The body, the delays, the Dantes, Amanda, and his own burgeoning hunger all fused together to set his nerves on fire. He felt a fine tremor in his hands as he waited for Amanda to finish with a guest. Looking down, he saw they were as steady as a statue's. Being undead did have its advantages.

Watching Amanda work reinforced his growing preoccupation with her. Was he in danger of losing control? No, he didn't think so, but he couldn't do anything about his feelings. Amanda Pearce was, after all, an employee, not a guest like Natasha's lover, Douglas Harper. That was merely inappropriate. This would be inexcusable. He looked at her hair, now coiled up behind her head, neatly and elegantly, and wondered what it would be like to unpin it, to run his hands through it. To kiss those full lips and taste her skin.

What's the matter with you? He was furious with his own thoughts, but as the guest moved away from the desk, he gathered himself together.

Amanda stood. "Stephen," she said.

Her voice . . . He wanted this woman. But he couldn't have her. *The corpse! Think about that!* But he could practically taste Amanda's blood. It would be sweet—*stop it!* "Where's Tyler?"

"On a break."

"Do you have someone else you can call on to man the desk?"

"Yes. Just a minute." Amanda went to the reception desk and came back with Carol Anne. "It'll just be until Tyler gets back. Not long," she told her.

"No problem! How are you, sir?"

"Fine, Carol Anne," Stephen said. This one was a gossip. As soon as they were away from the desk, he asked Amanda if she had told her anything.

"Well, she knows about the fake foot. So do at least a few others. I'm sorry, I told them at dinner. I was trying to find out who did it."

"Understandable. Have you said anything to her since you alerted me? Or to anyone else?"

"Of course not," she said, looking annoyed. "You told me not to."

"I had to be sure."

They stepped into the elevator and rode silently, both smiling and nodding at the guests they rode with. Fortunately, none of the guests got off at the first floor. "Where?" he asked as they entered the central hallway. Corridors led off in several directions.

She looked a little lost, then said, "The Arabian Nights room."

"Room 121."

"Yes, that's it."

"It's this way." He led her down a right-hand hallway, turning two corners before coming to Room 121. There was no laundry cart in sight.

"Damn," Amanda said softly.

Before he did anything else, it was time to make her forget. Stephen put his hand on Amanda's shoulder and turned her gently toward him. Her liquid eyes looked up into his, showing fear. He turned on the charm. "Amanda," he said, holding her gaze, "It's nothing. There was never anything here."

Her eyes flashed. "Of course there was. Do you think I'd call you if there wasn't?"

She wasn't supposed to respond like that. She was supposed to begin going under. He tried again. "There's nothing to worry about. It was a joke."

"Stephen," she replied, upset. "It smelled!"

"Shhh. Quietly, Amanda. Wet towels often smell, especially if they've been sitting for a while."

"There were suitcases and a foot under a sheet! Not towels."

"The towels were underneath," he soothed. "Underneath the luggage and manikin's foot that somebody thought they'd tease you with." He paused, redoubling his efforts. "Someone knew you were going to the Arabian Nights room, so they stuck the cart in there to tease you. Only, it wasn't a good joke."

She studied him, her eyes clear, not dazed. "No."

Amanda was the most resistant human he had ever come across.

"Why are you saying this? Why don't you believe me?"

"Amanda, I believe you," he began. "It's just that a body in a hamper sounds like a joke. If it's true, it's a serious matter."

"It's true."

He nodded. "Then I'll take care of it."

"Are you going to call the police?"

"Not now. Not until I have the body. And then, Amanda, you probably won't hear any more. We won't tell the staff. Only you and management will know. If it gets out it could destroy our business."

She considered, then nodded. "Okay. I won't say anything. But, Stephen, it's the second time I've seen it. Other people must have seen it too."

"But a laundry cart is a laundry cart. They're not likely to look inside."

"Well, you'd better find it before it gets any riper." She gave him a fathomless look. "If you want it to stay a secret."

"I want to talk to you again later, explain how these things work," Stephen said as they returned to the elevator. "What time is your next break?"

"About ten."

"Meet me in the garden, the one with the night-blooming jasmine. Do you know it?"

"It's near the side doors where we came in last night."

"Exactly. We'll talk there."

They parted in the lobby, and Stephen watched her as she walked across to the concierge desk and realized he was starving. Not only did he want her, he wanted her blood.

14

The thing was, Gabe Leoni didn't know why the laundry cart parked in the hall outside Room 121 seemed so familiar. But it was. He looked inside, repelled by a faint repulsive odor, and when he saw the suitcases and toes, it all came back to him. It was the cart he'd found this morning, the one he'd told Ori about. *Isn't it? Didn't I?*

How could I forget about this? Instead of stopping to ponder the question, he quickly pushed the cart down the hall and around a corner, stashing it in a dark corner. He wondered if he was losing his mind.

It's the Dantes! The thought popped into his head with stunning strength. Ori had warned him. *The Dantes put the body here!* He ran to his room to call Ori.

Opening his door, he saw the sheer white curtains blowing in the cool wind through the open balcony door. "What the fuck?"

"Hello, Gabe," Nicholas Dante said from the balcony. Leaving the door open, he pushed away the sheers and stepped inside, then walked to the right edge of the sliding door and shut the heavy blue drapes over the window and sheers. "How've you been?"

"Fine. Just fine." Gabe tried to hide his nervousness, but doubted he was doing a very good job. "I was going to call you tonight."

Nicholas smiled, all gleaming teeth and short dyed-blond hair. "Now there's no need. I'm here." He walked around the room, looking at the ceiling and corners, the lamps and furniture, and bent to study the dark television set. "This place is clean."

"Yes."

"Did you check it for bugs?"

"Oh, a hotel like this doesn't have bugs," Gabe told him. "It's a class joint."

Nicholas walked up to him and slapped his face. "Listening devices, cameras. Don't be stupid."

"I'm sorry. It's just that I wasn't expecting you. I wasn't thinking."

"Thinking's not what you're paid to do. You're supposed to look. So tell me, what have you looked at?"

Should he mention the body? Probably not. "Ori liked the DVD player. You were right; it made him friendlier."

"Good. What else have you got for me?"

"Nothing yet. I haven't been able to get him to talk about the tunnels."

"Have you tried?" Nicholas blinked slowly, like a snake.

"Not directly."

"Shit, Leoni, just come right out and ask him when he's in a good mood. It's not like the stories about tunnels and the treasure, for that matter, are a big secret. You're just asking about rumors as far as he's concerned. He's not gonna be suspicious, you pussy."

"I don't want him to think I'm just interested in him for that."

"Listen. He already *knows* you're interested. He knows you're a two-bit crook who'd love to get his hands on some gold. He's not stupid like you." Dante laughed. "He's stupid different from you. He doesn't know you're working for me and he's going to say something to you he shouldn't. Okay? Now look in the closet."

"What?"

"Look in the fucking closet, barf-bag."

Gabe did as he was told, and found a garment bag that hadn't been there before.

"It's Italian," said Dante. "Tell him it's right off the boat. He'll love it. It'll buy you some points, Gabe. Use them wisely. But use them before I run out of patience."

Gabe swallowed. "Sure, Boss."

"It's months you been hanging out with Ori. I want some results. Putting you up here's costing me a fortune. Who said you could get massages every day?"

Gabe looked sheepish. "Sorry."

"And eat in the coffee shop more often. It's cheaper."

"You got it, Boss."

Dante stepped closer, moving behind Gabe and around him, sniffing. "You stink like a fucking corpse. What've you been doing?"

"Nothing. It's just sweat. I need a shower. That's what I was gonna do when I came in."

Dante eyed him suspiciously, then shrugged and walked to the door. "One other thing. I want you to pay attention to who's staying here. I'm looking for a guy named Julian Valentyn. Might be using a different name. You can't miss him, though. He's real white, maybe albino. Tall, long blond hair. I want to know if he's here and what room he's in."

Gabe decided not to tell him he already knew. "Do you want me to talk to him?"

"No. The bastard killed my brother, Leo. I want that fucker on a platter. I'll take care of him myself." He paused. "We're watching you, Leoni. Don't you forget it."

An instant later he was gone.

Gabe couldn't stand the idea of stinking. Before doing anything else, he shucked off his outer clothing and stuffed it in the laundry bag for the maid. He washed his face and put a lot of good smelly gel in his hair to mask any remaining odors, then dressed in a nice charcoal suit. He put his shoes on as he called Ori.

"I gotta see you, Boss. *Now.* It's real important. It can't wait."

"That's the second time today something can't wait." The man's gravelly voice sounded amused. Which was good. "Where are you?"

"In my room. I found it."

"Found what?"

"You know, what I was talking about earlier." Sotto voce he said, "The corpse," then raised his voice again. "You want me to bring it with me?"

"What? No! Absolutely not. Someone will be there shortly. Wait for them."

Hanging up, Gabe rubbed his hands together. This was getting good.

Ori, seated behind his massive desk, gazed at his niece and nephew. Natasha was enjoying her second glass of B neg and Stephen, who had just arrived, was pouring himself a goblet. They were drinking more than usual, but then so was he. He cleared his throat. "Gabe Leoni has, once again, found the body."

"Good," Stephen said. "Because I didn't find it. But I checked in with Ellen in Housekeeping. She says that Room 142 is rented to a Jennifer Brown of Beaver's Neck, Oregon. It had a Do Not Disturb sign on the door all day, and Miss Brown hasn't been seen today. Ellen checked her room and she wasn't there. Neither was her luggage, but she's not due to check out until day after tomorrow."

"Any other irregularities with guests?" Ori asked.

"No. Ellen says everyone else is accounted for."

"Did you tell Ellen about our problem?"

"No details, but, yes, I did."

"Good," said Ori, punching in the number for Housekeeping. He spoke into the receiver, asking for Ellen, who was the nighttime head housekeeper and part of their fanged extended family. "Yes. Would you go see Mr. Gabriel Leoni in Room 102? He believes he's found that item you and Stephen talked about a short time ago. If you find it, put it somewhere safe. Send Mr. Leoni to me immediately after he shows you where it is. Allegedly is. Thanks." He hung up. "Let's hope this isn't another false alarm." He rose. "It didn't take long to finish that bottle off."

Stephen finished his drink in a gulp and gave Ori the goblet. Natasha did the same. As Ori rinsed, Natasha asked, "Why didn't your charm work on Leoni?"

"It did," he said, turning. "The only reason he remembers is because he found the cart again. That brought it all back."

"And Stephen, what about our young concierge?"

"Bad news. She's resistant. I ended up swearing her to secrecy for the good of the hotel. I gave her our stock story. She understands discretion."

"That's not good enough, Stevie. You know that."

"I know," he said regretfully. "Perhaps you can charm her. I seem to have some sort of emotional tie to her. That may be all that's wrong."

"You're emotionally involved with an employee?" Ori asked, raising an eyebrow.

"No. I simply feel drawn to her. I don't know why." He glanced at Natasha. "Perhaps in the same way you're drawn to Mr. Harper."

'Tasha had been poised to say something nasty, Stephen could see that, but now she settled back in her chair. "You can't act on impulses you may have. She's an *employee*. And a dangerous one if she's resistant."

"What if he bites her?" Ori asked suddenly. "That's a surer way to gain control of a subject, combining the bite with the charm. He could go to her room tonight."

Natasha nodded. "Maybe in this case we should try that before anything else. If she is resistant to hypnosis, it would be best if she didn't catch me trying it on her, as you did, Stevie."

Stephen, aroused, did his best to hide it. "Whatever you say, 'Tasha. Whatever you say."

Nicholas Dante was nothing if not observant, and finding the laundry cart had been easy. Having smelled the putrid odor on Leoni's clothing, he was alert for the odor of death as he left the man's room and walked into the hall. He had a superior sense of smell, even for a vampire. A human would not have been able to pick up the scent, not until he was right on top of it, but Nicholas Dante followed it around corners until he came to the prize.

If you could call it that. What had Leoni been doing with a corpse? Surely the Darlings didn't know about it—they would never allow such a thing in their precious hotel. Had Leoni done it? He didn't think so, he didn't think Leoni had the balls to kill. Why would he anyway? And if Ori wanted someone killed, he'd have much better ways of taking care of it; he'd do it himself or have one of his family do it. It was truly an interesting little mystery.

Now that he had the cart, Dante wondered how he could use it to his advantage. There was no time for anything elaborate—he had to leave the hotel without being noticed. He could leave the body in plain sight, but that would require touching the corpse and he didn't want to do that. Then he had an amusing little idea. He pushed the cart into the middle elevator and sent it to the third floor. Meanwhile, he took another elevator to the lobby and didn't wait around to see what happened. He'd get back to Julian and his secrets later.

When Lucy and Ivy had entered the women's spa for a little pampering, they were finally free of Ivor. "He'll probably wait for us," Ivy said in a poisonous tone.

Lucy shrugged. "Fuck him. I'm starving."

"Me too. But it'll be hours before Natasha lets us have dinner." Bare, Ivy lay on her stomach on the highest bench in the steam room. Her sister reclined on her back on the middle bench, similarly attired. They were the double-nude twins.

Lucy, who was extra juicy from all the wonderful oils and emollients that had been rubbed into her skin by the masseuse, was in a mellow mood. "We'll lose Ivor." She thought a moment. "Maybe we could go see Julian. He'll give us a drink. We need to tell him the cart's gone again too."

"That's a good idea." Ivy sat up. "You know, next time we should go in the men's steam room."

"Yeah," said Lucy with an evil grin. "I'll bet *they* wouldn't all leave just because we take our towels off."

The attendant, Kayla, opened the door. "Um, excuse me, girls, but the guests have been complaining."

"About what?" asked Lucy, lusty with hunger. Kayla, a young African-American, looked good enough to eat. She exchanged glances with Ivy, who shook her head no. She was always the voice of reason. Sometimes it was a real drag.

"Your attire. Lack of it, I mean. Some of the guests are uncomfortable with nudity, even in here." Kayla gestured at the room and smiled. "Would you mind draping a towel, you know?"

"I don't know," Lucy said innocently. "Drape it where?"

Kayla looked uncomfortable. "Over your privates."

"My cunt or my tits or both?" Behind her, Ivy giggled softly.

"Your—your breasts aren't the issue. You can leave them bare."

"So we should cover our cunts?"

"Um, yes."

Lucy plucked a towel off the bench and dropped it on her crotch. "Like this?"

Kayla looked like a statue in the mist. "Yes," she finally said, and with that, headed for the door.

"Wait." Ivy stood and walked to the young

woman. "We're getting dressed now. In about five minutes, would you check and see if Ivor is out there?"

Kayla smiled. "Sure."

"Thanks. Has anyone ever told you you have a beautiful neck? It's long. Regal."

"Thanks." She was out of the door like a shot.

"You shouldn't have said that," Lucy chided. "You scared her. She thinks you're from the Isle of Lesbos."

"I'd like to do more than scare her."

"Me too. We've got to refill some of our bottles so we have something to drink in our rooms. This is ridiculous."

"Yeah, Natasha'd have a fit if she knew ours were all empty already."

"I know. But she doesn't know, so let's go see Julian!"

Up and down. Down and up. Mezzanine, lobby, first floor, second floor, third. There were three elevators in the lobby, but no employees had happened to use the middle one, nor did any guests happen to complain. Up and down. Down and up. Jennifer Brown's body rode the rails.

If Nicholas Dante had stuck around, he would have been amused to see how people instinctively avoided being near the cart as they made their way to and from their rooms. The McLeods of the Arabian Nights room, on their way out for a lobster dinner at the Seaman's Shanty on the beach a few miles north in tourist-friendly Caledonia, edged away from the cart, Randy surreptitiously sniffing his jacket, just in case. They eyed another couple in the elevator suspiciously. That pair didn't meet their eyes, and by the time they reached the lobby, the McLeods had decided it was the other duo stinking things up. The feeling was probably mutual. "Smells like someone spent too much time at the cemetery," Susan told her husband as they walked through the huge lobby.

When the Hunts, allergy sufferers both, got on, they didn't noticed the odor, but their three-month-old infant, Mikey, did and set up an embarrassing wail. And little Marsha Martinez, whose incredible sense of smell had been dismissed by her parents as an annoying streak of imagination, said nothing but stuck her fingers in her nose and breathed through her mouth.

Then there was Douglas Harper, who looked at the bottoms of his shoes to see if he'd stepped in something. He forgot the vague odor as his thoughts turned to Natasha Darling, whom he was planning to immortalize as the heroine of his next book about a bra-busting hotel-keeper and her misadventures while finding her true love. On the elevator with Douglas was twenty-five-year-old Annette Chen, who didn't notice the odor at all; her impressions were purely visual and centered on Harper's modestly pleated trousers. The only trouble was, the pleats couldn't hide anything. Short of strapping his pride and joy to his inner thigh, which negated the action because it aroused him, there was no way to hide Mr. Chubby.

And so it went. Down and up, up and down. Finally, two young vampires bound for the third floor boarded the elevator for the upward trek. There was only one other rider in the car.

"Do you think that's it?" Ivy asked quietly as they looked toward the laundry cart.

Lucy wrinkled her nose. "It has to be."

The other rider got off at the second floor. "Julian will help us," said Lucy.

"He said to leave him out of it."

"He has to help us. He likes us. He'll do it." Lucy never questioned such things.

At the third floor, the girls got off, both pushing the cart. An old geezer they passed cast a curious look their way, but no one else paid them any attention, and after they turned down the corridor leading to Julian's suite, they saw no one.

Lucy knocked on his door, then looked at her sister. "God, that stinks."

"Isn't it awful?"

They waited a minute, then knocked again. "I hope he's there," Ivy said nervously.

"Me too. What if he's gone? What should we do?"

"What should you do about what, ladies?" Julian asked as he opened the door. He was dressed in gray trousers and a black sweater and his long pale hair lay loose on his shoulders. His narrow, high-cheekboned face was lupine and, in an odd, regal way, handsome. "Ah, I see your problem. And smell it." He turned away. "Jinxy! Jinxy, come here immediately." He looked at the twins. "Did anyone see you?"

"A few guests, but not nearby."

"This is dangerous. I wish you hadn't brought it here. I don't want to lose the trust of your family."

"We didn't know where else to take it!" cried Lucy.

"I know."

"We just found it in the elevator."

"Master Julian?" Jinxy came up behind Valentyn.

"Ladies, come in," Julian said, standing back. "Jinxy, this is the cart that disappeared from our door this morning. We need to do something about the body. Wheel it in."

The twins entered, followed by Jinxy, pushing the laundry cart. Julian locked the door and waited as Jinxy pushed the cart into a hall leading to the bathroom. He disappeared, soon returning without the cart. "What do you want me to do with it?"

"Do we have plenty of those heavy garbage bags?"

"Yes. Enough for both bodies."

"Both?" began Lucy.

Valentyn ignored her. "Very well. Do you think you can fit them both into the suitcases?"

"It'll be a tight fit, but we've got five cases."

"Then take off your clothes and get them into the tub. You have a lot of cutting to do. And Jinxy?"

"Yes?"

"Neatness counts. Now, my dears," he said, turning to the girls. "You look famished. Would you like something to drink?"

"Yes, please," they said together.

While he poured, Lucy spoke. "There are two bodies?"

Julian looked up and smiled gently. "We can't just leave our empties lying around, now, can we?" He brought their drinks and sat down in his chair.

"Is it a guest?"

"Heavens, no, ladies. I wouldn't do such a thing. This was human trash which won't be missed. I was craving something fresh and didn't feel like going out myself, so Jinxy did a bit of hunting for me. It wasn't much, but it was warm and pumping."

"Do you go hunting yourself?"

"At times."

"Maybe we could come with you sometime?" Lucy gave Julian her most winning smile.

"We'll see. You realize, don't you, that I have no business socializing with you? I doubt that your elders would approve." He looked at Lucy, then Ivy. "And to let you bring a corpse in here, well, I don't know what I was thinking. I must have been blinded by your charms," he added smoothly.

"We'll never let anyone find out," Ivy said.

"We promise."

"The best intentions. Your family has cameras all over. They could have seen you wheel the cart up here."

"Yeah," said Lucy. "Did you know they know about it? The body?"

Julian sat forward. "Tell me."

"One of the employees saw it and reported it. Natasha asked us a lot of questions, but we never let on we knew anything."

"Then they haven't actually seen the body?"

"No!"

"Good. Do you understand if they find out about you, I'm going to admit you came to me and asked for help? I must retain their trust."

Lucy and Ivy nodded. "Please, Julian," said the latter, holding out her glass. "May I have some more?"

Julian poured them each another glass, then settled back, ignoring the occasional grunts and thumps and bad odors that came from the bathroom. "What do you know about your new employee, the concierge?"

"Who?" Lucy asked, not hiding her surprise.

"The young lady at the concierge desk in the evenings."

"Oh, her. Nothing. She's the one who saw the body, though."

"I haven't talked to her. Have you, Lucy?"

"No." She leaned forward. "Why? What do you want to know?"

"I'd like to know more about her. She reminds me of someone I once knew. Find out her name, her background. You can do that, can't you, ladies?"

Both nodded, then Lucy said, "But she's just a human female."

"Not always, my dears. Now, but not always." A serene smile followed a moment of silence. "Half a millennia ago, I last saw her. I know she's been in this world some several times since, but never again have I found her. Never. Until now." He sounded wistful. "Perhaps."

"How can you know that?" asked Ivy. "How can you tell?"

"My darling girls, one never forgets one's queen."

15

"It's probably beautiful out tonight," Amanda said to Stephen shortly after they met in the foggy garden near the side entrance. It was a masterpiece of terraced walls rising up from the ground to about ten feet. Lush, beautiful greenery spilled over the walls, with sprinklings of delicate flowers, visible in the fog-muted lamplight. Behind the benches were walls of night-blooming jasmine. From an arbor, cedar pots hung, heavy with philodendrons of many varieties, crested white, dark greens, spring leaves. Purple wandering jew, dotted with lavender flowers, trailed among the green leaves and, in the brick planters, red begonias were massed among the ferns and caladiums and all sorts of other semitropicals whose names Uncle Ori would know. It wasn't so much a colorful garden as a green hideaway. As in many of the gardens, a life-sized gray plaster Green Man head was mounted above the bricks. This one spouted honeysuckle from its eyes and mouth and its features blended eerily with the fog. It was a favorite of his.

"It *is* beautiful," Stephen agreed. "At least we can see a little. The fog's not too bad. Would you like to visit another garden?"

She smiled. "Can you find the way?"

"I have special eyes. I can see in the fog." He offered her his arm and as she took it, he felt a shiver of pleasure and a pang of hunger.

He led her past the herb garden with its savory scents, and into a very private circular garden. The ground was paved with red cobblestone, and a large wedding cake redbrick planter, iced with thick mortar between the bricks, was the centerpiece, while honeysuckle vines hung like screens all around them. Heliotrope, rich violet and sweet, with dark fuzzy leaves, bloomed between four iron loveseats spaced around the circle.

The planter, about twelve feet around at the base, held blooming spring bulbs. Anemones, crocus, and freesia flowered sweetly, and purple irises with yellow combs shot between them on the lowest level. Multicolored tulips mixed with lavender hyacinth in thick masses on the middle tier. The small round top of the structure was crowned with a blaze of gladiolus. Silver-leafed salvia bearing small brilliant blue flowers trailed down the bricks to flirt with the hyacinth. Sweet violets and pansies, primrose and peonies, bloomed among the bulbs. Sweet fragrances filled the still night air, and Stephen inhaled deeply. "The air is so sweet," he said.

"It is," said Amanda as they sat down on one of the loveseats. "I'll have to come back in the morning. If it's this strong now, it must be heavenly when the sun is up." She paused, then bluntly said, "Tell me about the body."

"Well, we haven't found it yet," he told her, then reminded her that if they did, she probably would never hear about the police investigation. He claimed that in the past there had been a few other deaths—including a murder—at the hotel, and the police of Candle Bay were very delicate about such matters. They understood the value of the hotel for the local economy. All the while, he tried to charm her, to hypnotize her, but his attempts failed. She looked skeptical, and insisted that the police would want to interview her. She looked even more skeptical when he said they'd probably be satisfied without doing so.

She studied him a long moment, then nodded. "All right, but I still think it sounds fishy."

"Don't worry, it's not. One of the first things you learn in the real world of hotels is that unless a slipup occurs, virtually all deaths of any kind are kept quiet."

"What about explaining to the survivors where and how their loved one died?"

"I don't know about other hotels, but with the help of the police, we can usually minimalize the attention our hotel receives. Keep the press out of it." The truth was, of course, the police were rarely involved. The other truth was that he would have to bite her to make sure she did as asked. He looked forward to it.

She raised an eyebrow. "Nothing illegal?"

"All within the bounds of the law. We only ask that you, as our loyal employee, keep everything you know to yourself. Will you do that?"

"Yes. I suppose."

He looked at her face, at the soft curl of hair clinging, fog-dampened, to the smooth smooth skin of her neck. He could see the faint throb of blood flowing through her carotid artery. He licked his lips. He could bite her now. *No! Not while she's awake. It's too risky. What the hell is wrong with you?*

"What are you thinking?" she asked, studying him.

"Nothing."

She might have been a beautiful spirit if it weren't for the beat, beat, beat of her heart. He could nearly hear it. He looked at her lips, the lower one so full it begged to be bitten. Her eyes were deep mysteries in the misty lamplight. He wanted to suck her lip into his mouth, to feel her heat, to taste her. His eyes on hers, he bent his head a little, moving closer to her. Her eyes searched his, her pupils large, her nostrils flaring. He knew he could kiss her, that she was attracted to him as well. He hesitated, then drew back, not because she was his employee—at that moment, it never even entered his mind—but because if he kissed her, he would bite her. He had to wait.

"Riveting, as always," Ori Darling said as the *Sopranos* episode he'd replayed rolled credits.

"That Tony," Gabe Leoni said, "he sure gets a lot of pussy."

"The ladies like his power."

"I like his daughter," Gabe mumbled.

Ori gave him a disapproving look, then went to the drink cart and poured two glasses of a mild-mannered red wine. The maid, Ellen, had not found the body in the laundry cart, but he was sure that it existed. He believed Leoni. Carrying the glasses over to the leather chairs, he handed one to Leoni. Seating himself, he said, "I never interrupt *The Sopranos* with business. Now we shall talk. Tell me about that." He nodded toward the garment bag hanging on a coat hook.

"It's a Hugo Boss, right off the boat. Ori, that's part of what I need to tell you."

"Tell me."

Gabe felt pinned under Ori's dark eyes. It was a familiar sensation. "You know the stuff I've been giving you? The cigars, the DVD player, the suit?"

"Courtesy of the Dantes?"

"Yes."

"I knew that as soon as you confessed to me the identity of your original employer." Ori sipped from his glass, then sipped again. "I like to drink wine more than I used to." He paused. "Anyway, I drink more." He looked at the wine glass, then set it down. "What else do you need to tell me?"

"Nicholas Dante was here tonight."

That got Ori's attention. Maybe Dante really did have something to do with the missing body. "In the hotel?"

"He was in my room. He brought the suit."

"Why was he here? Do you know?"

"I know he was here to put the squeeze on me." Gabe looked into those mesmerizing eyes again and told him about the visit. All about it. "He wants me to find out about the tunnels and your treasure," he finished.

Ori sat back. "He does, does he?" He smiled slowly and steepled his fingers before taking another drink. "Let's give him a little something."

"What do you mean, Boss?"

"Tell him I talked about the tunnels. Tell him I inferred—not told you, just inferred—that there's an entrance to the tunnel hidden in the gardens somewhere."

"Not in the hotel?"

"Tell him the gardens. Tell him when you asked if there really is a treasure, that I said we've never found it and we don't believe it exists."

"Does it exist?"

"It's not healthy to ask too many questions, Gabe."

"Sorry."

"I'm not going to tell you anything, true or otherwise, my friend. Nicholas and Christopher Dante are masters of the lie and you won't be able to fool them."

Gabe cleared his throat. "There's something else. I don't know how, maybe he's got super senses or something, but Nicholas, he said he smelled death on me. You know, like from the corpse."

"Why? Did you touch it?"

"No, but I sure got a whiff of it when I looked in the cart. He must have a hell of a nose."

"That's fine then. Don't worry about it. As I told you, it's probably his doing anyway. Now he's wondering about our reaction to it."

"What happened to the corpse, Boss?"

"It's been taken care of," Ori lied. "That's all you need to know."

Ori rubbed his chin thoughtfully, then wrote down a name. "Dante will probably show up again soon. If he does, send me a message. I'm counting on you."

"You got it, Boss."

It rose straight and sturdy like the Washington Monument and it cast a shadow nearly as long. It gleamed, the proud pink of a salmon sunset, blue pulsing veins like rushing rivers coursing with life. It was the staff of life, the shaft of delight, a rod with two round reels, ready to cast its pearly lines to Natasha.

She gazed in perpetual amazement at Douglas Harper's pole, a pole she had vaulted once already since arriving in his room a half an hour earlier, seeking to forget her troubles. Douglas had come out of the faint that inevitably occurred at the moment of his orgasm—there just wasn't enough blood in his body to keep his brain from blitzing at times like that. But he was recovered now and ready to blast off once more. She cuddled next to it, the only stake she wanted to pierce her, thought of kissing it, to pay it homage for what it had done to her. But she knew she shouldn't. It was too dangerous. She might bite.

Natasha's first orgasm had shocked her in its intensity. She'd nearly lost control, and had had to concentrate hard to keep her fangs from emerging. She had never had a climax like it before, at least not during human sex. Normally, an orgasm like that was only possible if you drank the blood of your lover at the climactic moment, and that wasn't a good idea because you tended to kill your lover and wake up with a terrible hangover and little memory of what you might drunkenly have done to the body. It wasn't pretty.

But Natasha was. Douglas was staying in the mirrored room, and his massive monument to love reflected in a million facets. Natasha stretched out on the bed, eyeing herself in the mirrored ceiling. Thank heaven the myth about vampires and mirrors wasn't true because she loved to look at herself, at her forever-firm breasts and her perfect silhouette. At her thick crush of pubic hair gleaming in the faceted lights, almost as shiny as the hair on her head, which flowed across pale blue satin sheets and spread over Douglas's tan belly.

"You're beautiful," he said, watching her watch herself.

She stretched and twined her leg with his, let her

fingers comb slowly through his pubic hair, barely brushing his penis. Still, he trembled at her touch.

"Mr. Chubby needs you."

If she could change one thing about him, it would be the name of his prick. "Mr. Chubby" just wasn't dignified enough. "You should change its name to David," she murmured.

"Why?" His hand found one of her breasts and stroked it. "Why David?"

"Because it's a work of art."

He chuckled. "Okay, Natasha. Just for tonight. David needs you."

She couldn't resist. She nuzzled David, baptized him with her tongue.

"Ouch!"

"Sorry." She concentrated on making her fangs recede, then sat up. She couldn't go on without something to drink or she would kill him with passion. She began dressing.

Douglas watched in amazement. "What's wrong?"

"Nothing. It's just a business matter I forgot to tend to. I'll be back in fifteen minutes."

"Don't be late. I'm getting pretty light-headed."

"For God's sake, rest up. It's going to be a long night." She threw him a kiss and was out the door. It was too early to feed on a guest, so she went to her suite, opened a bottle of simple A negative, and drank straight from the bottle. She didn't stop until it was three-quarters empty.

Natasha felt the rush in her body and brain. She'd overdone it and was rapidly getting tipsy. She forced herself to put the blood in the refrigerator as warmth suffused her, the same warmth that alcohol had given her in her human days. Her legs were a little weak. *It wasn't that much blood, was it?* It was affecting her strongly. Then she remembered the glasses she'd had with her uncle and brother. *No wonder.* She should stay here until it wore off, but what about Douglas? Her crotch was on fire for him. Should she return to him? *Why not? The blood lust is sated.*

A little voice warned her she was taking a risk, but she didn't listen. She brushed her teeth and gargled, then left for Douglas's room. Halfway there, she met Ivor in the hall.

"Natasha," he said. "I've been looking for you."

She smiled, feeling a little drunk. "How are you, Ivor?"

He eyed her carefully before speaking. "Fine. But Lucy and Ivy have disappeared."

She knew he knew she was drunk. And he knew she knew he knew. And so on and so forth. The thought was stunning in its complexity, and she still couldn't wipe the grin off her face. "What?"

"I can't find the twins. They sneaked out of the spa. Are you all right?"

"I've never been better, Ivor. You know, you're a very large man, dear brother? And there's another very large man waiting for me in his room." She was vaguely aware she was upsetting Ivor, but couldn't quite bring herself to stop. "As for those twins, sweetie, you'll find them. You always do. Maybe while you're at it, you'll find that body too."

16

Having had just a little too much to drink, the twins were giggling. After they finished the first bottle, Julian had opened another, this one stronger stuff. The bouquet, while acceptable, was odd, with a hint of saltiness that clung to the nose. It was a cocktail, a mixed drink. It was BO negative.

He wasn't sure why he gave it to them; perhaps he simply enjoyed the girls' company. Watching them helped pass the time while Jinxy butchered the bodies. "Excuse me a moment, ladies." He rose and went to check on Jinxy.

"Daisy, Daisy, give me your answer true," sang Jinxy, who stood nude in the tub, bloody and stinky, a twine of intestines in his hands.

"How are you doing?" Julian asked, standing just inside the doorway. Two suitcases bulged and a third lay open, almost full of black plastic-wrapped packages.

Jinxy turned and almost slipped. He was breathing through his mouth to avoid the smell. "Damned guts. I got her all done and I'm working on him now. He's little. Won't take up so much room."

Julian nodded. "Very well, I'll be in the living room. Remember—"

"Clean everything up."

"Good man." Julian, nose wrinkling, returned to the living room and threw open the doors to the terrace. "Come, ladies, let's enjoy the evening." He stepped out into the fresh, fragrant air. As with the terrace at his own house, this one overlooked the gardens. He liked that. Positioning chairs around the glass-topped patio table, he pulled one out for each girl. Both carried their goblets, Lucy also had the bottle of BO, and Ivy brought Julian's glass.

"This is great," Ivy said.

"Fucking great," Lucy echoed. As soon as she spoke, she seemed to sense her language offended Julian and mumbled an apology.

He patted her hand. "Sip your blood slowly." He looked from girl to girl. They'd nearly killed the second bottle with very little help from him. He decided to open a third, something that appealed more to his palate than the BO. He excused himself and retrieved a good-quality B negative and a clean wine glass. He sat down again. "Young ladies, this bottle is not for you. You've both had plenty. A little too much, in fact. This is for me. My body has need of much more sustenance than yours do."

They looked disappointed. Then Ivy said, "What's it like being a pure vampire? As compared to being like us?"

"Well, I don't know what it's like being you, but I suppose I can tell you what it's like being me." The girls looked on expectantly as he poured himself a drink. "What would you like to know?"

"That concierge girl," said Ivy. "When was she your queen?"

"After you find out about her for me, I might tell you that story. What else would you like to hear about?"

"Where were you born?" Lucy asked. Wisps of fog, fluffy cattails, eeled around them.

"I was born in a land called Euloa thousands of years ago," Julian began. "As were all my kind. You may know it as the lost civilization of Atlantis. It's off the coast of Florida. The Bimini Islands are all that remain above water." He paused. "Silly name, Atlantis. Euloa suited it. Soft and smooth with rounded edges, swaying palms, and lush tropical forests. Fields of grain waving on the high ground; lower down, healing waters, pyramids and the great stone walls. Beautiful frescoes and friezes, statuary, a haven of art. That was Euloa." Closing his eyes, he tilted his head back as myriad images came to him. Vast echoing buildings made of stone and marble. Elaborate pillars and columns ornamented nearly all the public buildings. "In Euloa, a sense of grace prevailed. Every building, every walkway, every garden was a work of art. Everyone had tapestries and wall cloths covering interior walls. Windows of stained glass were covered by fine draperies and wooden blinds by day." He drank deeply. "The moon was full and white and stars gleamed as you have never seen them. The world was young and beautiful."

"Were there humans to feed on?"

"Oh, yes. We bred them, used them as slaves, but they barely knew it, so well were they treated. We let them grow their crops by day and tend to us by night. The humans were prolific—they thrived in the tropical sun—and we had plenty to drink as long as we didn't succumb to our hungers. That happened several times in our history, once in my lifetime, and it decimated our human and vampiric population. We nearly killed off our humans, then killed the animals, and finally fed on one another." He smiled thinly. "We bred what few humans we still had, but it took many years for them to support the vampiric population again. It seems even the trueborns don't always learn by our mistakes. But for the most part, it was a beautiful place, and a wonderful life."

"Do all pure vampires come from Euloa?" Lucy asked, stretching, catlike, nails shiny and red as blood.

"It was our home. Our scholars never found any prehistoric traces of our kind away from Euloa, so we believe that we evolved there and stayed for many years. It was hard to travel in the sun, as you well know."

"How was the vampiric race created?" Ivy asked.

He shrugged. "How were humans created? We evolved as your parent race did, but our numbers were always small. In the long ago, there was one who claimed to be the first and he was our king for a time. The first human vampires were the results of perversions carried on between the trueborns and our humans, of that we are certain."

The twins looked at him, not sure how to take such a comment. Finally, Ivy spoke. "Did you have a mother?"

"Yes."

"And a father?"

For a long moment, he was silent. "Yes, a father."

"Then you grew up," Lucy said, oblivious to his mood. "You aged. When did you stop aging?"

"I don't know that I have stopped. I'm only about five thousand years old and there were vampires that were twice that when I was young. They looked mature, but not old in the human sense."

"Were you a child for a thousand years?" Ivy asked, leaning forward.

He laughed. "No. We age at about a fifth of the

speed that humans do until we reach maturity. Then the process slows drastically, until a millennium is but a moment. Aging virtually stops."

"But you'll die of old age someday?"

"I don't know. The oldest vampires I ever knew, if they still exist, are perhaps fifteen thousand years old now. When I last saw them, they might have been taken to be thirty-five or forty, in human years. The aging either slows to a virtual stop or stops altogether. No one knows for certain."

Ivy cleared her throat. "Are they dead now?"

"What can kill you?" Lucy interrupted, rude child that she was.

"There is no true death for us. We are part of the earth, we are trueborn. We are forever."

"Where are the older ones?" Lucy asked.

"I don't know," he said, although he knew one was near. *The Father.* "Though we do not die, we can lose our physical bodies. Then we remain on earth in energy forms. One of us might be a strange cold breeze in a closed room, another, a rush of warm water in the ocean tide. We are only vampires in physical form. In this incarnation. We are trueborn. We are less and more than everything you know."

"Do you know any other trueborns now?"

"My last contact with one was in Russia perhaps three hundred years ago."

"Are there any on this continent?" asked Ivy.

"At least one other. I sense him occasionally, but we do not try to make contact."

"Why not?" Lucy asked.

Julian decided it was time to change the subject. "Is aging on your mind?"

"We'd like to be twenty-one in human years," Lucy said without hesitation. "Can you make us age a little? It would be so much easier getting into nightclubs and seducing men."

"It didn't used to be a problem, but now more and more of them are afraid of us. We're jailbait," Ivy explained.

"It's not within my power to age you," Julian said gently. "If you wear more mature-looking clothes and makeup, you should pass easily. Perhaps if you wore your hair up." Julian reached over and ran his long thin fingers through Lucy's flowing locks. She petted her cheek against his hand, almost purring with pleasure.

"You don't know of anything else we can do?" Ivy persisted.

"No. I'm sorry."

Ivy gave Lucy a dirty look as her sister continued to let Julian fondle her. She took his other hand and put it to her own cheek. "Do you like us?" she asked.

"Would I have helped you if I didn't?"

"She doesn't mean that kind of like," Lucy explained. "She means *really* like us. Do you find us desirable?"

"Because you are human-born vampires, you have human lusts as well as vampiric. I am of the pure race, the trueborn vampiric race, and I don't feel lusts the same way as you."

"But you have a mother and a father."

"There is a cycle involved which occurs no more than twice a millennia. Sometimes it does not occur at all. The last time I felt it, was during the time of the Incas."

"Wait a minute," Ivy interrupted. "What happened to Euloa?"

"The land broke and sank under the weight of a flood, perhaps caused by a meteor. We don't know.

Most of our race were victims of the sun. Euloa, even under the waves, is a haunted place. It's the reason there is a Bermuda Triangle." He studied the girls, waiting.

"That's too bad," Ivy said at last; then sure enough, the conversation reverted to sex. "We're beautiful. Aren't we?"

"Of course you are. Very beautiful."

"But it doesn't make you want to make love to us?"

"No. Generally, I only feel pleasure through the bite."

"Do you ever bite without killing?" Lucy asked, tasting his fingers.

"When it suits me."

"You're not salty."

"I'm not human. What do I taste like to you?"

"Jicama," Lucy said after a moment's consideration.

"Come on." Ivy licked the back of his hand, her brow furrowed in concentration. "Maybe you're right, Lucy."

"What does jicama taste like, ladies?"

"It's bland."

"Almost tasteless." Ivy paused. "But good."

"What's it like to bite a vampire?" Lucy asked. "A human vampire. Have you ever done it?"

"Yes. It is wonderful. The blood is sweet like honey. Intoxicating."

"Do you want to bite me?" Lucy asked.

"And me?" added Ivy. "Sometimes we bite each other and pass the blood back and forth."

Julian sat forward, fascinated in spite of himself. "I would like to see you do it. Then perhaps I will give you each a little bite."

The twisted sisters giggled with pleasure.

17

She thought she was sated, but the bloodlust came on Natasha again with a fierceness that scared her into sobriety. It happened on the heels of another killer orgasm brought on by Douglas's tremendous member. She wondered if the orgasm brought on the hunger as she sat up in bed.

"What's wrong?"

"Nothing, Doug." She looked at him, saw warm blood pulsing in those veins and arteries under that tasty masculine flesh. David—née Mr. Chubby—lolled sleepily on his master's thigh, but it occurred to Natasha that when he was at attention, he'd make a wonderful all-day sucker. All that blood . . .

"Why are you looking at me like that?" Douglas grinned. "You look like you want to eat me all up."

"Believe me, you don't want that," she said, uneasy with her thoughts and desires.

"Well, in a little while, I might."

She rose from the bed and began pulling on her clothes. "I have a low blood sugar problem, Doug. I need to go get a snack."

"There's the honor bar." He pointed across the room.

"Not what I had in mind." She paused. "Why don't we get together again tomorrow night?"

"Not tonight?" asked Mr. Eveready.

"We could, but I have some business I should attend to tonight." She kissed him on the nose and pulled back quickly, realizing she was about to take a bite out of it. "I've neglected my work tonight."

"I thought I was your work tonight." He smiled.

"No, you're my reward for tonight. And you look exhausted. How many times have you fainted in the last two hours? Three times?"

"Four," he said proudly.

"Well, I don't want to damage you or anything, so why don't we call it a night?"

"If you insist."

"We'll have dinner tomorrow, okay?" She slipped into her shoes.

"It's a date. How about a kiss, right here." He pointed at his lips.

She bent down and pecked him quickly, before she could be tempted to bite that succulent lower lip. "Good night, Douglas."

"Are you mad at me?"

God, I'll never get out of here. It occurred to her that she could bite him and hypnotize him, but it was risky. Like the new concierge, there was always the possibility he was resistant. *No!* "I'm not mad at you, but this blood sugar thing really gets to me quickly. I've got to go."

He looked persuaded. "Are you all right?"

"I will be, as soon as I get a protein drink."

"She didn't even notice us," Lucy whispered to Ivy as they watched Natasha leave a guest room and walk rapidly toward the elevators.

"That's all we need. Christ, I'm glad she didn't."

"What do you suppose she was doing in that room?" Lucy nodded her head toward 314 as they drew near.

"Getting her dinner?"

"No. For one thing, dingle-brain, it's still too early for dinner and you know how Natasha sticks to the rules. For another, that's the mirror room. Theme room, remember? There aren't any cameras in there."

"I wish there were. Cameras in theme rooms would be great. Natasha's such a tight-ass."

"I wonder what the tight-ass was doing in that room." Lucy grinned, feeling foxy. "Want to find out?"

"Yeah. But let's go back to our room first. I spilled some blood on my shirt and I want to change."

"It hardly shows."

"I know, but it's sticky."

"You could just suck it out."

"Go fuck yourself."

"I did. It was fun. Come on, I want to change too. My pants aren't tight enough."

"After, we could find out who's in that room before we go in."

Lucy rolled her eyes. "Where's the fun in that?"

Natasha arrived in her office three minutes after leaving Douglas's room. Entering the back room, she quickly scanned the cameras and picked out a nice hot meal. The man in 236 looked good.

"Natasha?" Stephen's voice came over the intercom. "Natasha? Are you there?"

She groaned, then buzzed him in before grabbing a bottle.

Reentering the office just as he walked in, she saw him eye the bottle. "That looks wonderful. In the mood to share?"

"Of course." Relieved that he didn't seem to disapprove, she took glasses out of a low cabinet while he opened the bottle. The vintage? Who cared? Stephen didn't bother to examine the label either, but poured immediately, taking a gulp as he handed Natasha her glass, filled nearly to the brim.

They sat down and didn't speak until seconds were poured. Then Natasha said, "I think we've got a drinking problem."

"So do I. I'm thirsty nearly all the time."

"Me too. I've had enough for four nights already and I'm still not satisfied." Natasha shook her head. "What about you?"

"Just the drinks with you and Ori, but it was all I could do not to drink from Amanda Pearce. And when I walked in here, I felt nearly incapacitated from the hunger."

"Miss Pearce," Natasha said. "She continues to resist?"

"I haven't tried again."

"I suppose you're looking forward to biting her tonight?"

"Very much."

"I nearly bit Douglas several times, and I'm not sure I could have controlled myself if I had. I might have killed him. Do you feel in control, Stevie?"

"Yes, 'Tasha. I think so. For now."

"Good." Natasha leaned forward. "As for Amanda, if the bite fails, she'll have to die. We can't take a chance on her talking about the body."

"We should give her a chance to prove herself.

Remember, we have several humans working for us who know what we are."

"And they've all been charmed. They can't betray us."

He nodded, obviously distressed but trying to hide it. "Do you think it's time to talk to Ori, Ivor, and the twins about the hunger?"

"Ori and Ivor. I don't know about Lucy and Ivy. If they're not feeling the urge, they would probably use knowledge of it as an excuse to go on a binge or two."

"You're right, 'Tasha. We should make sure they know we're keeping a close eye on them. For whatever reason. I wonder . . ."

"What?"

"Is it possible they're responsible for the body in the laundry cart?"

"We were so rushed when we talked to them—let's be honest—we were so thirsty, that I didn't give it much thought. But it's a definite possibility. How shall we handle it?"

"We could pressure them. Sit them down, force them to talk." He smiled. "If we make them sit long enough, they'll get so bored they'll be bound to talk."

Natasha rolled her eyes, then said, "We can also keep Ivor, or at least one of his team, with them constantly. I think we should do both. Do you agree?"

"Yes."

"Did you know that the twins went into the spa and ditched Ivor tonight?"

"Yes. Ivor told me about it. There's been no sign of them since, as far as I know. He's looking for them now."

"How about the body?" Natasha asked. "It hasn't shown up, has it?"

"Not a trace, to my knowledge."

She shook her head. "We're losing control here, Stevie. We have to regain it."

"We have to figure out what's causing our hunger. Our *hungers*. I think that's the key. What's changed around here recently?"

"Nothing much." Natasha thought a moment. "In the last month, we repainted the lobby and we've hired one new employee. The one you have a problem with."

"You have a problem with her, 'Tasha. I have a yen for her."

"Don't be impertinent, Stevie," she snapped. "You know what I mean."

"I'm sorry. I do know, and I don't think she has anything to do with it, no more than the fresh paint does. I've been coping with an extra-large appetite for the last month. It's just getting worse now."

"I agree, but I wonder if our appetites—blood lust and physical lusts—aren't related. I'm certainly feeling both more than normal. I'm eating more human food than usual too. I crave it, though not like the blood."

"You're more temperamental too."

She gave him a dirty look. "I know. What about you? You've always had good emotional control. Your obsession with Amanda Pearce seems peculiar."

"It's not an obsession, Natasha. I wish I'd never told you—"

"Goddamn it, Stephen!"

"You high-handed bitch!" He paused, looked at his hands. "I'm sorry. I think I've answered your question, though. I'm experiencing everything you are."

"I'm sorry too. If this is happening to the twins, we're in real trouble. They're going to be volatile."

"At least they haven't caused any public spectacles."

"Yet."

"Yet," Stephen agreed.

18

"That was a long shift," Carol Anne said as she and Amanda walked toward the elevators. "I'm tired."

"You worked hours of overtime tonight," Amanda pointed out. "I'm exhausted and I don't have any excuse."

"It's your second day and you're working weird hours. That's the only excuse you need." She pushed her hair back from her face. "Hey, do you want to go change, then meet in the Pelican Bar for a drink? In the mezzanine? You'll probably get to meet more of the staff."

"And you claim you're tired?" Amanda's first thought was that hanging around in the mezzanine would be a good way to run into Stephen. *Don't go there.* He had almost kissed her tonight in the garden, and she would have let him, even though she knew it was wrong. She was disappointed when he pulled away, but he had such longing in his eyes that she didn't question his actions or lack of them. Still, she had a feeling he would hold off forever unless she encouraged him. After all, he knew it was wrong too. "Okay. I'll come." It was against her better judgment, but she thought it would be smart to make some more friends. But her mind was on Stephen. His electric touch, his dark eyes that she lost herself so easily in. Sure, he'd said a few weird things—trying to talk her out of thinking that she'd seen the foot foremost among them—but he was just too interesting, too compelling, not to . . . *Stop it! You're not going to dirty your own nest!*

But she wanted to. Oh, boy, did she want to.

"Amanda?" Carol Anne was staring at her.

"What?"

"The elevator? You want to get on?"

"Oh, yeah. Sorry."

"Daydreaming?"

"No . . . Yes, I guess so."

The elevator stopped at the second floor. "Here's where I get off," Carol Anne said. "I'll meet you in the Pelican in fifteen minutes."

"Okay. See you there." She watched the little blonde walk down the hall. Amanda couldn't match the spring in her step. *Just one drink,* she thought as the doors closed and the elevator started up. *Just to be sociable.*

The doors opened at the third floor and Amanda found herself face-to-face with two teenage girls who looked like they'd been poured into their clothes. They had to be the twins, the ones she'd been warned about. *Not now! Please!*

"Hey," said one. "You're the new girl."

The one who spoke wore tight black jeans, a low-cut scoop-necked black top that ended below her breasts, and a short black leather jacket. The other was also dressed in jeans, but skipped the jacket in favor of a clingy red sleeveless top cut down to there. Then, the similarities increased. Both had the pale skin and dark hair. She could see their resemblance to Stephen in their dark flashing eyes and slightly Slavic cheekbones.

"I'm Amanda. Amanda Pearce. Assistant concierge." She couldn't remember their names, but it didn't matter—she was too tired to care.

"I'm Lucy," said the one in black. "She's Ivy. You work for us. We're Darlings."

Not Darlings. Sluts. Skanky ones. "It's nice to meet you." She extended her hand, but the girls ignored it. Next, she tried to step past them, but found herself flanked by them instead.

"Where are you going?" asked one.

"To my room."

She slipped her hand onto Amanda's elbow. The other one did likewise. "We'll go with you."

"I'm meeting someone in a few minutes," she said, suddenly nervous. Their touches were cool, insistent, thin hard fingers pressed into her arm.

"Who?" Lucy asked.

"Carol Anne, from reception. We're having drinks with some other employees." *Why are you afraid of a pair of teenaged sluts? What are they going to do, rape you?*

They were walking now, the twins evidently aware of where the employees were quartered on this floor. Amanda nearly shivered with fear. It crept up and down her spine, raised the hairs on her neck. Her body was afraid but she didn't know why.

"Carol Anne is an airhead," said Lucy. "You look smarter than her. Or are you an airhead too?"

"I—no." Words escaped her grasp. "I mean—"

"What's the matter, sweetie?" Ivy asked, her mouth close to Amanda's ear. "We won't bite."

Her knees went weak for an instant, then she got control of herself. She was behaving like an idiot. "Carol Anne is a very nice person."

"Carol Anne is a very nice person," Lucy mimicked.

Ivy laughed. "Are you a nice person?"

They were making fun of her, but what could she do? "Yes, I'm a nice person." She sounded surer of herself, irritation coming to the fore to rescue her. "Are you?"

The twins giggled madly. Finally Ivy spoke. "You're funny."

"Yeah, funny," said Lucy. "Where are you from?"

"Seattle."

"How old are you?"

"Twenty-two."

"Legal. She can buy us drinks!" said Lucy.

"Look at her face! We scared her."

"I'm not scared."

Ivy looked past her, at her sister. "What else should we ask her?"

"I don't know, but we need more."

"Need more what?"

"More information," said Lucy. They were approaching Amanda's room.

"About you."

"We're curious. I know," Lucy added after a pause, "What do you like to eat? Spaghetti? Steak? Cocks? Pussy?"

Save me, God! "I like steak," she said as if she hadn't heard the rest.

"You can eat our pussies if you like," Lucy offered.

They are *going to rape me!* "Look," she said, stopping dead outside her door. She crossed her arms. "I don't eat pussy, and I'm very selective about cock. Children and animals are definite turnoffs. Satisfied?"

Ivy grinned. "You're funny!"

"She is," Lucy agreed.

"Please excuse me now." She tried to sound forceful. Though she'd been warned about the twins, she'd had no idea how obnoxious they were. No idea at all. "I have to go change clothes and meet my friend."

"We'll help you," Ivy said, crowding her up to the door.

"We want to see your tits. Are they real?"

"Yes, they're real!" she snapped, then blushed. "I'm not into women."

"We are. And men. And big fat dildos," Lucy announced.

"That's nice. Now, please—" How was she going to get out of this, short of walking away from her room? *Don't let them intimidate you into running! They'll never stop hounding you if you do!*

"Miss Pearce?" It was Ivor Darling, a knight in a charcoal suit. He stepped up close and loomed over them. "Lucy? Ivy? You're wanted in Natasha's office." Big hands clamped down on their shoulders and the girls looked royally pissed off. "Good night, Miss Pearce."

"Good night." She wanted to add a thank-you, but thought it wasn't such a good idea, not in front of the twins. She opened her door and stepped inside, realizing she now knew that the term "evil twins" wasn't just a cliché.

Exhaustion hit her as she threw all the interior locks. She kicked off her shoes, suddenly not wanting to leave her room, not wanting to see anyone else tonight. Dialing Carol Anne's room, she made her excuses, considered the TV, rejected it, then turned on the radio and got ready for bed. By the time she slipped between the cool sheets, Coastal Eddie had assured her that the fog monsters were out in force, warned her that they could take any shape—she knew the shapes they took tonight!—and then accused the President not only of prematurely donating his brain to science, but of having sex with small gray beings from another planet as well.

"Thanks, Eddie," she muttered, smiling, as she reached over and turned off the radio. She picked up her copy of Chelsea Quinn Yarbro's novel *Come Twilight,* and started to read, but she was just too tired to even hold up the book. Amanda went out almost as fast as the light.

Late night. Early morning. The hotel whispered quietly, hummed softly, the signs of life almost imperceptible. Water, moved by filter jets, slurped gently against the sides of the indoor pool; no guests swam at this hour. The spa was closed now as well. The gardens held secrets in their foggy shadows; faces seemed to grow out of the green darkness, grinning or screaming, stern, solemn, forever changing. Eliot Lucre finished burying a body deep beneath the soil of a half-finished garden; he'd been out hunting and had taken more blood than he should. The victim was a girl who looked like a hippie from the sixties, with long greasy hair parted in the middle of her forehead. She had come to the gatehouse begging for money and he'd given her something else instead.

She wasn't the first human he'd attacked in the past few weeks. It seemed like he was hungry all the time. There was talk among the other vampiric employees; everyone was hungry. Most of the others fed on their assigned guests, some admitting to taking a little more than they should, but all claiming to exercise self-control. However, every one of them was hitting the bottle too. If they hadn't, who knows what might have happened? Shaking his head, Eliot tamped the last of the earth down and walked toward the toolshed to put the shovel away. Already, he was feeling hungry again.

Meanwhile, author and lover Douglas Harper never knew that, thanks to Ivor Darling, he'd been spared the gruesome midnight ministrations of Lucy and Ivy. For that matter, neither did Amanda. Gabe Leoni dreamed Robert Duval was his brother and Robert DeNiro his father, while Ori spent the early hours with *Miller's Crossing* and a good bottle of an unassuming O positive, as he turned over in his mind the talk with his niece and nephew about the growing problems. The twins were stuck with Ivor, and Natasha drank too much and resisted the urge to revisit her lover, while Tyler Shane thought about Natasha while reacquainting himself with Madame Palm and her five sisters. Carol Anne got drunk and did the deed with Billy the Bellman. Stephen . . . Stephen sat in the Pelican Bar and nursed a Bloody Mary, consumed with thoughts of the bite he would soon bestow upon Amanda.

Julian thought about the Dantes and the Darlings as he played a game of chess with Jinxy, who was surprisingly adept at the sport. Later, at daybreak, the servant would take the suitcases full of body parts and bury them in a garden when no one was around to see him. Meanwhile, they had time to kill.

In their rooms, some guests read or made love, but most of them slept, blissfully unaware of the fact that their innkeepers were losing their minds.

* * *

There were two dreams really, two that intertwined like grapevines to become indivisible from one another, to defy logic or explanation. Amanda was vaguely aware of them, and on some level knew they were separate but inseparable. Occasionally, she wondered why she had them. She couldn't remember them very well, just bits and impressions, but she knew well the terror she felt the moment she awakened from them.

Tonight they came, twisted about each other, stronger than the night before. Normally she might have one or two of the dreams in the space of a year. Not now.

Tonight, it began on a mountaintop, the air thin and cold, the night sky glittering with diamond-chip stars. She heard chanting, rhythmic male voices with higher female ones answering in eerie counterpoint. Then came a shadowed figure, a tall man. Terror filled her as he approached, dressed in pale robes embroidered with symbols she could almost discern, but not quite. He wore a mask of gold.

He touched her shoulder and her robes fell away. She screamed.

And night turned into day, the sun shining brightly in an azure sky. People moved around her but she was alone, filled with emotions she didn't understand. She trembled with them. She was ready to scream. Then something new invaded the dream. A voice whispered to her, a soothing, masculine voice. Everything faded away, except for the voice. The words continued, and though she couldn't understand the whispered words, they calmed her and stopped her trembling.

She began to feel a warmth, a glow from within. Sweet syrup filled her body, and she briefly tried to see who spoke to her, but all was in darkness. She didn't care. The warmth grew in her belly until it became fire, and now she was filled with physical need that transcended everything else.

Am I awake? She couldn't be sure, there was no way to tell. The voice tickled her ear with its nearness, the tickle increasing her desire until she felt as if she were in heat. Now she felt a hand on her belly, gently moving lower in a slight circular motion. She strained against the hand, trying to push into it, but she couldn't move; her muscles were paralyzed. *You're half awake,* she told herself. *When you can't move, that's what it means.* It was half-real, half-dream, but she didn't know which was which.

The voice continued, and she began to catch words here and there. "No death . . . Amanda . . . No death, just a joke . . ."

Stephen! She tried to say his name, but couldn't speak anymore than she could move. It was his voice tickling her ear, telling her things. It was his hand teasing her, moving close but never touching. *Or am I dreaming? I must be dreaming!*

"Just a joke, you barely even remember it, it meant so little to you. There was no body in a laundry cart. You only saw a plastic foot."

What was he doing? What was she doing? *You're dreaming about everything that happened today, that's all. Oh, my God . . .*

There was a prickling pain in her neck, just for an instant, and then a new warmth began spreading through her, a giddy, euphoric sensation. *Stephen!* This was turning into a hell of a great dream. It had to be a dream. You didn't feel this good when you were awake.

His mouth was on her neck. What was he doing that gave her so much pleasure? *It's all in your mind.* But the feeling built. His hands were on her shoulders now, but her crotch throbbed hard, faster and faster as the giddiness and desire built. Suddenly, she came so hard that her body shook and shuddered, that she thought she might die, but didn't care. It was all worth it. All of it, every bit.

PART TWO

It hath often been said,
that it is not death,
but dying,
which is terrible.

—Henry Fielding

19

"I can't sleep," Ivy told Lucy. It was eight in the morning, past time for all good little vampires to be in their beds or coffins (it was strictly a matter of personal choice), and Lucy and her sister had stretched out together on their black satin bedsheets an hour and a half ago. "Can you sleep?"

"No," Lucy replied, rising and moving to her dressing table. It was weird too, because vampire sleep was heavy and relentless. You couldn't fight it. "I'm hungry." She looked at herself in the mirror, touched her lips, then opened her potion bottle and rubbed a little on. Immediately, they looked better, moist and full. "Do you think Ivor's still in our living room?"

Last night, after Ivor took them to Natasha's office, where they repeatedly denied knowing anything about the body, Ivor had stuck like glue, refusing even to let them stay alone in their apartment. He was a real pain in the ass.

Ivy came up behind Lucy and put her hands on her shoulders. "I love the way the potion makes your lips look. It's better than lip gloss."

"Here." Lucy handed her the bottle and Ivy dabbed on a drop or two, then gave it back.

"I'll check on Ivor," Ivy said, running her hands

over her breasts. Naked, she left the bedroom and returned a moment later. "He's on the couch, dead to the world."

"It's weird. I almost feel like it's nighttime. I mean, my brain's working pretty well. Is yours, Ivy?"

"Yes. I wonder why? Do you think it's because Julian drank from us last night?"

"Probably not. I wish he'd let us drink from him, though. Who knows what would have happened?"

"I don't think he trusted us. Or maybe trueborns just don't let us mere immortals bite them." Ivy paused. "Do you think Natasha and the others are up too?"

"I don't know. Probably not, if Ivor isn't. It's just us," Lucy said. "Maybe we're changing."

"What do you mean, changing?"

"Getting to be more like Julian? You know, he acted like it was nighttime yesterday morning."

"It's because he's trueborn."

"Okay, but we were falling asleep. Why aren't we *now?*"

"Maybe he'd know. Maybe there's something special in the blood he gave us. Or in his bite." Lucy licked her lips, her eyes sparkling. "He'd probably give us more to drink now, if we asked."

Ivy didn't look convinced. "I really feel like sinking my teeth into something fresh."

"Me too, but most of the humans are awake and, anyway, we can't go roaming around in the daylight." Full of strange thoughts, she walked to the heavily draped window and carefully parted the material, squinting as a ray of drab daylight entered the room.

"What are you doing?"

"Watch this." Lucy put her hand into the light. It felt strangely warm, and she suddenly remembered a time when she went on a picnic with her sister and two boys. The sat on a blanket on the ground and ate chicken and dark bread beneath an oak. Sunlight dappled them from between the leaves, changing its spots with the direction of the wind. She wore a long, sky-blue dress, and her sister . . . her sister wore something similar; she couldn't remember what. It seemed like yesterday, but it was centuries ago.

"You'll burn yourself."

"No, I don't think so. It doesn't hurt."

"Don't take chances. Come on, stop it."

Lucy widened the part in the drapes and Ivy jumped out of the sun ray that burst across the dark rug.

"Goddamn it, stop it, you bitch!"

Lucy smiled and held her arm under the light. "We're changing. Do you think Julian can take sunlight?"

"I don't know. We could ask him. I mean, he likes to talk about himself. He'd probably tell us."

"Wouldn't it be great if we could go to the beach, Ivy?"

"You're dreaming, unless you want to go at night."

"I want to go."

"Now?"

"No." Lucy dropped the drape. "Don't be an idiot. But I'd like to go swimming now, in the pool."

"Lucy, what's gotten into you? Why do you want to do that?"

"I want to suck on a lifeguard!"

"We don't have lifeguards."

"Too bad. Let's go get something to drink."

"You mean at Julian's, right? Or fresh?"

"I don't know what I mean, Ivy. I just want to eat

and swim." She opened a drawer and pulled out a black bikini swimsuit and put it on. It was nothing but strings and triangles and it stood out starkly against her pale skin.

"But you hardly ever use the pool. Why now?" As she spoke, Ivy slipped into her own red suit, then pulled on a short pink T-shirt and blue jeans over it.

"I feel like it." Lucy finished dressing, in jeans and a black tank. "I feel like fucking too."

"That sounds good. Let's go pick something up at the cemetery tonight. Remember those two dope smokers we found last year?"

"They were fu-un!" Lucy grinned. "But I can't wait that long."

"We have to be careful not to do anything that Natasha and Stephen will find out about. And we have to ditch Ivor."

"We can hang out somewhere else today and when he wakes up tonight, he'll just think we've already gone out."

"Good idea. So let's go see Julian. Maybe we can stay there."

Minutes later, they arrived at Julian's door and knocked. And knocked again. And once more. There was no reply. "He must be asleep," Ivy said.

"I'm dying of thirst," Lucy muttered, trying her passkey in the lock. Nothing happened. "Special lock. We can't get in. We have to do something!"

"Where can we get a bottle of blood? I swear I'm going to bite the next human that comes along." Ivy nervously plucked at her shirt.

"We could sneak into Uncle Ori's office—"

"We can't get in there. He'd have to be there to let us in. Remember?"

Lucy remembered. He'd put a special lock on his

door, the same as Stephen and Natasha, because bottles of blood occasionally disappeared. They shouldn't have stolen it just to get drunk. Now they were paying. "What about sneaking into one of their bedrooms?"

"And if they catch us? They probably aren't awake like we are, but what if they are? They'd murder us."

Lucy was at a loss. Then she brightened. "Let's go into the tunnels. I think they store bottles in there."

"Do they? It's been ages since we've been down there."

"I bet they do. I mean, they've got to keep them somewhere, right?"

"Do you remember how to get in?"

"I think so. It's the second stall on the right. I think I remember how to do it."

"What if someone sees us?"

"They won't," Lucy said. "We'll be careful."

"How do we get out?"

"Same way as we get in. We just have to listen before we open up."

"Okay. But if you're wrong I'm going to suck *your* blood."

"Is that a promise or a threat?" Lucy dimpled up. "Come on. Let's go!"

They rode the elevator down to the lobby and stepped out. No direct sunlight hit the area—and Lucy didn't think the muted, foggy light would hurt them—so they walked into the lobby itself. There were patches of dim-colored sunlight coming from the stained windows, but they were easy to avoid. Even Lucy, for all her talk, didn't want to chance it in public. What if she caught on fire? *How embarrassing!*

They walked down through the lobby, away from the desks where people might recognize them, trying to maintain a slow pace and not attract attention. It wasn't difficult since there weren't many people in the lobby and the staff seemed unaware of them. Still, Lucy wished they'd practiced the art of blending in in the vampire way. She wished she could just turn it off and on at will, but it took practice and concentration. Their siblings and their uncle could do it, but they were patient sorts. Lucy and Ivy just never had the time to work on it. There was always something better to do.

They walked among the chairs and tropical plants, crossing a little bridge over the fountain stream running down the center of the lobby, then made their way back up to the area leading to the pool and spa. There, they stopped near a simple wooden door bearing the word, "Gentlemen." They waited for five minutes and no one came out, so they let themselves in.

As the door shut behind them, they looked at each other, controlling their giggles. Somehow, they just never got over the tiny thrill of entering a men's room—be it bathroom, steam room, or locker room—and Lucy was glad. After the first few years of immortality, she'd feared the thrill would wear off, but it never really did. Appetites were too strong, the feel of human blood coursing through your veins too thrilling, and even the little things— like going in the men's room or pulling a practical joke—still held her interest. Ivy's too. Maybe other vampires got bored, but *they* didn't, not as long as there was some kind of fun to stir up.

The door to the men's room, renowned for its luxury (it was even fancier than the women's room), opened into a lobby. It had coat and hat

racks and was carpeted in dark blue dotted with
gold. Something Mozarty played in the background.
There were masculine-looking leather armchairs
and a mirror that covered one wall above a long,
narrow walnut table.

"Ready?" Lucy said softly. Ivy nodded as Lucy
opened the door to the rest room proper.

Builder Joshua Case's special baby (and who
knew what that said about him), it was magnificent, with gleaming marble floors and walls, all
with a slight pink hue. A double row of booths
ran across the back wall, another held ornate
swanlike sinks, coral pink to accent the marble,
and a third had a baby-changing station and a
mirror etched with rounded art-deco patterns
above a table similar to the one in the lobby, but
twice the length. Small porthole windows lined the
long wall above the corridor of booths casting
drab circles of light on the floor.

The centerpiece was the urinal. There was only
one, a huge round sculpted fountain-like work of
art. It dominated the center of the large room, a
masterpiece of pinkish marble veined in black,
decorated in art deco madness. The base trough
had a wide curved lip, and drain holes and jets
dotted it. Water swirled constantly within. The wide
rise above it narrowed gracefully until, at the four-
foot level, there was a fountain bowl into which
water fell from above, through a huge fish that
stood on its curled tail and spouted water from its
mouth.

They rounded the urinal, hearing nothing but
the gurgle of water; then, as they neared the stalls,
there came a sound: "Unhhh." *Plop!*

Lucy put her finger to her lips, then looked under the doors. The man was halfway down the cor-

ridor, eight stalls from the one they sought. Lucy in the lead, they tiptoed past it to the second stall and shut the door behind them.

"Now we wait," Lucy whispered.

Five minutes passed and the grunter remained in his stall. Two other men came in and used the urinal. Their heels clicked on the floor as they left. Finally, when Lucy thought she was going to have to bite the man on the toilet (an odious thought, but she was starving), he flushed. Then he loitered after washing his hands, combing over his bald spot or pulling nose hairs, maybe both. Finally, they heard the door open and close. Ivy peeked out. "We're alone."

They turned their attention to the stall. The toilet was plumbed through the floor and behind it, pristine and white against the marble wall, was an overlarge toilet seat tissue-cover holder, three feet long, two wide, that also held paper towels and extra rolls of toilet paper, so that a guest would never be caught with his pants down. The holder was the same as the ones in the other stalls, but it was what was behind this one that mattered. Lucy stood on the toilet and reached down into the top of the contraption, felt around, and undid a latch. The holder swung away from the wall, and if a guest opened it, all he would see was the plate attaching the holder to the wall.

Carefully, Lucy pushed on two of four innocent-looking little screws. If you touched the other two, it would stop the process, but Lucy remembered right and after she pushed up on a tab in the metal, she heard a creak and whirring sound, and suddenly the plate swung away from the wall.

"You did it!" Ivy said softly. "Let's go."

"You first." Lucy stood down and let Ivy climb

into the dark hole. If there were any spiderwebs, she could deal with them.

Ivy turned and looked at her as she took the three short steps down to the floor. "Where's the light switch?"

"On the right."

"Got it." The wood-lined tunnel loomed behind Ivy.

Behind them, the bathroom door opened and heels clicked toward the stalls, toward this stall. *Why did they put the opening here? There has to be another one!* Quickly, Lucy hopped onto the toilet lid and practically threw herself through the opening. She turned and pulled the whole paper holder contraption back against the wall. It slid smoothly into place. An instant later, she heard the stall door shaken. The damned lock slipped and the door creaked open. Lucy signaled her sister to remain quiet, just in case somebody had heard them. But within thirty seconds, it was obvious the man was taking care of business. A slight fecal reek wafted in. "Come on," Lucy said. "Let's find the stash!" She started walking down the long corridor, which deadended into another passage, where a bulb was burned out. There, the wood floor turned to hard-packed dirt. Feeling her way along, her sister's hand on her shoulder, Lucy moved on. It was really creepy in here, worse than she remembered. She tried not to think about the Treasure.

She didn't wake up until noon, but when she did, Amanda felt like a million bucks, alert and re-freshed, and a little lazy too. After dressing in khakis and a camp shirt, she went down to the employees' cafeteria and picked up a beef-and-bean burrito and a Diet Pepsi to take back to her room to eat in front of the television. She wanted to enjoy some downtime.

She turned on the TV and switched to *Mephisto Palace* on HBO. It was a favorite movie of hers, and although it didn't follow the David Masters novel to the letter, it was a good little ghost story. She bit into her burrito and settled in to watch it.

Amanda's love of scary movies began when she was little. Her mother claimed she was born that way, but maybe it was due to the fairy tales and Oz books Mom had read to her when she was very little. However it happened, she loved them all—trolls, werewolves, ghosts, and especially vampires—but she tried to keep it a secret when she found out other girls thought she was a geek if she talked about such things. Only one trusted friend knew the truth and to this day, she kept her preferences to herself like dirty little secrets. Oh, it was all right to like movies like the *Scream* series, *Halloween,* or *The Sixth Sense*— everybody liked those—but admit to a love for the old Corman flicks? Not a chance!

She had been drawn to this particular place, but she thought that part of the reason she was here, working at a hotel, was due to a horror movie— well, really, the book was the real influence. *The Shining* had stirred up a fascination with hotels, big honeycombed ones that held their secrets in myriad rooms and hallways. Places alive with the past. Alive with ghosts.

The Candle Bay Hotel reminded her of the hotel in the book. It didn't look at all like the Overlook, but she could sense its personality beyond the stucco and tiles, the heavy colored glass and bright awnings. Its otherworldliness enhanced its beauty. She loved the exterior, but it was the lobby that hooked her. The high arched ceilings suggested echoes of laughter and screams (there had to be screams in Amanda's imagination); the elegant furniture and fountain and the dark imposing reservation desks spoke to her of murder and romance. The hotel had called her for years, and now, she had answered the call.

The Candle Bay reminded her of another hotel too, the one in the old Eagles song "Hotel California." This one was by the sea, not in the desert, but it looked the way she imagined the hotel in the Eagles song looked, rising out of the mist, bejeweled with sparkling lights. To her, the song was about a haunting, not drugs or sex or rock and roll, though they played a part in the haunting. It was a song that inspired daydreams and nightmares. *You can check out any time you like, but you can never leave.*

Involuntarily, she shivered. The Candle Bay, so far, hadn't really frightened her, except that first night when she thought someone was in her room. *In my room!* Suddenly, last night's incident—*dream, it was just a dream*—came rushing back to her. She remembered stars and sunlight, and then the voice. That was what she remembered clearly; Stephen's voice, her heat. She blushed.

Pushing the sexual thoughts away, she concentrated on trying to remember what he'd said to her in the dream. Something about the body in the laundry cart. He told her it wasn't real—just as he'd tried to do in real life yesterday. So, the dream wasn't too surprising, was it? Just a simple rehash of the day. *Typical.*

She wondered if they'd found it yet. She wasn't going to ask; Stephen had not wanted to talk about it yesterday, and he surely still felt the same way.

She could see his point of view, keeping it all a secret for the sake of the hotel, but it seemed strange that he didn't think the police would want to talk to her. *I should be happy about that!*

She watched the movie for a few minutes, but her thoughts drifted back to the dream, to the erotic aspects. She felt a little rush just thinking about it. She remembered the feel of his body, lying next to hers, pressed up against her. The tickle as his lips touched her earlobe. His hypnotic voice, lulling her into depths of sensuality she had never experienced before. His mouth on her neck, kissing her, *biting me—*

She jumped up and looked in the mirror, but there were no marks on her neck. *Idiot!* she thought, sitting back down. *Now you want to pretend he's a vampire!*

She smiled to herself. *I could use a good vampire lover.* Her imagination had always run in overdrive. *Still . . .* She smiled again. She would settle for a good lover, the human kind. But she only wanted Stephen, and although he had nearly kissed her in the garden, she knew she couldn't have him. That was probably the psychology behind the dream of him biting her neck; vampires and employers were both forbidden fruit.

"Rats," Lucy said, throwing one across the dirt floor of a little room off the main tunnel. "Big fucking rats." She wiped a drop of blood from her chin.

"Better than nothing," Ivy said. She turned her own rat over, examining it for any more traces of blood, but didn't find any. "Maybe we'd better go back. It must be getting late."

Hours had passed; Lucy could feel it. They were

tired now, ready to sleep, but the hunger kept them awake. They had been underground forever, but hadn't even found the catacombs—not that they wanted to, the whole place felt haunted, threatening—let alone a wine cellar used for storing blood. She was almost sure one existed, but there were so many little offshoot tunnels, most twisting into claustrophobic crawl spaces that couldn't possibly lead to a useful storage room, others dead-ending into solid rock. It seemed like they'd been down every one of them, looking for any sign of a cellar, but they had found nothing so far. Where was the fucking blood? Feeling lost, she wondered where the catacombs were; she hadn't been near them in years. She didn't even know if the Treasure could really be down there.

She had rarely gone beyond the wood-paneled area, and while she'd never admit it, the place scared her. *It's just Ori's stories that scare you.* She peered at Ivy, wan in the dim, flyspecked yellow light cast by the nearest bulb. "Maybe we'd better stay here and catch a few more rats, Ivy. I know it's disgusting, but I'm really tired." She brushed a smudge off the back of her hand. "We're dirty too. Sit very still," she added, seeing movement out of the corner of her eye. "Dinner's coming."

She caught the rat and shared its gamy blood with Ivy. It would hold them a little while longer, and they could always draw blood from one another, as they'd done for Julian the previous night. It didn't do any real good because they needed new, human blood, but it helped psychologically. It would buy them time.

"This is awful," Ivy said. "We shouldn't be hungry. We shouldn't even be up."

Lucy stood, her head an inch from the ceiling.

Those monks Ori talked about thought the tunnels were a big deal, and the really old stories—well, those were the ones that frightened her. *Stupid.* But whoever built them had gone to a lot of trouble. There had to be something here. Didn't there? "Come on." She led the way out of the room and down ten feet of tunnel, where she flipped the light switch off and stepped into the main corridor, which they'd left lit up. It was scarier than ever.

She looked both ways. Here the tunnel ran straight, and for a minute she lost her sense of direction. Her stomach flipped; then she realized that if she went down the incline, she was heading back to the hotel. "Let's go up a ways, Ivy."

"I really think we should go back."

"If we don't find anything in a few minutes, we will, okay? We're probably under the cemeteries by now. There ought to be rats."

"Oh, joy."

Ivy trudged behind her until they came to a Y that Lucy suddenly and clearly recognized, though she'd only seen it once. *The Treasure.* Hairs prickled upon her neck and arms. No way were they going down the right passage. *It's down there.* She could feel it. "That way," Lucy said. "Let's take the left-hand path." She paused, feeling for a light switch, finally found it. Yellow light dimly illuminated the steeply rising tunnel.

They followed it, walking on stone for about twenty-five feet, fear receding. Then Lucy stopped. "Dead end. No, wait. There's something here. An overhead door. Duck your head, Ivy, I need more light." A bolt had been thrown across a dark door. She tugged and yanked until it finally came free. Above her head, the door creaked and groaned. It was wood, very thick and heavy. "Ivy, stand back," she said, holding the door, which wanted to swing downward. "There might be sunlight."

"We can't take the chance—"

"It might be what we're looking for, and remember, the light didn't bother me."

"Well, be careful." Ivy paused. "What *are* we looking for?"

"I don't know." Slowly, she eased the door until it hung free to her left. There was no light. Ivy reached up and her hands touched cold, smooth stone, straight and flat. She pushed. It moved, but it was heavy, even for a vampire. "Help me."

Together they moved the slab until dark shadowy light seeped through. "I think it's safe," Lucy said. "Let's get this stone out of the way."

They emerged into a small, shadowed vault, climbing through what looked like an empty tomb. Others were built into the walls, and Lucy noted that the family's name was Banning. Fog sifted into the little mausoleum through black iron bars, and last autumn's leaves still littered the floor. "It's safe," she said, climbing all the way out. "Come on."

She helped her sister up into the vault, then stood in the shadows and peered out the doorway. "Just great," Ivy complained. "We have to go back the way we came or stay here and starve all day."

"Shhh! Look!"

"A rat?"

"Better than that." Lucy felt Ivy behind her, peering over her shoulder. A homeless man, maybe thirty with dark greasy hair and a dirty green knapsack, was approaching. He sat down on the steps outside the mausoleum and lit a cigarette.

"Help?" Lucy said coyly. "Mister, will you help me?"

He looked around, but couldn't see them. "Who's there?"

"I'm in here. I—I don't have any clothes."

"Bullshit," he said, sounding interested.

"Really, mister, we were having an initiation, my girlfriends and I. I was joining their club. They made me take off all my clothes and then they left with them. Do you have something I can wear?"

The man was on his feet, trying to peer inside the mausoleum. "Where are you? I can't see you!"

"Of course not. I'm naked. Can you give me a shirt or something?"

"I gotta come in first."

"Well . . . Okay. But don't look!"

"I won't."

His face wore a leer and a question as he stared into the mausoleum. Lucy and Ivy stayed out of sight and waited while he fiddled with the rusted iron latch until it broke off in his hand. He stepped inside, his eyes on the open sarcophagus. Lucy and Ivy leapt on him, Ivy's hand over his mouth to keep him quiet while they drank their fill.

Finally, he was still. The twins dropped him. "Look at his neck," Ivy said.

"Oops."

"What a mess."

"Feeding frenzy," Lucy joked. "Is he still alive?"

"A little bit."

Lucy took her potion bottle out and poured most of the remaining fluid on the torn flesh. The fluid began doing its job.

"What should we do with him?" Ivy asked.

"Well, we can't leave him in here. It might cause somebody to discover the opening to the tunnels."

"If we roll him out, police might still come in

here." Ivy made a face. "I guess we have to take him with us."

"I guess." They dragged him to the open sarcophagus and muscled him in. He dropped with a thud to the tunnel floor below. "Grab some leaves, Ivy. Let's clean up the spilled blood." They set to work, avoiding sunlight that broke through the fog.

"We should come back after dark and lock this place up." Ivy stood and dropped bloody leaves down the tomb.

Lucy did the same. "We'd better."

"Carefully, she approached the door and peered out at the lock. "How do we repair broken metal?"

"Bring a chain and a padlock?"

"Okay." She squinted, studying the landscape. "We're in the oak grove at the top of St. Mark's." Looking at her sister, she added, "I don't want to go back through the tunnels!"

"But we have to," Lucy said.

They climbed down through the sarcophagus and together, moved the stone back into place.

"Oh, yuck. I stepped on him!" Ivy jumped back and waited for her sister to join her. In the semi-darkness, they saw that the torn throat on the reprobate continued to heal. The bum was still alive, but probably not for long, not the way he looked.

"Let's go home," Lucy said. "I feel pretty good, for daytime."

"A good meal helps, doesn't it?"

They started walking. "We're filthy," Lucy said. "When we get out, we'll scoot over to the pool and swim ourselves clean. Then we can sneak in and be in bed before Ivor wakes up."

"Sounds like a plan."

20

Ori awoke at two in the afternoon and was unable to go back to sleep. He was logy, not fit to talk to anyone about anything important, but far more capable of thinking than he ought to be at this hour. He took a book—*Wiseguy* by Nicholas Pileggi—from his mahogany bed stand and propped himself up on pillows against his ornate, heavy headboard.

Shortly, he put the book aside, unable to retain what he read. Getting up, he pulled a silky black robe over his equally silky pinstriped black-and-white pajamas, donned his slippers, and walked across the elegant room, which was decorated in the same manner as his office—vintage Godfather. He opened a pair of large cabinet doors to reveal a thirty-five-inch television. He flipped a few switches and *Godfather 2* began to play. He knew this one by heart, and it wouldn't strain his tired brain.

He sat and watched for a few minutes, then picked up the phone and rang Gabe Leoni's room. "Yes, Gabe? I have a job for you."

Shortly, he hung up. Gabe would go to the Dantes tonight with the false information about the opening to the tunnels being in one of the gardens, a rear one that was under construction. It held only a little brick-work, a stone lion or two, and a lot of dirt to dig in.

He knew it would have more impact if Gabe went to the Dantes before they could come to him. He would take them the news and the Dantes would show up, right where he wanted them. It would be a feast, and Ori would supply the stakes.

Pleased with himself, he took a bottle of B neg from the cabinet and poured himself a glass. He noticed his supply was running low, but in his less-than-brilliant mental state, it never occurred to him to wonder why he was hungry during the day. Instead, he took the drink, sat down in a round, leather tufted armchair, and settled in to watch the movie.

Meanwhile, Ivor slept well on Ivy and Lucy's sofa, his dreams filled with images from days gone by. Unconsciously, he smiled. He was reliving a wild night in Stonehenge hundreds of years ago. The neo-pagans were celebrating the winter solstice and they thought he was a god. One after another, beautiful young women offered their necks to him. He drank lightly from each of them.

Ivor was a conscientious vampire who rarely over-indulged. Being head of security, he also tended to be extra cautious and when he went into a room for his evening meal—which was rarely—he always wore latex gloves. The potion hadn't touched him.

Others in the vampire family, like Ellen, the night-time head of Housekeeping, slept on, dreaming of rich, red blood. They had been given smaller amounts of the potion, and had been less liberal in applying it than the Darlings, and so had absorbed less through their fingertips. Their self-control was also stronger because of the knowledge that if they attacked anyone, the Darlings would end their existence. Still, hunger taunted them.

Natasha slept fitfully, plagued by nightmares in which she bathed in the blood of Douglas Harper.

And Stephen. Stephen dreamed only of Amanda.

But the twins were still wide awake.

Like all indoor pools, the one in the Candle Bay Hotel and Spa seemed wrapped in an air of watery eeriness. Every splash echoed, every voice and footfall carried. The entire room was tiled, even the arched ceiling far above the pool. It was meant to look like the sky, light blue with white clouds and birds here and there. The walls were mosaics of sea-themed art. One long wall displayed King Neptune on his throne, Venus emerging from the sea, voluptuous mermaids, and a sea serpent that probably scared little kids. The other long wall was an underwater view of colorful fish, a pod of dolphins, octopi, and gold-etched shells. The porthole windows near the ceiling of the King Neptune side cast bobbing light on the ocean scene. The far short wall showed the beach with 1920s bathing beauties and handsome young men, and the other, mainly a wide door, was edged with a nouveau fish-and-shells motif.

Amanda, dressed in a blue-and-white bikini, stood on the low diving board and looked down into the pool. It was lit from below—the window light only touched the water in small patches. The tiling was deep, dark blue, relieved only by Grecian-looking gold borders and, on the bottom, gold stars. If you looked carefully, you could make out constellations.

As she dived into the pool, Amanda felt a little thrill of fear; it looked bottomless, as if it would hold her down and never let her up again. But the water was warm and inviting with the clean light smell of chlorine scenting it. She knew she was strange, but Amanda loved the smell. It brought back childhood memories of spending summer days in the huge pool at the high school.

Only a handful of people were in the room with her, two in the pool, the rest lounging beside it. It was perfect. Amanda swam a lap, then went for several more. Finally, she stopped to rest, treading water lightly at the pool's edge.

In walked Lucy and Ivy Darling. Maybe walked wasn't quite right; they did more of a quick slither through the doorway, immediately went to one side of the door, and began undressing.

Amanda wondered why they didn't use the dressing rooms, and decided it was because they were in a hurry. They were dirty. She could see smudges on them and their clothes even from here.

Now what do I do? She watched as the twins came toward her. They hadn't noticed her; their eyes were on the pool. Amanda edged toward the shallow end, not wanting to run into them. *But there are other people around. They can't gang up on you here!* The thought didn't help much as the two girls simultaneously dove into the pool from the deep edge near the diving board. They swam like fish, gliding underwater all the way to the shallow end before their heads came up. They walked out to the four-foot marker and began washing one another, gliding their hands over each other's bodies with obvious enjoyment. Or, maybe it was just an act.

Then the one in red saw Amanda.

"Look who's here, Lucy!"

Lucy looked. "Hey, hi, Amanda. Do you like our pool?" She sounded harmless, nothing like last night.

"Yes, it's great." Amanda moved into a patch of sunlight and continued to tread water as the twins swam toward her. They stopped just short of the five-foot-round patch of light.

"Did you see us come in?" Ivy asked, eyeing her.

"No," Amanda lied. "Why?"

"Just wondered." The pair edged in closer and traded glances.

"Do you like our bikinis?" Lucy asked.

"They're very nice." She made herself look at them. *And very small.*

"Do you like our bodies?" Ivy asked.

"I can't really see—"

"We can't see yours either. Why don't you get out of the pool and model for us?"

"Actually, I have to be going. It's time to get ready for work." Amanda moved out of the sunlight, and immediately the two followed her, moving in close, like sharks. Amanda turned and swam toward a ladder, the twins behind her. She climbed out and felt their eyes on her body. It made her flesh crawl.

"Do you want us to come with you and help you dress?" Lucy asked.

"No, thanks." She turned and walked toward the dressing room, where she wrapped a towel around

herself and grabbed her clothes. She wasn't taking
any chances on getting cornered by those two
again.

She needn't have worried. The twins were washing each other as she walked out, and didn't even
seem to notice her. *What a relief!* She wasn't sure
what they were—smart-asses, lesbians, S&M freaks,
or all three. It didn't matter. Amanda hated them
because they scared her unlike anyone had ever
scared her before. What was it about them that
made them so—evil? She could think of no other
word for it. *The devil's daughters,* she thought as she
climbed into the elevator. *That's what they are.*

21

The Darlings held a short meeting of the entire vampiric staff as soon as everyone had risen for the night. The news wasn't good. Many of the employees had admitted to feeling "strange" in recent days. Natasha bet all of them felt that way and that "strange" meant excessively hungry.

She looked at them all, gathered around a rectangular table in the meeting room. "It may be necessary to supplement your evening meal with bottled blood. I'm sure you all have a small supply in your rooms, but we'll be bringing in more, hopefully tonight or tomorrow. For now, we'll issue you each two bottles. Don't waste it, but if you need more, come to any of us and say so. I promise you, there will be no problems as long as you're honest."

She smiled at them. If there was trouble, it was easy enough to incarcerate a problem vampire. Or stake one, if necessary. "We've told you all about the body in the laundry cart. It's still missing. If any of you see or hear anything, if you suspect something, even without an obvious reason, I want you to come to me. Okay, everyone. Let's get to work."

After the employees left, Natasha looked at her family. All of them were in attendance, even the twins. They looked a little hollow-eyed, and Natasha and Stephen had decided it was time to talk to them about the problem.

"Lucy, Ivy, do you have anything to tell us?" Stephen asked.

"Well," Ivy said. "Now that you mention it, we *are* a little thirstier than usual."

Lucy made herself look as young and innocent as possible. "We'd like some bottles of blood. They would help a lot."

"Do you have anything to tell me about that body?"

"It wasn't us."

"Honest."

Natasha gazed steadily at them. She was almost sure they were responsible for the corpse—they had gone on binges before—and she felt her fury growing. She should have staked them a century ago. Two centuries ago. *The day they were made. Damn Ori for turning them! He should have known better. They're nothing but trouble.* She started to open her mouth to say so, then closed it. *Control yourself. Don't let them see you lose your temper.* "Ivor or one of his guards is going to stay with you two. You're going to do whatever he says without any complaints."

"Who died and made you queen bitch?" Lucy glared at her.

"I've had just about enough—"

"Lucy," Stephen cut in sharply, "We aren't kidding. Don't try to put anything over on us."

"Any of us," Ori added sternly.

"For the moment, I'd like you both to go to your suite and stay there until Ivor or someone else comes for you," said Natasha.

"What about the blood?"

Natasha eyed them. "He'll bring the bottles."

Their eyes brightened at that, just as she knew they would. "Don't be too long, Ivor," Lucy said, and she and Ivy went to the door. "I want to take a walk tonight."

After the pair left, Natasha looked to the others. "What do we have in the way of bottled supplies? Ori? What's in the cellar?"

The so-called cellar was originally a room that led down into the tunnel system, but they had closed it off from the corridors so that it was now accessible only through a secret panel in Ori's office. "We have forty-eight bottles. Normally, that's a reasonable supply, but during this—emergency—it's far too little."

"I'll call Slater Brothers right away and order a dozen more cases," Stephen said.

"Three dozen," said Natasha. "Four. We can't have too much and it won't go to waste. Make most of it good house quality." That was type O, the least expensive. "Get a dozen cases of A, half that of B, and a couple of ABs. None of the unnaturally mixed vintages."

"Those are usually terrible," Ori said. The others nodded. Even Slater Brothers, the best of the vampire blood vintners, rarely got it right. Nature knew best.

"Do we have anything else to discuss?" Stephen asked.

"Yes," Ori replied. "I've sent Gabe Leoni to the Dantes with news that there's an entrance to the tunnels via the garden—the unfinished one with the stone lions and lots of room to dig."

"Why?" Natasha asked, not happy. She knew about Nicholas Dante coming to the hotel last night, but this seemed like a minor concern right now, considering the hunger problem. "Why encourage them now?"

"We can trap them and get rid of them once and for all," said Ori. "It's important now that they're after something very tangible."

"They're scum," Stephen said thoughtfully, "But we've coexisted for years. Do we really want to stir things up?"

"They already have—remember the stake?" Natasha asked impatiently. "They don't usually communicate that aggressively."

Stephen nodded.

"They could still be after the Treasure, I suppose," Ori said. "They obviously believe the stories. But they're certainly interested in the potion. That's the main thing. That's what's causing their aggression. As you know, Julian killed Leo Dante when he came to his home wanting to buy—and I use that term *very* loosely—the elixir. If we stake his brothers, I don't think their underlings will dare bother us again."

"Good point." Stephen rubbed his chin and glanced at Natasha. "But what makes you think the brothers will show up to do the digging?"

"Julian says they don't trust their own. With any luck, at least one of the brothers will show to supervise at dusk. We can start with that one. When he doesn't come home, the other one will come looking. It's all very simple. All we have to do is post a guard. We can rub them out on the spot." Smiling serenely, Ori took a cigar from his pocket and held it under his nose, inhaling the fragrance.

"My guards can handle that," Ivor said. "But I need to be there as well. Can someone else stay with the twins? There are many things I should be handling personally now."

"You're right, Ivor. You shouldn't be baby-sitting. We'll work something out," Natasha said. "And Un-

cle Ori, you're right too. It's best to rid ourselves
of the Dantes. Otherwise, they're not going to stop
bothering us. Tell me, has Julian asked about the
tunnels or what might be in them?"

"No, he has not."

"Frankly, I'm surprised."

"He's being cagey," Stephen said.

"I think he's above such things," Ori replied. "After all, we know the Treasure is probably nothing but
a myth. We don't even know it's really down there.
In fact, it might be very interesting to ask Julian what
he knows of the facts behind the myth. If it is true, if
there is *any* truth to it, he is likely to know."

"The only thing that lends credence to the Treasure myth is that Valentyn is a trueborn and he's
here." Stephen shrugged. "But it's a coincidence."

"Well, the Treasure, or at least its tomb, is safely
locked away and Julian doesn't know how to get to
it," said Natasha. Involuntarily, she shivered. "As if
anyone would want to go down there." The only
time she had gotten close to the vault, the suffocating dread she experienced didn't stop until she was
well out of the catacombs. All she really knew of
the Treasure was the myth as Ori told it. She was
more inclined to think the dreadful atmosphere
had to do with restless spirits of those buried below.
Ghosts could easily upset a vampire's sensitive
senses. Though by tacit agreement they rarely spoke
of it, she thought the rest of the family felt the
same way. And if indeed there was a Treasure and
the old stories were true, then they were its caretakers. "Did Julian suggest the Dantes are after the
Treasure?"

Ori mused. "I believe he mentioned it."

"There you go," she said. "He's planting all the
ideas he can."

"You may have a point," her uncle said slowly. "But I believe he was only trying to be helpful. Your dislike of him colors his words for you."

"Perhaps so, Uncle. But take everything he says with a grain of salt." Natasha folded her arms across her breast. "His interests and ours are not the same."

"I disagree," Ori said. "At least to the extent that he doesn't want the Dantes here any more than we do."

"Still, keep your counsel. Don't volunteer any information, but take all he gives."

Ori nodded. "I will. But don't you think we ought to talk to him about our growing appetites? He's been around for thousands of years. He may know a reason and a cure."

"I don't want him to see any weaknesses," Natasha said slowly. "But you're right. He might know something. Tell him one or two of our staff members have the problem."

"Why not Lucy and Ivy? He knows we have trouble with them anyway."

"All right. But be very casual about it."

"I will." He put the unlit cigar back in his pocket. "Come Ivor, I'll fetch those extra bottles for the twins."

Only Stephen and Natasha were left in the meeting room. "Did your bite work, Stevie? Has Amanda Pearce forgotten about the body?"

"I believe so. I haven't had a chance to speak to her yet tonight."

"Do so soon."

"I will."

"We should lock up that mausoleum tonight," Ivy said as she and Lucy lounged on their balcony, enjoying the evening sky. There was no fog, at least not yet. "How are we going to do it with Ivor all over us?"

"We could leave now, before he gets here—"

"Too late." Lucy rose and went to the door. "At least he's bringing blood." She licked her lips, then smiled, looking up, expecting Ivor. "Uncle Ori! I thought Ivor was coming."

"Come in, Uncle," Ivy said as she approached them. "Let me take that for you." She reached out, took the paper bag from him, and looked inside. "Lucy, he's brought us *five* bottles, not four! Thank you, Uncle."

"Yes, thank you!" Lucy took his arm and steered him to one of the heavy black upholstered chairs near the sofa. "You haven't visited us in a long time, Uncle Ori."

"I have been remiss," he said, smiling at them.

They both smiled back. Uncle Ori was a soft touch. Despite the trouble they sometimes caused, Ori was always the first to forgive them, and he almost always spoke to them without condescension, something the others rarely did.

"Why don't we open the extra bottle, my dears? We'll have a little toast, just the three of us."

"I'll get the glasses," Ivy called. She was back in a moment's time, and before she could sit down, there was another knock on the door. "I've got it."

Lucy and Ori both turned to look at the caller, and Ori rose the minute he saw who it was. "Julian!" He spoke before either twin could. "What brings you here?"

Julian, dressed all in deep navy, his platinum hair pulled back in a ponytail, smiled smoothly. "Why, looking for you, of course. I was told you were here and I hoped these young ladies wouldn't mind too much if I stopped in." He raised one hand, revealing a bottle. "I've brought refreshments."

"We've just opened one," Ori said as Ivy escorted Julian in and showed him to the other plush chair. "Join us. Have you met my nieces?"

"Briefly, yes. Ivy and Lucy, isn't it?" Julian smiled serenely. "Which one of you is which?"

"I'm Lucy," said the one in the tight purple shirt.

"And you must be Ivy," Julian said to the one dressed in a shrunken black T-shirt.

She dimpled up at him. "That's right. Will you have a drink with us?"

"I'd be delighted."

"I'll get another glass." She hurried toward their small kitchen.

"So why were you looking for me?" asked Ori.

"Mainly social. I haven't seen much of you for a few days."

"Any other reasons?"

Julian glanced at Lucy, then said, "Nothing important. Why don't we just enjoy some conversation?"

"That sounds like fun," said Ivy, returning with the glass.

Ori poured, they toasted the waxing moon, then all settled back. There was a moment of silence; then Ori said, "Why don't you tell us a story, Julian?" He looked at the twins. "Julian is famous for his stories."

Lucy and Ivy exchanged glances; then Lucy said, "I'd like to hear about your greatest lost love. Do you have one?" she added, in case he didn't want to talk in front of Ori.

"Lucy, I don't think such a personal question is appropriate," Ori said.

Julian regarded the girls approvingly. "It's all

right. Yes, I have a lost love," he began. "As you may or may not know, we of the trueborn race of vampires are only susceptible to the vagaries of love once or twice in a millennium. Our race is virtually immortal, and we only need to mate to keep the status quo due to the occasional change of form that occurs among us—the very rough equivalent of human death. However, once a connection is made, the lust for one's mate may resurface frequently and unexpectedly. It is rare, but it happens."

"Has it happened to you?" Ivy asked.

"Yes." He paused. "I fell in love with a human woman."

22

His name was Aardvark Wicket and he wasn't feeling too well. Weak. Shaky. Drained.

Like the boy named Sue, Aardvark was plagued by his moniker. Unlike the boy named Sue, he didn't learn to whup ass to defend his honor and good name (good being a relative term). His lack of whup-ass ability was to be expected, not only because of his slight build, but because his parents didn't give him the name to build that kind of character. They had been tree-hugging hippies, animal activists, and eco-threateners (they didn't quite qualify as terrorists). Sunny and Barnswallow Wicket (those were the only names Aardvark ever knew them by) had always been more concerned with the dwindling panda bear population than with little Aardvark, whom they expected to be one with the earth and the animals, to follow in their sandal-steps.

After years of teasing by other kids and hastily hidden smiles from adults, quiet little Aardvark had built a healthy disrespect for his parents. In fact, he hated them.

So, he killed them and they were at one with their precious earth.

Slish slash, that was all there was to it. It was so easy. He still carried the knife he'd killed them with in his ragged and stained green backpack. In fact, he'd used it many times since, preying on liberals wherever he found them. (To be entirely honest, he was around the bend and had long ago become an equal-opportunity slayer.) He traveled America, keeping to the coasts, to big cities, where he fit like mud in a puddle.

He hadn't really intended to kill anybody here in this little coastal town. He was on his way to San Luis Obispo, which was a metropolis compared to Candle Bay—but when the naked girl in the mausoleum had called to him this afternoon, he knew he was going to fuck her and kill her, *slish slash.* Maybe not in that order. Definitely not in that order.

But the naked girl wasn't naked and there were two of them, dark-haired beauties who attacked him, biting and licking. It hurt, but it made him come. Twice maybe, once for each girl. He'd barely been conscious after that, but as he felt the life pouring out of him, something new went to work on his neck, something wet-oily and warm. It felt like little tiny pins and needles, sewing him up. Vaguely, he remembered being tossed in a hole, and now, weak but conscious, he sat in the utter darkness, wondering where he was and where the girls were. Something scuttled over his legs, a rat probably. It stopped moving, and he could practically see it looking at him, thinking, *meat.*

Aardvark made one quick move and had the rat by the throat. His parents would be so unhappy; he'd long ago given up their vegan ways. He couldn't simultaneously hold onto the squirming rat and retrieve his knife from the pack, so he bit the rodent's neck until his teeth met. Hot blood poured into his mouth, taking the edge off his hunger. Still holding the rat, he felt his own neck. There was nothing wrong, but his shirt and jacket felt stiff and sticky, full of blood. *What the fuck happened?*

One-handed, he felt around, found his pack, and took out the knife and a squat candle. Putting the rat in his lap—he didn't want to get it dirty—he dug a lighter from his shirt pocket and lit the candle. He couldn't see much, but he would worry about that after he finished his *rat tartar. Spaghetti and rat balls,* he thought as he skinned the creature. *Ratatouille, Ratsaroni, the San Francisco treat.* He slit the belly, *slish slash,* and scooped out the innards with a grimy finger. If he was hungrier, he would have eaten them too, but they weren't exactly haute cuisine. They were *rat cuisine. Splat cuisine.* He snickered to himself as he started chewing the rat meat. It was tough and sinuous. A rat leg couldn't compete with a chicken drumstick, not on its best day. But rat brains, he thought as he cracked the skull and sucked, those were something special.

There probably wasn't anything he hadn't eaten at one time or another.

Done with his meal, he took the candle and started looking around the old tunnel with its wood framing. He could still remember Barnswallow's face when she'd seen him come in with a lizard in his mouth. He must've been about six. The tail stuck out, twitching between his lips, and when he tugged on it, it came right off. He offered it to her as he swallowed the rest of the reptile. It was trying to climb down his throat anyway.

"Well," he said now, spotting an electrical wire near the ceiling. "Well, well, well." He followed it to the end of the short corridor and found a light switch. God love him, the bulb even worked. He turned back the way he'd come, dim yellow light showing him the steps in the wall leading to the opening. That was where he'd come through. He climbed a couple steps, then tried to move the stone slab, but it was impossible. Those girls had moved it, though, and he was pretty strong for his size; he should be able to do it too, no sweat. A wave of nausea and weakness swept over him and he sat down to rest, ignoring his own nervousness.

Maybe after a nap. Maybe then he'd be strong enough. *A nap and a rat. That's the ticket.*

"In Euloa, there were two castes of humans, the workers, who were also the food, and those few of exceptional intelligence who helped the trueborns run the land. These humans saw to the law by daylight, to crop distribution and other daily human concerns, medicine, schooling, building. They managed the workers, and so were given preferential treatment by the trueborns." Julian sipped delicately from his glass.

"Loyalty was all-important in our land. Human loyalty to us—we were their gods. If one of them rebelled, he was dealt with most severely. We did not want to have to contend with an organized uprising. As their rulers, we were loyal to our humans. As long as they deserved it.

"There was a human woman who did not rebel, not in any way that can be detailed, but I knew her heart longed for freedom. Her name was Talai and she worked for my household, managing my workforce and seeing to it that everything stayed in order."

"She was your head housekeeper," Lucy said.

He considered. "Yes, in a way, since she ran the entire household, but she was more than that. The position she held was very important. I relied on her to make decisions that would affect my life in many ways."

"Was she pretty?" Ivy asked.

"Yes. Tall and dark, as were all the Euloan humans. Huge eyes, perfect lips, long neck. But there was something wrong. I didn't trust her entirely, though I didn't know why. I had no reason for it. I think now that it was her intelligence that intimidated me.

"I was a young adult at this time, a prince, and my first mating time arrived over the course of a few nights. I hid this from all, for I was not interested in the marriage my father had arranged for me. One twilight, after awakening from dreams I'd never had before, dreams of a sexual nature, I wandered toward my favorite balcony in my villa. I wasn't fully awake yet and as I approached, I saw Talai leaning against a column, watching the last dabs of purple and peach staining the sky. My time had come and she was my vision.

"I knew my lust for her—and love, for a successful mating ensures that the couple remains together—was a perversion and I tried to deny it. It wasn't unknown for a trueborn vampire to lust after a human, but it was seen almost as a form of bestiality. What could I do? My urges were overwhelming, I was a rebel, and I was afraid I would be found out. So I did what trueborns occasionally did when they didn't quite trust a valued human but didn't want to kill them. I turned her into a vampire."

Julian poured more crimson fluid. "It was an excuse. Making her into a human vampire ensured her loyalty to me and began to feed my craving for her. Not only did creating a human vampire have a bonding effect between the trueborn maker and the new vampire, but it bestowed a status on the human that was otherwise unknown." He laughed gently. "At the same time, it was not a practice highly endorsed by our kind. They tended to ignore the human vampires. As I told you, they were of a worry to them. They were very nearly beasts."

"Why?" Ori asked.

Julian looked at Ori and his nieces in turn. Human vampires were impure, that was it in its entirety. Making one was like giving the former human a minor membership in an otherwise exclusive club, and after all these years, eras, eons, Julian still felt the stigma attached to these half-vampires. They couldn't reproduce with humans or trueborn vampires, and their humanness caused them to do stupid things, like fall in love. Julian, to his shame, knew about that. It was a simple quirk of timing, one any trueborn could have experienced. "It's just the way things were," he said, deciding to spare the others' feelings. After all, they already knew they were his inferiors. "It took three bites to change her, and I was nearly overcome with lust with the first one. I barely controlled myself, such was the emotion upon me. It had to be done; I wanted her and would not mate with a human. Could not. But I could with a human vampire, though it would not yield offspring." Telling them this story was intriguing, a confession, yet not, since they could not possibly judge him.

"Weren't there any female trueborn vampires around?" Lucy asked. "I mean, besides the one you didn't want to marry?"

"Not too many. There were never many of us, as

I've told you. When the lust came, it tended to cause a trueborn to fixate on one female, one you perhaps thought about regularly. Even before the lust I thought about Talai—I had to, I dealt with her constantly—so it was no surprise when I wanted her. I fought the urge unsuccessfully. I don't think anyone knew—my status was high and I had to answer no one's questions, except my parents', and I stayed away from them. My father, who was very powerful, and I did not get along.

"If the trueborns had known of my lust, it would have lowered my respectability in their eyes, at least if they thought I changed her for lust instead of business reasons. Business was my excuse.

"The second bite began to change her. Unlike you, who must cause a human to drink your blood to complete the change, my kind secretes the substance in our bite, should we choose it to do so. I so chose.

"I watched her as she became, more and more, a creature of the night. On the fifth day, an hour before sunset, I arose and watched her through colored glass as she stood on that same balcony. Tears flowed down her face. She could no longer take the sun on her skin and she knew what was happening to her. She turned and saw me watching her through the glass.

"That night, I administered the third bite and I took her to mate as she was changing. I could wait no longer. I took her again and again, and by morning, she was changed and frightened, clinging to me in her newfound fear of the sun. Secretly, I took her to bed in my inner chamber, and there she stayed each day and often much of the night. I taught her to drink and she seemed to take to it, but there was always an air of sadness about her. I loved her more for it. Eventually, though, she killed herself."

"How?" asked Lucy.

"Why?" asked Ivy.

"I've never known why, but I know how. She sat on the beach, in the sand, waiting for the dawn. She would not leave with me, and I finally fled as salmon light appeared on the horizon. She remained and let the sun turn her to dust."

"Eww!" Lucy made a face similar to the one her sister was making. "Oh, Christ, how could she?"

Julian, never quite as susceptible to sunlight as a human vampire, now able to withstand it for short periods due to the potion, smiled gently. "The sun inspires terror in the human vampire, the terror you exhibit now. It was very brave of Talai to do as she did."

"So she wasn't your queen?" Lucy asked.

He remembered the other story he'd promised them. Since Ori didn't know he had spoken with the girls previously, he kept his answer bland. "She would be my queen eventually."

"How?" Lucy and her sister were wide-eyed.

"I'll tell you another time."

The phone rang then, and Lucy answered. "Uncle Ori," she said, taking the phone to his chair. "It's for you. That Gabe guy."

He took the call, said very little, then returned the phone to Lucy. "Girls, I have some business to attend to. Will you promise to stay put until I get back?"

Lucy dimpled up, all sugar and spice. "You didn't mention you were baby-sitting us, Uncle."

"I'm simply spending some very enjoyable time with my nieces." He grinned at them. "And your elder sister will want me to spend some more. Do you promise not to disappear while I'm gone?"

"I'd enjoy the pleasure of your company, ladies," Julian said. "I'll stay, if that's all right with your uncle."

"It's a fine idea." Ori didn't hide his relief. "I'll be back as soon as I can." He hesitated, and Julian sensed he wanted to tell him something. But it wasn't to be. Not now.

As soon as he was gone, Julian asked, "Who is Gabe?"

"Oh, you know how Uncle Ori likes all that gangster stuff? *The Godfather* and *The Sopranos* are practically all he talks about?"

"I'm aware of his predilection. This Gabe has something to do with that?"

"He's just a lowlife human who treats Ori like he's the Godfather. Gabe's his little pretend-gangster buddy. He kisses his ass."

"Does he know Ori's a vampire?"

"No," said Ivy. "But he gives him stuff."

"What does he give him?"

"Like suits and VCRs and stuff. Once he gave him a peacock," said Lucy. "It lives in the gardens." She paused. "Julian? We have something we need to talk to you about. Can we talk?"

"By all means. What is it?"

"Can we go talk in your suite?"

"Certainly. Just leave Ori a message so he can find you again."

"What's the problem, Gabe?" Ori asked. He'd seated the man in his office in a comfortable chair and given him a brandy. He had one himself and found it agreeable. He poured another.

"I keep trying to leave the Dantes and they keep pulling me back in."

"Did something go wrong with your meeting?"

"No. I told them about the garden entrance, just like we planned."

"And?"

"They ate it up, Big O."

"I prefer not to be called that."

"Sorry, Boss. No disrespect. Anyway, I think they'll show up soon, maybe even tonight. But they want more. They just keep pulling me in. They want to know things."

"Well, that's all right. It lets us know what they're up to. What are they after?"

"Well, they're asking about that guy Julian. They want to know what he does, where he goes, you know, everything. I barely even know who this guy is."

Ori nodded.

"They think he has something to do with the treasure, I think."

"What do they think the Treasure is?"

"They never say." Gabe paused. "I assume it's gold and stuff? Jewels, maybe? You know, Boss, I don't think they know exactly what you've got. They're hot for me to find out, though. I need to tell them something." He paused, his eyes filled with dramatized terror. "I'm afraid they might whack me."

"They won't, Gabe. You've already given them invaluable information." He smiled thinly. "Or so they think. They know you can provide more as long as you're my friend."

"What should I tell them about this Julian guy?" Gabe bleated.

"Let me think about it."

"But I need to tell them something *now*. What should I tell them?"

"Never mind now." Ori glared at him, temper flaring. "You are beginning to get on my nerves, my friend. May I suggest a little more respect?"

"Sorry, Boss, sorry. I didn't mean to—"

"Hush." Ori lit a cigar, thinking that Gabe Leoni was asking questions on his own behalf. Ori assumed the mythological Treasure, not pirate gold and jewels, was what the Dantes were after, but Gabe was craving some of the latter for himself. He wanted a cut. *A cut of what?* Ori smiled. "Tell them you've found out that Julian is a friend of mine—a *close* friend. As for the Treasure, tell them I'm being recalcitrant."

"Rectal—what?"

"Re*calc*itrant. Never mind. Just tell them I'm being very mysterious."

"Maybe I'm safe until they dig for the tunnel entrance," Leoni said doubtfully. "But what about after? When they find out I gave them false information?"

"We'll concern ourselves with that if and when we need to. Stop worrying, Gabe. Things will work themselves out." Ori made two smoke rings, a small one moving through at larger one. Leoni, who was doing his squirming best to sit still, had started to smell delicious. All that hot blood. Briefly, Ori considered biting him. *It wouldn't be prudent.* It was time to open a bottle of something salty, yet piquant, instead. A nice little B negative would do nicely. "Gabe, you must excuse me now. I have other matters to attend to."

23

Tyler Shane had aspirations, lofty ones. Soon he would be part of the management team of the Candle Bay Hotel, and after that, who knew? He would go as far as he could here—he had his sights set on day manager, a position now held by a sixtyish asshole named Hooper, who ought to get a clue and retire. In his quest for the job, Tyler would make sure that happened. It wasn't hard to show someone was incompetent, even if they weren't. He'd done it plenty of times before, as often as it took to make sure the people he worked with fit the right mold.

He was considering doing it to Amanda Pearce, even though she was his most immediate ticket up; he needed her to take his lowlier position. But she was getting too much attention from the Darlings. He'd seen the whole clan (not counting the twins, of course) going out of their way to be friendly with her. Especially Stephen. Stephen had a hard-on for her.

All that attention turned Amanda into Tyler's competition. The Darlings usually maintained more distance from their employees. Maybe it simply had to do with the ridiculous foot-in-the-hamper incident that Amanda had made a big deal about. Whatever the cause, he didn't need any competition.

He would bide his time for now, and it would probably all die down. All except for Stephen's interest. Tyler had a feeling that was only going to worsen. But he could get rid of Amanda if he really needed to. A faked letter from an irate guest. A little petty cash found in her desk drawer. The possibilities were endless.

Taking delivery on a monstrous bouquet of red roses addressed to Natasha, he continued to think about Amanda. She was good, a breeze to train, and she gave him no shit. He thought he could probably lay her if he wanted. *And that might not be a bad idea.* He could get her hooked on him instead of Stephen, who probably hadn't made a move yet. The Darlings were pretty uptight about employees dating, and it would take a while for Stephen to talk himself into it, having to set a good example and all. In fact, he might not even do it at all. He was one of those ultra-moral types, that was obvious.

"Amanda," Tyler said.

She looked up from her paperwork and smiled. "Yes?" Her lips were full and friendly and her eyes sparkled.

Fuck her for sure. She wants it. She wants you. "I have to take these roses to Natasha, so you're on your own for a while."

"That's fine."

He took the flowers and walked toward the upstairs offices, vaguely disappointed at Amanda's response. He'd thought she was flirting with him. *Tease.* What did he expect? That she would fall all over herself? *Oh, Tyler, fuck me here, right on the desk! Oh, Tyler, you're so much more handsome than Stephen! You're such a great lover, I've never had anyone like you before.* As he was buzzed into the office area, he realized he was kind of looking forward to fucking her, even though she wasn't really his type.

Natasha Darling, however, was his type. As she buzzed him into her private office, he realized he was holding his breath. She wore a form-fitting black dress with long sleeves and a V-neck that hinted at cleavage but didn't come right out and say it. Simple gold jewelry. She was breathtaking.

He held out the flowers. "These are for you."

"Thank you, Tyler." She smiled. Amanda wore lipstick that enhanced the natural color of her lips, but Natasha chose a deep glistening red that reeked of sex. But then she reeked of sex from head to toe. She was the object of all of Tyler's favorite fantasies. She took the bouquet. "They're beautiful."

They matched her lips. "Oh, they're not from me," he blurted. "I mean—" *You asshole! You sound like a moron!*

"I know." She laughed gently, and took the envelope from the floral pick and opened it. Whatever it said made her smile, but she didn't tell him who they were from. "There's a vase under the sink in my rest room," she said, pointing toward a door to the side of the room. "Would you take these and put them in water?"

"Of course. I'll be glad to."

In the small but luxurious lavatory, he found the heavy, square crystal vase and took care of the flowers before glancing around. On the counter was a small blue dish of shell-shaped soaps. Not pastels, but bright greens and purples. Quickly, for the hell of it, he sniffed them. Mulberry, and something that reminded him of a rainstorm. *Nice.* Next, he opened the medicine cabinet and peered inside. There was a toothbrush, paste, a bottle of Scope, and three packs of dental floss—plain, peppermint, and cinnamon. Natasha was into oral hygiene in a big way. There were a couple of lipsticks and some other makeup, plus a small flat vial of amber liquid. *Perfume. What kind?* It had no label, so he took the bottle from the upper shelf and opened it.

"Tyler? Did you find the vase?"

"Yes. I'm just wiping the dust off. I'll be right out." Hastily, he sniffed the fluid. Its fragrance was faint but very nice, musky and weird at the same time. Almost irresistible, it was a fragrance he'd never encountered before. After a second's hesitation, he poured some in his hand and applied it to his cheeks, like aftershave. It was slightly oily, but soaked in quickly. It tingled a little on a shaving cut, but stopped almost immediately. Maybe it was Oil of Olay or something, damned if he knew, but his skin looked and felt great and he couldn't even see the shaving nick anymore. He capped the bottle and put it away, then took the roses and returned to Natasha's office. "Here you go."

Sitting at her desk, her legs crossed to reveal lots of thigh, she indicated a narrow table next to the bathroom door. "Put them there. Yes. That's perfect."

His cheeks felt warm and suddenly, Tyler had a boner the size of Cincinnati. Embarrassed, he moved to the front of her desk to hide it. "May I do anything else for you?" He was bursting at the seams.

She smiled, and he could swear she was looking at his crotch, but then, he was afraid to make eye contact, so he didn't really know for sure. Maybe he was just being paranoid. *Or maybe she wants to fuck me!*

"What else would you like to do?" she purred, putting her legs up on the desk, and crossing them at the ankle. Her nose twitched and she opened her mouth slightly, reminding Tyler of his mom's cat when it was sniffing something. But she couldn't possibly smell the oil, it was just too faint. He dismissed the worry.

Her legs went on forever, and he wished he could see behind the desk. *Heaven awaits.* "What would *you* like me to do?"

"Why don't you sit down and tell me a little about yourself. You'll be in management very soon and I like to know my men." Emphasis on *men*.

"Okay." He could barely think. His penis had taken over his mind. As he sat, the material rubbing over his crotch nearly set him off.

"Would you care for a drink?"

"Yes, thank you."

She lowered her legs and disappeared into the back office, soon returning with a wine bottle. "A nice merlot."

"I'm on duty."

"I won't tell if you won't."

"Just a small glass." Ordinarily, he would have refused the alcohol to preserve his impeccable reputation, but between Natasha's legs and his erection . . .

"Here you are." She came around the desk and handed him a full glass of purplish-ruby liquid, then poured one for herself, half that size. *Is she trying to get me drunk?* No, that was ridiculous. Wasn't it?

Natasha bent and sniffed his face. She frowned. "I think you've been snooping in my bathroom."

His face was on fire. "No. I just tried on—"

"You tried on"—she paused—"my skin toner. I can smell it."

"I'm sorry." What else could he say?

She kept her face close, her eyes locked on his, and ran her fingers over his throat. "Do you feel different than before you used it?"

He couldn't lie to her, couldn't look away. "Yes."

"In what way?"

He tried not to say it, but out it came. "I want sex." *I want sex? I want sex? This is what you say to her?* Her eyes were driving him crazy.

She took the glass from his hand and set it down next to hers, her gaze never wavering, as deep and black as the ocean at night. "You won't remember our conversation. You will only remember delivering the flowers. You'll forget about putting the toner on your face. Do you understand?"

He did.

The next thing he felt were her lips on his throat, exquisite torture, warm and cold, harsh and gentle. Suddenly, he felt a bright pain, and with it, sexual release. He opened his eyes and saw Natasha go into the bathroom. She came back out with the vial of amber oil and dabbed his neck with it.

"This did not happen," she said forcefully. "Nothing happened. You merely delivered the flowers."

"Yes." Even as he agreed, his memory of the last few minutes fogged over.

"I need more potion," Lucy said as soon as she, Ivy, and Julian were comfortably ensconced in his apartment.

Julian, relaxing in a leather armchair, cocked his head and let his chin rest on two of his long fingers as he studied the twins. They were abusing the potion in some way, that much was obvious, and not only because of their hunger. It showed in their eyes and voices; they were edged with it, limned with it. He could smell it. "Why do you need more potion?"

Lucy licked her shiny lips and put on a seductive smile. "I spilled it."

"Where did you spill it? On a human? On your-self?"

"No, on my dresser."

She was lying, but he decided not to push it. Julian stood and stepped over to the girls on his couch. Both their lips shined. He bent and put his face close to Lucy's, and sniffed. Then he sat down again. "The potion is not makeup, ladies."

"We only used a drop," Ivy said.

"One drop for you, and one for your sister. It adds up. You can't waste it. I don't have an unlimited supply. When I run out of the main ingredient, I'll have to send a team of explorers to South America for more. It's not something I care to do too often." He smiled. "I have to have the team members killed when they are almost home." He steepled his fingers, an enigmatic smile stealing across his face. "It's very frustrating for them. And very expensive for me."

Lucy and Ivy smiled back, a bit tentatively. Lucy said, "I really did spill it."

"She did. I saw her do it."

"I'm sorry." Lucy tried to look sweet and innocent, but it didn't quite work.

"We won't use it on our lips anymore," Ivy assured him. "We promise."

"We promise," Lucy echoed. "May I have some more?"

What funny little liars they were. Perhaps the time had come to encourage a bit of abuse. "Give me your vial. Yours too, Ivy. I'll fill them both, but I expect you to use the elixir only for its intended use." He smiled as he spoke.

After refilling the vials from the bottle he kept in the wall safe Jinxy had installed in his bedroom, he gave them to the girls, who were spread out on his Grecian sofa like temple keepers, like the *ajllas* of Peru five hundred years ago, and those before them over the millennia. His earlier storytelling had made him nostalgic and his thoughts turned to other things.

He wanted it. Sex. Hot and stinky. Real hot. Real stinky. Tyler Shane's manhood was nearly unmasked, such was his excitement as he scurried upstairs to change his underwear. Fortunately, no one saw him on his journey across the hotel and he was soon safely in his room.

God, it looked like somebody had spilled mayo in his shorts. He threw them in his hamper and tried to clean himself off with a damp washcloth, but it was too much; his penis wanted the washrag for a girlfriend. His penis wanted anything for a girlfriend. *God, I want more!*

More? He hadn't had any lately, except for what he provided for himself. *Why am I feeling like this?* He searched for an answer, remembered thinking about how good Natasha looked, but he'd only seen her for a moment. Earlier, he'd been considering laying Amanda, for business purposes, but it now became an urgent desire, uncalculated and scary and sexy.

Glancing in the mirror, he saw that he looked reasonably normal (above the waist) except for mussed hair and slightly flushed cheeks. Quickly, he turned the cold water on and splashed some on his cheeks. *That's better.* He took his wayward organ and held it under the stream—*Oh, God, that's cold!* He was never so happy to see an erection fade away, not even that time in eighth grade, in Miss Scott's class, when he had to walk up front and do a math problem on the blackboard. Miss Scott was wearing a turquoise sweater that fit all her curves, and Tyler's response was a healthy one. Lord, was the walk back to his seat ever humiliating.

"Damn it!" Thinking about Miss Scott had undone the effects of the cold water. He had to get back to work and he couldn't like this. Suddenly, he had an idea. In the kitchenette, he put a couple of ice cubes in a Baggie, zipped it shut, and stuck it in his shorts. "Oh, God," he muttered. He could barely stand it, but he had to do it. He couldn't go back to work in this state.

He was dressed and riding the elevator down to the lobby when he thought about Amanda and sprang back to life, ice cubes be damned. He tried thinking about Carol Anne—definitely not his type—but it made no difference. He thought of Ori Darling, and the hard-on remained. Baseball scores? Even those didn't work. At least his pants were black and pleated, a good hiding place for things that go *boing* in the night.

Things suddenly subsided—*thank God for the ice!*— and he smiled at Amanda as he approached the desk. "I'll bet you could use a break!" He showed his pearly whites. *God, she looks good! I wish I could lick my forehead—that would impress her!* "Go on, I've got the desk." He wanted her to leave before something embarrassing arose again.

"Thanks. Tyler? Are you all right?"

"Sure. Why?" *God, don't let her look at my pants!*

"You just seem excited."

No, no, no! "Excited?" His voice cracked.

"You know, excited. Did something happen?"

He realized she didn't mean *that* kind of excited. "Oh, no. Everything's fine."

He watched her walk away, heading as usual toward the side garden entrance. He'd never noticed before how her hips moved beneath her black suit skirt. Wondering if she was going to meet Stephen, he felt a surge of jealousy. Then Carol Anne came into view.

"Hi, there, Tyler. Slow night, huh?"

Oh, yeah, she wants me!

"We meet again," Stephen said to Amanda as he approached her in the wisteria garden. Since leaving the meeting, he'd taken care of the blood order—half would arrive tomorrow night, the rest was on back order and would come in a few days—and conducted some hotel business, doing some spot inspections and a little paperwork. All the while, he was aware of Amanda, where she was, what she was doing. Now, finally, he could speak to her. He could find out if last night's bite had worked or not.

"It's a nice night, isn't it?" Amanda sat down on one of the benches.

"May I join you?"

She looked surprised that he would bother to ask. "Of course." Patting the bench, she smiled a smile that could take him to the moon.

"It *is* beautiful this evening," he said. The fog covered only the lowlands by the shore; the stars and moon were bright in the sky, and you could see the Milky Way clearly. The wisteria filled the ocean air with sweetness, mingling with fainter flower fragrances from other gardens. Above it all, he was aware of Amanda's scent, her warm skin, her hot blood. Just sitting next to her was exciting. "How's work?"

"Fine. No problems." She looked at him and said softly, "I did meet up with the twins last night and again today."

"I should have formally introduced you." He studied her, thinking she seemed a little nervous. "Did they do anything to upset you?"

Amanda chuckled nervously. "I guess you could say that. They followed me to my room and wanted to see me naked."

"What?"

"Ivor came along and took them away. Stephen, may I be totally honest?"

"Of course."

"They're scary."

"They can be. I'm sorry they bothered you." He paused, then added, "I'm not going to say their bark is worse than their bite. It *usually* is, but don't go anywhere with them or invite them into your room. You said you saw them again tonight?"

"Today. This afternoon. I was swimming and they came to the pool."

"What happened?"

She thought a moment. "Well, basically, they asked me if I liked their bodies, then offered to help me dress. Are they actually lesbians?"

"No. They like both sexes. And they were trying to upset you by talking like that."

"I know."

"Remember my advice concerning them. Usually they're all talk. *Usually.*"

"I'll remember."

"What time did you say you saw them?"

"I didn't say, but it was somewhere between one and two this afternoon."

"It couldn't be them then. They're at school," he lied. *She saw them in the daytime? What's going on?* He himself had actually been awake and reading— of all things—part of the afternoon. Being awake was strange; being cognizant enough to read was practically unheard of. And yet the twins were walking around.

"Well, maybe they'd gone on a field trip or something," Amanda said. "They were using the pool to bathe. They were filthy. You know, dusty, dirty."

"Really? I wonder what they were up to."

"I don't have a clue." Amanda turned to face him. "Please don't tell them I told you anything."

"Don't worry. I'll be very discreet. Any number of people could have seen them."

"Stephen?"

"Yes?"

"What's the thing with the Darlings and daylight? Before I saw the twins today, I was beginning to wonder if I'm working for a family of vampires."

"Vampires?" He couldn't believe his ears.

"I'm sorry. I didn't mean to upset you. I was only joking."

"I know." He managed a smile, knowing it had to be a chance comment. "We do avoid sunlight. We have an inherited medical condition that makes us extra-sensitive. The sun can burn us even on a foggy day. Now tell me, what made you think of vampires?"

She hesitated. "I like them."

This was getting really confusing. "What do you mean, you like vampires? And why are you blushing?"

Her eyes traveled over his face before she spoke. "I mean exactly that. I've always been a secret vampire lover, ever since I was little. I like ghosts and goblins too, but vampires are my favorite."

"Oh! You mean *movies!*"

"And books. What else could I mean?"

He recovered himself nicely. "For a moment, I thought you meant you believe they really exist."

She smiled. "Who knows? Maybe they do."

* * *

Amanda was embarrassed about making the vampire remark. *Rule Number One: Never call your boss a vampire.* Stephen would make a great one with his broody good looks, but that was beside the point. She couldn't take back her remark, but she could change the subject before he thought she was even more of a dork. She opened her mouth to say something about the weather, but he beat her to it.

"Any sign of that mysterious foot in the laundry cart?"

"Until you brought it up, I'd almost forgotten about it." She paused, remembering his insistence that it was a prank. "Why do you ask?"

"Just curious."

"You haven't found it?" She could feel tension in the air. *What does he want me to say?* It suddenly seemed important to say the right thing.

"I'd imagine the plastic foot's been removed and the cart is back in use." He half-smiled. "Don't you think?"

"Yes," she said slowly. "I suppose so."

"You don't seem sure."

Smiling, she said, "I'm sure." That was what he wanted to hear, so that was what she told him. God knew why, but her answer made him smile, for real this time.

"Hopefully that's the end of that mystery."

"I'm sure it is." The tension had dissipated and she decided to press her luck. "You were in one of my dreams last night."

"I hope it was a pleasant dream," he said. "Tell me about it." He sounded concerned.

She felt herself blush again, realizing she shouldn't

have told him. "I—I don't really remember much
about it, but it was very pleasant."

Relaxing, he reached out and pushed back a lock
of her hair that the breeze had blown out of place.
"Did we talk much?"

Well, you told me I imagined everything about the foot.
But he hadn't really been there; it had only been
a dream. Her annoyance passed, but she spoke
carefully. "I don't think so." She thought that was
the safest thing to say at this point. Anyway, the
important part of the dream didn't involve speaking. And she wasn't about to tell him about that.

He locked her into his gaze, and she felt a thrill in
her stomach. Touching her hand, beside his on the
bench, he spoke. "I won't question you further."

"Why not?" *What a relief!*

"Because you're blushing, and a gentleman
shouldn't ask questions of a blushing woman."

*He knows it was a sex dream. Oh, God, why did I say
anything?* "Thank you." She tried to sound dignified. "I should probably get back to work."

He still touched her hand, watching her, and now
the only tension between them was sexual. "You
can always come to me, Amanda. You can tell me
anything."

That was a weird thing to say. "Um, okay."

They rose and walked together until just out of
sight of the garden doors. He touched her hand
again, just a brush, but it felt like fire. "You go in
first, I'll wait a few minutes. We don't want anyone
to get the wrong idea."

Or the right one. "Okay. I'll see you later."

His voice followed her, light and pleasant this
time. "Perhaps we'll meet again in your dreams."

24

Natasha paced like a lioness, stopping only to drink from the glass on her desk. *I can't believe I did that! I don't believe I did that!* "You did it," she said as she grabbed up the phone and punched in Douglas Harper's room number.

"Doug," Natasha said with false calm. "I love the roses. Unfortunately, I'm running late." *I can't believe I bit Tyler Shane!* "I have a few more things to do before I can even think about meeting you. It might be best if we wait until tomorrow night."

"Things got busy, huh?"

"Some problems have come up." *How could I do that to Tyler? What if I do it to Douglas?* "Can you manage without me?" she asked reluctantly.

"I suppose I'll have to. If you change your mind, I'll be in my room. I don't care what time it is, use your passkey and come visit. Mr. Chubby and I miss you."

"If I'm not too tired, I promise I will." *If you don't mind me taking a bite out of you.* The thought was simultaneously disturbing and appealing.

She put down the phone. *How could I have done it?* If she could so gracelessly charm and bite someone like Tyler, how could she trust herself to behave around Douglas, someone she was attracted to? She wondered if she should admit to her family what she'd done, but quickly decided it would only dishearten them. She was, after all, their leader, and leaders needed to be strong. And she didn't want to tell; it would be too humiliating.

She would, however, tell them about her mistake of leaving the potion out, and warn them to be cautious. But first, what she needed to do was talk to Julian Valentyn about the incident—how it had affected the human—and get him to refill her potion bottle.

She hated going to him, and had avoided him ever since his arrival. It was a basic distrust; why would a trueborn vampire want the Darlings' protection and why did he choose to give them the potion? His motives might really be as they seemed—they probably were—but she had to have more proof. She was skeptical of everything, as her family well knew. Unfortunately, Uncle Ori, in his zest for drama, was easily influenced by Valentyn. He reveled in his reflected glory, enjoying the notion that he was protecting this trueborn from other vampires. *The Dantes. Blood-sucking trash.*

She picked up the phone to let Valentyn know she was coming, then put it back down. *I'll surprise him.* The idea pleased her; she hoped she'd interrupt something.

Her office door shut behind her as she strode away. When she exited into the mezzanine, she saw Stephen. Nodding at him, she continued walking, not wanting to talk to him, not now. He would know something was wrong.

"Natasha." He took her arm as she passed, and brought her up short.

"Stephen. Is everything all right?"

"Yes and no. The good thing is that the charm took last night."

"You mean Amanda?"

"Who else would I mean? But the 'no' part is upsetting. Amanda told me the twins went swimming. This afternoon."

"This *afternoon?* No. She has to be wrong, Stevie."

"She's not. She even told me what time they were there."

"We'll have to do something about this. I can't believe it."

" 'Tasha, you look like something else is wrong. What is it?"

She hesitated, wondering what she should tell him. "Do you have a few minutes?"

"Sure. What for?"

"I'm on my way to Julian's suite."

"Why?"

"An incident with the potion. I need information. We all do. Come on. I'll tell you what happened on the way."

The knock on the door was sharp and business-like. "Ah," Julian said to the twins. They all sat on his terrace, enjoying the clear night. "That's probably your uncle." He raised his voice. "Jinxy, the door."

Julian had been thinking about going out himself tonight for fresh, living blood. In order to get what he required without incapacitating the humans, he needed to accost three, preferably four, people. Unlike human vampires, the trueborn could virtually always be sure of going unnoticed. He could make himself appear to disappear; it was a trick of shadows and light, not true invisibility. His bite, if he willed it, could not be felt, and a person sitting quietly in the shadows became the perfect dinner guest, especially if his or her state was somewhat altered. Julian often found the meals he was looking for getting high in the cemeteries above.

As he had in San Francisco, he preferred to do his hunting in the fog, and it looked like he wouldn't get much of it tonight, at least not near the hotel. He'd have to go into town, down to the pier or the boardwalk. That was a long way and would require driving, a true annoyance. But first, he had to dispense with his guests, and he wasn't ready to do that yet.

He and the girls had gone through several bottles since coming to his suite. He wanted to find out what really happened to their potion supply, and he'd thought drink would do it, but they kept up with him, barely acting drunk. It was the increased hunger caused by the potion, and with increased need came decreased drunkenness. He wondered what trouble they would get into because of their appetites, and smiled.

"Master Julian?"

"Yes, Jinxy? Is Orion here for the twins?"

"No, sir. It's Natasha and Stephen."

"Really. Well, ladies, it appears we're found out. Bring them out here, Jinxy." He quickly set the empty bottles on the floor behind a potted asparagus fern, then smiled at the twins. "I'll explain things."

"But—"

"Don't worry." He rose. "Natasha, Stephen, this is a pleasant surprise."

"Julian," Natasha said. Her eyes moved from him to the twins. "What are you two doing here?"

"I brought them here," Julian said quickly. "Ori

had something to attend to, so I invited your sisters to visit me until he finishes. In fact, I thought that you were him. Now won't you each have a seat?" He gestured at two empty patio chairs.

"Thank you," Natasha said as she and Stephen sat. "We have something we need to talk about." She glanced at the twins, then looked at Stephen.

"I think they should be told about it too," Stephen said.

The doorbell rang, and they waited while Jinxy escorted Ori out to the terrace. He looked surprised to see most of his family there. He looked from Natasha to Stephen to Julian. "I'm glad you're here. I have news that affects all of us."

"If it's business, Uncle—" began Stephen.

"It involves Julian." Ori tugged one cuff, then the other, then sat down in the last vacant chair. "It involves the potion."

Julian watched the looks exchanged between the three of them. Stephen looked concerned, Ori excited, and Natasha was darting her eyes from Ori to Julian, looking less than pleased.

"As I suspected, the Dantes are actively seeking the potion," Ori said. "And they're asking questions about you, Julian."

"Have you spoken to them?"

"No." Ori briefly explained about Gabe. "Nicholas Dante was here last night. They mean business."

"I could leave Candle Bay for a while if you'd like, Natasha." Julian looked around and called, "Jinxy, a bottle and glasses, please."

Natasha had started to smile at Julian's offer, and caught herself. She looked seriously at him. "I appreciate the offer, but it won't get rid of the Dantes. They'll assume there's potion here because you were here." She sat back. "Not only that, but we

Darlings keep our promises. Uncle Ori promised you protection, and you shall have it. I'll send Ivor to have another chat with you about your security here."

"Perhaps you'd like to keep your elixir somewhere safer than in your suite?" Ori suggested.

"I'd rather have it under my direct protection than in a safe away from my immediate presence." Julian smiled, locking eyes with Natasha. "Unless you have an even better hiding place? A locked room in those tunnels of yours? A room protected by locks *and* sorcery?"

The twins giggled.

"The tunnels are in ruins," Natasha said. "Earthquake damage. I don't know about you, but I have a fear of being buried undead." She didn't crack a smile. "There's nothing down there now except the catacombs, quite a distance up the hill. I'd imagine rats are the most interesting things you'd find in the tunnels."

The twins giggled.

"What?" Julian laughed lightly. "No Treasure? The tales hold no truth?"

"Would we leave it there if it existed?" Natasha accepted a goblet of A positive from Jinxy. "This is lovely. Thank you."

Julian watched her and the others as they drank. They all tried to hide their hunger, but it was as plain as a full moon. "Jinxy, another bottle, please." He turned back to Natasha. "Tell me something. Do you believe it ever existed?"

"I don't know. Perhaps, in some form." Her family looked at her in surprise. She never said such things. "I wondered how long it would take for the great Julian Valentyn to get around to asking." Irritation rode her voice.

" 'Tasha," Stephen said gently. "Everybody wonders about the Treasure." He looked at Julian. "We've had guests try to find the gold and jewels hidden by monks and pirates ever since we opened."

"Natasha, I didn't mean to upset you, though I must admit I'd love a look, especially at the catacombs," said Julian.

"I'm not upset." She had settled herself admirably, he had to admit, because there was terror in her eyes. "I'm wondering why Lucy and Ivy snickered when the tunnels were brought up. Girls, I'd like you to come and see me in my office later. Thank you, Jinxy," she added, accepting a refill. "I came here for another reason and I have to get back to work soon, so let's talk about that."

"I am at your service." The graciousness annoyed her, Julian could tell. *Good.* He was thinking about the twins now, the twins and the tunnels.

"It's about the potion," Natasha began. "A human found mine and put some on his cheeks."

"Which cheeks?" Lucy interrupted. Ivy giggled.

Natasha ignored her sisters. "I could smell the potion on him. As for what happened, suffice it to say that none of you should leave your bottles in your office rest room, or anywhere that an employee might possibly go." She cleared her throat. "What I want to know is this, Julian; can the potion do anything to humans other than heal them? This one nearly emptied my bottle."

She was getting too close to the truth, but he had to give her something, if only to distract her from thinking more about the elixir. "He had no wounds?"

"No."

"Ordinarily, all it will do is heal wounds. If there are none, there can be . . . side effects in humans."

"Which would consist of?"

"Flushing." He had to be careful of what he said, since these vampires were unknowingly experiencing most of the same effects. "It can give them tremendous energy for a while."

"Which causes what?"

"It depends entirely on the human. One might jog to excess. Another might sing. Yet another might clean house." He waited, hoping that was enough to satisfy her.

"What would you recommend doing with this particular employee? He's experiencing an excessive libido."

"What's his or her job?"

"He's the head concierge."

Julian smiled and sipped his drink. "I'd advise giving him a sedative. Something mild in a drink. That should ensure his behavior isn't too outrageous." He wasn't really sure it would work, but it sounded good and would keep her mind off what the potion was doing to her.

"I'll do that." Natasha rose. "I'm going to give him the night off. Will he be normal tomorrow?"

"Oh, yes, I should think so. The potion's effects are brief."

"No, don't get up. I'll see myself out. Thanks for the drink." She stepped inside the apartment, where Jinxy hovered. "Ivor will be calling on you."

Stephen started to rise. "Won't you stay a little while?" Julian asked. "Have one more drink?"

"Thanks. I believe I will. 'Tasha, I'll see you soon."

She nodded and left.

The ice in his shorts was melting quickly, and Tyler suspected there might be a pinhole leak in the

Baggie. Things were feeling cold and damp, and on top of everything else, he was still aroused.

It had taken every ounce of willpower he could muster not to proposition Carol Anne when he'd first returned to the desk. Hell, he'd almost jumped her bones when he flirted with her and she flirted right back. He was pretty sure she would have let him too, but there was a flurry of check-ins, mostly women. They all looked fuckable and he had to stop himself from staring.

When Amanda returned from her break, it just got worse. She set down next to him at the desk, and he could feel her presence, her pulsing sensuality. He smelled her femaleness, her skin, her hair, the faint scent of her perfume. It was something flowery, like jasmine or heliotrope, and it made him want to take her to the gardens and ravish her.

"You spent your break in the garden again, didn't you?" He spoke in an attempt to forget about sex.

"Yes. Why?"

It was obvious she hadn't liked the question. "I just wondered. You must like it out there. Which garden is your favorite?"

"The wisteria. But they're all nice."

He wanted to ask about Stephen, if she'd met him out there, but she'd turn into an icicle if he did. What did she see in the guy? His eyes, that had to be it. His eyes were like Natasha's, dark and hypnotic. At the thought of her, his shorts got even tighter, despite the cold dampness. He shifted uncomfortably.

"Earth to Tyler."

"Oh, sorry, Amanda. What?"

"Which is *your* favorite garden?"

"I like the one with the green man heads hanging in it."

She smiled. "So do I. It's kind of eerie with all those faces peering out of the leaves and vines. If it had fragrance, it might be my favorite too."

He barely heard her. He was thinking about being the hot dog inside a Natasha-Amanda bun.

And then it was for real. Well, sort of. Natasha appeared in front of them, holding two large coffee cups. "I thought you two could use these." She set one in front of Tyler, and one before Amanda, then let go of several sugar and cream packets, which dropped on the desk between them.

"Thank you," Amanda said.

"Yes," Tyler said, unable to stop staring at his employer's breasts. "This is very nice of you."

"You're welcome."

She bent a little, and Tyler could see down her dress just a tiny bit. He forced himself to look at the coffee cup, take off the lid, and put in cream and sugar. Amanda took hers black.

"How are you doing tonight, Tyler?"

He felt a blush. Natasha's voice was so sexy and she had called him by name. *Oh, Tyler, fuck me, Tyler! I want your big hard cock, Tyler!*

"Is something wrong?" she asked. "Your breathing sounds hard."

"Nothing's wrong." *That you can't fix!* "I'm fine."

"Feeling well? You look flushed. Why don't you have your coffee and then go up to bed? Amanda, you'll cover the desk, won't you?"

"Of course."

"I'm fine. Our shift is almost over, so I'll stay." Tyler didn't want to miss a minute of being close to Natasha or Amanda. Or any other women that came along. He had to get one in his bed tonight. Natasha was out of reach, but Amanda might not be.

"Very well, but I'm trusting you, Amanda, to send him to bed if he seems ill."

"Sure. I'll keep an eye on him."

Maybe I can get her into my room if I act like I don't feel good. "Don't worry. I'm fine." Sipping his coffee, he watched raptly as Natasha walked across the lobby to the mezzanine. She disappeared into darkness under the stairs, where there was a seldom-used private elevator.

"Tyler, put your eyes back in your head." Amanda laughed softly. "You're being way too obvious."

He looked at her sheepishly. "Sorry." He tried to convince himself she was jealous, but he knew it wasn't true. "If you don't tease me about this, I promise not to tease you about Stephen. I know you've been meeting him in the garden."

"Deal."

"Now we each know a secret about the other. I promise not to tell yours if you won't tell mine."

She cocked her head, looking at him. "You *are* acting weird, but okay. Now, drink your coffee."

25

"We've gone through several of your bottles, Julian," Stephen said. "We've just placed an order with Slater Brothers for ourselves. Would you care to add to it?" He set his glass on the coffee table, feeling slightly drunk, but sated for the first time in several nights, and that felt good.

"It would simplify things. Thank you, Stephen." Julian opened a wooden inlaid box on the side table and took out a small leather-bound notebook and a pen. He began writing his order.

Ori sat nearby, quietly contemplating his nearly empty goblet. He had imbibed slowly but steadily since his arrival, and appeared to be feeling it, if only mildly. The twins were still out on the terrace, watching the night, doing a little eavesdropping, giggling, occasionally arguing. Their voices rose and fell on the ocean breeze.

"Here you are." Julian handed him the note and Stephen scanned it. The trueborn had expensive tastes.

"I'll reimburse you, of course," Julian added. "When do you expect delivery?"

"Soon. I'll call this in tonight."

"I appreciate it. Would you, or you, Ori, care for more to drink?"

Both declined. "We do have something we want to discuss with you, however," Ori said.

Julian cocked an eyebrow, then pulled his chair closer to the other men. "What is it?"

"The twins," Stephen told him, "are out of control."

The eyebrow raised higher. "In what way?"

"They're harassing our employees, for one thing."

Ori looked at Stephen. "I didn't know about that."

"They're picking on our new concierge, and several of the food employees have complained about them picking through food they're preparing for the restaurants."

"Food? That *is* strange."

Stephen nodded. "They seem to have little self-control. They've always been marginal, but they usually did as they were told. Not now."

"We have to watch them every moment," Ori added. "As you know."

Julian nodded sagely. "Go on."

Stephen pondered how much to tell him, and decided to be more forthcoming than his worrywart sister would be. "They were seen in the daytime yesterday. They were swimming and evidently had full use of their mental functions. They made sexual advances to a female employee."

"The concierge?"

"Yes."

"They're drinking too much as well," Ori said. Stephen looked at him sharply.

"Yes, I've noticed," said Julian. "You all are."

"We seem to require it," Stephen told him. "It doesn't intoxicate us like it normally would."

Natasha's not going to like this, but what can I do? Julian's no fool.

"How long has this been going on?" the pale vampire asked.

"A few days, though I think the first symptoms appeared weeks ago. They're worsening rapidly."

"Do the rest of you feel out of control, as well?"

Stephen considered. "To some extent. You told Natasha that the potion excites humans. Is it doing something to us?"

"Oh, heavens, no." Julian looked from one to the other. "I can tell you what's wrong."

Stephen waited, hiding his impatience.

"It's inherited from the trueborns. I told you about the mating urge, how strong but infrequent it is in a trueborn vampire?"

"Yes."

"You're experiencing the human vampire version. It happens to your race sometimes, just as it does to us, but it's a milder phenomenon, and comes out in increased appetites. Human appetites as well as vampiric."

"Why is it happening to all of us?"

"It's catching, like a virus."

"And Ivor is immune," Ori observed.

"Is he?" Julian rubbed his chin thoughtfully. "How fortunate for him."

"How did we catch it?"

"It's part of your vampiric heritage. I've only seen a few manifestations."

"What can we do about it?"

"Not very much. You'll have to let it run its course."

"How long will it last?"

"It varies in length just as it varies in strength from vampire to vampire."

"I've never heard of this, this virus," Stephen said. "I've met human vampires much older than myself and none of them ever mentioned it."

"It doesn't happen to everyone." Julian sat back. "Do you want my advice?"

"Yes," Stephen said. "We do." He almost choked on the words because he sensed Julian was enjoying it all.

"You have to ride it out. Lay in a good supply of blood and drink all you need. It won't harm you and you need it." He paused. "Be on guard against emotions taking over. You probably aren't sleeping very well."

"No."

"You can't do anything about that, but it won't hurt you. What you do have to be careful of is human guests and employees. You'll want to bite them. That's why it's important to keep yourselves sated with bottled blood until this passes. As for the twins, if they're volatile to begin with, you might consider locking them in their suite by day so they won't go wandering. At night, do as you are now, and keep them close. Don't let them make you angry—you're likely to overreact. Keep an eye on each other. And wait. It's unlikely to get much worse. Talk about it with every affected vampire and reassure them it's a normal occurrence and nothing to worry about if all of you control yourselves."

"Thank you. That sounds like good advice." Stephen realized the trueborn was sincere, not gloating, and regretted they hadn't come to him sooner. Of course, he'd have to have Ivor hold onto Natasha while he told her about the conversation, but she'd soon see the wisdom of it.

He had a sudden thought. Quickly, he told Julian about the trouble with the corpse in the laundry cart. "And it still hasn't shown up. What do you make of it?" He watched Julian closely, for it had occurred to him that he might have killed the woman himself.

"That was an act due to the virus, I'm sure."

"We suspect the twins," Ori said quietly.

Julian nodded. "That makes sense. Just keep them close. That's all I can counsel."

"I'd like to know what happened to the body," Stephen said.

"Perhaps they buried it," Julian suggested. "Or they might have taken it into the tunnels, if you have any entrances left." He lifted an eyebrow.

Stephen nodded, thinking about what Amanda had said about the twins being filthy when they came to the pool. Either suggestion could cover that.

The human vampires, all four of them, had left his suite shortly after he'd told them the tale of the mysterious vampire-attacking trueborn "virus." Presumably, they would call a meeting of their kind to discuss it. Julian smiled to himself. They had believed him—and why not? It made perfect sense. It was not a new story; he had used it before, though not for centuries, and it always worked.

Ori had been reassured, as had Stephen, and that was the important thing. His surety would rub off on Natasha; Stephen acted as her advisor, that was obvious. She would listen and believe.

And none of them would be ready for the invasion of the Dantes. He had feigned ignorance when Ori told him about his little shill, Gabe something, and now he picked up the phone, ready to rat him out, as the gangsters liked to say.

26

"It's a beautiful, clear night here in Candle Bay, that is, if you're perched above the fog. Friends and neighbors, say hello to the stars and moon, our infrequent but welcome visitors. Here at the station, the fog is licking our toes and ankles and from the big KNDL bay window, I can see Orion the hunter aiming his arrow, his dog, Sirius, nipping at his heels." Coastal Eddie's voice lowered, hushed. "I wonder what he's aiming at. The amphitheater? It's dark tonight, so that's probably not his target. Could he be sighting one of the cemeteries in the hills? Why shoot his arrows at the dead? To rouse them perhaps?

"Ah, I see the gleam of the Candle Bay Hotel and Spa cradled in the hills. A beautiful building, stately, graceful, its lights like jewels shining in the darkness, it calls to us with its sweet song. It pulses with life, but is its heart surrounded by darkness and death? Is that where Orion aims his arrow? I think so, my friends. The question is, is it an arrow of love or of terror?"

A chill ran down Amanda's spine at the DJ's words. "Which is it?" she murmured, brushing her hair in preparation for bed. *Silly*. She didn't even know why she had turned the radio on. Coastal Eddie was full of it. *So corny.* But . . . The crazy things he said, his talk about monsters in the fog, about the hotel, drew her in. She'd always been a sucker for a spooky story, and Eddie was still delivering.

"The creatures of darkness are out there now, dear listeners, and they are searching for their dinner. And their dessert. Don't be fooled into thinking you're safe because the night is clear. They are there, in the shadows of buildings, lurking beneath the pier, or hiding behind the trees. If you're driving right now, use your rearview mirror to make sure nothing lies in wait in your backseat. If you see a strange shadow there, pull over now and exit your vehicle. Caution, my friends, is the watchword tonight."

"What about the creatures *outside* the car, Eddie? Are they less scary than the ones inside?" *What a flake!* She smiled as she untied her robe, ready to turn off Eddie and climb into bed, but a knock on the door brought her up short. Reknotting the tie, she put her eye to the new peephole. It was Tyler, and he was carrying a sprig of purple snapdragons from the arrangement at the end of the hall. *What now?*

She opened the door and peered at him. He wore baggy shorts, a long T-shirt, and a big stupid grin. "What do you want?" she asked, keeping her voice low.

"For you." He held out the snapdragons.

She didn't take them. "Tyler, what are you doing?"

His other hand came out from behind his back. It held a bottle of premixed strawberry margaritas. "I thought we could have a drink. Can I come in?"

"It's late." He was flushed and a little crazed-looking, just as he'd been during their last hours on duty, when he'd refused to leave his post even after Natasha told him to. He had stuck it out, acting weird and flirty the entire time. And he hadn't just flirted with her. He'd come on to female guests and employees alike. *He's an equal-opportunity slut.* But that wasn't really fair, calling him a slut, since he hadn't acted this way before. *Maybe he has a virus or something. Maybe he's on drugs.* "I'm really tired, and I'm ready for bed," she said.

His leering smile unnerved her. "So am I."

"Then you should go to bed."

"A drink will help us sleep."

Us, Tonto? "It won't help me, Tyler. Why don't you go back to your room now?"

"I think I love you."

"You're just tired. Go to bed, Tyler. You probably have a fever."

"You could take my temperature." He made puppy-dog eyes.

"No." She began to shut the door. This was unreal.

"Wait!" he cried in a strangled whisper.

"What?"

"Are you turning me down because of Stephen?"

"No, Tyler. I'm just turning you down. Believe me, you'll be thankful in the morning." She paused. "But we won't bring it up."

He opened his mouth to say something, then glanced down the hallway. "There's Carol Anne. I'll see you later." He trotted away.

Shutting the door, Amanda shook her head. What was with him? As she took off her robe, she hoped that whatever it was, it wasn't catching. She slipped between cool sheets and stretched out

"Don't forget, folks, this Saturday night I'll be broadcasting live from the boardwalk. Look for the

KNDL van near the merry-go-round. Stop by and say hi—that is, if you can find us in the fog. And now a word from our sponsor, the Marital Aid Museum and Emporium, located in beautiful downtown Caledonia, just a few miles north of Candle Bay."

Amanda turned off the radio. She was having enough trouble with men. She didn't need a fake one too.

Three A.M. Amanda sat up in bed, her eyes on the alarm clock's glowing display. It wasn't a dream that woke her tonight, but a certainty that someone was in the room with her, a certainty that came rushing up from somewhere deep inside to bring her bolt upright, out of a dreamless sleep.

"Who's there?" She whispered the words. Moonlight from the open sliding glass door slanted across the carpet, illuminating the room enough to let her see the grayish forms of the furniture and the outlines of paintings on the walls. She noticed that she hadn't closed the closet door. The open side yawned blackly, while the closed half mirrored moonlight and shadows. It didn't bother her. Much. She glanced at the bathroom door, saw nothing unusual. Everything seemed to be as she'd left it. But someone was in the room. She could feel it. "Who's there?"

Of course no one answered. The same thing had happened her first night here, and no one was in her room then either. *What about the man leaving the corridor? Maybe he was in your room. Maybe he's back.* But that was just first-night jitters. *There was no one in the room that night.* She put her hand to the side

of her neck to rub an itchy spot. The skin felt oily
there, but she barely registered it.

She could feel a presence, its eyes on her, its emotions, so alien. *It's not human.* She touched her neck
again. *You just listened to too much Coastal Eddie.* But
she continued to search the shadowed room, barely
moving her head. *Something's here. You sat up, so it
knows you know. You talked to it, for Christ's sake. So
why not turn on the light? Because I'm afraid, that's why.*
Afraid that light might not make the intruder flee,
that she'd see it was really there. *That's silly.* Making
up her mind, she reached over to turn on the bedside lamp, and as she moved, something whooshed
past her like a cold breeze. She saw a fluttering out
of the corner of her eye and paused, her fingers
on the switch. It had to be the wind.

Then there was a sound, small but real. She
looked toward it, toward the door to her room, just
in time to see a shadow pass over it. The door
opened and closed quietly, smoothly, all by itself.

"Holy crap!" She turned on the lamp. *A ghost!*

More excited than scared, she hopped out of bed
and crossed to the door. The dead bolt was undone.
Something was *in here with me! Something invisible!*

*An invisible something that had to use a door, to undo
a lock.* Well, there were plenty of stories about
ghosts manipulating material objects. It had to be
a ghost. What else could it be? "Wow," she whispered.

Locking the door, she moved to the balcony. The
sheers fluttered, ghostly themselves in the mild
breeze. The sea rode the wind, the sea and fog, a
damp, strange smell. Amanda opened the screen
and stepped outside. There was nothing there, no
clue, and she spent a long moment looking out,
studying the mostly dark hotel and the glittering

lobby. The stained glass gleamed in rich reds and blues, yellows and greens, and she thought she caught music on the zephyr, but at this hour it had to be her imagination. Beyond the hotel, she saw a few street lamps in the misty ocean air, and below, the sea and town lay muffled in fog.

Should she tell someone? Wake someone? *But what would I say? A ghost was in my room?* The thought made her smile. *I don't think so!* She returned to her bed after locking the sliding door and double-checking the room door. The locks probably wouldn't keep a ghost out, but despite the terror she had felt, she knew ghosts couldn't really hurt you.

She had seen him, yet not seen him, been both aware and unaware of his presence in her room. Julian Valentyn had decided not to slake his thirst on the homeless sleeping in the cemetery or beneath the pier, but rather to partake sparingly of Amanda Pearce's exquisite lifeblood. It was the second bite. On his original visit, he had administered the first.

Now he supplemented his diet with bottled blood, nourishing himself for the night as he wondered how Amanda had sensed him. Was it simply coincidence? He doubted it. There was more to Amanda than showed on the surface. Much more. Stephen sensed it, but only he, Julian, *knew* it. The Father would know it too.

Something resembling fear wandered across his consciousness.

His terrace faced northwest, allowing him a view of the gardens, the rolling hills, and the ocean. He looked toward the water. Waves crashed, their roaring muted in the low-lying fog, and the sky was beginning to pale with the dawn, fingers of reddish light edging gray-bottomed cumulous clouds. A storm? Perhaps. He lingered, remembering the sunset so long ago in Euloa and his lost love, Talai.

He didn't know how much time had passed, but Aardvark Wicket had consumed six more rats, *slish slash,* eating their flesh, drinking their blood, and he was getting damned sick of them. Rats for breakfast, rats for lunch, rats for fucking afternoon tea. He didn't know what the rats themselves ate, but it was probably something he didn't want to know about anyway. The meat tasted old and rancid, and if he hadn't been so hungry, he would have puked it up.

His strength was returning slowly but surely, and now that he could stand up without having to rest every other minute, he was ready to explore the tunnels; so far he had stayed in or near the Y arm where the exit he knew about was located. That sucker just wouldn't move. He thought there was a trick to it, since those girls had done it, but he'd torn his nails and bloodied his fingertips trying to get the goddamned thing to open.

Right now, he was headed up the other arm of the Y, and it was getting creepier by the second. Even though he wasn't the type to get scared, this place was trying to freak him out. He hadn't tackled the wide stem of the Y yet—he was saving that since it led downward and away from the only opening he knew about. He sure as hell didn't want to get lost. Even now, going up the other arm, he was dropping rat bones to mark his way. You couldn't be too careful.

The tunnel narrowed as he moved farther from the single overhead bulb. His flesh prickled up. There was no sign of another light switch, so he took his cigarette lighter from his backpack and flicked it on. He saw a doorway ahead, without a door. It was just sort of an ovoid opening into darkness. Aardvark paused, letting the lighter have a cooling rest. Should he go on? *Yes.* A shiver ran down his spine, but the hope of finding another exit compelled him. Or maybe something else did.

Trembling, he approached the open space and thrust his hand and lighter inside. In the flickering flame, the passageway appeared to widen out and lead to another, blacker entryway. "Shit!" Aardvark almost dropped the Bic as, in the darkness, he sensed eyes watching him, many eyes. And something more. Death was in the air. He could feel it. There was an odor of old brittle bones and papery skin.

Come to me.

What the fuck was that? His first instinct, and his second, was to run, to get the hell out of there just in case he wasn't hallucinating; then he thought that maybe here he would find a gateway to the outside world, to the cemetery above. His salvation might be inside. Snapping the lighter back on, he moved into the larger chamber and walked to the inner entry. The darkness was thick, and he had to kneel and hold the flame close to the bottom of the doorway in order to make out the stairs leading down deeper into the earth. The air was frigid.

The feeling of being watched was overpowering, and the dusty dry scent of old death surrounded him. Panic welled; he began drowning in it. Turning, he skittered back down the limb of the Y, gathering his rat bones as he went. If there were an exit back there, he didn't think he would resort to it. Never had he felt such apprehension; it would be better to die than face whatever was down there.

He reached the end of the arm and began dropping rat bones again as he started down the main shaft. At least there were dim yellow lightbulbs here to help him on his way.

He wondered if it was day or night.

27

Ori liked to think of them as the Goon Squad, though he never said it aloud for fear of hurting Ivor's feelings; his nephew was very proud of his charges. The core security team was an interesting lot, a crew of six, excluding Ivor, made up half of vampires, half of humans. These humans were loyal subjects, the most loyal, for their secrecy was doubly insured by both hypnosis and the bite.

Ivor, quiet, yet possessing a powerful and inspiring presence, held the disparate lot together, kept personalities from clashing, made them into a team. The vampires included Dilly Landsdown, who had been a nurse in the War Between the States before Ori changed her. The two male vampires were brothers (but not twins) who fought in World War I. They were called Nipper and Snapper; their real names were less than memorable. The humans were Dale, Ed, and Nadine, an ex-Marine who was deceptively small and feminine-looking. Dale had wanted to be an FBI agent, but couldn't pass the background check, and Ed formerly ran a gas station up in Washington State. Both men were reasonably tall, strong specimens. They all followed orders well, and all of them very much desired to be brought over to the vampiric life.

This evening, the team had gathered in Ori's private suite. Ordinarily, the vampires never took a drink in front of their mortal coworkers, but tonight was not ordinary. Ori served coffee to the humans and blood to the vampires. Only Ivor demurred, and Ori, who thirstily joined in the drinking, wondered at his nephew. Whatever really was increasing the hunger, he was immune to it. *Why? How?*

Drinking problems hadn't been the point of the meeting, however. Its purpose was to plan the watch on the unfinished garden of the stone lions; the one Gabe Leoni had told the Dantes contained an entrance to the tunnels.

"So it's decided then," Ori told the team. "You'll take turns on a rotating watch. In the evening, you will contact Ivor, then your teammates, the moment you see any signs of activity. You know what to do. Any questions?"

"Why are they interested in the tunnels?" Dilly Landsdown asked.

Ori cleared his throat. "They believe that we keep treasure there. The treasure I speak of in this case includes the elixir we've been using to heal bite wounds on humans. They are after that, we know."

"Is it down there?" Dale asked.

"The elixir? No. The main danger we would experience if they found their way into the tunnels would be if they found their way out again via the hotel itself."

"Could they?" Nadine asked, smiling.

"Highly unlikely," said Ivor. "The tunnels are impassable in places."

"There is another danger," Ori continued. "If they did figure out how to get in and out of the tunnels, they could do something very antisocial, such as killing some of our human guests. Certainly, they would snatch a few for feeding purposes."

"We ought to know where all the tunnel openings are," Ed said. The others murmured agreement.

"What do you think, Ivor?"

The tall man considered. "I think we should concentrate on keeping the Dantes out of the tunnels."

"It's possible they could find entrances up in the cemeteries, isn't it?" Snapper asked. "I mean, there are some up there, right?"

"Correct. The original ones are long gone, but there are two small mausoleums containing passages we've constructed."

"I think we should seal them," Ivor said. "I'll do it myself."

"I want you—and your team—nearby," Ori said. "I'll ask Stephen to take care of it."

Ivor nodded.

"As for telling you all where the entrances are, it may come to that. But for now, the less you know, the better." It was a family secret, one he didn't care to share even with these trusted employees. Tunnels and rumors of treasure were hard for anyone to resist. The fewer who knew anything, the better.

"What about weapons?" asked Snapper.

"Excellent question. Your .38s day and night, and by night, stakes and crossbows. Be careful to keep them hidden as best you can." He smiled thinly. "The guests wouldn't understand. If one of you humans stands guard at night, don't do anything that will reveal yourself to the invaders before backup arrives. The Dantes don't care about being subtle; they'll kill you in a minute."

"What about the guests?" asked Dale. "What do we do about them?"

"The lions' garden is already cordoned off to keep people out while we finish designing it, but I want you to make certain the guests stay away. Be polite but firm. And keep a particular lookout for illicit lovers. They seem to like to make love among the lions."

"Where else would they keep it but in the tunnels somewhere?" Nicholas Dante asked. He sat with his brother and the others at the rectangular table in the conference room of the Dante Medical Waste Management, Inc., in San Luis Obispo, the biggest city anywhere near Candle Bay. They had several other offices scattered up and down the coast; beach and fishing towns were always concerned with medical waste.

"In a safe?" suggested Christopher Dante. "I don't understand why you believe the elixir has to be in the tunnels."

"Because they keep all traces of the tunnels hidden. They want them kept a secret, so why wouldn't they hide it there?"

Christopher shook his head. "We don't even know if the tunnels really exist or if they're accessible. We've never been able to find out. The elixir could be kept anywhere. I wouldn't be surprised if it is kept off the property. Maybe they *want* us to think it's in the tunnels."

"Okay, okay, I get what you're saying. But humor me," Nicholas said. "Gabe Leoni got us the information on how to get into the underground. Let's see if it's for real."

"The underground?" asked a bucktoothed vampire two seats down.

"Yeah, the tunnels. Got the info from Orion himself, the old blowhard."

"You think they're feeding Leoni bogus information?" one of the other vampires asked.

"Maybe. Maybe not—Orion likes to talk. Or maybe something else is going on. An anonymous individual called to say Leoni's changed sides, that he's kissing Orion Darling's ass now. It might be a frame, but it's also believable. You all know how much those two fucks like mob culture. That's why we sent Leoni in the first place. They've got something in common. Orion makes like he's the fucking Godfather. That impresses Leoni. A lot. He easily may have turned on us."

Nicholas looked at Christopher, seated at his right hand, and then the others. Most were blood Dantes, cousins and such, created back when they were competing with the Darlings and other families to increase clan size, before they knew better. Others were unrelated and had been carefully selected according to their talents and predilections. Altogether, ten sat at the table. These were the best of the bunch. There were other vampires in the business with them, but not many—obtaining blood without getting caught was always a problem when the population increased. That was why there were suppliers like Slater Brothers and Crimson Tide. The vampires had learned the hard way that numbers didn't necessarily mean power, not when you had to feed the troops. Like the Darlings, the Dantes used humans wherever they could. Most of them were relatively easy to handle and very well behaved. All it took was a little nip now and then.

"One thing we have to remember. The Darlings

are housing the trueborn vampire who killed our brother. They're our enemies, along with Valentyn. We do in the Darlings as they come along, and after we have the elixir *and* the recipe, we kill Valentyn."

"Is that possible?" asked one of the cousins. "To kill a trueborn?"

"You don't see many around, do you?" Christopher said.

"We stake him out and let the sun take care of him. But that comes later."

They spent some time discussing tactics, deciding to enlist humans to begin digging well before dusk. Then Nicholas said, "We have one other piece of news from our nameless source." He smiled, his fangs half out. It was past time for a drink. "The Darlings are expecting a large shipment from Slater Brothers night after next. According to the source, it's the second in three days. Something's going on. I suggest we amuse ourselves by intercepting the truck before it arrives at the hotel. Does that appeal to everyone?"

It did.

Back at the Candle Bay Hotel, few guests were awake. The mezzanine bar and Satyrelli were closed and dark, as was the spa and pool (though vampires sometimes swam there in the dark, white bodies gliding in the moonlight like long, pale fish). The lobby remained well lit and inviting with its lush tropical gardens and bubbling fountain. The guitarist was gone, and a Mozart sonata played softly in the background. Tonight, the lobby felt pleasantly warm and dry compared to the cool foggy air outside, but only the employees were there to enjoy it.

In his office, Ori relaxed with a good bottle of blood and watched *Godfather II* while he pondered problems in the back of his mind. Meanwhile, Stephen spent time in the cemetery, sealing the two mausoleum entrances to the tunnels with heavy chains and padlocks, securing them through pre-drilled holes in stone slabs. When he came to the second mausoleum, which had a broken latch, he found an old drunken bag lady sleeping in the doorway. He had a drink, and it took great effort to not take too much of the woman's hot, fresh blood. The drunk never awoke, and after Stephen had sealed the opening within and padlocked the ornate black iron bars, he put the sleeping woman back in the doorway.

And then there was Ivor. He and his team prowled the hotel and grounds, paying particular attention to the garden of the stone lions. A few other employees had been tapped to add to security within the hotel, but they had little to do; things were quiet and sleepy in the public areas.

One guest was awake, barely, and that was Douglas Harper. Natasha, well fed, had allowed herself a visit. They made love twice and she had not lost control, though she came close to biting him during her orgasms. Now, he accompanied her to his door, where they kissed passionately. He watched her until she turned down a bisecting corridor, then closed his door and fell asleep almost as soon as his head touched the pillow.

Unseen by either of them, Julian Valentyn watched from the shadows. He could smell the sex on Natasha as she swept by. An hour before dawn, he joined Ori for a nightcap. It took little prodding to get the mobster-loving vampire to talk about Natasha's human lover.

28

The knock on her door startled Amanda, causing her to close her novel without marking the page. More raps followed, sharp and insistent. She glanced at the clock; it was three in the afternoon. *What if it's the twins?*

KNDL was having an Eagles hour, and she turned down the radio, muting "Smuggler's Blues." Brushing a few cookie crumbs off her lap, she rose, telling herself not to be paranoid; it wasn't the twins. *But Stephen warned you.* Well, if it was them, she wouldn't answer, she'd go directly to the phone and call Stephen's private number. As silently as she could, she tiptoed across the room and peered out the peephole Stephen had had installed for her.

With a sigh of relief, she opened the door. "Carol Anne," she said. "Hi. Come on in." She stood back, and the little blonde entered the room, looking around.

"This is nice, but you've gotta put up some of your own pictures and things. I'll show you my room for inspiration. I have a really great collection of ostrich art. You know, drawings, paintings, little statues, and stuffed toys. I've been collecting them since I was six."

"How nice." Amanda didn't think Carol Anne's taste would inspire her, but she nodded, smiling. "I'd like that." At least it wasn't a bunny-rabbit collection.

Carol Anne, dressed in pale pink shorts and a white blouse printed with little bunches of pink and blue balloons, walked to the open balcony. "You've got a nice view. All the rooms on this side of the hallway do. I wish mine was over here." She turned and plopped down on the couch, then picked up Amanda's novel. "You *read?*" The girl looked genuinely surprised.

"Voraciously," Amanda said. She wondered if the other girl even knew the word. *Don't be cruel.*

"What's this book about?"

"A vampire."

Carol Anne's eyes widened. "Isn't that scary?"

Amanda grinned. "I like scary books. Movies too."

"But they're so—so scary!" Carol Anne set the book aside. "I only read magazines like, you know, *Elle.* Stuff like that. But I like scary movies if I'm with a guy." She giggled. "Then you get to hang onto him." She paused, then blurted, "Guess what!"

Sitting down on the short couch next to the girl, Amanda smiled. "What?"

"Guess!"

She quelled the urge to groan and roll her eyes. Carol Anne was nice enough if you liked sitcom-fluffy girls, but she was an energy drain on Amanda, who forced another smile. "I can't guess. You tell me."

Carol Anne wiggled with excitement. "No. Guess! Once, at least."

"You got a promotion?"

"That's not even a good guess. Try again."

"Sorry. I'm out of guesses."

The girl was ready to burst, and burst she did. "We did *it!*"

"What?"

"You can't tell anybody!"

"Okay, but I don't know what you're talking about."

"Tyler and me. We did *it.* You know, we—"

"I know." Amanda remembered the way Tyler had lit up at the sight of Carol Anne after she herself had turned him down. The guy had been desperate for sex. "Last night?" she asked sweetly.

Carol Anne nodded. "Yeah. You were talking to him right before he came to see me. He said you were just talking about front-desk stuff." She hesitated. "You aren't jealous or anything, are you?"

Amanda laughed at the thought. "Not at all."

"But he's really cute."

"Not my type," Amanda assured her. An image of Stephen entered her mind, and lingered until the other girl spoke again.

"We had margaritas—do you like margaritas?"

"Sure."

"Well, he brought my favorite, strawberry margaritas. Do you think he already knew, or that it was just a coincidence?"

Amanda realized she was still smiling, and it was legitimate. "Maybe you told him."

Carol Anne lit up. "I bet I did! Anyway, I invited him to my room and he said yes. Once before, I asked him, a while ago, like months, and he said he couldn't, so I wasn't real sure if I should, but . . ."

"You went for it."

"Yeah!" Her eyes sparkled. "I went for it. And it

was grrr-eat!" She did a pretty good Tony the Tiger. "Unbelievable!"

Amanda had a hard time believing that. Tyler had seemed so desperate; she didn't think he'd have lasted a minute.

"We did it six times! He couldn't get enough!"

"*Six* times?"

Carol Anne nodded. "He was like a redwood." She considered. "Well, more like a cherry tree, I guess, but he sure knew how to use it. I bet he doesn't have a drop of sperm left in him."

Too much information! "I'll bet."

"Is Stephen big?" Carol Anne asked abruptly.

Amanda stared at her. "Big?"

"You know." That annoying tittering giggle. "*Big.* His *thing.*"

She didn't know whether to laugh or get angry, so she said, "I have no idea."

"You haven't laid him yet?"

"No, of course not. What made you think that?"

"I see you guys talking in the garden sometimes. You're always staring at each other like you want to do it. He watches you when you're working too. Did you know that?"

"No, he doesn't, and nothing's going on. We're just friends. I barely know him."

"But you want him."

Amanda half-smiled and said quickly, "So tell me more about Tyler. Was he inventive?"

"Uh-huh. The first time we did it, his thingy was really cold."

"Cold?" Maybe this was interesting after all. She refrained from suggesting he might be the devil.

"Yeah." Carol Anne paused, cocking her head. "It was kind of weird. He had a plastic bag of cold water in his underwear. He tried to hide it, but I saw. That *is* kind of weird, isn't it?"

Nodding, Amanda laughed. "What did he say about it?"

"That he was keeping himself fresh for me." She giggled like Betty Boop. "Then he said he'd been thinking about me and he had to put an ice pack on his thing because I turned him on him so much. But it melted."

"Wow. He must really like you." *The guy really is in heat. Or he's kinky. Or Carol Anne's exaggerating.* She restrained a chuckle. "I'm glad you had so much fun. Have you seen him today?"

Concern flitted across her face, just for a second, then she was smiling again. "Yeah. In the dining room. He acted real cool, like nothing happened, and that's why you can't tell I told you. He wants it to be a secret. At least for now."

Amanda nodded. "Did he tell you that?"

"No. There were other people around. I wonder if I'll see him again tonight. I hope so." There was that look of concern again.

"I hope so too." *You've been used, honey.*

"A few of us are going out Saturday night," Carol Anne said abruptly. "Do you want to come along?"

"Where are you going?" Even though Carol Anne wasn't ideal company, there would be other people. Going out sounded great and she had the night off.

"The boardwalk. It'll be open and KNDL is broadcasting from there."

"Coastal Eddie," Amanda said. "I heard."

"You listen to Coastal Eddie? Isn't he cool?"

"He's interesting." A throwback was closer to what he was, but he intrigued Amanda. She'd like to get a look at the guy. She already pictured him as an old hippie with long straight hair and wire-rim glasses and she wanted to know if she was right. "That sounds like fun. Who else is going?"

Carol Anne looked at her hands, then dimpled up. "Well, I thought I'd ask Tyler. Maybe we could ask Stephen too. There's going to be dancing at the old pavilion. There's a band from Red Cay that's going to play. Plastic Taffy. Or maybe they're from Caledonia. I forget. Anyway, all the rides will be running, even if it's really foggy."

"Wait a minute. You've only asked *me* so far?"

She nodded. "I thought—I thought I could ask Tyler if other people were going. Then it wouldn't be like I was asking him out on a date. What about Stephen? Would he come?"

"I doubt it. You wouldn't want to go someplace with your boss anyway, would you?"

"Well, you could ask."

"No." Amanda was firm. "It's not appropriate."

"Well, I'll try and get some other people, but it's you and me for sure, right?"

"Yes." *Arghhh. Alone with Carol Anne.* "But maybe you should ask Tyler without telling him you already asked me."

"Why? I don't want him to think it's a real date."

"Just say you asked other people. I don't think Tyler and I can both take the night off. If he says yes, I won't go, and you can ask other people along or just tell him everyone else canceled."

"You'd do that for me?"

"Sure."

"Okay, thanks."

After Carol Anne left, Amanda realized that she hoped, just a little, that Tyler would say no. She really wanted to go out, even if it was with Carol Anne.

* * *

"We're locked up."

"Like rats."

Lucy and Ivy were wide awake and raring to go. They had slept a few hours, but now they paced their apartment like caged lions. They had been doing so for most of the afternoon. Their hunger consumed them, and they'd already gone through all the bottles they had in their room. It was a good thing, Lucy thought, that more blood was being delivered. She wanted gallons and gallons. She wanted to drink until it seeped out her pores.

"I wonder why we don't get drunk anymore," Ivy said. "We've been drinking so much."

"Yeah. I miss it. I really miss it." Lucy pushed dark curls back from her face and tugged on her short black T-shirt. Her belly flashed white between the shirt and her jeans. "Maybe I should get my belly button pierced."

"Isn't that getting a little old by now?"

"Yeah. It'd heal over in a day or two anyway." Lucy shrugged. "It's four in the afternoon. How do we get out of here?"

"Have you ever looked for secret passages in here?" Languorously, Ivy draped herself across the black leather sofa, resting her head on a paisley purple and red pillow.

"Of course. So did you, stupid, and we didn't find squat. Now, how do we get out of here? Think." Lucy rubbed her chin, thinking, then crossed to the curtained balcony, cautiously plucked up some of the heavy material to let a few rays of muted sunshine in.

"Hey!" Ivy jumped off the couch as the light shimmered toward her. "Watch it."

"Remember the pool? There were windows in that room and the sun didn't bother us."

Ivy looked deep in thought. "Yeah. I guess not, but the glass was thick and hazy, plus it was really foggy."

"It's foggy now. Watch." Lucy pulled the drape open farther open and put her hand directly in the light. She waited. "See? It doesn't burn at all."

Looking uneasy, Ivy kept to the shadows. "Stand in it. Get your whole body in it."

Lucy suppressed a cringe at the thought, and reminded herself that they really had been exposed to light during their swim, no lie. Resolutely, she used the wand to open the drapes about eighteen inches, and she stepped into the rectangle of light falling across the carpet.

Standing with her back to the window, she was alert for the smallest sensation of burning, but so far, she felt nothing except a hint of warmth from the rays. A good kind of warmth.

Ivy squinted at her. "The light hurts my eyes a little."

"A *little*," Lucy repeated. She turned to face the light, her eyes closed. Through the lids, she could see red, but it wasn't painful until she tried to open them; then it was just too bright. "Wait a minute." She walked to their bedroom and dug through her dresser drawers until she came up with a pair of very dark sunglasses.

Slipping them on, she moved back into the sunlight. This time, she could open her eyes. Opening the sliding door, she stepped onto the balcony. "Get your shades and come out," she called to her sister. "It's great!"

"Are you sure?"

"Hurry up!" The fog was thick today, but if it

thinned much, things might get dangerous. By the time Ivy arrived, wearing sunglasses and a coat, Lucy was feeling the first small prickles of the bad kind of heat, but it was amazing that it had taken so long. To stand in a stray sunbeam should have begun burning her immediately.

"How?" Ivy asked as she looked at the foggy air, at the looming limbs of an old oak near enough to see and touch.

"I don't know," Lucy confessed. "I bet it's got something to do with not getting drunk anymore. I guess it's just that virus thing." She leaned over the balcony, skin lightly prickling. "I was thinking. We could climb over and down to the balcony below us." Even as she spoke, she realized it couldn't be done, not yet. "I'm starting to burn," she said abruptly, brushing past her sister to return to the safe shadowy apartment. Ivy followed, drawing the door and the drapes closed behind her.

"Are you all right?" Ivy shucked her coat, letting it drop to the floor.

"Yeah," Lucy called from the bathroom. She'd removed her glasses and was examining her skin. "It just got a little intense all of a sudden." There was a faint blush of sunburn on her exposed abdomen, her arms, face, and neck. She wished the burn would turn to tan. *Oh, well, fuck it.*

She returned to the living room and began to pace. "I can't wait until they unlock the door," she announced. "I *really* can't wait. I'm starving."

"Me too. But they locked the door from the outside. What can we do?"

Lucy tapped her forehead with the palm of her hand. "Julian." Why hadn't she thought of him before? He was a trueborn. Maybe the rules didn't apply to him, or maybe he was like they were, awake and bored, waiting out the sun. Hell, he was a true-born. Maybe he was sunbathing.

"Ivor is dead to the world," Natasha told Stephen. "Just as Uncle Ori said."

For a moment, they watched their brother getting his beauty sleep on the massive bed in his darkened apartment. He hadn't budged when his siblings came in, which was the way it was supposed to be. Not like Stephen and 'Tasha. "So Julian claims we have a virus," Natasha said, irritation in her voice. She still hadn't forgiven Stephen for talking with the trueborn so frankly, but on the walk to Ivor's apartment, she had admitted interest in what was said.

"Not a virus—but it spreads like one. And Ivor is evidently immune."

"I'm still not sure I buy that story."

" 'Tasha, it makes sense. Just because you don't like Julian doesn't mean he's telling tales." *Why am I defending him?*

"I know, I know," she said quietly. "Let's go. I don't want to wake Ivor up."

They left, exiting into the dimly lit hall. Stephen spoke. "It's at least two hours until sunset. Perhaps we should try to get a little rest."

Natasha eyed him. "I'm not tired, are you?"

"No." He paused. "But I am thirsty."

"So am I." She took his arm. "Come on. Let's share a bottle and go over the accounts. If that doesn't bore us into relaxation, nothing will."

"You're right about that." As they walked toward Natasha's office, Stephen was tempted to beg off. If the twins could go in the pool room and endure that much sunlight, he could traverse the shadowy corridors and pay a visit to Amanda. He wouldn't bite her. They would talk, get to know one another. Well, he would get to know her, at least. But he knew it was a bad idea. It wasn't professional, and he couldn't go there on an empty stomach; that would endanger Amanda. *Well, maybe after a drink . . .*

When the twins phoned, Julian was reading a terrible little tome concerning Napoleon and the Peninsular Wars. Though well researched, the book was dry as dust. *Bloodless.* And there had been so much blood. Bodies and parts of bodies scattered over the land. The stink of dead flesh had eventually driven him away from the dying. But that was history. Now was the time to have some fun with the young ladies. "Jinxy," he called as he hung up the phone.

Jinxy was by his side in a matter of seconds. "Master Julian?"

"Take your lock-picking tools to the apartment of Misses Lucy and Ivy and let the poor girls out. Bring them to me. They're very thirsty, and I believe I have just what they need."

29

"Julian!" Lucy said.

"Julian!" echoed Ivy.

The pair went to him and kissed his cheeks. "Thank you for letting us out!" Lucy cooed. "It was like being chained in a coffin in there!"

"I'm sure it wasn't so bad as that." He smiled at the grateful girls. "But I am pleased to be of service. Sit down." He gestured at the Grecian sofa and the girls sat, alert as puppy dogs begging for a bone. Lucy's foot tapped, scratching for fleas.

They were agitated, just as he had hoped "Would you ladies like a drop to drink?"

Their eyes lit up. "Please!" they chorused. Lucy's foot beat faster. Ivy began twirling a lock of hair around her finger.

"Jinxy, go to your quarters and stay there until I summon you."

The assistant nodded and headed down the hall toward the door to his connecting room.

"Why'd you do that?" Ivy asked.

"Because I wish to be alone with you two lovely creatures." The truth was, he didn't want either of them to try to bite his servant, and looking at them, he thought there was a chance they would. A good chance.

"But the blood," Lucy protested. "He always gets it for us. For you."

"I will retrieve it in due time." He rose, taking a vial of the elixir out of his pocket. "First, a treat for you. Open your mouths."

They looked like baby birds awaiting a meal. Standing over them, he opened the vial and let a few drops fall into each mouth before stoppering its top. "Now, just relax a few moments while I retrieve the blood."

He took a few moments in the kitchen, letting them begin to absorb the potion. Given their present state—agitated and hungry—the few extra drops he'd given them would send them over the edge before long. Then the trouble would begin. He smiled to himself, thinking of his plans. *Such fun.* He returned to the living room with bottle and glasses, judging that a fifth of blood split between them would keep them from succumbing to pure blood hunger. He wanted them to take their time. He wanted to watch. It would be amusing.

He poured and handed them the goblets, then sat down in his leather chair and watched as they drank, both too thirsty for polite conversation. When they finished their first glasses, he poured more. "My dears," he purred. "How would you like some fresh, hot blood?"

Their eyes twinkled. "Really?" both asked.

"How would you like to have an adventure?"

The twinkling redoubled as they nodded.

Glancing at the clock, he said, "Well, then, finish your bottle and we'll have a little fun. No, no. Don't gulp. Sip. We have plenty of time."

* * *

"Am I interrupting anything?" Stephen asked as soon as Amanda opened the door to her room.

"No." She stepped back. "Come in." *What's he doing here?* "I have some time before I have to get ready for work." She blushed and tingled at the thought of changing her clothes in front of him. "Please, have a seat." She pointed him toward the couch. "Excuse me just a moment."

He sat. "Of course."

Amanda stepped into the bathroom. Her hair was a mess; there was a little fleck of something, probably a cookie crumb, on her cheek. Quickly, she fixed herself up, brushing, flicking, and lipsticking. She couldn't do anything about her clothes—khaki shorts and a Hawaiian camp shirt—but they weren't too bad.

When she walked out, she saw that Stephen had drawn the drapes and turned on a table lamp. He smiled, mouth closed, serene, and she went straight to the couch and sat down, leaving a cushion length between them. "What can I do for you?" She felt herself blush again as she spoke.

He captured her in his deep, dark eyes. She was a willing prisoner. "I was passing by and I thought I'd stop in and ask you how you like your job. I'm not asking as your employer, but as a friend. Are you happy?"

Her hands trembled, and she held them tight in her lap to hide it. It was suddenly too hot in the room. *Those eyes. Those lips.* "I'm enjoying it very much." *Is he really only here to ask me that?* She hoped there was more, dared not believe it. "It's nice of you to ask."

Holding his gaze on hers, he barely nodded. "I'm

glad you're happy. Is there anything that bothers you at all about the hotel?"

Well, there was that foot in the laundry cart. His not wanting her to remember that little detail was what really bothered her, but she was afraid to come out and say so. She sensed danger behind that calm gaze. And it excited her, but, oh, was she hot, her skin felt afire. She was about to get up and open the balcony door when she remembered he was sensitive to light.

"Amanda?"

"Oh, sorry. You asked if there is anything I don't like?"

"For instance, my younger sisters. Have they left you alone?"

"I haven't run into them again." She cleared her throat. "But there is something."

"Tell me."

"I don't want to sound like an idiot. It's silly."

He reached out and patted her hands. His lingered an extra second. "You can tell me anything."

"I might have seen a ghost."

Douglas Harper, napping, groaned in his sleep. He dreamed of Natasha, reliving moments they had shared. His hands cupped her breasts as she rode him toward orgasm. The dream continued, sweet and seductive, keeping him on the verge of release.

And then it began to change, to become more exotic, if that were possible. Feminine voices whispered in his ears, telling him things that would be done to him, making promises in the dark. Still asleep, he tried to turn over, but in his dream, hands held him down, kept him on his back.

"Don't move, Dougie," a feminine voice said in

his left ear. A tongue tickled his right lobe, followed by another voice, the same yet different. "Lie back and enjoy it, Dougie. Let us do the work." In stereo, voices giggled and tickles of breath danced on his neck. *Two Natashas?*

Natasha never called him Dougie. She wouldn't dream of it.

Consciousness tried to intrude on the dream, but failed. He felt hands on his wrists, tying them and pulling them up to the corners of the bed. It turned him on, but it hurt too. *Gently,* he tried to say, but nothing would come out of his mouth because he was gagged. They took his feet and spread-eagled him on the bed. Helpless, silent, blind. *Stop now! Wake up!*

His mind raced. Natasha didn't go for this stuff—she'd let him lightly bind her once but she refused to tie him, smiling and claiming that she didn't trust herself. *Goddamn it, wake up!* He twisted in his bonds but he couldn't move. *Wake up! Now!* He struggled to open his eyes, to tear his way out of the dream.

Then he felt tongues laving him, bringing his erection back despite everything else. He relaxed, just a little. *Maybe this isn't so bad after all.*

Suddenly, sharp teeth sank into him. He came awake instantly, screaming behind the gag. Unable to move in his bindings, he raised his head enough to see two dark heads hovering over his crotch. One of them looked up, and removed her unbelievably long teeth from his flesh. She smiled, blood dripping from her mouth, then, teeth flashing, she lowered her head again.

Douglas's head dropped back, and he saw a man with platinum hair standing over him, his eyes too dark for his pale skin. "I have lived thousands of

years and rarely have I seen a man built as you are,"
he said. "You must be very proud."

"A ghost?" asked Stephen. "You saw a ghost?"
He had been trying to hypnotize her from the moment he walked in the door, but no matter how
hard he tried, it wouldn't take. It frightened and
elated him. *She's someone who can stand up to me.*

"Well, I thought I did."

"When?"

"Last night. Around three a.m. I woke up thinking somebody was in my room." She smiled nervously and added, "Maybe it was the wind."

She was lying. She didn't think it was the wind;
she was worried—and embarrassed. He sat forward
and took her hand. *I shouldn't do this.* The very
touch of her warm skin aroused his burgeoning
lusts for sex and drink. *If I hadn't just split that bottle
with 'Tasha, I'd be in real trouble.* "Amanda," he began. Her eyes seemed almost to mesmerize him,
and that aroused him all the more. And scared him.
He let go of her hand. "You can tell me anything.
I'm not going to laugh at you."

"But you'll think I'm an idiot," she said gamely.
"Smart people don't talk about seeing ghosts because they know everyone they tell will think they're
idiots." She looked down at her hands.

"I don't think you're an idiot and nothing you
could say would make me think so. Tell me what
happened." When she continued to hesitate, he
added, "All hotels worth their salt have a ghost or
two."

"Do you believe in ghosts?"

She looked up again, and he was swept into fantasies the colors of the ocean, deeps blues and

greens, teals, sparkling sunlight on water, fondly remembered. He could almost believe she was one of their own. *Maybe she should be.* He forced the thought away. "Yes," he told her. "I believe in ghosts. I've seen one or two right here in this hotel. Now, what happened last night?" If something had occurred, he doubted it was due to a ghost. More likely, his sisters were at work.

"There was no one in my room, but I could feel someone. . . ."

He nodded. "Go on."

"Then I couldn't believe my eyes. My door opened and closed by itself."

"You saw this directly, not out of the corner of your eye?"

"Yes. There was moonlight. I could see it as clearly as I'm seeing you now. Unless I'm crazy, of course."

"You're not crazy." His mind raced. Who among them could blend in with backgrounds well enough to do that? Not the twins, at least not to his knowledge. *Maybe I should pay more attention to them.* The rest of his family was fairly adept, but none would be able to disappear under a head-on stare. *Julian!* He'd done it before. Anger flared. *I'll kill the bastard!*

"What?" Amanda asked, watching him. "What's wrong?"

He composed himself. "I remembered a similar incident."

Her eyes lit up. "Really?"

"Yes. Some years ago, a former employee described the same thing." He took her hand again. Kept it. "I think that he might have been assigned this room."

"I'd like to talk to him."

"I'm sorry, but that's impossible. He died last year."

"Oh." She laid her other hand on their entwined ones, her cheeks flushed. "That's too bad. But I'm really glad you remembered that. Now I don't feel so idiotic. Maybe this room is haunted." Her voice was soft and unafraid.

"Would you like to change rooms?"

A moment passed. Deep oceans swirled in her eyes as her gaze intensified. Finally, she spoke. "I think I'd like to stay here. At least for now."

Her lower lip trembled, and he fought the urge to kiss it. "Are you sure? You're not afraid?"

"I like this sort of thing. Remember? Vampires, ghosts, zombies? When I was younger, I fantasized that I was *Buffy the Vampire Slayer.* How can I walk away from my very own ghost?"

He wished she'd stop mentioning vampires. Normally, it wouldn't have fazed him, but coming from her, it was different. Scary. His arousal grew. "You're very brave," he told her. "If you change your mind, I won't tell anyone why you traded rooms." *What is it about her?* He was nearly trembling because of her nearness.

"I appreciate that. Stephen . . ."

Kiss her. Kiss her now. "What?" Propriety forgotten, he started to lower his head toward hers.

Their faces were inches apart. The tip of her tongue came out and wet her lips. Then she said, "Stephen?"

"What?"

"I have to get ready for work."

30

"Let's bring him over," Lucy said as she, Ivy, and Julian stood before Douglas Harper, sprawled on his blood-soaked bed. He was arguably conscious; his eyes glazed with terror despite his blood loss.

"Why?" asked Julian, though he already knew. He hadn't seen such a large yet functional male member since a late-night swim with John the Baptist a millennium or two ago. Douglas Harper was a king among humans, enormous, but not freakish. It might be interesting to create such a gifted vampire if there weren't too many half-breeds already. "Why should he be changed?" He smiled sleekly. "Other than for the obvious reason?"

The girls traded sly glances, then Ivy spoke. "As a present for Natasha?"

"I believe that if Natasha wanted to change him, she would do it herself. I very much doubt she would appreciate your doing it for her." Julian smiled. "Don't you think?"

"Let's do it anyway," Lucy said. "He's so beautiful and he's like the Energizer bunny. He just keeps coming, and coming, and coming."

"That's going, stupid," Ivy sniffed.

"Your elder sister's wrath will be great," Julian

prodded. "And it will make no difference that you changed him. He won't be yours. He's already Natasha's. He always will be."

"Natasha can go to hell," said Lucy. "Fuck her."

"Yeah. Fuck her."

"If you really want to upset her . . ." Julian teased. "You do, don't you?"

"Yes!" times two.

"Then I would suggest doing something else to Mr. Harper. Something . . . theatrical."

"Natasha will lock us up forever," Ivy cautioned.

"Only if she finds out it was you."

"Everybody's going bugfuck around here," Ivy said. "Nobody'd know it was us. Anyway, Natasha deserves it. She's such a bitch. She's the one who had us locked up."

"I'm sick of her. I'd like to stake her."

Julian could hear the fury in Lucy's voice. She meant what she said, and that could prove highly entertaining. The elixir was steadily heightening the twins' raging emotions, and the others weren't far behind. Natasha was decidedly unstable, and although Stephen had more control, he was a source of great annoyance due to his obvious fixation on Amanda Pearce. That wouldn't do at all. The thought caused a surge of unpleasant sensations, and Julian quelled it instantly, turning his attention back to the twins. "Stake her?" he asked, displaying surprise. "She's your own sister." He nodded toward Harper. "Why don't we concentrate on the matter at hand? I'm quite thirsty, girls. Do you mind if I partake?"

The twins didn't look particularly happy, but they nodded assent. Julian moved to Harper's neck and bent over him, drinking until the veins collapsed and the man's heart stopped.

"We could still change him," Ivy said.

"No, he's dead."

"But *you* could still change him right now, couldn't you?" Lucy asked, ever hopeful. "Since you're a trueborn, I mean."

He straightened, delicately touching the corners of his mouth to make sure he hadn't spilled any sustenance. "No," he claimed gravely. "Even I cannot bring back the dead." He favored them with a patrician smile. "Now. What shall we do with the body? Be creative, my dears. Be creative."

Digging. The Dante shills were digging and they'd been at it for some time. Now, daylight was beginning to fade and the vampires themselves would soon appear. These two were merely humans dressed like the gardeners that came every Tuesday. But it wasn't Tuesday and these guys didn't have green thumbs.

Security man Dale Tucker stood amid neatly trimmed hedges and delicately shaded flowers in the English garden, the best vantage point. Silently, he watched the men through a froth of leaves. They were digging in the center of the would-be lions' garden, where the dirt had been loose and mounded to begin with. Now, freshly turned earth encircled a depression that might be four feet deep.

Dale backed up a little, and that allowed him to better observe the movement of the two men as they bent to their work, oblivious to his presence. Their shovels bit into the soil with a sound like hatchets slicing through gravel and old bones. He could hear their ragged breathing; they were working hard.

He spoke softly into his transmitter. "Ed, you there? Nadine?"

"I'm here," Nadine said, a fly in his ear.

"Yeah," Ed said, another fly. "What've you got?"

"Same as before. Two male humans still digging. I guess none of the vamps are up yet?"

"Haven't seen any," Nadine said. "It's a little early."

"Meet me in the English garden. Out."

Within two minutes, Ed and Nadine showed up, moving so silently that he barely heard their approach. Like him, they were itching for action.

"Let me look," Nadine said, pushing forward with a pair of binoculars.

"Don't you think we ought to do something now?" Ed asked, patting the holster under his jacket. "We can take them down before they know what hit them."

"No." Dale sighed reluctantly. "We haven't cleared for guests. Besides, we don't want to be in the middle of something when Dante's vamps show up. We wait for the rest of the team, per Ivor's orders." He checked his watch. "If no one shows up in ten minutes, I'll go wake them."

"Stephen and Natasha might be up already," Nadine volunteered. "I thought I saw them in the hall."

"No. It's too early," Dale said.

"Swear to God. I saw them."

"Once the Dante vamps arrive it'll be a lot more dangerous," Ed said. "We shouldn't wait."

"I'll go alert the Darlings," Dale told them.

"Hey," Nadine said. "Something's happening. They've stopped digging."

Dale peered at the lions' garden. "I don't like this. Keep an eye on them while I go after the Darlings. Don't do anything unless you have to, and if you do, make sure you've got your silencers on."

* * *

It certainly wasn't the proper time, but Natasha, well fed, had just left her office, intending to go to Douglas's room for a little relaxation and recreation, when Stephen stopped her. "We need to talk."

"Now?" she asked in exasperation. "Can't it wait an hour?"

"Now."

"Half an hour?"

"Come on."

He led her to his office and shut the door behind them. As they stood before his desk, she glared at him. "This had better be important." She was practically climbing the walls. She needed Douglas, and she needed him now. Her desires had never been so strong.

" 'Tasha, do we have any records of hauntings occurring in Amanda Pearce's room?"

"You stopped me for this?" she snapped.

"It's important. Tell me."

"No, not in her room." She hesitated, surprised at his intensity. "There is a another one in that corridor with one though. The footstep ghost." It was nothing but a psychic loop that occasionally activated. It didn't scare anyone much, but it had been reported many times by guests over the years. "Why? What happened?"

He told her Amanda's story. "She thought it was a ghost. I think it's Julian."

Natasha nodded. "You're probably right. Could it be anyone else? The twins? They love to pull stunts."

"No. She saw the door open and close straight on. I don't think anyone but Julian could pull that off."

"Damn it," she fumed. "Damn Ori. Why did he ever bring that creature here?"

Stephen smiled dryly. "Julian made him an offer he couldn't refuse."

"Yes, well. This poaching has to stop. Valentyn is dangerous. I think we caught that damned virus from him. And it's not just that. He's slippery, smart, and treacherous. And he's got Ori in his pocket." Anger bubbled. "And the twins. You saw them with him. He's obviously charmed them behind our backs." She heard her voice rising as her anger flared. "Those two are horrible as they are. We can barely keep them under control—"

"We can hardly keep ourselves under control, 'Tasha," Stephen said soothingly.

"I know! I know! You don't need to tell me that." Even through her fury, she felt a sexual pull. *Douglas.* She wondered if Stephen might be feeling the same toward Amanda; that would explain why he was so upset about Julian feeding on her. "Don't try to placate me, Stevie. You know exactly what I'm talking about. What kind of influence is Valentyn? I'll tell you: the worst imaginable. He's evil, pure evil. And the twins are nearly as bad. Because of him, we'll probably have to kill them." She nearly smiled at the idea.

"Natasha!" Stephen took her by the shoulders. "Get a grip on yourself. Don't let them upset you! Imagine how happy they'd all be if they knew what they've done to you."

She took a deep breath and let it out slowly. "Logical Stevie. Where would I be without you?"

He smiled. "I can't bear to think about it."

He had calmed her, and she was about to thank him when the buzzer sounded. Stephen answered.

"This is Dale, Security. They're digging. And they've found something."

My son.

Lying on his bed, Julian stirred fitfully, his brief rest disturbed by the voice. *Father.*

It is time. I arise. I will take what is mine, just as I told you so long ago.

No. Julian came upright on his silken silver sheets. "I will not allow it!" As he jumped from the bed, he turned, looking in all directions.

The bedchamber was quiet. No breeze stirred the heavy brocaded drapes, deep, royal purple to repel the sun. No whisper echoed across the room. Only the heavy golden masks stared at him from the ivory walls, their features inscrutable.

I arise.

The voice came from all around him. From within him.

It was true. He knew it, had always known, but it had all happened so far in the past that it had come to seem academic. Even when he moved into the hotel, he'd refused to admit to himself he was doing it because of the Father, but rather had nearly convinced himself that he was simply here to amuse himself, to stir up trouble and destroy the Darlings so that he could take control of the hotel. Behind all that, however, was the Father, the Treasure. The Treasure was not a myth. But now he could no longer deny it, and he had to find a way into the tunnels before it was too late.

Aardvark Wicket awoke in a cold sweat from a fitful, nightmare-filled sleep. His belly was cramp-

ing—evidently he'd gotten hold of a bad rat—and
he held his gut as he crawled away from his backpack, his way lit by dim light from the corridor.
Reaching a dark corner of the dank little room, he
pulled his pants down an instant before Montezuma
hit. He squatted, moaning, ass on fire, for what
seemed like hours. Finally, the cramps subsided.
Disgusted by his own acrid metallic stink, he pulled
up his pants and took the Bic from his pocket,
flicked it for a better look. He always looked. The
huge shit storm was swirled with bright blood. *Fucking rats.* They'd given him that e-coli crap or something like it. Quickly, he grabbed his backpack and
slung it over his shoulder. He had to get out of this
fucking place. Now.

When he stepped into the corridor, the terror
really hit, a dread nearly as debilitating as the
cramps had been. He'd felt it while he was asleep,
growing, cloaked in nightmares, then in pain, but
it hadn't been so strong, so overwhelming. Aardvark had long ago lost track of real time, and now
it came to him that the only way he knew that time
was even passing was by the slow creeping apprehension that was eating him up, instant by passing
instant. A second clicked by, a moment. An hour
would kill him.

*You're just freaking, that's all. You got sick because a
rat had cancer or something. There you go. That's all it
is. You got a bad rat. It probably had cancer. That's why
you're freaking. There's nothing down here but rats. Just
me and the rats.*

But he couldn't swallow his own bullshit; he knew
that wasn't why he was nervous. No, something else
was causing it. At first he tried to tell himself it was
his imagination, but that was just more bullshit.
Something *was* down here. Something was down here

with him, and it knew he was here. "Gotta get the fuck out of here," he murmured, looking around.

From the beginning, he'd been repelled by the dark downward stairwell at the end of other fork of the Y, and now, he glanced that way and shivered. It was too close by. He could feel it, waiting, calling to him. *Come to me.* He wondered if he'd imagined the voice just now. If anxiety didn't get him first, *it* would, and it would try to kill him the way he killed the rats. *Slish slash.* But he wasn't scared, he reminded himself, just edgy.

The room he'd slept in was just below the point where the two arms of the Y joined, and his first impulse was to head back up the other arm, the one he'd first been in. But he didn't want to go a step nearer the dark arm, not even to pass it. What good would it do him to go back again anyway? He couldn't get the opening to give; he wasn't going to get out that way. No, it was time now to head down the long main corridor and see where it would take him. It was the only possible path to freedom, unless there was an opening down those dark, dark stairs. But how could one be down there, deeper in the earth? Even if there was, he didn't think he would survive to see it.

The main corridor, the long part of the Y, led downward, and it occurred to him now that its gentle descent probably followed the hill's natural downward slope. He had avoided going this way; what little he had explored had yielded offshoot tunnels, some as wide as the main one, and he was concerned about getting lost. But staying here, near that stairwell, near *it,* that was worse. He turned off the string of lights behind him, not wanting to leave a trail. He didn't like the dark, but it was also a friend that would hide him. Shivering, covered in icy sweat, he began walking, his lighter in his shirt pocket, open knife in one hand, his other trailing along the invisible bumpy walls.

Sitting idly at the quiet concierge desk, Amanda had never missed Brenda Newly so much in her life. But Brenda was in Massachusetts working on her masters in botany. She always was a plant person. Brenda had been Amanda's best friend since second grade, and she was the one and only person Amanda could confide in. Brenda knew everything about her; even about that embarrassing crush she'd had on Mr. Thurman, her junior high school science teacher. Amanda smiled, thinking of the adventures they'd shared. Together, they'd sneaked into the boys' locker room, drilled a hole in a closet door, and watched the guys shower and dress. Once, when they were nine, they'd cut each other's hair and had begged in vain for wigs for six months thereafter. They never did that again, but she and Brenda had pierced each other's ears and eyebrows. She smiled to herself. *Fortunately, time heals all things.*

There were other adventures too. The day they got kicked out of Disneyland for harassing the Mouse, the morning they left an open can of tuna to rot all week in the back of a humid Sunday school room, the time they put a jockstrap under her hated Aunt Vicky's pillow. Aunt Vicky said nothing and the jockstrap never resurfaced. It had been Amanda and Brenda's considered opinion that the old witch wore it over her nose at night, because that was the only way she could get close to a man.

Amanda and Brenda had spent a year or two anxiously comparing their pubescent breasts to those in an old *Playboy* Amanda found in her father's

dresser drawer. They told each other their darkest
secrets, and Brenda even knew all about Amanda's
love of horror, which only boys were supposed to
like. They dressed up like vampires at Halloween
once in high school and went out to scare the little
trick-or-treaters, and although Brenda teased her,
she always watched scary movies with her. She even
admitted liking them, especially the one with Brad
Pitt's whiny vampire, which she was willing to watch
over and over. Amanda preferred the take-charge
Tom Cruise. But since she was a plant person,
Brenda's favorite movie was *Day of the Triffids*.

Amanda wished she could talk to her now, not
about vampires, but about Stephen. She was so confused. *Why did I stop the kiss?* That question was driving her crazy. She just couldn't figure it out. God
knew she wanted the kiss. *What stopped me? Am I
afraid of him?* Could it be true? *Maybe.* Stephen's
eyes were so intense that they both excited and
scared her. And then there was his weird insistence
that she didn't remember the foot in the laundry
cart. It was sort of like he was attempting to hypnotize her. *What's that all about?* Whatever it was, it
was a good reason not to get involved. *But . . .* She
flushed with sudden warmth. *Maybe it's a stupid reason not to kiss him.*

"Penny for your thoughts."

Amanda looked up into the blandly cheerful face
of Carol Anne. "What?"

"Penny for your thoughts," the girl said, grinning
like a Girl Scout. "You look so serious! Is something
wrong?"

"No." Amanda created a smile. "Everything's
great." No way was she going to confide in Carol
Anne. She was no Brenda. "Have you asked Tyler
to the boardwalk yet?"

"No." She frowned. "He hasn't talked to me yet tonight. I think he's avoiding me."

"Nonsense." Actually, he'd been avoiding Amanda as well, which intrigued her no end. Obviously, he was embarrassed by his own behavior. It was pretty hilarious, if you thought about it. What she really wanted to do was corner him and watch him squirm over last night's antics. *He doesn't deserve that.* A slow smile quirked up her lips. *Or maybe he does.* She wondered what he might have tried if Carol Anne hadn't come along last night. "Why don't you go ahead and talk to him?" she said cheerily as she saw him heading their way. Handsome in his dark suit, he looked uncharacteristically shy, and he slowed his step, probably horrified at having to face both of them at once.

Amanda smiled at him, but he wouldn't make eye contact, so she said, "Look who's here."

Carol Anne glanced back, then began blushing furiously and kept her back to Tyler. "I don't know what to say," she whispered.

"Say hi," Amanda advised. Tyler had stopped two feet behind them, and was fiddling with a stack of brochures he held in his hands. Amanda raised her voice. "Hi, Tyler." *Is that ice in your pants or aren't you glad to see us?* She wanted to say it, but decided to be nice.

"Hello," he said without his usual smooth-guy attitude.

"Hi, Tyler." Carol Anne spoke coyly. "How are you?"

"Uh, fine." He set the brochures in a display next to the desk before turning to face her. "How are you?"

"Fine," she bubbled, instantly aglow.

He's her new reason for living. "So I hear you two

went on a date last night. Have fun?" Amanda asked sweetly. She shouldn't have said it, but it was already there, hanging in the air. *Sorry, Carol Anne.*

Tyler still wouldn't meet her eyes, but he tried for a little bravado. "We just got together for a drink."

"That's right." Carol Anne winked at Amanda, then looked at Tyler. "We had drinks. Strawberry margaritas. They were yummy."

"Maybe next time you'd like to join us," Tyler said with all the innocence of a spring lamb.

Not on your life! Amanda suppressed a giggle. "Maybe," she said, distracted by movement at the garden doors across the lobby. *Stephen?* No. There were several hotel people there, but he wasn't among them. "Maybe sometime."

"If you ladies will excuse me," Tyler said, "I have some errands to run." With that, he escaped.

Carol Anne stared after him, but Amanda's eyes were back on the garden door. She was fairly sure the man and woman hurrying outside now were Stephen and Natasha. "Carol Anne? Will you watch the desk for just a minute?"

"What? Oh sure."

Amanda hurried across the vast room to the garden entrance, where someone had taped up a hastily written sign on the glass. "Garden temporarily closed." She peered out, but couldn't see anything through the foggy mist shrouding the evening.

"Miss," said a plainclothes security guard as he came in from outside. "Please go back to your station. There's nothing to see here."

"What happened?"

"A guest sprained her ankle on a broken paving stone. Now please, go back to work."

Reluctantly, Amanda returned to the desk.

"What's going on?" Carol Anne asked, right on cue.

"Nothing," Amanda said as she sat down behind her desk. "Nothing at all."

The girl nodded, satisfied, and returned to Reception. Amanda, however, kept her eye on the garden doors. Something was happening, she was sure, and she wanted to know what.

31

"All the guests are inside?" Natasha asked for the second time. She and Stephen stood with the guard just outside the garden doors.

"Yes, ma'am," said Dale. "We double-checked and guards are posted now. Ed's watching the door inside, and Nadine's in the English garden keeping an eye on our diggers."

She nodded. She had seen Amanda Pearce's face at the door a moment before, and Ed shoo her off. Still, the girl worried her. She glanced at Stephen protectively. Amanda held some kind of fascination for her brother, and she might have to put a stop to it to keep Stevie safe. Now the door opened, startling her out of her thoughts. It was Ivor, looking sleepy, followed by Nipper and Snapper. They all wore overcoats to hide their weapons.

"Dante vampires will show up soon," Ivor said after being quietly apprised of the situation. "They're probably holed up nearby."

Natasha knew he was right. They could be hiding in one of the mausoleums on the hill, or in a hotel room or even a van. Anywhere dark and quiet. During the morning, the human security people had patrolled the roads to at least make sure no Dantes were anywhere near the hotel.

Nadine appeared out of the mist, moving as silently as a ghost. "They've definitely dug something up. A box maybe. I couldn't see well enough to be sure."

"What?" said Natasha. "They're not supposed to *find* anything!"

"It's time to take action," Ivor said.

"Just scare them off," Natasha directed. "We don't need a mess to clean up. But take a Dante brother if you can." Disposal of human bodies was always an unwanted chore. Then it occurred to her that feeding on them would kill the hunger pangs. And she wasn't the one who had to do the clean up after. It started to sound like a good idea after all.

"Maybe you and Stephen should go inside now," Ivor said, all dark and somber.

"Maybe," she said, but didn't move.

"What the fuck is this stuff?" Lenny Bentwick asked Sid Cox. They were hip-deep in the broad hole they had excavated in the unfinished garden outside the hotel. He couldn't believe how smoothly things had gone so far. No one had bothered them. It was great, but it also worried him a little.

Sid leaned on his shovel. "It sure as hell ain't a tunnel. If you ask me, somebody gave the chief bum information."

Lenny was thinking the same thing. He was already worried about the Dante brothers and how they'd react if a tunnel wasn't uncovered by dark. He scooped up another mound of earth, the shovel uncovering more of some kind of hard plastic. "You smell something?"

Sid sniffed. "No. Well maybe, a little. Oh, shit, you hear something?"

"Shhh!" Lenny crouched, motioned for Sid to do the same. The thick atmosphere played with sounds, muting some, making others seem louder, and right now, the footsteps sounded pretty loud. Somebody was coming and chances were it wasn't their employers. He studied the gathering gloom, waiting.

They had started digging a couple of hours ago, when the day was foggy-bright. The idea was to find the tunnel entrance by dusk, when the Dante vampires would arrive. All had gone well; no one had given them a second glance. But now was the hour to be nervous. You couldn't trust vampires, not even those on your own side. Not really.

The footsteps veered away down another path. After a moment of silence, Lenny bent and pushed soil off the hard plastic. "Hey, look at this!" he whispered. "It's a suitcase." As he pulled it free he nearly retched. The stench of decay was faint, but it didn't take much to set off Lenny's gut.

"Here's another one." Grunting, Sid pulled a large case free. "It's heavy as hell."

"Yeah." Lenny climbed out of the hole to escape the odor, which Sid seemed oblivious to, then peered down at his coworker. "Open one."

"Yeah? You think I should?"

"No. I just told you to open it so I could see if you understand fucking English. Now do it. Open one."

"Sure." He bent, straining with effort. "It's stuck. No wait. There." The latches snicked open, and Sid raised the lid to reveal black-plastic packages of varying sizes. "Jesus Christ!" Sid yelped, and scrambled out of the hole. "That's rank."

"Hello, fellas. Working a little late, aren't you?"

Stomach tightening, Lenny wiped his mouth and turned, taking in black cross-trainers, dark trousers, dark shirt under a windbreaker, and the bland face of a fortyish, balding man. "Just finishing up," he said.

"Yeah," seconded Sid.

The guy was dressed civilian, but Lenny didn't think he was a guest. When the man drew a .38 from inside his windbreaker, Lenny knew he was right.

"Come on. Stand up straight and leave those shovels on the ground."

A small woman appeared out of the fog. "Need any help, Dale?"

"Sure, Nadine. Cover them."

Nodding, she drew her gun and waited while Dale attached a silencer to his own weapon.

"There now," he said, training his gun on Lenny and Sid again. "We wouldn't want to disturb the guests." He gestured at Lenny with the gun. "Down in the hole with your friend."

Lenny stood his ground, praying the Dantes would show. They were probably up by now, maybe even on their way over from the cheesy little motel where they'd hidden from the day. But could they get here before the hotel vampires came out? *Not likely.*

From behind, hands suddenly clamped onto Lenny's shoulders. They pressed into his flesh with a strength that could only mean one thing—vampire.

* * *

He smelled of dirt, of sweat and fear, and the combination excited Natasha no end. She slowly turned the man to face her, her eyes boring into his, instantly knowing his secrets, mesmerizing him.

Without taking her gaze from his, she spoke to the security man. "Dale, did you intend to shoot these men?"

"That was our plan."

"Don't you think that's a waste of perfectly good food?"

"Uh, yes, ma'am, but your orders were to—"

"Your coworkers are on their way. If there's time, give the other one to them." Out of control, not caring, she moved in closer to the man in her grip and put her lips to his neck, tasting him, just a flick of the tongue, before sinking her teeth into his flesh. His blood was salty, earthy, and she drank and drank, lost in the heated pulsing of the blood, in perfect harmony with her victim.

" 'Tasha. 'Tasha. That's enough." Reluctantly, she let Stephen tug her back, his hands firm on her shoulders. Her food dropped to the ground, but was still breathing.

"Have some, Stephen. Don't let him go to waste." She smiled at her brother as she wiped a drop of blood from the edge of her mouth. He looked from her to the victim and back again.

"Here, 'Tasha? Now?" His expression was disapproving, but blood lust gleamed in his eyes. *"Now?"*

"Why not?" She looked past him, nodding at Ivor and his three vampiric security people as they approached. They all walked to the edge of the pit together. Natasha looked down at the cowering man and then at the shadowy forms of the suitcases, the dark packages spilling out the open one. "Why don't you three go down and take a bite out of that one?''

"Look at the sky," Ivor cautioned. "We need to take care of business now."

"I'm going back in," Stephen said, turning quickly. She watched him fade into the fog, knowing he was fighting his own urges. She wished she could be so stoic.

As for taking care of business, Ivor was right, of course. She had to keep control of herself. Dante vampires could show up at any time. If the security team fed now, they might not be as quick and vicious as they would be hungry. She nodded slowly, then looked at Dale, whose silenced weapon was trained on the human in the pit. "Do it. Kill him."

A smile stole across the security man's face, evaporating as quickly as it had come. "Yes, ma'am." He took aim and fired before the victim could cry out, the sound muted in the fog. The man fell back, a bullet through the brain.

Natasha glanced at the man she had half drained. "Throw him in too. And a couple of you, climb down and see what's in those suitcases." She knew it was something dead, but she wanted to know if it was human or animal.

Brothers Nipper and Snapper hopped down. Nipper pulled open one of the plastic bags, then let it drop, stepping back as a putrescent stench arose, permeating the air. "Dismembered human," he choked.

Natasha glanced at Ivor. "Our missing guest?"

"I wouldn't be surprised. But we'll worry about that later," Ivor said. "After we deal with the Dantes."

"It's human," Nipper affirmed. "Can't tell who or what. Too dark."

Natasha turned to Ivor. "I'll leave you and your crew to do your magic."

She strolled along the pathways toward the hotel, not really wanting to go. No, she wanted to fight, to kill, but it wasn't her job. *Perhaps it's time for a drink.*

The thought disturbed her. It came so easily, yet she had just fed heavily and should have been sated. In normal times, she couldn't drink as much as she just had; she would have passed out and been stuporous for nights after. Yet she wasn't. She wasn't starving, but another drink sounded good. Damned good. *Do they have twelve-step programs for vampires?* Shaking her head, more amused than concerned— *it's just the trueborn virus*—she turned her thoughts toward Douglas. *Maybe I should pay him a surprise visit now.* She would, she decided, as soon as she apprised Stephen and Ori of the situation in the garden. *Then, just a quick visit, to take the edge off.* She tingled all over at the thought of seeing her lover.

"Good evening."

"Good . . ." Amanda looked up into burning eyes set in a pallid face. "Evening," she finished lamely. The nearly albino man had platinum white hair pulled severely back, making his angular features stand out. He looked feral, hungry. And she knew him. From where, she didn't know, but he was disturbingly familiar. "How may I help you?" Her voice trembled slightly, but he didn't seem to notice. Instead, he smiled at her.

"I'm sorry," she blurted before he could answer, "but have we met?"

His slow closed-lip smile chilled her. And warmed

her. And fascinated her. "I cannot imagine forgetting your face."

She blushed. "Thanks. I'm sorry if I was rude."

"You are anything but rude."

"How may I help you?" His eyes were fathomless, cold and deep. *Reptilian.*

"I am Julian Valentyn. Julian, to you. I'm a permanent resident here at the hotel, Miss Pearce."

How does he know my name? After an instant of confusion, she realized he had read her name tag. "I'm pleased to meet you." Feeling foolish, she extended her hand, but instead of shaking it, he took it briefly in both of his dry chill ones.

"The pleasure is all mine."

Was he hitting on her? Why did he seem so familiar? *He was the one in the hall that night.* The thought hit like a rock as she recalled the flash of moon-white hair she had seen on the man leaving the corridor. *You can't know that for sure.* She wished Tyler were here, but so far, he'd barely made an appearance, running errands, still avoiding her. She cleared her throat. "What can I do for you?"

He continued to stare at her, that small thin smile staying in place, mocking, promising, *knowing.* She felt like she was under a microscope. "Theater tickets?" she asked, filling the silence. "Let me guess. The opera house in Caledonia? *Don Giovanni* is getting excellent reviews."

He cocked an eyebrow. "You take me for an opera lover?"

"I'm sorry."

His smile returned. "Don't be. I enjoy opera and many other forms of music. What about you? Tell me what you like."

She felt drawn to his eyes, drawn to him and repelled too. There was something in his smooth, cultured persona that was profoundly disturbing and attractive. "I like music," she said, feeling flushed and stupid. She wasn't about to tell him she knew all the words to the songs in *The Rocky Horror Picture Show* and that she liked show tunes, not operas. She couldn't think. What did he want? Relief flooded her as she spotted Stephen coming her way.

Valentyn caught her gaze and turned. "Stephen, good evening."

"Good evening, Julian." Stephen stepped around him to stand behind Amanda at her desk. "Do you need any help, Amanda?" He put his hand on her shoulder.

What's going on? "Everything's fine," she said. "I was just going to help Mr. Valentyn."

"How may *we* help you?" Stephen interjected. Amanda glanced back at him, and saw that he was staring hard at the pale man.

Valentyn returned the gaze steadily. "A ticket," he said. "For *Don Giovanni*." He looked down at Amanda. "I've always been fond of Mozart, particularly in his darker moods."

Amanda was almost certain he'd only ordered the ticket because she had suggested it. *What does he really want? Is he flirting?* Whatever it was, he gave her the creeps. Maybe it was the creeps, she wasn't sure. She thought that if he'd had dark hair, he would have made a perfect vampire or warlock of the evil persuasion. *He's like something out of a movie. Maybe that's all it is. He doesn't seem real.* "I can arrange that for you," she said. "When would you like?"

"Tomorrow."

"Matinee or evening?"

"Evening. A box seat."

She made the reservation and gave him a ticket

voucher, all the while acutely aware of Stephen's presence behind her.

"Thank you very much, Miss Pearce. I'm sure I'll see you again." He turned and walked toward the elevators. Amanda watched him move, fascinated; he almost seemed to glide.

Stephen sat down in Tyler's chair. Maybe it was her imagination, but he had seemed protective of her in Valentyn's presence.

"Is the woman all right?" Amanda asked.

Surprise showed. "Woman? What woman?"

"The one who hurt her ankle in the garden."

He hesitated briefly, then smiled. "She's fine."

"Why are the doors to the garden still locked?" She'd noticed several people try them unsuccessfully.

"We don't want anyone else getting hurt. The garden will reopen tomorrow after the problem's fixed."

She nodded. "I was wondering. . . ."

"Wondering what?"

He was her employer and she was hesitant to ask the question because of that. But they were, evidently, friends too. She decided to go ahead. "Julian Valentyn," she began. "He seemed, um, unusual."

Stephen smiled thinly. "He is. He's a very old friend of my uncle's."

"What does he do?"

"He's independently wealthy. I don't know how he occupies his time." He paused. "Amanda, be cautious around him."

"Cautious? What do you mean?"

He studied her a long moment. "I'm not exactly sure what I mean."

Could he be jealous? The thought thrilled her. "He

did seem a little flirtatious. In a weird sort of way."
*You don't know that for sure. What an obnoxious thing
to say.*

But Stephen merely nodded. "I didn't like the
way he was looking at you."

He's jealous! On the other hand, maybe it was just
a warning he'd give any employee. Valentyn had
seemed like someone to be wary of. "What—"

"I can't answer any questions. It's just a feeling
I have." He stood. "Duty calls. I'll see you later."

She watched him go, and wondered what was
happening. First, he'd warned her against his twin
sisters, and now against Julian Valentyn. She knew
why she cautioned her about the twins, but hadn't
a clue about the Valentyn warning, though she was
sure *he* knew exactly why. And she was going to find
out.

PART THREE

When I am dead, my dearest,
Sing no sad songs for me.

—Christina Rossetti

32

The twins were pure delight. Julian, seated in his curule chair, smiled as he watched them sprawling languorously, half on the sofa, half on the carpet, a tangle of arms and legs, pale skin gleaming in the lamplight. One—they were difficult to differentiate when they were nude—sipped red nectar from her sister's femoral artery, then moved up to her mouth and fed it to her. She drank greedily.

It was an orgy of two that helped distract him from the voice he had heard during his rest. That voice—the Father's voice—was the reason he had gone downstairs and introduced himself to Amanda so suddenly—time was of the essence now—and when he returned from that pleasant task, the girls were waiting for him, just as he had requested. After their fun with Natasha's well-endowed lover, he had seen them back to their apartment and locked them in, with the understanding that, after dark, they would let themselves out via the balcony and return to his suite. *Voila.*

He vibrated with sensations rarely felt; vibrations near-dormant for half a millennium. It was nothing like the Darlings were experiencing, rather a deep tugging, a primal call. The cycle was beginning again at last. Because of *her.* She was here and everything was in place.

He watched the twins, and one caught his eye. "Come join us," she said, her lips and tongue red with blood, her fangs fully released. "Come join us, Julian."

"Thank you, but proceed by yourselves. I will watch." They wanted to taste his blood, his true-born blood, and while it was tempting in a twisted sort of way, he did not care to feed them any of his power. The pair was feral with elixir-induced blood lust, but would not attack him; he was clearly their master. However, if he allowed them to drink his blood, they could become uncontrollable, even for him. The combination of the elixir and true-born blood would be unconquerable.

He watched them roll and writhe, nip and suck while he thought about Amanda. She was beautiful, intelligent, and quick. Wary too. An innocent.

As she must be.

As she always is.

But there was danger in her innocence. Stephen sniffed about her like a rutting dog. *He senses it. He senses what she is.* But he didn't *know.* He couldn't. He could only be drawn to it. *Has he tasted her?*

The thought distressed Julian even more than the thought of what waited below in the catacombs. That Stephen Darling might taste her sweet blood, that he might defile her or even change her in an effort to make her his own, made more dormant emotions surge into Julian's blood. He felt true emotion now. Rage. Lust. Emotions similar to those of humans, but sharper, clearer, cleaner. He would savor them.

Unlike the human vampires, he was in control of himself, and he would handle Stephen in such a way that no blame fell upon himself. He might give him to the Dantes. *Or the twins.* They would soon be far enough gone to mutilate their own brother. He smiled to himself. *The possibilities. Oh, the possibilities.*

But he also had to attend to the Father. The Treasure. *Treasure.* The very word angered him. He wanted to push it to the back of his mind, to concentrate only on Amanda, but he could not. Not after tonight, not after hearing the voice.

"Girls." He clapped his hands quickly, twice in succession. "Girls. That's enough."

They looked at him, all red blood, black hair, and white flesh.

"Clean yourselves up, ladies. I wish to tell you a story."

The twins. The damned twins. In the excitement outside, Natasha had forgotten all about them; they were still locked up in their suite. As far as she was concerned, they could rot there, but she knew they wouldn't. Now that the sun was down, they would soon escape over the balcony, and the last thing she needed was to have those two running loose tonight. Who knew what kind of trouble they'd stir up?

She wondered if she was ever going to get a chance to see Douglas as she approached her sisters' door. It had been one thing after another, and now she was stuck with the twins; Stephen was taking care of business, Ori had holed up with that little drip Leoni, all the vampiric help was busy, and no human would last five minutes baby-sitting the little bitches. She adjusted the shopping bag she held containing four chilled bottles of blood and unlocked the door to the girls' apartment.

"Ivy?" she called. "Lucy?" Stepping inside, she pulled the door closed behind her. The twins were nowhere to be seen, so she took the bottles into the kitchen, shaking her head at the mess on the counters. In addition to all the inevitable empty blood bottles, there were open bags of beef jerky, an overturned quart tub of beef liver, half eaten, the remainder drying in a shiny blob on the Formica, and an empty Doritos bag. Fuzzy with fake flavorings and drops of spilled blood, unnaturally colored chips crunched underfoot. In the sink was an open, full bottle of the hotel's best champagne, the bubbles long gone. *Little bitches.* They never thought about budgets and finances, only themselves.

Human hunger rose suddenly. After glancing at the shiny liver, she grabbed a jerky stick to gnaw on, then groaned around it when she looked at the refrigerator. The girls, decoratively challenged, had glued razor blades to its black exterior. Cheez-Whiz drawings of breasts and penises broke the monotony of black and silver. Natasha opened the door and placed the full blood bottles inside, doing her best to ignore the open containers of black olives, caviar, goose liver pate, and a plate holding a stick of butter coated with blood and marred by fang prints. *What were they thinking?* There was also what appeared to be the back half of a chihuahua. At least that wasn't pilfered from the kitchen, but if it belonged to a guest, she'd see to it that the twins would wish they'd never been reborn.

Fuming, she slammed the door and reminded herself of Stephen's warning not to lose her temper. He was absolutely right. She walked across the living room and checked the bedroom and bath before going to the unlocked balcony to confirm what she knew: The twins had already flown the coop.

The twins, each with her very own fifth of blood (Julian insisted they use goblets; they might be animals, but they didn't have to act as such), sat at his feet. He had sent them to shower while his servant cleaned the blood spots they had spilled on the carpet while they were entertaining him. Before they returned, to keep him out of harm's way, he had sent Jinxy out to procure something fresh to consume later in the evening.

"Have you ever wondered what the Treasure really is?" Julian asked. He watched them charily, hoping this conversation might inspire them to lead him to one of the tunnel entrances the Darlings had created during their remodeling. He suspected that if properly motivated, they would, and that the main reason they hadn't spoken up yet was their absolute fear of Natasha. No doubt, the stake was the promised punishment and Natasha would keep her promise. At this point, given the influence of the elixir, she might even be looking for an excuse to remove her siblings, so he would have to be judicious in his use of the twins until he got what he wanted. "Have your siblings or your uncle told you the entire story of the Treasure?"

"I don't know," Ivy said pensively. "We're not supposed to talk about it."

"We can talk about it with Julian," chided Lucy. "He's not a guest. Well, he is, but you know, he's not like human or anything and it's a really old story and he's really old—"

"So it's all right?" Ivy looked from her sister to

Julian. "I thought you said you were going to tell *us* a story, not ask us to tell you one."

Little idiots! He chuckled benevolently, silently amazed that the temperamental Natasha hadn't staked them already. He had underestimated her self-control. "I will tell you a story, but you don't want to hear one you already know, do you?" He folded his long fingers together in his lap. "Tell me your tale."

The twins looked at one another, then Lucy sipped her blood and spoke. "You'll keep it a secret, what we tell you?"

"Naturally, just as I expect you will keep my secrets."

Lucy looked surprised and both girls sat up a little straighter, intrigued by the notion of secrets. "Okay. Well, it's not a very long story. Uncle Ori heard it a long time ago from a vampire who was a friend of a trueborn. You know, like you."

"I know. Go on."

"Tell him what the Treasure is."

"I *will,* Ivy. Shut *up!*" Lucy pushed a tangle of curls back from her face. "This part of the story is probably true. Way before the monks came here, there were vampires, but hardly anybody knows that. The American Indians really, really far back, thousands of years ago, knew about them and told stories and stuff and they worshipped them and made sacrifices, you know? Blood sacrifices?" She licked her lips.

Julian nodded, wondering why these two chose to speak such poor English. He supposed it was to fit in with the human youth, but he found it tremendously annoying.

"So anyhow, the vampires used up the Indians after a while, and there wasn't anything left except animals, and they drank from them, but the vampires were really violent and primitive, so they kept attacking each other. So, pretty soon there were hardly any vampires left. Maybe ten or twenty."

"Tell him where they lived," Ivy prompted.

"Oh, yeah. It was kind of like a castle and it was right here where we are now. It was big and beautiful. The vampires dug the tunnels and catacombs. They mostly lived in the castle, but they could hide out down there when they needed to. Anyway, the vampires were still starving, so they started luring Indians to the castle from the closest village, which was miles away. But not enough of them came because they knew the stories their ancestors had handed down and thought the place was cursed. So anyway, the vampires ended up trying to fix things by turning some of the Indians into vampires because they thought that they could lure more of their people here. You know, convince them the curse was over. But those Indian vampires just left and lived in caves."

"There are caves all along the coast around here, caves in the cliffs," Ivy explained.

"Yeah, so the Indian vampires knew where all the caves were and they stayed in them. They could go all over the place because they knew all kinds of places to hide during the day, so they got all the food before the vampires in the castle did. So the castle vampires had to hunt them down and kill them." Lucy paused dramatically. "Okay. Uncle Ori says this is where the story probably starts getting silly. This special trueborn vampire came to them because he knew they needed help. He told them he was the Trueborn King of all vampires, and they believed him because there had been a prophecy about him. He said he was the first vampire, the son of God."

Julian hid his reaction to that statement. *Hah!* "What god might that be?"

"I don't know. Just God." Shrugging, Lucy took a long drink. "The king trueborn fixed everything. Even though the castle vampires that were left were the best ones—they didn't kill each other—they'd gotten sort of gross, you know, they'd suck anything."

"They had to. They even sucked fish," Ivy said, nose wrinkling in disgust.

"Yeah. They had become like embarrassments to other vampires, except there weren't any others around so they just embarrassed themselves," Lucy informed him.

"An astute observation," Julian said, musing that while one could turn a human into a vampire, it was impossible to turn an idiot into a scholar. "Tell me what happened after this special trueborn arrived. This king, this son of god."

"He showed them how to get humans to live near them and how to farm them instead of using them up, just like in your story about Euloa." Lucy's eyes sparkled darkly. "They called him the Treasure."

"Do you know his real name?"

"No. He was supposed to be the trueborn son of God." She smiled devilishly. "I guess that means he was Jesus's half brother," she added with a giggle.

"Do you mean to tell me that Jesus wasn't human?" Julian asked, bemused. He had seen so many religions come and go, so many gods, but these two young ones just assumed there was nothing before Christianity, even if they joked about it. In all their time on earth, they had never bothered to study the history of human beliefs.

The girls looked at one another, then back at him in surprise. "Well, of course Jesus wasn't a human. He rose from the dead so how could he be human?"

Julian smiled benignly, dazzled by the twins' utter lack of intellect. "Perhaps Jesus was a human vampire."

Lucy rubbed her chin, frowning. "Nah. Yeah, well, maybe there's a human God and a vampire God?"

"Or perhaps there is no god," Julian said to add to their confusion. "Or there could be many."

Ivy shrugged, unswayed. "The trueborn son of God was the King of the Vampires, which means he was our king too, and he foretold that he would sacrifice himself to save our kind," Ivy said, irritated. "The Christians just stole the story from us."

"I see." Julian chuckled.

"They *did!*" Ivy insisted. "I mean, they pretend to drink the blood of their Jesus. Where'd they get that? Shit, they even pretend to eat his body, and that's just *totally* gross."

"So, anyway, the castle vampires all lived happily with the Treasure as their ruler until these other human vampires showed up," Lucy continued blithely. "The band came from far away and were led by a powerful trueborn named Keliu. They were searching for the Treasure. Keliu claimed he was the true king and that the Treasure was really a demon who was going to kill all human vampires."

"Wipe out every single one because they weren't pure," Ivy added.

"Like Hitler," Lucy chirped, clearly pleased with her vast store of knowledge.

"The castle vampires didn't believe it because the Treasure helped them so much, and so they fought, but Keliu and his vampires killed them," Ivy continued. "They were like warriors or something. But not even Keliu could destroy the Treasure, but he captured him and made him into a mummy. He paralyzed him with sorcery and maybe took his guts out and put them in jars and shit like that, then put him in a sarcophathingy, you know, and took it all the way down through the tunnels into the deepest catacomb of all. Then he did some more magic and stuff to keep him trapped there for a thousand years or something like that." She took a breath and lowered her voice dramatically. "So the Treasure and all the dead human vampires are still down there."

"It's so creepy down there," added Ivy, brilliant as the plant for which she was named.

"The newcomers lived with their king, Keliu, in the castle until an earthquake knocked it down. It happened in the daytime, and some of the vampires burned up but the rest got away. The quake had been prophesied by the Treasure as the first sign of his resurrection."

Julian nodded. That was a logical prophecy since the likelihood of a devastating earthquake in California occurring sometime during many centuries was enormous. The other so-called prophecies were equally ambiguous. Only three out of more than a dozen were actually true. "Where did the surviving vampires go?"

"Oh, they all went up to Icehouse Mountain. It's near the Oregon border, deep in the forest. They dug new tunnels, and now they live in their own city under the mountain. There's a human town nearby called Eternity, so they have plenty of food. They're probably still there. Hey, Ivy, we should go and see sometime."

"Cool! Maybe we could meet them!"

"And Keliu?" Julian prompted. "What happened to him?"

"He led them to the mountain, which he said was a sacred place. Uncle Ori says that to this day, Keliu travels but always goes back, and sometimes he comes out and answers a human's questions and stuff because he's wise and mostly because he has this humongous ego. I mean he thinks he's totally hot shit, hotter shit than the Treasure. People believe he's this old count or something. Not Dracula, some other guy. Count St. Geranium. Yeah, that's it. He makes them see, like, golden buildings and stuff on the mountain, but they're not really there. He can make people see anything he wants." Lucy scratched her chin and yawned. "I wonder if he really still hangs out there. I mean, there just couldn't be much to do."

"No, I don't suppose there would be." Though annoyed by the remark about Keliu's ego, Julian was pleased that they had no real idea where he was; in point of fact, they sat before him now. Their story, discounting their Christian babble, was essentially correct, particularly the details of the latter times; he had masqueraded as St. Germaine (with apologies to the true count), when he occasionally spent time on the mountain, where the small clutch of human vampires worshipped him as their king and food was ridiculously easy to obtain. "What of the Treasure? What did your uncle tell you?"

"He's supposed to be reborn," Ivy said. "You know, grow all his guts back and stuff after some things happen. Prophecy stuff. Then he'll rise again. Of course, it's just a story."

"Will he help you or destroy you?" Julian asked helpfully.

"I think the Treasure is good and Keliu was full of shit, but Ivy thinks the Treasure wants to kill all the human vampires. Either way, if it's really true, the Treasure will rise as long as nobody does the magic on him again. That's how you keep him from being reborn. Do sorcery stuff. That's why we have to keep the tunnels a secret; so that nobody can find him and fuck with him. A lot of vampires believe the story, you know."

"What are the signs that he is about to be resurrected? Other than the earthquake."

"We don't know. I think Natasha wouldn't let Uncle Ori tell us," Ivy said.

"Stupid bitch," Lucy grunted. "Do you know what the signs are, Julian?"

He shrugged. "Not really."

"If the Treasure's real, you must have met him." Ivy went all goggle-eyed as the proverbial lightbulb lit above her head.

"There was one trueborn who claimed to be the first vampire, the direct creation of the gods," Julian said offhandedly. "But he was insane and I've met no other. Now, tell me what your family believes of the Treasure? Is he the true king?"

Ivy smiled. "I think he's a vampire killer."

Ivy was right, Julian mused, amazing as that seemed. But the Treasure's true preference was to kill his competition, his fellow trueborns and his own son, who would be king. That was why so few were left.

"Shut up, Ivy, you weirdo." Lucy turned to Julian. "They don't believe any of it, but they don't want to take any chances. At least that's what Uncle Ori says. And Natasha. She says it's all probably just a nice or awful fairy tale, depending on how you look at it, and that the tunnels are off-limits because other vampires believe the stories and some of them believe Keliu was right, that the Treasure will kill them, so they want to stop him from being reborn. But most think the Treasure will make human vampires the rulers of humans, so they want to take him to their own homes so they have him with them when he wakes up." She ruffled her fingers through her hair. "Also, lots of humans think there's jewels or gold down there, which there probably is since it's supposed to be a really cool tomb. We've gotta keep them out too."

"You haven't been down there yourselves?"

The twins exchanged glances. "Well, we haven't been all the way into the catacombs. Not that far." Ivy made a face. "Not past where the monks are buried."

"Why not?"

"Like Ivy said, it's way spooky down there," said Lucy. "I think it's haunted by those old dead vampires. That's what *almost* everybody else thinks too." She pointed her sharp gaze at her sister.

"I think it's the Treasure," Ivy said darkly. "I think he's coming back to life soon. And he's going to kill us."

"You think?" asked Lucy, dripping sarcasm.

"Well." Ivy drew out the word. "It'd really piss off Natasha."

They giggled.

"Girls," said Julian. "Letting the Treasure out, if indeed he exists, is not a good idea."

"He's real?" they chirped in unison. "It's true?"

"Then he's *evil?*" Ivy beamed. "See, Lucy, I told you!"

"I don't know if he's real," Julian lied. "Or if

he's evil. That word has many interpretations, but if he is evil by your family's definition, you shouldn't take such a chance." He paused. "Perhaps we should find out the truth. Would you like to know if the Treasure truly exists?"

"You mean go into the tunnels? Into the catacombs?" Ivy's eyes widened.

"We can't," Lucy said.

Julian smiled gently. "What do you fear more, Lucy? Natasha's wrath or the catacombs?"

Lucy's lower lip stuck out stubbornly. "We took an oath never to reveal the entrances. And it's creepier than ever down there now. And you promised to tell us a story."

"So I did." He steepled his fingers, studying the human vampires. "Let me fetch you fresh bottles."

The girls, bottomless gullets both, nodded eagerly. Julian walked into the kitchen, curious about Lucy's sudden streak of family loyalty. He suspected it was due more to fear of what lay below than of Natasha. More elixir might overcome that problem, but it might also send her over the edge before it was desirable. Meanwhile, he decided, he would regale them with some harmless tales of vampiric romance. It might help soften them up. He shook his head. *Son of god indeed.*

33

"Jinxy, hey Jinxy," hissed Eliot Lucre, appearing phantomlike behind him in the dark shadow of the roadside guardhouse, far from the gardens. "Where're you going?"

Jinxy took a deep breath, willing his heart to stop racing. The fog cloyed in his lungs. He wasn't going to give Lucre the pleasure of knowing he'd scared the shit out of him. "Master Julian's hungry." Fucking filthy Eliot stank of God knew what. Maybe he'd rolled in rotten corpses like a dog.

Eliot leered. "Aren't we all?"

Jinxy sniggered. "Yeah, we are." He was hungry for some tail and intended to make use of Julian's dinner, which would be female, before handing it over. "Want to go hunting with me?"

Eliot shook his head. "Wish I could." He held up a radio transmitter. "We're on alert tonight."'

"Why?"

"You don't know?" Eliot seemed surprised. "Well, I guess it doesn't have anything to do with that master of yours. You know who the Dantes are?"

"No," he said, though he'd seen them with his master and knew Julian was fucking around with them somehow.

Eliot, his voice loaded with swagger, explained who they were, making them sound a whole lot scarier than Jinxy knew they were. "So, I'm supposed to call in the second I see them coming. But I'm going to stake them all myself before Ivor's crew even gets here. See if I don't."

It all sounded like bullshit to Jinxy. "They're not coming through the front gate, are they?"

"Well, they could disguise themselves and try to drive in, but I'll spot them, even if they park and walk in."

"So you're watching for what? Slow-moving cars?"

"Or maybe a van."

"Well, there goes one now." Jinxy pointed toward the road, where a dark van was crawling by, probably only going slow because of the fog, just like every other vehicle would be doing. He glanced at Eliot. Jinxy had met a lot of vampires and this one was one crazy motherfucker. He'd been nuts even before Julian gave him the potion.

Eliot squinted after the van and called it in on the radio, then turned to Jinxy. "Thanks."

"Sure you don't want to go hunting with me?" Jinxy asked again to sound friendly, which was always a good idea.

"Sorry, can't. Too much going on." He tugged the belt of his pants. "There were a couple kills out in the gardens a few minutes ago. Humans working for the Dantes, Ed says."

"Ed?"

"Security. He said Natasha Darling did one herself." He licked his lips and leered. "Sucked him half dry."

The look in the vampire's eyes gave Jinxy the willies. He'd seen it before, and it meant he should get the hell out of there before he got himself bit. "Well, see you around."

"What's your hurry?"

"Julian wants his dinner." Jinxy turned, deciding to go back up to the parking lot and get the SUV to drive into town instead of prowling the cemeteries. If there were a bunch of unfriendly vampires near the hotel, he sure as hell didn't want to be around.

"Jinxy."

He turned and found himself nose to nose with Eliot, who smiled, baring white fangs. His eyes glinted. His breath stank of old blood.

"Julian will kill you if you touch me," Jinxy warned.

Elliot's smile broadened. "How would you like to be one of us?"

Jinxy studied him. "I've heard that line from a lot of vampires. Sorry. Not interested."

"I can't believe that."

"Julian will turn me himself when the time is right."

"How long has he been promising you that?"

It had been thirty years. Jinxy shrugged. "A while."

"How many years?" Eliot prodded. "Ten? Twenty? More? Getting a little past your prime, aren't you, Jinxy? A little long in the tooth?" He chuckled.

It was true, of course. He was well into middle age, and he'd begun feeling the aches and pains that went with it, but when he complained, his master would simply give him a drop of his potion and the arthritis would go away. Occasionally, he asked Julian when he would change him over, and the trueborn would always smile implacably and say, *In due time, Jinxy. In due time.*

"Well, Jinxy? What do you say?"

"I can't do it. I'm faithful to my master. And Julian doesn't have a replacement for me."

"That's too bad."

Eliot Lucre's grimy hands shot out, one pinching into Jinxy's shoulder, the other grabbing his chin and turning his head to expose the throbbing artery. And then the biggest question in Jinxy's life was answered. As Lucre sank his fangs into his flesh, he experienced a brief burst of pain and then bliss, sheer utter bliss. *So that's how it feels.*

"The bumbling idiots got themselves caught." Christopher Dante, hidden in an ivy-strewn garden, spoke quietly to his brother, Nick, over his cell phone. "We got here just in time to see it. Big Sister fed on one—she's some hot babe—then they shot them both and buried them in the hole they'd dug looking for the tunnel entrance."

The phone sputtered, then he heard Nick clearly. "Okay, so we definitely got bum information. They definitely know Gabe Leoni's ours. They're using him."

"I think Leoni changed sides," Christopher murmured. "Our little Fredo, he loves that Godfather shit just like Orion Darling. I still think they bonded."

"You could be right. I'll find out. Either way, Leoni's dead meat walking." Nick's laugh staccatoed through the static. "Hey, Chris, let's hope he doesn't have too much garlic in his blood, huh?"

"Yeah, right. Listen, Nicko, I'm losing the signal. I'm going to try to catch us a prize, like we planned."

The connection died before Nick answered, but that was okay. Christopher looked at the two vampires who worked for the Dantes. "Forget the tunnel for now, boys. We're just going to go hunting tonight."

"Vampires or humans?" asked Bleeder.

"Darlings?" Garth asked hopefully.

"No. Not Darlings. Not yet." Christopher paused, staring into the murky dark in the direction of the garden where Bentwick and Cox had unknowingly dug their own grave. The Darlings had killed two of his humans, and his urge was to take down two of theirs in return. But that didn't fit the plan. "Since we're taking a prisoner, we'll stick with a human. Remember, it has to be one that's important to the Darlings." He smiled, knowing the enemy was nearby. "Humans are easy. Of course, if a vampire wanders into our path, we could stake him. Just for fun. We'll just stay here a little longer first. Maybe some of them will go in." He nodded toward the place where he knew the Darling crew was gathered. "Then we'll spread out and catch ourselves a prize."

Stephen, in an effort to stop fantasizing about Amanda, slipped silently into the quiet gardens to join his brother and the security people. Of the humans, only Dale remained on site, but vampires Nipper and Snapper had joined him and made quick work of covering the Dante corpses and filling the hole. Ed, Nadine, and Ivor, along with the third member of the vampire guard, Dilly, were patrolling the hotel itself, blending in with guests in the lobby and elsewhere to watch the entrances in case the Dantes attempted entry. That was assuming they would recognize whomever they sent, which Stephen thought unlikely.

"Seen any Dantes?" he asked quietly.

"We think there are a few over there," Nipper said, nodding toward the southwest.

"Have you seen them?"

Nipper shook his head. "Just heard some little noises."

"There's a Dante stench in the air," Snapper added.

"Feels like we're being watched," Dale said.

"Since about the time we finished with the suitcases," Nipper added.

Stephen had nearly forgotten about them, his thoughts back on Amanda. "Any ID on the bodies?"

"Yes," Snapper said. "On the woman. Her name was tattooed on her ass. I guess it was her ass. She's your missing guest. The other one looks like a junkie. Stinks like one too. Got that druggy smell under the rot."

"Somebody's pretty hungry," Dale said. "The kills couldn't have been too far apart time-wise."

"Do Natasha and Ori know yet?"

"Ivor's telling them."

"Good. What orders did Ivor leave for you?"

"Don't attack until we see the white of their fangs," Dale said solemnly. He said everything solemnly.

Nipper rolled his eyes as Snapper spoke. "That's about right. We're ready for them if they attack, but we're not going after them first. I know your sister wanted us to, but Ivor didn't think we should after we killed the humans."

Stephen nodded. "Good. Listen to Ivor."

"Ivor thinks the Dante vampires will leave once

they're sure their humans struck out. He'll be checking in any minute now. You want to talk to him?"

Stephen stared toward the place where the others
thought the Dantes were lurking. He saw nothing,
but he felt they were right. Or maybe it was just a
little healthy paranoia. "No, I'll catch him later. Be
careful."

He slipped away and reentered the hotel. The
guitarist was playing, but he could also hear irritat-
ing pop music coming from the mezzanine bar.
One of those metallic female voices that shrieked
of lack of training. Sometime during the 1980s, music had started going to hell again. Unexpectedly,
anger welled, and it took great effort to extinguish
it. Afterward, he told himself he would calmly go
upstairs and have them tone it down, then he'd
stop by the concierge desk to say hello to Amanda.
A visit would vastly improve his mood before he
had to speak with Natasha, who would undoubtedly
be a barrel of laughs since hearing about the identity of one of the bodies. Not that she would appreciate the other in her gardens either.

Surprised she hadn't already sought him out,
Stephen hoped for her sake that she was off making
love with Douglas Harper. And that she didn't kill
him in the process.

34

Natasha, sated with a fine, rare blood, wore Douglas Harper's favorite red dress, with nothing underneath, as she walked down the corridor leading to his room. Earlier, when Ivor told her about finding the missing guest dismembered in the garden, she had flown into a rage and ordered him to leave her office, to leave her alone. Her brother did as she requested without a word, knowing that she was on the verge of violence. After he left, her urge to rip off somebody's head, anybody's, remained, and only steely willpower kept her in her soundproof office, where she screamed and cursed for a quarter hour before she even began to cool down. Then her violent thoughts turned to the still-missing twins. She suspected they were with Julian, who wasn't answering his phone or door. This suitcase incident reeked of Lucy and Ivy, who shared a history of stuffing their oversucked victims into trunks and crates of various shapes and sizes. Long ago, they had severed a few heads, a leg here and there, as necessary, but they had never gone this far, never cut up bodies like so much steak, then packaged them, not even in the early eras, when they had run wild. The pair had been much better controlled in recent times, but now Julian and his virus, or whatever it was, had taken them to the deepest depths.

Thinking about it began reigniting her fury, so she had turned her emotions toward something more pleasant: a long-overdue tryst with Douglas. Soon, a little calmer, she retreated to her apartment, where she took two of her best bottled bloods and a crystal champagne flute into the bathroom and relaxed in a hot tub of fragrant roiling bubbles. She slowly sipped the exquisite liquid until every last drop of anger had given way to erotic fantasies.

Now, at her lover's door, where a DO NOT DISTURB sign dangled from the knob, she smoothed her hair and promised herself she would not lose control, even if it meant forgoing an orgasm or two. She rapped on the door and waited in front of the peephole. "Douglas?" she called softly. "It's Natasha." She knocked again, but he didn't answer. *Maybe he's gone to dinner.* But why leave the sign on the door? *He's napping.* She didn't have her cell phone with her, so she walked to a courtesy phone and tried his room number. No answer, just voice mail. She punched the key to get the operator, and learned that Douglas had left no hold on his calls, nor had he left any messages. So, if he were in the room, he would have heard the phone ringing; it would have awakened him.

A tinge of concern creased her thoughts, but she ignored it, knowing he most likely hadn't even realized the sign dangled from the knob. She went downstairs and checked Satyrelli, but he wasn't there. Neither was he in the other eateries. The spa and pool yielded nothing, and the wandering guards assured her they hadn't seen him, inside or out. Finally she walked out to the parking lot. His car was there.

Concern mounted as she retrieved a passkey and went up to his room. It occurred to her that he could have gone into town with someone else, but she knew he hadn't; he came to the hotel for solitude, and for love. She knew him; he was no socialite, but was invariably aloof around other guests.

She arrived at his door, pausing a moment to glance around the corridor. Closed doors stood silent sentry along the deserted hall. She saw nothing, sensed nothing, felt only a ball of dread forming in the pit of her stomach. She knocked. "Douglas?" She paused. "Douglas? I'm coming in."

She slid the key into the lock. It turned easily, and she withdrew it as she pushed open the door. "Douglas?"

Mirrors on the ceiling. She saw them first, beyond the foyer, reflecting nothing but part of the unmade bed and, further across the room, the edge of Douglas's laptop computer, where it rested on a writing desk near the sliding glass doors that led onto the balcony. The doors were closed, the drapes open, the sheers drawn and still, holding in the odor of death. Slipping inside and letting the door close behind her, she knew what she would find.

She flipped the light switch in the foyer, and light bloomed in the bedroom beyond. Now she could discern a spray of red spots on the patterned bedspread, and as she entered the room, dark stains on the sheets came into view. There wasn't a lot of blood . . . *but then there wouldn't be, would there.* A champagne bottle rested in a bucket of melted ice.

She didn't see him until she turned her gaze on the far side of the room. A small round table and chairs had been moved into the corner to make room for him. He hung from the ceiling fan, a pinkish-gray cocoon, his exposed toes just dragging against the blue carpet. "Douglas," she whispered, approaching. "What have they done to you?"

There was a gaping black gash in his abdomen showing where the loops of intestine had been pulled from his body to make a sausage of him. Looking up, she saw one clouded green eye staring at her from between the coils, the eyelid pulled up by his bindings. His nose poked out, a mummy trying to breathe.

"Oh, Douglas. I'm so sorry."

Natasha turned from the body, holding her anger deep and low, controlling and savoring it, even as her fangs released of their own volition. She touched the tip of one with her tongue, tasted a drop of her own blood. "You little bitches." She spoke softly. "You little bitches will pay for this. And you too, Julian. If you're behind this, I'll destroy you too."

"Shit. Oh, fucking shit. What have I done?" Eliot Lucre let Jinxy drop to the ground. "What have I done?" The man was still alive, though if he'd stay that way or not, Eliot couldn't tell. But he did know that Julian would have his head on a spike in the sun if Jinxy died. *But only if he finds out you killed him.*

Eliot, you idiot! He had never lost control like this before. Sure, he had killed on the sly, especially in recent weeks, and that was against the Darlings' rules, but he was always careful; they never found out. But this . . . *You fucking idiot. What the hell did you do this for?*

For hunger. The hunger was taking over his entire

existence. Stephen had told him about the virus and given him extra blood, but it wasn't enough, and he didn't dare tell them it wasn't; no matter what they said, the Darlings would lock him away— or worse—for losing control.

Looking at Jinxy, he considered his choices. He could get rid of the body, or he could force Jinxy to imbibe his blood and make him into a vampire. At least he'd be undead. But Valentyn would still kill him for what he'd done.

Wiping his mouth with the back of his hand, Eliot decided to ditch the body, dead or not. It shouldn't be too hard, not with his knowledge of the place. When the Darlings bought the abandoned hotel, Eliot had immediately moved onto the property, and he'd had the place to himself for nearly two years before restoration began in earnest. Not only had he happily cleared the place of human riffraff, stalking them one by one as they slept in their own filth in the empty hotel rooms, he had explored every inch of the property. Every nook. Every cranny. He had worked on the building and grounds, as well as below ground, shoring up the tunnels, stringing lights in the dark in the still hours after midnight. Sometimes, it was very difficult to remain in those tunnels, and he never did map the catacombs completely. He hated that place. It was pretty funny if you thought about it, a vampire hating a tomb.

He knew where all the older tunnel entrances and exits were, and he had shown the Darlings all but one. His cousins had promptly destroyed and closed off most of them, while changing the others so drastically that they would never be recognized, should any Treasure hunter ever come along.

Getting Jinxy's body to any of those entrances

would be almost impossible, but the one he'd kept to himself was another story. He looked around, saw no one, then easily hoisted the body over his shoulder fireman-style and carried him to the caretaker's cottage, located on a rise not far away, on the other side of the property from the gardens. Eliot unlocked the door to his little stone house and dropped the lanky bag of bones on the floor.

The old stone cottage predated the hotel, having been built in the time of the monks. Formerly covered with thick adobe, it had been refitted and modernized with all the basics. The outside was covered with a red clay tile roof and peach stucco walls that matched the hotel's own. Inside the postage-stamp living room, chocolate brown carpeting covered the floor, and one wall was nearly taken up by a massive stone fireplace. Heavy but attractive wood shutters, painted to match the carpeting, had been fitted to all of the interior windows in addition to heavy drapes. The furnishings all came from the hotel, including a few landscape prints that Natasha insisted upon because they made the cottage look homier. He didn't give a rat's ass, but he obeyed her wishes. The only room he really cared about was the bedroom, which he entered now. It had a double bed, shutters, drapes, and blinds for good measure, and a closet that Eliot had built over part of one wall. Now, he opened the door and entered. First he moved his extra shoes, placing them outside the enclosure. Then, pushing his clothes aside to reveal the ancient unfinished stone at the back, he took a straightened hanger he kept behind the shoes and carefully aimed it at a small hole in the stones. After he inserted it several inches, it clicked into place and he turned it, undoing the hidden latch. With a groan, the back wall moved back, revealing a hidden space big enough for a man to enter. The space was open on the bottom, and an old ladder led down into the tunnels. Satisfied, Eliot went to retrieve the body, which maybe moaned a little when he picked it up. Maybe not.

He dropped Jinxy into the tunnel and climbed down the ladder after him, his hackles rising as soon as he hit the ground. The darkness was thick, cold, almost pulsing, as if he were near the catacombs. It had never felt like that before, not in his cottage.

This narrow tunnel was an offshoot of the main tunnel that began beneath the hotel and led upward into the funereal hills. He had strung no lights in this passage, and now he felt around on the wall to his right, finally finding the kerosene lantern hanging on a nail driven into the rocky wall. Nervously, he fumbled in the dark, and finally managed to light the lamp. Holding it up, he was relieved to see nothing but Jinxy's body and the empty tunnel in the dim flyspecked glow. *What did you expect?*

Over the years, he had used the tunnel to dispose of bodies on numerous occasions, but this was the first time he ever felt like he was being watched as he dragged Jinxy, heels first, toward the main tunnel. By the time he reached it, the lamp, which hung from his mouth, was nearly dead and he was so spooked that he thought about leaving the body there in plain sight. After all, who would see it?

Someone might. Though he didn't think the Darlings used the tunnels, he couldn't be sure. He had to hide the body. After moving through forty more yards of darkness, he gratefully turned on the first light switch he came across, near the offshoot tunnel that led from the entrance in the men's lava-

tory. Here he doused the sputtering lantern and set
the lamp down. He'd retrieve it on his way out.
Glancing down the offshoot, he wondered if he
dared to exit through the hotel after he'd disposed
of the body. If not, he would have to find his way
back down to the cottage in the dark. His vampiric
vision was catlike, allowing him to see much better
than a human in the near dark, but if there was
no light at all, he was equally blind.

Dump the body and get out of there. That was
the plan. It was easier hauling Jinxy along in the
main tunnel, but Eliot's unease continued to mount
despite the light. Disgusted with himself for feeling
fear without cause, he determinedly headed up the
gradual incline. There was a place not far from the
catacombs where there was a small natural cavern
that dropped down a very long way. That was where
he had always dumped his empties.

He paused, thinking he heard something move,
but no other sounds came and he decided it had
to be rats. It was a strange place for the rodents,
this sometimes dank, sometimes dusty place, and
he wasn't sure how they got in—probably from
small openings among the mausoleums and graves
in the cemeteries of the hills above. Or maybe they
fed on the ancient dead monks in the catacombs.
Who knows? Who cares? He didn't want to think
about the catacombs.

His foot crunched on something. Looking down,
he saw a recently gnawed rat carcass. Only its long,
spindly tail appeared unmarred. *Other rats must have
done it. There's nothing else down here.* He continued
on, doggedly pulling the body, occasionally imagining he heard scrabblings, breathing, all sorts of stupid things, but he steadfastly ignored them. As he
neared the catacombs, the noises stopped. That was

even worse. He glanced toward the entry to the tombs and as he did, the sensation of being watched increased, while the air thickened and darkened until the dim lightbulbs were mere glowing circles, illuminating nothing but themselves.

Eliot hadn't felt such fear since he was human. *And even then . . . never like this.* With strength reborn of terror, he dragged Jinxy down the short, low natural passage that led to the cave, shuffling his feet to make sure he wouldn't miss its low lip and fall in himself. Reaching the edge, he pulled the body around and heard Jinxy groan as he pushed him over the edge. It was probably just a corpse sound, air and gasses; he'd heard those before.

Now he turned and saw nothing but blackness. The lights in the primary tunnel had gone out. If he'd been human, he would have wet himself.

He'd never bought into those stories about the Treasure before, not really, but now they seemed all too real. When he was alive, he'd been a devout Catholic. He could believe anything.

35

"As I told you earlier, I'd traveled to Machu Picchu, high in the Andes," Julian told the twins, "to find the bloodberry. Later, I would recreate the elixir for the first time in several millennia, for the first time since the continent of Euloa was destroyed." He smiled foxily. "The elixir that you two love so much."

They giggled. The pair was on their third bottle of blood each since they had drained Douglas Harper, and they were finally becoming calm, even logy. The amounts these two had ingested would have turned a normal human vampire comatose. Tomorrow, though, it would take even more to bring them to this state. Such was the power of the elixir.

"I was welcomed to their mountain as a god. The Incas were the caretakers and as a trueborn, I was their master. They and their forebears had known of us for many centuries."

"Did they know the Treasure story?"

"Yes," he said. "A similar tale. Most of the ancient races knew the stories in one form or another. The pre-Columbian races believed that trueborns came from the blood and flesh of the gods, that we were their physical incarnations. The pyramids and the temples crowning them were erected to honor and to thank them for their gifts by giving blood back to them. And flesh. The beating heart. I was associated with the sun god—"

"That's funny!" Ivy interrupted. "You and the sun."

"The sun god needed to feed on the blood of humans. I was light and bright like the sun, and they brought me the living blood of enemies and even their own people. It was an honor to be my meal."

The twins looked at each other. Lucy spoke. "It sounds like you really got off on that."

Julian ignored her, knowing her tongue was loosened by a surfeit of blood. "Only the most elite of the Incas were allowed to reside in Machu Picchu, where they gave me a villa. The elite included the shamans, the royalty, the wealthy and powerful, and the Virgins of the Sun. The most honored warriors were my guard and procurers of my food. I told them stories of the trueborns, of myself and other gods in faraway places. It was an idyllic time. It was also my time of mating."

The twins cuddled and stretched together like panther kittens, every move sensual and sublime, helping his reawakening urges to revive. He thought of Talai, and now Orzuca. "She was an Inca priestess of the sun, an *ajlla,*" he said softly.

"A what?" asked Lucy.

"Who?" queried Ivy. "Huh?"

"Orzuca is—was—to be my love, my queen." He watched them. "She was a temple virgin at Machu Picchu, the holiest place of the Incas, the city in the clouds in what is now Peru."

"What was so special about her? Was she a trueborn?" Ivy said.

"No. She was my lost love."

"Just how many lost loves do you have anyway?" Lucy said. She took a deep swallow of blood and licked her lips.

"Only one, my dear."

"But Talai was your lost love."

"Yes, she was. She always is, no matter what she is called."

"What the hell are you talking about?" Ivy asked, lazily curling a lock of her sister's hair around a finger. "I don't get it."

"Surely you've noticed." He folded his hands. "You've been on earth long enough to have witnessed it a number of times."

"Noticed what?" they asked.

"Humans. The same ones often come round. They tend to travel in the same packs, over and over, in one way or another. Oh, they have different bodies and voices, but when you've met one who impresses you in any way, you recognize their spirit in their next form."

"You mean reincarnation?" Lucy's eyes widened. "That shit's for real?"

"Of course."

"So, like, Talai reincarnated as this Orzuca?"

"Yes, and as others between those times. I've actually found her a number of times. You might say that I have a seventh sense for her." He smiled curtly. "Most of those times she was too old, male, or otherwise undesirable to approach, but as Orzuca, she was Talai. Oh, not in appearance, although there was a resemblance. She was beauty incarnate, untouched, waiting for me."

"But you turned Talai into a human vampire. Does that mean if we're staked, we still reincarnate, just like humans?" The twins sat forward, transfixed.

"Yes. Contrary to human myth, your souls, such as they are, are intact. Humans have mixed up ghouls with vampires. Ghouls are soulless and found mainly in Eastern Europe. They're the creation of other ghouls. You, on the other hand, can and do reincarnate. When you lose your vampiric life, you will come back as simple human beings."

"Oh, gross!" moaned Ivy.

"Not me!" Lucy insisted. "I'll always be a vampire. Humans are stupid."

So are some vampires. Julian nodded, bemused. "Perhaps some part of you will remember this life and seek out a vampire to change you back."

"God, I hope so!" Lucy looked at him. "Do you reincarnate?"

"No. My race is elemental. It is very difficult for me to lose my form as a trueborn. Nearly impossible."

Lucy eyed him skeptically. "How do you *know* that?"

"My dear young creature, would you question one who has lived so long as I?" He knew she wouldn't. "If I were ever to lose my form, I would live in the wind and shadows, in the night, in the leaves of a tree. I would be the chill breeze on the back of your neck or a storm at sea." He paused. "Whenever you feel eyes watching you and no one is there, it might be a trueborn in one form or another."

Ivy cocked her head. "Is the Treasure like that? In another form?"

"You said yourself that it is only a story."

"Come on, Julian."

"The power of the Treasure was such that even

Keliu could not take his trueborn form from him. Or so it is said."

"Oh." The twins glanced at each other; then Lucy said, "So what happened with Orzuca or Talai or whoever she was?"

"She was a woman exalted by her people. I met her shortly after I arrived in Machu Picchu on my quest for the bloodberry. That is how synchronicity works." He sipped from his goblet of blood. "It is a great force in the world, bringing together those things which are meant to be joined." He allowed them no questions, but continued quickly. "Orzuca was a passionate young woman, something of a rebel, yet deeply religious. Her desires and her beliefs were at odds.

"She did not care for the confines and restrictions of temple life, and was given to slipping out at night to enjoy the stars overhead. There were many to see so high on the mountain. That is how we met. Gazing at the stars."

"What happened to her?" Ivy asked, growing impatient. She wanted violence, not purity.

"She died by her own hand."

"Why?"

"Yeah, why?"

"Because she loved me but had taken the sacred vows of the *ajlla*. Before I changed her, she was gone." He sat back as a wave of humanesque emotion washed over him. He supposed it was a sadness, a longing. The feelings would continue only until his mating time had passed, but he would remember them. And if he joined a female permanently, the actual emotions might continue. He wondered if it were true and if he would enjoy it or not.

He hadn't told the twins the entire truth about Orzuca's death. It happened after he had administered the second bite, when she had realized what was beginning to happen to her. Conflicted by religion and passion, she had killed herself. The night that it happened was beautiful and clear, the Milky Way a sparkling band of diamonds in the crystalline air. Hearing deep male chanting, Julian had followed the sound, walking up the pale granite-lined path from his terrace to the small plateau just under a narrow peak. It was a place of sacrifice.

It was like a tableau of marble in his mind, etched in that instant in time. Red-robed figures were gathered behind her, shadowed by the ragged peak. The chanting abruptly ceased. Dressed in white, breast bared, arms raised, Talai—Orzuca—held a ceremonial knife high in both hands. It was too late and Julian, even with his trueborn abilities, could do nothing but watch the obsidian blade arc down into her breast. As the scarlet bud blossomed, she turned her head and looked straight at him, though she could not possibly see him with her eyes; he was too far away and the torches occluded her vision. But she saw him with her soul. He felt it shear down into his deepest depths. Then, with the barest of sighs, her body crumpled and her spirit fled from him once more.

"Julian?" That was Ivy. "Hey, Julian?"

"Have you ever seen her again?" Lucy asked.

Julian steepled his fingers and closed his eyes a brief moment, drawing a new vision into his mind. When he opened them, he said, "Yes."

"When? Where?"

He had their full attention now. He looked from one to the other. "Tonight, as a matter of fact."

* * *

Cradled in darkness, bathed in the stale air of the tomb, in bone dust and the cobwebs of ancient spiders, he smelled the monks, five hundred years dead, smelled the ghosts of their decayed flesh, caught the odor of the rotting robes as their skeletons lay moldering in the hollows of the walls. There were other odors as well. The stench of dead human vampires remained, though the bodies had long since turned to dust, and then to nothing.

He knew this: A millennium had passed. When last he had walked in the world, the European Christians were beginning to proliferate. Jesus was long dead and only the Church remained. He knew it had grown and swept over this land when he learned and listened to the monks above, talking and praying, prostrating themselves one moment and sodomizing one another the next. He had preferred the natives' pantheistic religions, but the monks took from them the knowledge of their own souls and replaced it with pap. With papacy.

Humans never changed. They wanted—nay, they craved and required—a god to tell them what to do, how to behave. A god to humiliate themselves before, to beg for forgiveness for sins that were not sins but only human nature. They were useful. They were amusing. They were food. Their adoration could be charming at times. And if a village became a problem, he created human vampires to help him wipe it out. The red plague.

The human vampires were not as pleasurable as the humans. They fancied themselves to be demigods and did not show the proper respect due him. Having had enough time to assimilate their current language, he knew something of the ones who lived above him now; they were too sure of themselves, and their leader was an arrogant woman. A woman! Worst of all, they, like all human vampires, dared to plunder *his* children, *his* humans. Human vampires were scum, nothing but leeches, and when he was done with them—he would kill them.

And his own kind? Once, he had ruled the true-borns for a very long time. Yet, for all he gave to them, they did not appreciate him, but turned on him, dethroned him. Even his own son tried to destroy him, and thus he had made him a wanderer in the wilderness. A wanderer who would be the last of his kind, the last of the gods, and the greatest.

He also knew this: His long rest was about to end, his self-fulfilling prophecies were at hand. His son had arrived. Keliu. Keliu the jealous, Keliu the weak. Keliu, who would be king, who would be God, though never would it happen.

And *she* was here, the one who had turned his son from him.

Lying utterly still in the darkness, he waited, content to feel his body readying itself to return to trueborn life. He would need to feed to complete his rebirth. Feeling a pang of hunger already, he sent his mind out, calling to any of his human or vampiric children that might be listening.

On her break, standing in the doorway of the steamy warm pool room, Amanda shivered.

"What's wrong?" Stephen asked, resisting the ceaseless urge to touch her, to hold her.

Amanda looked away, then into his eyes. "I guess someone just walked over my grave." She paused, then smiled. "It's time for me to get back to the desk."

"I'll come with you."

She looked at him oddly. "People might talk."

"Let them."

36

Sudden pounding on the door brought the twins bolt upright and startled even Julian. The bell began chiming, accompanied by more pounding.

"What's that?" a twin asked. "Who's that?"

Julian put his finger to his lips. "Shhh. We'll find out."

"Julian! Open up! I know you're in there!"

"It's Natasha," whispered Ivy.

"And boy, is she pissed," Lucy observed.

Julian rose. "Both of you, quickly and quietly, follow me. Bring your glasses and bottles."

He led them into his bedroom and opened the door of a walk-in closet. He swept the clothing to one side, slipped a piece of cedar lining up, and pushed a hidden button. The false wall slid away to reveal a hiding place that was a little tight for the two of them, but it worked. The chamber was the handiwork of Jinxy, and the Darlings had been unaware of it. "Stay in here until I come for you. Don't make a sound unless you're ready to experience reincarnation sooner than expected."

"What's happening?" Ivy asked.

"I think your big sister is onto us." Julian let the

door slide shut and pushed the clothes back into place. He could hear her pounding from here.

"Julian, you open this damned door!"

Quickly, he straightened the living room, then went to the door and opened it an inch or two. "Natasha, quietly, please. What is it you want?"

"You know what I want," she growled. "Let me in."

"Only if you promise to control yourself."

"You bastard, you give them to me!" Her voice lowered but remained harsh.

"I don't know what you're talking about. Will you contain yourself if I open the door? You realize I can easily overpower you if you force me."

She glared at him, her eyes wild and sparking with fury. "Yes, I do. Let. Me. In."

He allowed her entrance, and she strode to the end of the room and opened the balcony doors, stepped out and looked around, then came back inside. They stood face-to-face in front of the fireplace. Her hands began to come up, but he caught her wrists in a motion so fast it was nearly invisible, and held them still. "Now, what is it that I can get for you? What do I have that you desire?"

"The twins."

"I don't have them. You may look around if you wish, as long as you don't destroy anything." He chuckled softly. "May I ask what they have done?"

"You know exactly what they've done, you bastard. You're probably behind it, you son of a bitch, you fucking piece of shit!" Her voice rose and she struggled against his hands as her fangs unsheathed.

"This won't do, Natasha. Control yourself. What has happened? What is it that you think they did?" He used every ounce of his hypnotic ability as he spoke, and it had a slight calming effect on her, but she was far more animal than vampire at this moment.

Her fangs receded. "They've been killing guests. But you know that already, don't you." She spoke flatly.

Guests. Plural. That was interesting. "No, I didn't know that, but the effects of the trueborn virus would account for their behavior. They are not themselves." He added gently, "Nor are you. Come sit down and have something to drink. You'll feel better. We'll talk."

Glaring at him, she nevertheless let him lead her to his rounded leather chair. She sat carefully, very tense, as if expecting an electric shock. He let go of her wrists and, gaze unwavering, she adjusted herself in the seat. She looked small but dangerous in the big tufted chair, like a cornered cat, wary and ready to attack.

"Stay seated, Natasha. I'll be back in an instant." He raised an eyebrow, trying to press his mind into hers. "Or faster, if necessary."

She made no reply, and hadn't moved when he returned. He handed her a goblet, poured, then set the bottle on the side table next to the chair. She sipped, then drank greedily and poured herself another as he retrieved his own glass and settled onto the Grecian sofa. He turned so that he faced her, then sat forward attentively. "Now tell me about it. Perhaps I may be of service."

Another heated glare. "Quit trying to get into my brain." A swallow of scarlet. "I thought that was something you couldn't do, invade a vampire's thoughts."

"It is difficult, but it can be done, I admit. You're

particularly susceptible in your current state and I was only trying to calm you. I will stop."

She nodded curtly and simmered.

"Whom do you think they killed?"

"Tonight we found suitcases containing two dismembered bodies."

"Really?" He was surprised. Jinxy wasn't given to making such mistakes.

"Really."

"May I ask, how did you happen to find them?"

"Dantes dug them up. That doesn't matter. What does—"

"Have you considered that the Dantes might have killed them as well? It strikes me as something they would do."

She hesitated, and he knew his words had had an effect, but she denied it. "The twins did it, I know it."

"How do you know?"

"I just found the body of another guest. A friend of mine. A good friend. It's the twins, I know it. And so do you."

"Tell me what makes you think I'm involved in this."

She started to rise, then stopped herself, her nails digging into the leather arms as she inched back down. "How can you ask that?" she spat. "I've never trusted you, but somehow you've mesmerized my uncle, so I have tried to make you welcome for his sake. But you're up to something. You want something, and you don't care who you destroy to get it. You're using the twins. We've all seen them with you."

Julian set down his goblet and folded his hands together. "They amuse me, I must admit. But you misjudge me. I've been keeping them out of trouble by giving them the blood they crave. Just as I've given it to you. You need it." He smiled thinly. "After all, you don't want to have another tantrum in public. It's bad for business."

She was furious. Instead of answering, she poured another glass of blood and downed half in one gulp. "Ever since you arrived, things have been different. Wrong."

"I am sorry that you and yours fell victim to the vampiric virus. I wish there were a better word for it. I did not know you would be affected." He bowed his head. "So few are. I am not responsible for it, but I'm sorry for your trouble."

When he looked up, she was standing. "Show me the rest of your suite."

"Gladly." He took her into the small kitchen, the large bathroom, and finally, into his bedroom. She opened the closet and probed. Fortunately, the twins were quiet, and Natasha shut the door, satisfied he was not harboring them. They returned to the living room.

"You'll alert me if they show up," she commanded.

"Of course. Natasha?"

"What?"

"I know something of the Dantes' methods. Keep them in mind regarding the bodies." He paused. "They are very interested in the Treasure as well."

"Are you interested in the Treasure?"

"Why do you ask?"

"Do you want it?" she persisted.

"Heavens, no!"

She eyed him. "The myth claims that the Treasure will rise after several things occur. Two of the last three were that human vampires would return to this place and that a trueborn would arrive. That would be you."

He chuckled, and wondered if she knew of the third thing that had taken place. He didn't think so. "Surely you don't believe those old stories. Those ridiculous prophecies."

"No. But maybe you do."

"The Dantes believe," he told her. "They want to take the Treasure for themselves. One of the brothers told me that before I killed him. I didn't want to bring it up when I first arrived."

She watched him.

"It seemed silly to me at the time as well as secondary to their lust for the elixir. But you have found them on your property tonight and, as you mention, the so-called prophecies are in place. They may become extremely aggressive."

"I'll keep it in mind. Thanks for the drink." She strode to the door and put her hand on the knob before turning her head and saying, "I still don't trust you." With that, she was gone.

Julian walked out on the balcony for a moment alone before letting the twins out. His keen ears picked up fog-muffled voices somewhere below, but he couldn't make out the words.

He enjoyed the mist, cool and damp on his face. It wasn't only the effects of the elixir working on Natasha now. There was a feeling in the air. The Father's presence was so strong that the human vampires were beginning to sense him. For some reason, that made Julian think of Jinxy and wonder, a little uneasily, where he was.

Aardvark had gotten himself lost, and knew now how foolish he'd been to turn off the lights as he traveled because his sense of direction had vanished in the darkness. He could barely even discern the tunnel's grade most of the time. This place was unreal. Abnormal. For now, he sat cross-legged in a small low-ceilinged room just off the main tunnel. He had left the passage unlit when he came in here to take a nap and to escape, as best he could, the overwhelming dread that followed and called to him from within the tunnel. In here, he didn't hear the voice. Not so much, anyway. Abruptly, pale yellow light flickered across the threshold.

It was weird, feeling scared. It was a rare experience for him. The best and only real fear he'd ever felt occurred while hiding ten feet from a screaming woman who'd found one of his victims before he could get away; it had given him a thrill and a chill. *Slish slash.* But it hadn't really scared him. It happened in downtown Seattle, in the underground, which he'd become very familiar with over several weeks. That day, he'd gotten into the old subterranean city and lain in wait for some hapless, dawdling tourist to ambush. Just for fun. To ease the boredom.

After a while, he'd gotten himself a nerdy little man in a plaid shirt, who had stopped to examine a crack in a brick or something in a shadowy corner. Aardvark crept up behind him and cut his big bobbly Adam's apple in two, *slish slash,* before Plaid Man could make a sound. He croaked before he could croak. Aardvark smiled to himself. He had lingered over the body, taking a pinkie finger for a souvenir. (He only kept it long enough to slip it into a pot of soup in a men's shelter in Bellevue. He wasn't a fool; you couldn't keep shit like that on you and expect not to get caught.) Anyway, another tour arrived practically on the heels of the

other one, and he'd had no time to hide the body,
only himself, by crouching down behind a couple
of old shop signs propped against the wall.

The tour guide had begun talking endlessly about
a gold rush, when all of a sudden a woman stuck
her big nose in the corner and started screaming
her ass off. The tour guide ran to the rescue, and
then they were a screaming duet. Aardvark huddled
behind his skimpy billboards, sure they'd spot him.
But they didn't. Instead the guide, once he calmed
down, hurried the whole bunch back the way they'd
come. Aardvark quickly fled deeper into the underground, resurfacing in the mop closet of a Mexican
restaurant of ill repute a few blocks west. He'd
bought himself a burrito to go with the tip money
from a couple tables and sauntered into the day,
energized by the murder and especially by the intense fear of being captured he'd experienced so
briefly.

He loved the fear, but he knew not to indulge in
it. Like keeping trophies, it made you easy to catch.
But now, thinking about the fear, realizing it was in
him, he told himself to enjoy it, to relish how it
made his body feel, but to keep it down deep in
his brain so it wouldn't affect his thinking. He
didn't know what caused the fear—probably nothing but some forgotten childhood trauma—but he
would savor the sensation while he could.

Unfolding himself, he stood and slung his pack
over his shoulder. Gooseflesh rose as he peered into
the tunnel. More lights illuminated the path in
both directions. He looked at the upgrade, visible
now, and as he did, he saw another few bulbs come
to life. Somebody was headed up the hill. Somebody who could lead him out of here. He stepped
into the corridor, briefly considered following the

light downhill, then decided to shadow whoever it was, to keep to the nooks and crannies, to hide in false doorways until the other led him out. That would be the best thing to do. The most fun. If it didn't work, he could always go the other way.

Gooseflesh prickled and his stomach threatened to burn his ass again, but he waited out the cramp and took his first tentative steps up the tunnel. *Come to me.* The voice seemed so real, but he knew it wasn't, so it couldn't be what caused the fear. He didn't believe in spooks and goblins and all that shit. *Come to me, Aardvark Wicket. Come to me now.* He tried to will it away; he might be a lot of things, but no fucking way was he a schizo. Maybe it was the rats. Maybe they'd poisoned his stomach *and* his mind.

Urine trickled down his leg and his knees turned into jelly balls, but Aardvark didn't care. *Enjoy the fear.* Or as his parents might have said, *Be the fear.*

He pushed on.

Stephen wouldn't leave. Not that she minded, but it seemed out of character. Previously, he'd been careful not to give anyone anything to talk about. Now Amanda felt his gaze on her, even when she was helping a guest. She was really going to hear about it from Carol Anne, who kept smiling and making thumb's-up signs when Stephen had his back to her. Amanda had almost succumbed to hysteric giggles once, not so much because the blonde was funny, but because she was probably already telling all the staff, and because Amanda was confused, a little giddy, and very horny.

Stephen wasn't flirting, except with his eyes. Instead, he had been telling her about the restoration of the hotel. Finished with his story, he glanced around and said, "A very slow night."

"Yes." She nodded in the direction of a petite redhead in a navy pantsuit. "She works here?"

Stephen looked. "Yes. That's Dilly. She's a security guard."

"She sure is spending a lot of time up there by the front doors."

Stephen looked unhappy. "There are others patrolling too. You might see them. We've had a couple of pickpocket incidents today."

"You should have told me earlier. I've got a great view from here." She hesitated. "There's virtually nobody up there by the entrance. Why does she stay?"

"Ivor probably told her to. She's the type who follows orders to the letter." He grinned, his handsome face suddenly boyish. "I'll bet you don't."

"Follow orders? Not if I think they're stupid."

"Troublemaker." He put his hands on the desk and leaned closer.

"That's me. Um, am I keeping you from anything?"

His expression changed, and he looked up at the big art-deco clock face on the wall behind them. "I'm okay for a few more minutes." He looked at her. "Am I making you uncomfortable?"

He was, but it was a good kind of uncomfortable. Stephen was a mystery to her. He seemed dangerous tonight—just a little. Maybe because he was less somber and serious than usual. Maybe that was all it was. She half expected him to sweep her out of her chair and carry her to his bedroom. *Oh, Christ, where did* that *come from?* Clearly, her brains had traveled down and taken up residence in her panties.

She chuckled lightly. "No. You're not making me uncomfortable." *Rip my bodice, baby!*

He was silent a long moment, letting her hear the classical guitarist play something that had to be Vivaldi. The gentle murmur of business punctuated the notes.

"I've been wondering about an interest you mentioned," he finally said.

"What interest is that?"

"I'm just curious. Why do you like vampires so much?"

"Vampires represent sex and death. Everybody's fascinated by those things. Vampires are like a combo meal."

He cocked an eyebrow. "Do you believe they exist?"

"Sure," she said snidely. "They hang out with the Tooth Fairy and Santa Claus." She paused. "You *are* joking, aren't you?"

"But you believe in ghosts. You saw one."

"Well, more like I *didn't* see one. Yes. I believe in ghosts, but they're not anything real, they don't bite or bring you presents. They're just little movies playing over and over. They don't think or anything."

"So you believe in them because you can explain their existence?"

"Yes. I suppose that's it."

"What about demons?"

"Demons are for Christians. No disrespect, if you are one. A Christian, I mean, not a demon." She felt her cheeks flush.

He laughed loud enough to make Carol Anne gawk. "I was once, many years ago. I believe in many things, but I don't know if there's a god. I am agnostic."

"If there is one, he doesn't belong just to the Christians."

"You are also agnostic then?" His eyes bored into hers.

"Okay," she said. "Close enough."

"What do you mean? Are you an atheist?"

"Maybe. No. I'm a skeptic. Maybe there's a god, but I don't like that word. It's a human word. Too anthropomorphic. I read a book once where they used the word 'Tao' instead. As in *The Tao of Pooh*? The book I read implied that god is energy. The life force we all come from. We're all part of the Tao, and in between lives we rejoin it."

"Aha. You *do* believe in something. Reincarnation. Tell me what your last life was."

She rubbed her chin. "Well, I lived in Baltimore and was a powder boy for the Navy, killed during the War of 1812. Will that do?"

"Are you serious?"

"No. But I do lean toward reincarnation. But not religion. It's nice to be able to tell someone that without getting a sermon."

"You don't think religion is good for people?" he goaded.

Amanda considered. "Well, it's good for a lot of people. But I hate it."

"Why?"

"I don't know. It's always repelled me. I mean, the things people do in the name of god. Like sacrifice other people. Or themselves." She shivered.

Stephen briefly touched her hand. "Are you all right?"

"I always do that when I think about that." She didn't even want to say the word.

"I'll tell you why."

"Tell me."

"It happened to you in another life."

She felt weak in the knees, and was glad she was sitting down. "That sounds so right." Shaking her head, she said, "Let's change the subject back to something nice, like vampires."

"Vampires are supposed to be repelled by the cross. There's Christianity in the stories. That doesn't bother you?"

"Of course not. Christians made up a lot of vampire stories. It's in our culture. I enjoy the mythology as much or more than any others. *The Exorcist* is one of my favorite movies." She paused. "You must like vampires yourself, to ask about them. What's your favorite story?"

"Dracula," he said slowly. "No. That's not true. My favorite story isn't one that's been made into a movie, or even written as a novel. It's an offbeat little myth. Very old."

"I'd love to hear it."

"I'd love to tell it to you, but I'm sworn to secrecy."

"I'll take it to my death."

"In that case—"

"Stephen!" Natasha said, appearing suddenly. "What the hell are you doing?" She glared at her brother, then gave Amanda a poisonous look. "What were you two talking about?"

"Books," she said quickly. "Movies. We both like the same thing."

"And what would that be?"

"Natasha!"

"Quiet, Stephen. Let her answer." She smiled, but it looked more like a grimace. "I love teasing my brother. Now tell me, dear. What do you both like?"

Amanda met her eyes and lied. "Mythology.

Greek mythology. We both like how Greek myths are updated, you know, like Shakespeare's plays? It's fun to recognize the original story and—"

"Fine. We have some business to attend to, Stephen. Let's go." She took his arm, and Amanda could see her knuckles whiten from the pressure she put on him. Turning, she led him away without another word.

37

"It could be the work of the Dantes," Orion said, lighting a cigar. As usual, the theme from *The Godfather* played softly in his dark, paneled office. "Perhaps they're trying to set us against one another."

"You're just repeating what Julian told you," Natasha snapped. She stopped pacing. "He tried that one on me."

"My dear niece," Uncle Ori said darkly. "He repeated to you what *I* told him. Let's make that clear."

"Well, what made you think of it? Did that little twirp—Leoni—did he tell you that? Well, I have news for you, Uncle. The Dantes aren't the ones losing control. The twins are."

Ori gave her a long, stern look. "Sit down, Natasha. Have a drink. We need to talk about certain things."

"The Treasure," she said, filling a wine glass. She sat down in the chair between Stephen and Ivor in front of Ori's desk. "I know. Julian went on about the Dantes' belief in it and how much they want to get their hands on it."

Stephen shut his eyes a moment. He'd heard most of this before Ori and Ivor had joined them,

right after she'd lit into him about talking to
Amanda. Fortunately, she hadn't brought it up in
front of the others, but his sister had overheard
enough of what he had said to Amanda to strongly
suspect he was going to tell her the Treasure story.
And he had been. He seemed to have no control
where she was concerned. Never had he been so
affected. Sitting there, he wondered why, and didn't
tune in to his sister's words again until he heard
her say something about the prophecies. Then he
sat up straighter.

"I've never really taken the prophecies seriously,"
Uncle Ori said. "But you do make a point. We are
here and a trueborn has come among us." Cigar
smoke curled sweetly in the air between them. "But
there is still a third sign."

"The woman," said Ivor.

"Yes. But if the prophecy *is* real, there is nothing
left in the stories of the Treasure to tell us what to
look for or why. We don't even know if she is a
vampire like us or a trueborn. For that matter, a
simple human."

Amanda! The world twisted and turned.

"Stephen?" Ori said. "You have something to
share?"

"No. Just a hunger pang."

"Natasha, pour him a fresh drink. Back to the
matter at hand. I think that Julian might be able
to tell us something more."

Natasha handed Stephen the glass. "I don't trust
him. We're relying on him too much for information." Her voice arced up a notch. "I think he's
orchestrating something. I know that bastard is behind Douglas's murder, no matter what you think.
I know!" Two more notches. "And I know the twins
were part of it!"

"Natasha," Ori said sternly. "You have to get control of yourself. Otherwise, you'll force me to appoint Stephen in your place or take charge of the hotel myself."

"You are in charge," Ivor said. "You're the CEO."

Ori smiled with half his mouth. "Yes. But I prefer to act as *consigliere* and let Natasha—and Stephen—operate things." He looked at his niece. "Normally, I trust you implicitly, especially with Stephen's levelheaded influence to temper your decisions."

"Are you saying I'm not levelheaded?" she demanded.

"Don't force my hand, Natasha."

With a sulky look, she sat back and picked up her wine glass. "My instincts are good, Uncle."

"Yes. And so are mine. I'll speak to him shortly. Don't worry, 'Tasha, I'll be cautious."

"I'd like to come with you," Stephen said. The woman in the prophecies. It was Amanda, he knew it, and he was sure Julian did too. What he had to do now was make sure Natasha didn't find out. In her current state, she would kill her without a thought.

Ori nodded. "Yes, that's a good idea. Now, Ivor, anything to report?"

"Not at this point, but we believe there may still be Dante operatives on our grounds. We'll continue to patrol all night. There is one thing that Dale called in a while ago. It's probably nothing, but Eliot wasn't at the guardhouse."

"I told him specifically not to wander off." Ori shook his head. "Keep your eye out for him and send him back to the post. Tell him Natasha's very angry with him for leaving."

Stephen chuckled. Natasha's anger, even in normal times, was a much bigger threat than Ori's despite his Godfather demeanor. She was the muscle. Sometimes, even Stephen was intimidated, though more out of a feeling that he should be as forceful as she because of his gender. But it wasn't his nature. *You should be thankful for that!* The recent bursts of anger and emotions were more than enough to convince him. He was a self-control freak, whereas his sister was simply a control freak.

"I hope you kill at least one Dante tonight, Ivor," Natasha was saying.

"You participated in the death of two already," Ivor said reprovingly. "I thought we agreed. . . ." He looked to Ori for guidance.

"Maybe Natasha is right after all," Ori said. "I thought we shouldn't show our hand too much, but perhaps I'm being too cautious. What do you think, Ivor?"

"I think we should kill them whenever an opportunity arises. Like ducks in a row."

"Then do it if the opportunity arises. Cautiously."

Ivor nodded and rose.

"Ivor?" Stephen said to his looming brother. "Are you still feeling normal?"

"Yes. I'm not affected."

"You don't seem very affected either, Uncle."

"I am, but not so much as the rest of you. I think that perhaps Ivor is immune and that I was at an older, less hormonally driven, age than you when I changed. This would also account for the twins' extreme behavior. And you, Stephen. How are you faring?"

"As long as I ingest enough blood, I'm in control."

Natasha glared at him. "You just want to fuck that human girl, that's all."

"Douglas Harper, 'Tasha. Need I say more?"

She stood up and opened her mouth, but Ori cut her off. "None of that. You're on thin ice. Remember that."

38

At midnight, the Candle Bay Hotel seemed to sigh and settle in for the night, tucking itself into the heavy blanket of fog that had just rolled in from the ocean. The cathedral-like lobby contained only a few employees and they worked quietly, as if muffled by the fog that pressed insistently against the windows. From hidden speakers, *Fur Elise* waltzed softly in the air like a lovers' lullaby. That is how it seemed, so peaceful and sleepy, but looks deceived.

First, it wasn't fuzzy blanket fog. It was full-blown Jack the Ripper fog, all pea soup and damp cotton, a ground fog so heavy it hid your feet from your eyes. The lighter fog that clung routinely to the hotel was lost within it, eaten up, consumed. Cannibalized.

The hunters, invisible, moved with more caution now. Half an hour would pass before it was time for Christopher Dante, Bleeder, and Garth to come together behind an outbuilding at the rear of the garden to decide whether to continue the hunt. At this point, Christopher was trying to navigate through the invisible maze of gardens to get to the building, and hoped the other two were doing the same. Although they would go home empty-handed, it was just too dangerous to continue in the fog.

Not too far from Christopher, security man Dale hunkered in the bushes, silently wiping the dew from his .38 with his handkerchief. He felt like the very essence of a G-man as he patiently waited for something to cross his path. He was in his sixteenth hour of work, but didn't mind.

Nipper and Snapper, patrolling the grounds in search of the elusive Dantes, decided to visit Eliot's house for some libations. Finding their host away (he hadn't reappeared at the guardhouse either), they helped themselves to a bottle of O positive. They didn't bother with glasses, but passed the bottle and watched some Leno.

In the lobby, Dilly Landsdown sat near the massive entrance and watched custodian Jimmy Vasquez mopping a section of floor. He was handsome, with his black hair and sleepy brown eyes. His well-developed muscles rippled beneath his clothing, and Dilly could practically smell his blood. She smiled at him when he looked up. He smiled back, and she knew he would taste hot and spicy.

Nadine and Ed, the human guards, also in their sixteenth hours, were spotting for one another. Right now, Ed slept in a chair while Nadine walked the long service corridor that ran behind the lobby, restaurants, and pool, checking all the entrances. She was tired. Ivor had promised to relieve the humans at midnight, giving their patrol areas to other employees, vampires who were less experienced but fairly reliable. So far, they hadn't shown up.

Ivor was everywhere, checking on his people, patrolling the guest wings' entrances, checking on more of his people outside. He'd bring them in soon because of the fog. Nothing had happened, no one had actually spotted any Dantes, but Ivor felt as if he were holding his breath, waiting for something to happen. The atmosphere was charged with death.

Beneath the hotel, deep underground where the darkness was as thick as the fog above, Eliot was drawn to the catacombs after depositing Jinxy's corpse. His terror was extreme, but he was so attracted, so captivated, that he'd sat down on the top step in the ovoid doorway that led to the chambers. He began to watch the blackness like a television, wanting to leave, but unable. Something called to him, but he refused to go down the stairs.

Meanwhile, Aardvark Wicket hid in a closet-sized nook in the spooky half of the Y. He sat cross-legged for comfort, but in his hand was his knife, open and ready. In the dim, dim light, he could just make out Eliot's silhouette fifteen feet farther down. He knew this stranger was waiting, so he would wait too. Unlike Eliot, Aardvark was only half-aware of the thickening of the darkness, the way it swallowed everything. But he did think that the lights were less illuminating than before. He chalked the sensation up to imagination. Also unlike Eliot, who was fully aware of the terror he felt, Aardvark had turned his fear into a funhouse feeling to be relished and enjoyed. He refused to accept that it could be more than that because he knew himself to be one of the few men who barely even knew the nature of fear. He had felt it only once or twice and knew that fear wasn't terror—it was fun. Still, he could not stop the calling of the voice inside his mind or will away the sensation of pockets of cold air sliding over his body like the hands of the dead.

At the Dantes' medical waste office in San Luis Obispo, Gabe Leoni was currently undergoing questioning by Nicholas Dante. He was bound to a chair and Nick brandished a scalpel as he asked his questions. So far, he had only trimmed Gabe's nails, taking the very tips of his fingers with them. It was what might be called a close shave, and Gabe Leoni knew the first knuckle joints would be next. Then the middle ones, and finally, the fingers would be removed entirely. His memory dragged forth the unwanted sound of a chicken leg being cut from the bird. Crunchy sounds. He prayed, knowing he couldn't talk his way out of this, that no matter what he said, he would sleep with the fishes. Unless Ori Darling somehow found out and came to the rescue. But in the gangster movies he loved, as in real life, pretty much nobody ever came to the rescue.

Back at the hotel, Natasha still steamed in her office, drinking, softly cursing, and trying to shed no tears for Douglas. But a few still escaped. She was trying to see truth in her uncle's suggestion that the Dantes were responsible for his death. She suspected that even though Ori thought it was his idea, Julian had planted it. It was the kind of idea that played directly into Ori's Godfather obsession, and she'd had to say so, calmly and clearly, so he would listen and consider her suspects as well.

She turned her thoughts to the Treasure and the prophecies. It would be a while before anything Julian had to tell would reach her, but it didn't matter; she could not accept at face value anything the trueborn said about the myth or anything else. Could there be truth to the myth as she knew it? Her family had guarded the alleged "Treasure" for years, ostensibly to keep their hotel safe from vampires who believed in their own vampiric god, and humans who wished to plunder pirate treasure. When they first moved in, she, Ivor, and Stephen had visited the catacombs, but hadn't ventured behind the door that sealed the deepest tomb. By unspoken agreement, they'd left it unmolested. To this day, they didn't speak of it.

What they had seen by lamplight were the brown bones of monks and the dust of vampires a thousand years gone. Unfortunately, it was pure fable that vampires instantly turned to dust when killed; it would have been convenient considering the Dante problem. It was true that they decomposed more rapidly—the longer you'd been on earth, the faster decomposition occurred—but they were in real, physical bodies, their own human bodies, however modified.

Perhaps being a vampire was the result of Julian's so-called "virus" or something like it. Anxious not to dwell on her anger, she considered the idea for a time. It wasn't really a virus, he'd said, but it spread like one once in a blue moon. Could it have something to do with the mating cycle of the trueborn? Could Julian be shedding the "virus" now because he was in his own cycle? He would deny it, naturally, but it was an interesting thought.

The fugitives, Lucy and Ivy, found egress from Julian's suite via the balcony, thus ensuring no cameras picked them up. Now they were on the modest second-story balcony directly below it. There were no lights or sounds coming from the adjoining room, so they lazed against the railing, facing the garden. A view? Nonexistent. So far, they had had a whispered discussion about the current identity of Julian's lost love and if he would change her; they decided to work on that mystery later. They also had to make a decision as to whether or not they should take Julian to a tunnel entrance, but they put that off too; it was just too serious to think about.

When they left Julian's, he'd given them an ash stake for protection and cautioned them to be quiet and wary because of the Dantes and their own stake-happy guards. That was what concerned them most now. They were listening for Dantes. Lucy was feeling lucky, and convinced Ivy that she did too. She was glad the fucking Dantes were hanging around. She and Ivy would catch themselves one, and that would redeem them with Natasha so that they wouldn't have to hide out forever.

"Did you hear that?" Lucy whispered.

Ivy, barely visible a foot away, nodded.

Something had run into something else, making a crunchy, crushy shrubbery sound. It happened again a moment later, and Lucy guessed it came from someone—it might be an animal, but she doubted it—lost in the fog maybe two or three little gardens away. "Let's go," she murmured. She found her way to the wall edge of the balcony and climbed over the railing, the stake held firmly in her mouth like a dog with a bone. It was a little weird, but what else could she do?

She shimmied down a decorative beam, past the balcony of the raised first floor of guest rooms, to the ground, just four feet farther. Her sister followed, stalling out by the first floor before dropping to the ground. "I think people are fucking in that room," she whispered.

Lucy reached out and put her hand lightly against Ivy's mouth. "Listen."

They waited, and before long there was another noise, this one like a flower pot getting kicked over. *A Dante!* "Come on," she murmured, taking her sister's hand.

It could be hard to judge where sounds came from in the fog, but Lucy was pretty sure they'd find their prize in a brick-floored garden full of potted plants just a little ways away. When she heard a short scraping sound—flower pot on brick—she was certain of it.

She and Ivy knew the gardens better than anyone except maybe Uncle Ori and Eliot, and she found her way slowly but relatively easily along the path. The sounds were small but frequent now. Whoever it was, was getting frustrated.

A few cautious steps brought them to the brick-paved garden. She paused. The Dante guy had moved out of the garden now, but she knew he was close. *Fucking fog.* She put Ivy's hand on her shoulder to guide her so that both her own hands were free. Without disturbing a single pot, they made it to the other side where she heard a shoe scuff no more than a yard in front of her. Lucy raised the stake and, in a flash, reached out with her other hand, feeling for the chest, yanking the Dante around to face her. She didn't know if she was dead on target, but she sure as hell was close enough to bring him down long enough to stake him right. She plunged the stake into the vampire's breast as hard as she could. The sharp tip went between the ribs, all the way through, until it veered when it smashed into a back rib. All this in the same instant as a muffled gunshot sounded, a bullet flew past her cheek, and the Dante wrenched out a piercing scream. Then, the body dropped and the night was utterly silent. "I didn't know men could scream like that," she said to Ivy, who was now close by her again. "You good?"

"Fine. Let's see who it is. I hope we got a real Dante brother, not just one of the guys working for them."

"Whatever. I'm just glad we got one." Lucy put her foot out, prodding the body until she found the head. "Here."

They crouched low over the head, and Ivy pulled a cigarette lighter from her jeans. "Be prepared!" She giggled and flicked on the flame.

They still couldn't see who it was. They lowered their own faces until they were inches above the dead guy. His lungs or something gurgled. Ivy held the flame over the face.

"Oh, shit. It's Dale!" Lucy yanked her sister up, and pulled out the stake, quickly wiping it on the security guard's clothes.

"What the fuck was he doing out here in this kind of fog?" Ivy bitched.

"Come on. We've gotta get out of here. They'll blame the Dantes." She was on the move, if at a crawl, dragging Ivy along.

"Fuck!" Ivy said. "It's his own fucking fault for being stupid enough to be out here. Hey, he's human. Maybe we could have a quick—"

"No way! Get your ass in gear! We'll go hang at Eliot's. He won't give us away."

"What if we run into someone?"

"I'll stake them."

"What if it's one of our guys?"

"They'll blame the Dantes. Now shut up."

"Yes, there is a reason for the Woman mentioned in the final prophesies," Julian told Ori and Stephen over drinks. He was beginning to wish he had never started plying them with the potion—it cost him too many bottles of good blood. He could have just leveled with them about the Treasure. Ori would have listened and everyone would be happy, and Julian could safely renew the spells that held the Father within the earth. But it wasn't that simple. The elixir was necessary because he had to take control away from the Darlings in order to take possession of this piece of land for once and for all. He cleared his throat. "The Woman's tale somehow got separated from the primary myth, lost to time. But originally, she was integral to the story."

He began reciting the primary myth, sticking to the details the twins had given him, adding little of his own detail. He finished and then said, "The Woman came before the myth. She was the reason Keliu attacked the Treasure."

He had admitted to the twins that he was Keliu in order to more easily manipulate them, but he would not tell these two. However, he would tell them other things he hadn't divulged to Lucy and Ivy.

"Keliu was the Treasure's own son. A prince of the land of Euloa. His father was the oldest known trueborn and claimed to be the first, spun of the elements by the hand of Nature Herself. The Treasure claimed he had no name that could be spoken safely. And so he was called 'My Lord,' even by Keliu's mother."

"He must have had a name," Ori said.

Julian smiled. "I'm sure he did, but he kept it a secret. No doubt the mysterious power it implied delighted him."

"You call this story a legend," Stephen said. "A myth. But you were born in Euloa, weren't you? Weren't you there?"

He nodded. "Yes. But it was legend by then. Now, let me tell you the rest: Keliu's father eventually began fancying himself a deity. It was something of a joke to the trueborns, but they were peaceful people and ignored his posturing since it was aimed at the humans. He demanded they worship him as their god and build temples dedicated to him for this purpose. He gave himself a new name and commanded they use it: Father. The Father.

"Keliu's father did not like the trueborns to create human vampires. He hated the creatures. No offense. Keliu knew this, and grew up under the prejudice. Meanwhile, the Father began going too far. First he demanded that the trueborns also address him as Father, just as the humans had been doing for many generations. He had always been a good ruler, amusing and charming and fair, so for a time they humored him. Then he told them he was their god as well as the humans', and had a grand temple built in the city. There was resentment, but the trueborns were set in their ways and wanted no upheaval, so they gave him lip service. Keliu watched all this as he grew up. He knew his father was no god.

"By this time, Keliu was a young man. He had moved into a beautiful home of his own, next to his father's palace. The time of his first mating was upon him, but he refused to wed the trueborn woman chosen for him. His father was furious, but did nothing, knowing that the mating time would continue for many years if it wasn't quenched. Eventually Keliu would give in.

"But Keliu had refused the trueborn woman because he was in love with another. A human woman. A very special one, with special blood, a truly royal human, you might say. But still a human."

Stephen smiled. "What was her name?"

"That has been lost." Julian realized now that he shouldn't have told the twins her name or that he was actually Keliu. It made it too easy for their smarter relatives to put it all together and figure out his true identity. But everything was fine. Before sending the girls down the balcony, he had carefully fired up their fear of their sister, reinforcing their belief that she would kill them. They would stay away from their family as long as necessary. He had virtually total control over them now. He was sure.

"Such fog," he said, glancing at the balcony doors. "The Woman. She has always been known as the Woman to my knowledge. Keliu knew enough to hide her from his father. He turned her into a human vampire and they loved one another for a little while. But she craved sunlight and society, the latter unavailable to her because she had to be hidden from Keliu's hateful father. She grew more and more depressed, until one dawn she sat on the beach and let the sun burn her life away.

"Keliu was devastated. He blamed himself for not standing up to his father, but he blamed his father even more. He despised the prejudice, and knew now that it extended far beyond the walls of the palace. Although the Father had set no rules, he made it obvious he thought human vampires were to be scorned, and some of this prejudice against hybrids naturally wormed its way into society. It was a mild prejudice, one that could be overcome. Keliu knew that. Trueborns who created them treated their human vampires well, changing over favored humans so that their relationships could continue for more than the brief span of a human life. But officially, in society, human vampires were ignored. They had no place. They were the equivalent of homosexuals in this society a decade or two ago. They were the ones relegated to the back of the bus. They were an embarrassment.

"Keliu decided to change this view. Still overwhelmed by the death of his lover, still deadly furious at his father, he stormed into the palace and told him about the woman that he loved. He told him everything.

"The Father reacted in a strange way. He did not kill Keliu, though he threatened him with death if he spoke of this to any others. He put guards on his son and turned him into a virtual prisoner in his own home. And he did something else, which, had he not been so young and passionate, Keliu might have foreseen. The Father began turning his own opinions into laws. First he ordered all trueborns to attend temple services in his honor, this to make them more aware of his power and control.

"Keliu's father was a charming trueborn, and that is the main reason he had ruled for so long, that and the fact that no one could disprove his origins. But now his lust for power took first place. He outlawed the very existence of human vampires. He declared those who created them criminals unless they handed over the human vampires to his law enforcers.

"Some human vampires escaped, usually aided by trueborn friends or humans. The Father had all the others killed, along with their trueborn protectors.

And he ordered the trueborns to show their gratitude for this act, to bow and kneel before him. That was how he lost the throne and his godhood." Julian smiled thinly. "He traded his charm for force. That is never a good idea."

"What happened? How did he end up here?"

"Keliu, as the Father's son, was approached to act as ruler and he accepted, immediately striking down all the laws his father had declared. He began putting things back the way they had been. His father hated him for it and tried to assassinate him. Keliu had him imprisoned.

"Hundreds of years passed and his father was released, allowed to live in a fine home away from the palace, along with a servant. He also always had a guard, more to keep him from attempting to kill his son again than to protect him from his own assassination. He stewed out there in the countryside, a power-hungry trueborn with no power, watching as his own son betrayed him.

"Keliu came upon the mating time again and he could sense the presence of a young human woman in Euloa. His love, the Woman, reincarnated. He set out to find her, and that's just what he did. It took time, but eventually he traveled to a farming village near his father's residence. Everyone knew of his arrival and ran to meet him, humans and trueborns alike. And that night, he found her, looking much as she had before, living in a small cottage with her parents. That night he administered the first bite. Everyone rejoiced for him. Almost everyone.

"The next night, hours after Keliu had given his love the second bite, just before the dawn, the Father killed his guard and rode to the cottage, where he savagely killed the young woman. He tore her to pieces, along with her parents."

Julian paused to refill their goblets. "Keliu found out at dusk and, cold with fury, rode alone to his father's house to kill him. He found only the dead guard. His next stop was the docks, where he discovered that his father's servant had loaded a recently acquired schooner with trunks and a coffin and set sail well before noon. His father had fled, assuredly to this land, which was very close by.

"Although he had pledged to kill his father, Keliu stayed in Euloa until the sorcerers warned that the small continent would soon be destroyed. He and many others moved to the east coast of this land, and then on to many other continents, the humans seeding the planet with the beginnings of many cultures. I find that fascinating."

"How did Keliu find his father?" Stephen asked.

"With great difficulty. They had a number of run-ins, which was to be expected since each was out to kill the other. The Father was easy to find because he established little kingdoms—goddoms, if you will—wherever he went. There are many small stories of the battles of father and son, but there's time for those another night. Suffice it to say that Keliu, who lived in a very small group of trueborns, humans, and human vampires, learned much sorcery from a master who stayed with him for many eras, until the Father killed the master. That is one of the stories. Back to the point, the more Keliu learned, the more he realized how hard it would be to actually kill the Father, who also had such skills. He learned ways that might bind him away from the world in case he could not kill him.

"Keliu found him living with—of all things—a group of human vampires about a thousand years ago. He found them living like animals in the edifice that once stood here. They had left Euloa long before any trueborns did and had flourished for a while. But now their castle was crumbling. The Father took over as king and god and guided them into better times. He was always at his best when being benevolent.

"Keliu came to kill his father and . . . You know the rest."

"And the Woman?" Ori asked. "Was she reborn?"

"Yes, many times, and when she appeared as a young woman at the right moment in time, Keliu would usually find her. And she would die. This spans thousands of years. She died by the Father's hand more than once, and by her own even more often. And so she is the third prophecy. She will arrive before the resurrection of the Treasure." He sipped a few drops and looked directly at Stephen. "Perhaps she already has. If you believe any of this."

"Julian, let's say it is true, just for argument's sake," Ori said. "The trueborn who arrives would be you?"

"I don't know. Perhaps. Perhaps not. The resurrection may be years away."

"Are you Keliu?" Stephen asked abruptly.

Julian laughed. "It's a story, my boy. A story. Remember, I told you? This all began before I was born. If it ever really happened."

Stephen nodded. "From what you tell us, the version of the myth portraying the Treasure as a vampire killer is the true one."

"Yes. And if it is true, Keliu was the one who championed human vampires. His motives, I imagine, were not so much philanthropic as selfish. It would not have happened had he not loved a human."

Stephen nodded thoughtfully. "How can she be recognized? The Woman of the prophecy. And why would she come here if Keliu wasn't here as well?"

"I don't know if anyone can recognize her, if she indeed exists. Keliu would know and the Treasure would be aware of her—"

A muffled scream brought them to their feet. Stephen was out on the balcony instantly, but there was nothing to see. Or hear. He came back in. "Let's go, Uncle."

Julian watched them hurry from the apartment. He had been going to tell them that the Father had also tried to commit genocide, tracking down and killing trueborns who did not believe he was their god. He'd gotten most of them. There were perhaps a hundred still in vampiric form spread all over the world. In killing the rest, he had murdered Keliu's subjects—the people who had named him king. They had to be avenged.

Christopher Dante heard all the scuffling, the gunshot, and the scream, followed by feminine voices, unintelligible. Sadly, he knew it meant that the Darlings had gotten one of his vampires. *Shit.* As balcony doors opened, he was moving again, hopefully in the direction of the work shed.

39

Amanda, just off work, had retreated to her room to avoid the questions and teasing that would inevitably come from Carol Anne and the others regarding Stephen's long presence at her desk tonight. She stood on her balcony, letting the fog seep into the pores of her face. If she held out her hand, she couldn't see it until it was a foot away. She loved it. Breathing in the moist cool clouds calmed her body and mind, and helped her to will away the day.

A scream broke her calm and sent her pulse racing. It sounded male and far away. Her balcony faced the front of the hotel, but the sound came from the garden side—probably; the fog was tricky—assuming it came from the hotel grounds at all. Amanda had to find out what was going on. She reentered her room, swathed in puffs of fog. Shutting the door, she locked it, pushed her feet into her black penny loafers, grabbed her keys, and left Coastal Eddie babbling on about oil spills on the Kansas coast.

Downstairs, the small crew manning the desks was looking curiously toward the garden doors, but not venturing near them, probably because an employee, a big burly guy bulging in his suit, stood in front of them, his arms crossed like the Jolly Green Giant, though he probably didn't say, "Ho, ho, ho."

She sure wasn't going to get past him, so she went around the long reception desk, and worked her way back to the service corridor. No one was around, so she stole down to a back door and tried her employee's key card on the slider lock. The mechanism clicked, glowed green, and out she went, into the gauze-and-cotton night.

As long as she moved slowly and shuffled her feet, it was fairly easy to stay on the straight cement walkway to the northeast corner. There, after listening carefully for a moment, she turned west and followed the walk along the hotel's edge. To her left were rooms, to her right, the gardens. After a moment, she heard muffled voices on the garden side. They were coming closer. Quickly, she crouched down in the bushes on the hotel side and waited, heart pounding. After a lifetime, a tall form appeared, pushing something—a wheelbarrow, she realized when it was close enough to see. She clapped her hand over her mouth as the barrow turned onto the walk and stopped. Inches from her eyes lay a body, its chest slathered in blood. It was Dale, the weird security guy. His eyes stared sightlessly at her, so clear that she thought he must be alive. But his mouth lolled open and blood, still wet, ribboned down over lips and chin, down his neck, where it met the chest blood. *Bring out your dead!* John Cleese's voice called in her head. *Bring out your dead!*

"Are you sure you want me to leave him outside, Uncle?" The voice came from the man pushing the barrow. *Ivor!*

"Only for the time it takes you to change out of

your suit," Ori said. "Then I think the best thing to do, considering this fog, is bag him and store him in the tunnels for the day."

The tunnels. They really existed.

Ori continued. "We'll have our day crew dig a grave out near the work shed; then we'll put him in it tomorrow at dusk."

"Why can't we just put him in the lions' garden with the others?" Ivor asked. "It would be easy and over and done with tonight. We wouldn't have to open the tunnels."

"He's right." Amanda cringed as she recognized Stephen's voice.

"Well, it's rather disrespectful," said Ori. "After all, he's like family. On the other hand, we could do that and put him in a better place when things settle down." There was a pause. "All right, wheel him back out there. Nipper and Snapper can do the dirty work, but make sure they're safe while they dig."

Nipper and Snapper? Who were Nipper and Snapper? She probably didn't want to find out.

"I'll guard them myself," said Ivor. "Send me Dilly for backup, please, Uncle." The wheelbarrow creaked, and almost hit Amanda as Ivor turned it back the way they had come.

"Come, Stephen," said Ori. "We'll locate Dilly. Then we must consider a course of action regarding the Dantes."

"At least Natasha will believe you now."

Ori chuckled. "If we're lucky."

They moved slowly away, in the direction Amanda had come. *Oh, great.* Amanda remained crouched in the bushes, wondering if she'd be there all night. With Dilly away from the front doors, maybe she could just stroll in that way, right in plain sight. She could say she had just gone out to get some air. That was probably safer than trying to sneak back in. She would wait until Dilly passed by, then go for it. A tear ran down her cheek. *Stephen. What are you doing?*

"Amanda, are you working overtime?"

Headed for the elevators, she turned and saw Stephen coming toward her. She hesitated, wanting to run away but knowing she couldn't. When he joined her, she said, "No, I'm on my way up now." *Please, just go away.* Her mind swam.

"Have you been outdoors?"

"Why?" she asked, startled. *He saw me in the bushes!* She crossed her arms to hide her trembling hands.

He studied her. "Your hair."

"Oh, uh, yeah." She touched her drooping tresses, felt the dampness. "I stepped out front for a few minutes to get some air."

"More than a few minutes, from the looks of you." His voice was light, his face serious.

Dad always said to take the bull by the horns. She decided on just one horn. "I thought I heard someone scream and I stayed out, listening. I lost track of time." She paused. "Did you hear it?"

A long pause. "Yes, I did. There was an incident. And that means you don't wander around at night by yourself, okay? Not outdoors."

"What happened? Was someone hurt?" She put on her innocent face.

"A trespasser attacked one of our guards. He doesn't look good."

That's for sure! "The guard or the trespasser?"

"The guard."

"Did you catch the trespasser?"

"We're looking for him. Look, why don't you come up to my apartment for a little while? We can have a drink and talk privately."

That was a good idea since she suspected the staff spent most of its free time eavesdropping on guests and one another. The idea of seeing Stephen's apartment set all her chimes ringing, but one off-tone clang spoiled it: the dead body. *Well, he wasn't the murderer.* She was fairly sure of that.

"Well, what do you say?" He smiled. "I promise not to bite."

"Sure. Why not?" She couldn't believe she'd said it. It wasn't just men who thought with their sex organs.

Stephen's apartment was not what Amanda had expected. Stark modern furniture, black leather upholstery, very masculine. Lots of metal and glass. Low jazz on the stereo. Cool, darkish colors. That was what she thought she'd see. Instead, there was an eclectic collection of antiques, books, and art, comfortable furniture, and an entertainment center, surrounded by loaded bookshelves. Magazines weren't perfectly neatly stacked, every corner meeting, and the throw pillows on the couch were all at one end. A couple of empty V-8 cans sat on an end table. Stephen suddenly seemed more human. In his dark suit, with his perfect hair and handsome face, he was intimidating. But now she knew he liked to sprawl on the couch and watch TV, just like other people. The music that played in the background was Civil War-era stuff like you'd hear on PBS. Strange but very pleasant. Haunting and haunted with flutes and violins.

It was nearly two A.M., and she knew she should leave, but when he returned from the kitchen with two fresh drinks—another martini for her and a Bloody Mary for him—she decided to stay a little longer. She was more at ease now, thanks to the alcohol. They had talked seriously for a while about hotels and crime. He'd told her about a rival named Dante who sent spies around. Corporate espionage could be deadly; that was as close to an explanation of the dead guard as he came. Something didn't ring quite true, and she refrained from asking what hotel Mr. Dante owned. She also kept silent on the matter of police involvement. All in all, conversation aside, she was immensely attracted to him, but afraid too. *What the hell are you doing here?*

Now, he sat next to her on the couch and they toasted. "Maybe I should have tried a Bloody Mary," she said as he swirled a leafy little celery stalk in his red-colored drink. "It looks tasty."

He looked at her from under his eyebrows, his face unreadable. "It is. I've just run out of tomato juice, but I'll mix you one next time you visit."

She sipped her perfect martini, feeling its warmth send little swirls of pleasure down through her belly to her crotch. She adjusted herself on the couch, daring to end up an inch closer to him. He responded with his own inch. There were four to go, but he said, "Just a minute," and took two remotes from the end table. With one, he started a crackling blaze in the fireplace, and said, "I love this century." With the other, he changed CDs. "Chopin," he said as graceful piano notes trickled into her ears. "Nocturnes. Fitting background for the vampire tale I promised you. You would like to hear it now, wouldn't you?"

She looked into his eyes. *I'd like to make love now, please.* Blushing, she said, "Yes, I would." *This man is dangerous, maybe a criminal . . .*

He told the tale of a trueborn king, starting with his arrival on the coast. He told of Keliu and the battle, and ended with the destruction of the castle. "And so the vampires left this place. Except for the one buried in a deep tomb beneath us." He smiled. "Well? What do you think?"

"So the tunnels are real?"

"Yes. But keep it a secret, and never tell anyone the story."

"Why not?"

He ran a finger down her cheek. "Because it's a secret. Now tell me if you liked it."

She smiled. "I did. But there's no romance. You need a romance in a vampire story."

He hesitated. "Actually, there is a little adjunct to the story, one I just heard for the first time."

She listened to the prequel, and something about it chilled her.

"You're shivering," he said. "Do you want me to turn up the heat?"

"No. I'm fine. But that's a horrible story. The poor woman, dying over and over again. She didn't love Keliu, I don't think. At least not enough to give up the sunlight for him."

He came close as he spoke, then pulled back. "Excuse me just a moment." He rose, was gone for about a minute, then sat down again, taking care of those last four inches.

She could smell peppermint on his breath and that erased any doubts. Thoughtfulness like that deserved a kiss. *Even if he's a killer?* Without a word, she turned her head toward his. They hesitated, lips a hairsbreadth apart. Amanda savored that instant, letting it last as long as she could. Then his lips met hers, warm and welcoming. At first, it was an innocent kiss, and she felt him begin to tremble slightly, the same as she. She began to ache for him. He ran his fingers through her hair and held the back of her head, fingers splayed, trapping her.

On fire, pulsing and aching, she opened her mouth to him, and he immediately began to lick the inner edges of her lips, lapping softly with the tip of his tongue. She started to respond, but he stopped her tongue with his, making it clear he wanted to explore every inch of her first. He flicked over her teeth, and she felt one of his for an instant, a sharp sensation that lasted a zillionth of a second. His tongue kissed the insides of her cheeks, then lifted her tongue and poked underneath.

Amanda's heart pounded, her body ached. Finally, he twirled his tongue around hers and led it into his mouth. As she began her own explorations, he trembled harder. He acted as she had, holding his own tongue back until she finished exploring. Finally, his tongue met hers to swirl and dance together. When his hand cupped her breast, she had an orgasm.

"Oh, God!"

He pulled back. "What—did you—did you?"

"Yeah. Want to see me do it again?"

"I do. Excuse me just a moment, won't you? Don't move. I just have to—I had a lot to drink."

"You have to use the bathroom," she supplied.

He smiled, closed mouth, his eyes intense. "Yes. I'll be right back."

"I'll be waiting."

He left the room, and Amanda thought about going into the kitchen for water, but then she saw his glass still held a swallow of watery Bloody Mary.

She picked it up, put it to her lips, and poured it down.

Blood! Gagging, she dropped the glass. She jumped up, horrified. No wonder he'd brushed his teeth. He'd been drinking—*Oh, God*—blood. Trying not to retch, she turned to leave. Stephen appeared.

"What's wrong?"

"Nothing. I'm just not ready . . . I have to go. . . ."

She saw him look down and notice the overturned glass. His eyes traveled back and forth. "Amanda." His eyes brimmed.

"You're a pervert," she said.

"No. I'm not a pervert."

"You're sick. No wonder you told me that vampire story. No wonder you asked me why I liked them. You're one of those nuts who wants to be one so bad that he drinks blood!"

He started to protest, then just stared at her.

"I have to leave now," she said.

"I know. May we talk tomorrow? I can explain."

"You don't need to explain. We're employer and employee. That's all we are and all we ever were or will be. Understand? I don't date freaks."

As she left the apartment, she heard him say, "I'm sorry."

Julian, taking a stroll through the lobby at the quietest hour of the night, saw Amanda come out of the mezzanine door that led to most of the Darlings' quarters. She moved down the stairs, walking rapidly, trying to look businesslike, but he could see the tears on her cheeks and a smear of red next to her mouth. *Stephen! I will kill you for this.* Suddenly, the mating urge sparked harder. It wasn't a literal urge to mate, although that too would happen. This aspect of the urge, brought to life by her appearance, was concerned with jealousy and a need to protect his property.

As she neared, he stepped into her path. Using all his charm he said, "Amanda? Are you hurt?"

"No. Excuse me."

"You have a drop of blood by your mouth." He gently wiped it off with his finger. "See?"

She stared at it, looked hard at him, and said, "It's tomato juice. Please excuse me." She hurried away.

Watching her retreat, he licked his finger and knew that Amanda had lied for Stephen Darling. Women did that for their lovers. If that mere human vampire had touched her, defiled her in any way, he would disembowel him and leave him hanging by a hook while rats nibbled the intestines that dragged on the ground. Only then would he kill him, waiting until the instant before he began to heal. It was what he deserved.

Enraged, Julian returned to his apartment and drank a liter of blood. That calmed him a little, and he realized that Jinxy ought to be back with a human by now. He needed fresh blood. He paced, waiting for his servant.

"Remember, fog or no fog, KNDL radio will be at the boardwalk tonight," Coastal Eddie said. "Come and see me, friends and insomniacs. I'll answer your questions and tell you no lies."

No lies? That would be a nice change. Amanda lay in the dark, unable to sleep. *Why would Stephen drink blood?* The question haunted her. She wanted to get up and confront him, right now, but she was afraid of the answer. How could she have ever gone to his apartment after what she'd seen in the garden? How could she have kissed him? *Drinking blood. Oh, God.* Her stomach churned even though she had vomited everything up an hour ago. She should have known Stephen was too good to be true. *A freak. A goddamned freak.*

"Let me ask you this, dear listeners. Do you really know the one you love? Think about it and give me a call. Wives or girlfriends of serial killers are often in the dark. They don't know they love a monster. Do you love a monster in disguise? Does he bring you flowers and whisper sweet nothings? Does he take the kids to ballgames? Does he strangle hookers?" Eddie paused. "Sometimes people are funny that way."

"Oh, shut up." She switched off the radio and stared at the ceiling. If she closed her eyes, she'd see the dead man's eyes. Or Stephen sipping his drink, stirring its celery stick, swirling ice in blood. *But he couldn't be . . .* What couldn't he be? Evil? A criminal? A freak? She didn't know the answers. Talk about conflicted. She didn't want to believe any of it. She wanted him to explain it all and make it okay for them to be together. Maybe, she thought, not for the first time since going to bed, maybe it wasn't blood. Maybe it was some weird spice. Or medicine. She fell into fitful sleep as she tried to find an excuse that would make it all go away.

Julian, who had let himself into her room while she was showering, watched Amanda. She made little noises in her sleep, whimpers, and twitched fitfully with nightmares. Finally, toward dawn, she settled into a deeper sleep and he stepped from the shadowed corner.

Talai. He mouthed the word as he bent over her. His long fingers came out to caress her face, but he stopped himself. She was a sensitive and might feel the touch as more than a gentle breeze. He contented himself with staring at her, studying every curve of her face, noting the way her eyelids fit over her eyes, so like Talai's. Her cheekbones, her lips, he could see her former selves in Amanda's face.

She sighed in her sleep and shivered. Julian reached down and pulled the folded bedspread up to cover her better. He thought about the first taste of blood he had taken before. It was different from any other, with a magic of its own. Now, he would administer another bite. The second of the three it would take to change her. The first time may have left her a little tired, hardly enough to notice. After the second bite, she would feel tired and avoid sunlight, but revive with the coming of dusk. After the third, she would be his creation. Ordinarily, he would stretch the bites out over a week or two, making it easier for her to adjust, but now he needed to finish it quickly so that she was better protected against the Father's anger. He had heard the voice in his head several times in the last few hours. The Father was ready to rise.

Julian brushed Amanda's hair from her neck and watched the pulse of blood beneath her skin. In one fluid movement, he lowered his mouth to her neck, sensed the arterial flow, and made the bite. After waiting a second or two for the anesthetic to be secreted, he drank from her. Hot blood, spicy-sweet—*Talai's blood*—flowed into his mouth, exciting him in a way he had not experienced for five hundred years. Amanda, soundly asleep, made a pleasurable sound and her hips moved slightly in response to his bite. He closed his eyes and lost himself in her, finally forcing himself to withdraw before taking too much.

After dabbing a few drops of elixir on her wounds, he lingered over her, watching her sleep. The roiling hatred he felt for the Father and his fury with Stephen Darling remained in the background, serving to increase his passion for Amanda.

40

By noon, the fog had cleared, but the twins were stuck in Eliot's stinky little house, wide awake and thirsty. They'd decided to stay because it had been too risky to try to get back to the hotel without being seen. And where would they go anyway? Julian's suite was the only safe place they could think of, and they were tired of hanging around with him all the time. He was great to have around when you needed blood or help and stuff, but he was always so fucking serious. Lucy needed a break.

So they'd spent the night sampling Eliot's considerable blood supply and watching a *Brady Bunch* marathon. When that ended around three in the morning, they watched a two-hour infomercial on how to make money raising beavers in your basement. Or something like that.

The weird thing was that Eliot had never shown up. He should have come in before dawn. He must've gotten caught somewhere and was holed up for the day.

Ivy came out of the kitchen with a Mason jar full of red. "I think I found some more blood." She handed it to Lucy.

"It says *Ragu* on the label. And it looks like there's chunks in it."

"Clots?" Ivy asked hopefully. "I like clots."

"I don't think so." Lucy twisted the top off and smelled it. "It's garden style spaghetti sauce."

"Well, we could pretend it's blood. Spaghetti sauce is good. We could like have a tea party, you know, like when we were little."

Lucy looked her up and down. "You're a feeb." She stuck her finger in the sauce, her nail spearing a fleshy chunk of tomato, then sucked it into her mouth. "Not bad. A little heavy on the garlic. Taste." She thrust the bottle into Ivy's hands, but Ivy didn't grasp it quick enough and it crashed, dumping the thick, gooey contents on the rug. "Idiot," she said.

Ivy giggled. "It looks like somebody forgot to use a tampon."

Lucy cracked up. "Come on. Let's go see if he's got any bottles stashed in the bedroom."

She led the way, opened the door, and immediately upon entering got that creepy feeling that she'd had in the tunnels and that she sometimes felt around Julian.

"What's wrong in here?" Ivy murmured from the doorway.

"Don't know." Lucy motioned her into the room. "Just start looking." She went to the bed, which had stiff, creased sheets so dirty that she couldn't tell if they'd been white or blue or paisley. They looked like gray wax paper, but they smelled a lot worse. She got down on her knees and raised the edge of a filthy blanket. There were a few porn mags under there and a crusty-looking butt plug, but that was it. She dropped the blanket in disgust.

"Lucy," Ivy said, her voice muffled.

Lucy turned. Her sister was in the closet. "What?"

"Shit, look at this. Just look." Ivy stepped back and Lucy entered the closet. It was fucking scary in there.

"What the fuck? It's a hole. Ivy?"

"Hang on, I'm getting a flashlight."

She returned momentarily, and Lucy shined the dull beam into the hole. "Fuck. It really is. It's a tunnel opening. There's a ladder and everything."

"Do you think anybody else knows?"

Lucy backed out of the closet and turned off the light. "No. I think this is Eliot's little secret. Shit. He probably takes all his empties down there." She grinned. "Now we've got something on him."

"And we can show it to Julian because Natasha doesn't know! It won't be breaking our promise."

"Sure. Tonight. It'll really get his rocks off." She snorted. "You think he's even got rocks?"

"I don't want to know bad enough to look." Ivy giggled. "You think Eliot's down there?"

Lucy closed the closet door and went to a bureau. "Yeah, he's down there." She opened a drawer and started throwing stuff on the floor. There were wads of clothing, a coil of rope, some more whackzines, assorted knives, three bloody bras, and a dead snake rotting beneath it all, so old it didn't stink anymore. The next drawer yielded more bras—souvenirs, she figured—comic books, a Danielle Steele novel, some pants, and a blob of unwashed socks. But beneath those, at the very bottom of the drawer, lay two bottles of blood. They weren't labeled, but they were tightly sealed and would do the trick.

"Here we go," Lucy said. "We'll wait until it's dark, then go get Julian."

"Maybe we should try to nap," Ivy suggested.

"Do you feel tired?"

"No."

"Then let's watch television. Maybe some of those autopsy shows are on."

Amanda awoke from a sound sleep and lay stretching luxuriously in bed, letting herself doze a little, nuzzling comfortably into her sheets, a ray of sunlight warm across her exposed arm. She'd slept better than she ever had, with pleasantly erotic dreams of Stephen.

"Stephen!" She bolted upright and looked frantically around the room as memories flooded back. *The blood!* She slumped back, depressed. *You sure can pick 'em.*

She had hoped her bad luck with men was over, but obviously, she still had the touch. Her last boyfriend, Daniel, had seemed to be a great guy until the night he'd begged her to pee on him. Before that was Chip, who'd loved to come over and hang out at her parents' house. It was a little annoying, but he was so much fun, so sensitive, a great listener, a guy with a sense of humor. Unfortunately, it turned out that the reason he liked to come over was because he had a crush on her father, which became painfully evident one summer's day when they went sailing. They were both a little drunk and having a great time. Amanda was getting a big kick out of watching the two most important men in her life bonding, but right about then Chip asked Dad if he wanted help hoisting his mainsail.

She'd had a few normal boyfriends before that, but they were young and pimply and so was she.

But now Stephen, the first man she'd found attractive since breaking up with Daniel a year and a half ago, had proven to be the worst of the bunch.

Blood-drinking definitely beat golden showers in the freakiness factor.

"Christ." That was what she told her watch when she saw it was past one o'clock. She got out of bed and took another shower and brushed her teeth twice, then dressed casually in jeans and a tank under a long-sleeved chambray shirt. Examining the circles under her eyes, she sighed and decided she'd feel better after she ate.

Her phone rang and she stared at it then finally picked it up. *What if it's Stephen?* She sucked it up and said, "Hello?"

"Amanda? It's Carol Anne. What time do you want to leave for the boardwalk?"

"Carol Anne, why don't you just go with the others? I'm not in the mood."

"There aren't any others yet. I still have to ask Tyler."

"Ask him. I'll work his shift. You don't need me."

"Yes, I do! He can get somebody else to cover the desk. You know he can. I want you both to come!"

"The fog will probably be bad tonight. I'd rather not drive in it."

"Then I'll drive," Carol Anne chirped. "My car's at the mechanic. I can drive yours. I mean, it's not a stick or anything, is it?"

"I'll drive." Amanda heard herself say the words. *Shit. I fell right in.* "What time?"

"I dunno. Have you had lunch?"

"No. I haven't even had breakfast."

The girl's voice turned all-knowing. "Late night with Stephen?"

"No," she replied calmly. "I just couldn't fall asleep."

A snicker. "Because you were thinking about Stephen."

"Drop it or I won't go to the boardwalk," she said sternly.

A moment of silence on the other end. Then: "Okay. Come down and have lunch with me. I won't bug you. I promise."

Famous last words: *I won't bug you.* Lunch with Carol Anne was only tolerable because the blonde really wanted to go to the boardwalk and Amanda reminded her that she had the only car. To her credit, Carol Anne tried to keep Stephen out of the conversation, and once Amanda steered her onto the subject of Tyler's affections, she stayed there. And stayed there. And stayed there. Carol Anne had a bad case of motormouth. Amanda wanted to install a muffler.

"Let's go find Tyler," she said, laying her napkin on her plate as she stood. "If he can go, he can drive you."

"And you!"

"If we both can take the night off, I'll take my own car in case you two want some alone time." She made herself smile.

Carol Anne dimpled up. "Come with me to the lobby. He's filling in a half-shift for Jaimie. I'll ask him now."

"And you want me there why?"

"So it doesn't sound like a date."

"Okay. Fine. Let's go."

Tyler was signing for a beach-ball sized square box when they approached. After the deliveryman left, Tyler hefted the package, avoiding their eyes.

"Hi, Tyler," Carol Anne said.

He blushed. Time hadn't healed much yet. "Hi."

"What's that?" Amanda asked.

"I don't know." He sounded relieved. "It's for Ori." He picked up the phone and called the upstairs office, then stood and picked up the box. "He wants me to bring it up now. He's in today."

"Um, Tyler?" Carol Anne stepped in front of him, all powder puffs and popcorn.

"Yes?"

"We're going to the boardwalk tonight. Coastal Eddie's going to be there. And a cool band. Do you want to come?"

"I—"

"Jaimie will cover for you," Amanda said.

"Who else is going?"

"I dunno. People."

"Well, probably not." He looked at them, embarrassment on the wane. "But maybe. I'll tell you later, after Jaimie gets back. I've got to get this upstairs." He took off with the box.

"There," said Amanda. "That wasn't so hard, was it?"

Carol Anne giggled. "I've gotta go decide what to wear. You want to help?"

"Not today. I have some errands to run."

Carol Anne started to turn, then paused. "What are you going to wear?"

"Probably what I'm wearing now."

The girl looked her up and down like Amanda was nuts, and said, "Whatever," and flounced away.

After Tyler Shane left his office, Ori studied the package on his desk. It had no return address and was postmarked in San Luis Obispo. He considered calling Stephen and Natasha—if he was up, they would be too—before opening it, but decided that if it was a bomb, he'd rather leave them out of it.

He used a folding knife to slit the packing tape, then opened the flaps, revealing nothing but foam peanuts. He brushed away a little of the packing material and saw the top of a circular gold-toned handle. He grasped it and pulled, revealing two inches of staff attached to the handle. Cold radiated from it. Then black hair, vapor curling off it like smoke, came into view, and Ori pulled whatever it was the rest of the way out. Frozen for neatness and with the handle screwed in for convenience, the head of Gabe Leoni hung before him. *Poor fool.* A rat was stuffed in the mouth, its ass poking out, the frozen tail trailing down his stubbly chin. The message was clear.

"Bada bing," Ori said with finality. *At least they didn't stick it in my bed.*

Natasha, at her desk with her feet up, had sedated herself with blood since leaving the family meeting the night before. It helped for a time, but her supply was running low, so she'd tapered off and now anger and appetites were rising. If blood could boil (actually it could, she'd tried it in a hot toddy once and didn't recommend it), hers was at full-steam boogie. She picked the small vial of elixir from her desk and held it up to the light, studied its amber purity, then unstoppered it and put a single drop on her tongue. She thought it might have a soothing influence. Anyway, it couldn't hurt.

Between Ori and Stephen, they'd convinced her that Dante involvement in the murders was at least a possibility. That question, among others, had occupied her mind for hours. She forced herself to think instead of letting the rage build over Douglas's demise. She took another drop before closing the bottle. It seemed warming, it made her feel better. Hunger surged.

Looking up at the monitor covering the little lobby outside her office, she saw Ori's door open. Tyler Shane stepped out. She swung her feet off her desk and stood. Tyler was so easy to hypnotize. She could just call him in for a moment and have a quiet taste. No one would ever know.

You can't do that. It's against your own rules! But she watched herself go to her door and open it just as Tyler was about to leave the lobby. "Tyler, could you come in here a moment?"

"Sure." He grinned, his eyes taking a little trip up her body to her face. They took a short trek back to her breasts, then came back up and stayed there. He walked briskly through the door she held open for him.

The look he had given her excited her, but made her wonder if her previous hypnosis had taken as well as it should. Shutting the door, she realized that it was probably only a leftover reaction to his use of the elixir. *Oh, hell.* The bottle was still on her desk.

But he didn't give it a second look. "What can I do for you?"

Tell him something and send him on his way. But hunger surged and he looked so tasty. In more ways than one, she thought, remembering how he had reacted to the potion. "Sit down, Tyler. Let's have a little talk."

"Okay."

He sat before her desk, and she saw him notice the amber bottle. "It's a skin-toner," she said, sitting on the edge of the desk. Taking the vial, keeping her eyes on him, she opened it and let a drop fall on her finger. "It's wonderful for your skin," she murmured, seeing he was already falling under her spell. "Here, try this." She put her finger to his lip and lightly ran it from one corner of his mouth to the other.

"It's warm." His eyes glazed a little.

She applied one more drop for good measure, this time letting her finger linger, the nail between his lips. "What do you think?"

"I—I think it's nice. You're nice."

Natasha slipped the vial into the desk drawer, leaning so that Tyler got a long look at her thigh when her dress rode up. When she turned back to him, she slid herself forward a few inches, giving him a clear view up her dress. "Tyler?"

He looked up, his nostrils flaring, his face flushed. No words came. Partly mesmerized, partly stunned, and obviously affected by the drops she'd administered, he did nothing. She slid off the desk and stood directly before him, then reached under her skirt and slowly slid her panties down around her ankles and stepped out of them. Tyler trembled, his breathing loud. She took his hand and brought it up against her pubic hair, then took it away again. "Come with me," she ordered, going to the door. He stood and followed. Before they left the office, she said, "If we run into anyone, you're going to help me move a piece of furniture in my apartment. We won't tell them what you're really going to do. Or what I'm going to do to you. Do you understand?"

"I do."

41

It was another hour until dusk and Lucy and Ivy were really getting weirded out at Eliot's house. They'd found another two bottles of blood, so it wasn't that. It was the tunnel entrance, Lucy was pretty sure. It was letting something out. Bad-vibes-type stuff. At first, they only felt it in the bedroom, but now, hours later, even with the door closed, it had seeped out here. It made the lights less bright and the air feel thick.

"We should close the hole," Ivy said, doing her mind-reading act. "That would fix it."

"But if Eliot's down there, we might lock him in."

"We'll just close it until Julian comes. He can open it again."

"No. It's gotta be some secret mechanism. We'd better leave it alone."

Lucy made a face. "Are you gonna go down there with him?"

"Well, we were down there the other day."

"It was creepy then. Now it's way worse."

Lucy nodded. She didn't want to go, that was for sure. But she didn't know how to get out of it without looking like a weenie.

"We could show him how to get in and then ditch. He should know his way around. At least if he's really Keliu." Ivy cast a troubled look toward the bedroom door.

"Well, maybe. But don't you sorta want to see what's down there? I mean, like you say, he's supposed to be Keliu. That means he can protect us."

"But will he?"

Lucy didn't answer, but looked back to the TV and wondered if he would.

Earlier in the afternoon, Julian left a phone message for the still-sleeping Dante brothers, reminding them that a big blood order—a huge order—was being delivered to the Candle Bay Hotel. Shortly after that, he went to Ori's office to discuss ways to destroy the Dantes. Julian was having a good time. The Father's voice continued to intrude on his thoughts, but with the will only available to a trueborn, he banished it from his consciousness. He refused to worry about his missing servant for the time being.

Amanda was plagued by something ominous, but she didn't know what. It felt like something was about to happen, and she imagined several times that she felt a voice calling to her. *Maybe you're losing your mind!* She kept her brain busy thinking about the tunnels Stephen had mentioned, thinking how much fun they'd be to explore. *Fun? Are you nuts?* Nonetheless, she felt drawn to them.

After parting ways with Carol Anne, Amanda spent some time wandering the gardens, trying to sort things out, and half convinced herself for a while that it wasn't blood that she had tasted in Stephen's glass. That was absurd. *Blood?* Try as she might, however, she couldn't repress completely.

The sun was warm and bright and she felt tired despite her long sleep. Several times on her walk, she passed the unfinished lions' garden, but didn't dare linger in case she was being watched. The freshly turned soil fascinated her. The thought that there were bodies down there made her stomach turn, so she went back to thinking about her relationship with Stephen, but coming to no conclusions, she went in and swam for a while. She tried the sauna, but felt like it was suffocating her, and she ended up back in the pool to cool off. There wasn't a twin in sight, and for that, she was grateful.

Now, standing on her balcony watching the beginnings of the sunset, the first rays of peach and cherry and gold glowing in the clouds, she began to feel refreshed and more alive than she had all day long. She felt strong, and decided that she would confront Stephen sometime tonight. But first, the boardwalk. Going out tonight was beginning to sound like fun again, even if the fog was already starting to gather. It was time to get ready.

Stephen spent a sleepless day sitting in the dark and drinking while his mind crawled with contradictory thoughts and feelings. Risking the family's safety was unforgivable. He knew he never should have told Amanda the story of the Treasure. What had possessed him he didn't know. And leaving his cocktail glass behind was utterly thoughtless; he should have taken it with him when he left the room. He would have to try to mesmerize Amanda again because, if she remembered any of what had happened and Natasha found out, she would kill her on the spot.

Hypnotizing Amanda with his bite was a pleasant task, but the trouble was, he wanted her to remember what he'd told her. He wanted to share everything with her, including his vampiric nature. He wanted to change her and keep her with him for all time. Intellectually, he understood that the so-called virus was clouding his judgment and that he dared not act on his impulses. And because he loved her, he would give her a choice. *If it ever gets that far.* Her horror over the blood last night was not a good omen.

Love. The feeling amazed him. It wasn't caused by the virus, he was sure of that. It was real, a solid knowledge, a feeling so certain that it stood up to every attempt he made to write it off. When the virus ran its course, his love for her would remain. Perhaps then a relationship would be possible.

For now, keeping her out of Julian's hands was the pressing concern. Julian would make her into a vampire whether she wanted it or not and take her as his property, as only a trueborn could. If that happened, Stephen believed that history would repeat itself and she would die by her own hand. *You're assuming Julian's story is true. It is. You know it is.*

Someone began knocking insistently on his door. Startled, he jumped up and checked to see who it was, and recognized Natasha even though she was turned away from the door. *She knows about Amanda, she's going to kill her!* He smoothed his hair, calming himself—*don't be paranoid*—and opened the door. She flew in, throwing herself into his arms, sobbing.

He'd witnessed her anger many times, but he had never seen her like this.

" 'Tasha," he murmured as he stroked her hair. "What's wrong? Come on over to the sofa." He led her away from the door.

"I can't sit there," she managed. "I'll ruin it."

"Why?"

He turned on a table lamp and saw the crimson spray of blood across her shirt and face. "Come into the kitchen. We need to wash your face." Stunned by her tears, he guided her to the sink and used a damp paper towel to gently clean her face. After, they both washed their hands. She had calmed, but it wasn't the right time to leave her alone so he could change out of his stained clothing. The smears offended his senses and he tried not to think about it.

Silent tears still ran down her cheeks. She wiped them away. "Stevie, I don't know what to do. How could I do something like this?"

"What did you do?" He maneuvered her away from his knife block; she could be unpredictable in the best of times. "What happened?"

"You have to swear to keep it a secret."

"Of course I will, 'Tasha. Now tell me. What did you do? It couldn't be all that bad."

Her eyes were huge and for once she looked like a little girl. "Oh, but it is. I killed an employee."

His hands clawed into her shoulders. He barked, "Who?"

"Don't worry, it's not your precious Amanda." She sniffed. "It was Tyler. A crime of passion. I seduced him—Stevie, I was just so pent up I thought I'd explode, I never meant to kill him. I was going to hypnotize him so he'd forget it all. He was already half-hypnotized. I gave him a drop of elixir because, well, I wanted to fuck for hours. I needed it."

"I guess you needed more than that." *That could have been me with Amanda.* "Where is he?" He spoke gently.

"In my apartment."

"Oh, Natasha. Your own place?" He was one to talk; he'd done exactly the same thing with Amanda. "Let me get a change of clothes and we'll go take care of things. We have to get him out of your apartment."

"Then what?"

He studied her, his first instinct to go straight to Ori for help. But he couldn't. He had already made a promise to his sister. On top of that, they didn't need to be under Ori's Godfatherly thumb. With the viral influences, it might not be long before he'd be holding his hand out, hoping they'd kiss his ring. Their uncle tended to do a lot of role-playing in normal times, given the opportunity. Stephen told her so.

She nodded. "That's for sure."

"But Ori would approve; we'll do it mob style. We'll dump the body and let the Dantes take the blame." He smiled.

So did she.

Aardvark couldn't stand it anymore. He was still crammed in the wall cubby, and who knew how long he'd been there, but he'd pissed himself twice so far. He'd done so because he couldn't risk leaving his hiding place; the guy was still sitting in the dark doorway. Just sitting there like a statue, and Aardvark was pretty sure he knew why. It was the voice.

Something was happening in here and it emanated from that black doorway. The lights barely illuminated the tunnel now, and the air had grown thicker and colder. He was still grooving on the spooky atmosphere and the voice that kept calling him. That was why the other guy was there too. It had to be.

Aardvark was having trouble keeping the spooky feeling fun. He should be bored out of his gourd by now, but no, everything seemed eerier than ever. Not that he was frightened. No way. And it was good he wasn't bored, because otherwise this gig would be really, really bad. Suddenly he realized he was babbling to himself. *Okay, my brain's getting fucked up. I gotta eat.* Maybe the other guy had something he could dine on. *Time to make nice.* Aardvark, hoping the guy had some beef jerky on him, the kind with all the pepper, stepped out of the hollow. "Hey there," he called softly. "Hey, mister."

The man paid no attention. *Slish slash,* said Aardvark's brain. It was hard to really see much of him down there where the light petered out, but he didn't think the guy even turned his head. "You deaf?" he called louder.

Blade in hand, he started stiffly walking toward the man and the darkness beyond. Every step seemed more difficult, like walking in molasses. Deep inside, a part of him screamed to turn and run and not look back. Any regular guy would do it, but Aardvark knew he was extraordinary. He was fearless. That's what he kept telling himself. "Hey, mister. I'm gonna come right up beside you, okay?"

Come to me.

For an instant, Aardvark thought it was the guy talking, then realized it was the voice, strong

enough now to sound real. It seemed to come
from outside him, not just inside, from all around,
from the walls themselves. He hesitated. "Who's
there? That you, mister?" He moved forward. Nobody was gonna fuck with Aardvark Wicket and
get away with it. "Here I come." He held out his
knife and flicked on his lighter. Piss ran down his
leg, but it only registered as welcome warmth. One
step. Two. Three. He was right behind the guy.
Panning down the flame, he saw stringy hair.
Where it was thin on top, the scalp looked kind
of peely and funny. Aardvark's skin did a spider
walk all over his body.

Taking a deep breath, he poked the guy's head
with his knife. The man fell over like he weighed
nothing. Aardvark bent and used the flame again.
"Holy fucking shit!"

It was a mummy, a fucking mummy. It had regular clothes on, but beneath them was nothing but
skin dried on bones. Its eyes were really fucked-up,
but still there, way down deep in the sockets, as was
part of a nose, that not-quite-bone stuff. The mouth
hung open. The thing looked like it was laughing
at him. Mocking him.

And it was. Whoever had come down here had
set this all up to fuck with him. It was probably that
guy in his head. *No, the guy's not really in your head.
It just sounded that way.* He started to panic, then
caught himself. *Nobody fucks with Aardvark Wicket!*

Come.

"I'm coming, you motherfucker." Hand on the
cold stone wall for guidance, he started down the
stone steps. They seemed to go on forever, and by
the time he reached the bottom he felt like he was
breathing molasses as well as walking in it.

He was still in a tunnel, but it was different. It

smelled different, kind of chalky or something. Nor did it feel so closed in. He used the lighter again, and found himself in an underground mausoleum, one of those places with holes in the wall for bodies, like where they buried monks under churches way back when. He checked a few indentations and each one had a skeleton in it, old as fucking hell. There were even shards of colorless cloth clinging to some, and one had an iron cross inside its broken rib cage. More than one. Monks. Had to be.

Come to me.

Aardvark jumped and dropped the lighter. Scrabbling around in the thick dust—*dead body dandruff*—he finally found it and wiped it clean. When he stood, he called, "Who said that?" but nobody answered. Drawn by the voice, by some pull he didn't understand, he continued his slow journey downward through the tombs.

The Father, self-appointed god to all, stirred in his dark tomb. Recently, he had fed psychically upon a human vampire that came close enough to draw energy from. He'd taken the vampiric and human fluids for his own, a process that was not even known to his would-be sorcerer of a son. These fluids nourished his body, bringing it closer to resurrection. It was not yet enough; he still needed more human blood to complete the process of regeneration.

And a human was very near now. It was either brave or stupid; few of their kind would heed the call and come so close. Keliu had sealed the tomb well with his magic. But not well enough. He could not stop what was prophesied.

The Father continued to send out his psychic call.

Others, vampires and humans both, were beginning to feel it; he sensed their energies. He cast about for the whore, Talai, but could not locate her. That was curious.

42

The boardwalk on a Saturday night in spring seemed like a living ghost town. The pea-soup fog hovered far out to sea like a long roll of cotton, but there was still the usual land fog eddying and oozing between the rides and buildings. You couldn't quite see the ocean because of it, but you could hear the breakers crashing onto the sand of the broad beach, and you could smell that saltwater tang, especially when the breeze picked it up and sprayed the cool brine mist across your face.

Amanda licked salt from her lips. She watched white ghosts swirl and twist among the arms of a brightly lit Octopus. Not all of the rides were open, and some of the tacky little wooden buildings remained boarded up, dark and spooky in the middle of all the life around them. Voices, screams and laughter, overrode the distant carousel's calliope (Daisy, Daisy, give me your answer true; she thought she would hum the tune for hours after), and above the sounds and the saltwater and the blaze of lights, she caught the scents of pink cotton candy, popcorn, and cinnamon-drenched churros.

The wooden roller coaster, a vintage Wild Mouse, roared and screamed invisibly at the far end of the park, near the old pier. She'd already heard the locals' favorite story about how, back in '54, or maybe '48 (hey, and again in '65, right?), the cars flew off a high curve of rail and landed in the ocean. No one survived, but the riders' ghosts wandered among the rides. Sometimes you could spot one in particular, a little girl dressed in yellow who'd died of a broken neck. She looked real, and when people stopped to ask if she was lost, they would suddenly realize that her head tilted at an impossible angle and blood drenched the front of her pinafore. (Amanda's dad had told her the same story about the Cyclone at the old Pike in Long Beach, only there it was a woman in white instead of a girl in yellow.)

She realized she was smiling as she strolled with Carol Anne along the cracked midway. She was so glad she had come; it felt exhilarating to be out in the night, and she decided right then to talk Carol Anne into riding the coaster.

"That rotten Tyler," grumped Carol Anne. "He never even bothered to tell me if he'd come with us or not."

"Definitely rude," she agreed. "He just sort of disappeared. Maybe something came up."

"I guess. That prick! I'm never going to speak to him again."

Amanda laughed. "You work with him. You have to speak to him."

"Well, I don't have to like it." Her lower lip stuck out.

"Give him a chance to explain," Amanda said, thinking of Stephen. *Take your own advice.* "Just one chance."

"Well, maybe. Let's get our palms read." She pointed at a fortune-teller's booth.

"Oh, come on. That's such a crock. And it's ten bucks. I don't want to spend that much on one thing!"

Carol Anne took her hand and dragged her toward the purple shack. "My treat. My daddy sends me a hundred dollars a week. He says it's fun money."

"That's some daddy you've got there."

Carol Anne dimpled up. "He's a honcho at an international financial company and he was never home, so I got lots of presents."

"You still do." Amanda felt sorry for her. Her own father didn't buy her lots of presents, but he gave her plenty of attention. That was better. But a hundred dollars a week to throw away. *I know me. I'd just save it.* That decided her. For once, she'd be frivolous, even if it wasn't with her own money. "Okay. Palm reading it is. But then you go on the roller coaster with me."

"I scream," she warned.

"Just so you don't throw up." They walked under the fold-out awning and through a doorway draped with red-and-white bunting. In the middle of the purple-and-gold-draped room was a round table where a 250-pound woman dressed in flowing—what else?—purple awaited them.

"What can I do for you young ladies tonight?" she asked. "A palm reading, the crystal ball, or—"

"We want our palms read." Carol Anne was bouncing on the balls of her feet. Amanda felt seasick.

"You want to know about your true loves, I'll bet."

"Wow. You *are* a mind reader," Carol Anne gushed. Amanda tried not to roll her eyes.

"Well, sit down."

Amanda went first, fighting embarrassment all the way. A handsome man awaited her, they would have four children (she wanted one, tops), and live well because she was going to become a famous Hollywood screenwriter. She was also informed that she'd had an unhappy childhood (not), a dog (it was a cat), and loved to read romance novels. (She wouldn't be caught dead with one.) It was nice to hear that she'd have a very long life, though.

Carol Anne's turn came at last. She sat down and held out her hand. The woman examined it a long time before looking up. "You have had a happy life."

"Exactly."

"You were a cheerleader."

"Wow! How could you tell?"

How couldn't she tell, Amanda wondered.

"I see that your favorite color is pink."

Gee. She has to be psychic. The pink sweater and pants couldn't give it away.

"What about my true love?"

The woman actually looked troubled. "I can't see him clearly."

"Why not?"

"I don't know. There's a veil sometimes. It separates us from the psychic sphere and makes it hard to see."

"I'll have one though, right? A husband?"

The seer smiled and squeezed her hand. "What do you think?"

Carol Anne giggled. "He'll be blond and own lots of houses. He'll give me diamonds for my birthday, and we'll have three kids and five horses."

"Yes." Then the fortune-teller did a strange thing. She took the ten dollars and handed it back.

"I can't get a full reading on you. Please come back later and we'll try again."

"Is anything wrong?"

"No. But be careful, honey. You're a little accident-prone."

"Wow! That's for sure." She thrust the money back at the woman. "You keep it."

The fortune-teller hesitated, then put the money in her bra. "Thank you. Be careful driving home in the fog tonight. Both of you."

"We will," Amanda said, and dragged Carol Anne out of there.

"She wasn't telling me something," the girl said excitedly.

"She just couldn't read you. And she was all wrong about me anyway."

"How do you know if it hasn't happened yet? What do you think she was hiding from me?"

She gabbled on all the way to the roller coaster. While they were standing in line, she suddenly squealed, "Look! They're here! Joey and Tom! Hey, Joey! Tom!" she yelled.

Two guys in jeans and cammie T-shirts loitering at a churro stand nearby looked up. They both had short hair and looked like they'd have no trouble beating up the biggest gay guy around. "Carol Anne," Amanda began. "I don't think—"

"I went to high school with them," she explained. "They're great guys. I dated both of them."

"At once?"

Carol Anne looked at her, then said, "You're funny."

The alleged boyfriends were coming over. Carol Anne waved them on. "You want to go on the roller coaster with us?" she squealed.

"Sure," said one.

"How you doin'?" asked the other one, trying to look cool.

They were gross close up. "I'm fine," Amanda said. "And you?"

The guy just sort of snickered. "I'm Tom. Who are you, besides hot, babe?"

"Amanda."

Carol Anne was already hanging on Joey's arm. "Joey and Tom are in the Air Force. They're stationed up the coast at Fort Charles. They're on leave tonight." She blinked at Joey. "I wish you were wearing your uniform."

"It's in the car," he said, his arm tight around her waist. "I'll go put it on if that's what'll do it for you."

"Really? That's so nice! It's okay, though." She snuggled up. "You smell good."

Amanda shut her eyes. Evidently, Carol Anne got off on stale sweat and beer.

"How about you, babe?" asked Tom. "You like men in uniforms?"

"No. They make me think of Nazis."

"Whoa! You're a wild one." He sidled closer. "You like Nazis too?"

Amanda stepped back and glared at him.

He started blabbing on about being all he could be or being one of the proud and few—something like that, she wasn't really listening. They finally got to the front of the line, and by that time Carol Anne and Joey were doing tongue dances. Amanda knew she should have realized the innocent-looking puffball of a girl was a slut in disguise.

Her last hope, that the boys didn't have tickets, was shot down when they whipped them out at the gate. Carol Anne and Joey got in the front car. As she bent to climb into the car behind them, Tom rubbed against her ass. And when he sat down, he tried to put his arm around her. She put it back in his lap. It didn't faze him. "You'll be hanging on tight when the ride starts. Just try not to leave marks."

Asshole. Stinky asshole. God, his breath. It reminded her of a seedy casino in Las Vegas at about five in the morning.

Ignoring him, she enjoyed the ride, but refrained from whooping it up, not wanting to give Tom any excuse to try to touch her. When it was finally over, the four of them stood in the shadows of the pier. "Amanda? Do you and Tom want to pair off?"

"What?"

"You know. Me and Joey. You and Tom. Joey's going to drive me home."

Skanky little cheerleader slut. Amanda smiled. "You go ahead. I'm meeting someone."

Idiot Carol Anne blurted, "Stephen? He's coming?"

"Who's that?" Tom asked instantly.

"Her boyfriend. He's so great—"

"Shit," Tom said. "Why'd you lead me on, you bitch?"

Amanda smiled, deciding to go with the flow. "See you later." She turned and quickly lost herself in the crowd, wanting to make sure Tom didn't follow her. It was time to go check out Coastal Eddie.

Julian had spent a restless day, his carefully maintained calm disturbed by a barrage of increasingly powerful thoughts from the Father. Fortunately, he was unaffected by the fear spell he'd cast so long ago, but it troubled him that it was spreading, growing strong enough for human vampires in the hotel to sense (and soon, humans, many humans). He had designed the spell not only to repel humans and vampires venturing near the tomb, but as an early warning system that had the ability to spread in response to the Father's imminent resurrection. It was this terror spell that lent the taint of fear to the Father's voice, isolating him even when he raised his otherwise charismatic voice to call the world to him. The good news was that it was working. That was also the bad news. Time grew short.

Julian was pacing when he heard the knock on the door. He hoped it was Jinxy but was not surprised to find the twins instead; he had been counting on their arrival. They were disguised in maid's uniforms and looked on the verge of panic. Again, unsurprising. "Come in, ladies."

They practically fell over one another in their hurry to enter and they started stripping off the uniforms as soon as Julian shut the door. Underneath, they wore yesterday's clothing—shorts and T-shirts. Lucy kicked her discarded clothes in the general direction of the fireplace. "God, I didn't think we'd ever get here."

"We almost got caught," Ivy added. She didn't bother to kick her maid's dress, but left it in a puddle where it dropped and stepped away. "Can we have some blood?"

"May we," Julian said. "And yes, you may." He retrieved two bottles and glasses and came back to find them sitting close together on the sofa. Not sprawled, but sitting up straight. They *were* nervous. He served them before sitting down opposite them in his curule chair. "Where did you spend the day?"

"At Eliot's," Lucy said.

"We went there last night."

"He's not there."

"Yes, I heard from your uncle that your cousin is missing. So is my servant, Jinxy. You haven't seen him, have you?"

"No." Lucy poured a fresh goblet for herself. "But we maybe know where they are."

"There's a tunnel entrance in Eliot's house," blurted Ivy. "It's open."

"You bitch! I was supposed to tell him! I said so!"

"Fuck you."

"No, fuck you."

"You said you were, but I didn't say okay, you stupid twatsickle!"

"Butthole!"

"Barfboobs!"

"Cuntrot—"

"Girls!" Julian roared. "Stop it at once!" He fought the desire to rip out their throats. While he composed himself it struck him that the time of mating was nearly full upon him, his needs more urgent. Perhaps he should administer the last bite to Amanda tonight. His preference was to put a night between the final bites, but she was young and healthy and the proximity would do her no real damage. He would have her before the first rays of light burned across the sky. Arousal replaced rage. *You will die!* came the Father's voice, reminding him of what he must deal with first. He looked at the twins, who sat, quiet as stones, staring at him, glasses on the coffee table, hands folded in their laps.

"Did you enter the tunnel?"

"No," Ivy said politely.

"It was scary," Lucy added. "This creepy feeling—I can feel it here, even—was just pouring out of that hole in the closet. We closed the door to the closet and the bedroom it's in, but it was still awful in the whole house."

"And we had to stay there until dark!" Ivy bleated.

"If it had been a foggy day, maybe we could have run for it," added Lucy.

"It's everywhere now," Ivy said. "We feel it everywhere, even here. But it's strongest at Eliot's."

He decided against telling them he was the creator of the fear since it might cause them to question his motives. Unlikely, considering their mental acumen, but nonetheless possible. He looked at the duo. He didn't need them now that he knew of a passage to the tunnels, but he didn't care to leave them alone in his suite, nor did he wish to leave them running around loose. If they were caught by their family now, they would undoubtedly implicate him. He would just have to take them with him. "Put your uniforms back on, ladies. I want you to meet me at Eliot's."

Ivy looked horrified, and Lucy spoke. "We can't go down there."

"Not in the tunnels." Ivy looked near tears.

"You don't have to. I merely want you to stand guard while I do."

They looked at one another, then at him. "Do we have to?"

"Yes."

Still meek, still frightened by the moment when they first arrived and he raised his trueborn voice to them, they meekly rose and began dressing. When they were done, Julian produced a vial of the elixir; the time was coming for them to lose control. "Put a few drops on your tongues," he told them. "It will fortify you."

Standing in the lobby, keeping an eye on the garden door, Nipper was nervous. So was Snapper. The two security vampires, like the other vampiric employees, had been living on bottled blood on the orders of the Darlings, who feared for the safety of their guests until the virus ran its course. But the bottled blood was running low and the atmosphere all over the hotel was tense and thick. The hotel held its breath, waiting. Waiting for what, Nipper didn't know. "Snap," he said, "I'll be right back. I'm going to check the men's room again."

He walked into the ornate lavatory, passing the grand urinal fountain and the three men relieving themselves. He slowed when as he turned the corner into the long corridor of stalls and watched cautiously for anything that looked suspicious. The farther in he went, the darker it seemed and the higher his hackles rose, though he did not know why. He wanted to turn and leave, but he made himself walk all the way to the end, continually sensing that something was wrong. The air pulsed with a danger that was almost a physical threat. *Don't be a jackass. You're imagining things.* He opened the door to the next-to-the-last stall and nearly leaped backward as waves of fear washed over him, through him.

Taking his elixir vial from his pocket, he placed a drop on his tongue. It was like taking a swig of brandy in his human days. Fortified, he forced himself to walk into the stall and closely examine the interior. The oversized toilet seat tissue and paper towel holder looked slightly crooked, so he pushed on it and it moved oddly. Fighting fear, he craned his neck down to see underneath it, feeling around at the same time. Nothing. He stood on the toilet seat and felt the top, touching something he couldn't see and suddenly, the whole thing, including the large frame it was mounted on, slowly swung

out away from the wall. A moment later, the metal
plate swung away as well, revealing yawning blackness. Shuddering, he forced himself to stick his
head in, and thought he could make out dim light
far in the distance. Then a fresh wave of horror
passed through him, and with it he heard a voice.
Come to me.

43

Waiting for Uncle Ori and Ivor to arrive in her office, Natasha looked at Stephen with renewed respect. He had taken over and fixed things, getting rid of Tyler's body for her without a lecture. He never judged. That was her job. It was a joke between them but it was also a truth. "Thanks again," she said. "I won't forget this. Ever. I owe you one." She sipped blood from a coffee mug.

He did the same. "You're welcome."

"Here they are." She buzzed Ori and Ivor in. They sat down and Ori pulled out a cigar.

"Oh no you don't, Uncle. That stays in your pocket in my office."

Ori tucked it away. "I hear these things can kill you," he said solemnly. Ivor's mouth twitched, but he didn't believe in smiling.

"We have several things to discuss," Natasha said. She was full of blood and felt fairly normal. "First, the twins. They're still missing."

"They know they're in trouble," Stephen said. "They're probably hiding around here somewhere."

"I agree," said Ori. "They'll be on the property."

"Has anybody checked with Eliot?" Natasha asked.

"He's missing," Ivor said. "No one's seen him since last night."

"Nor Jinxy," Ori added.

"Jinxy is Julian's problem. Has anyone been to Eliot's cottage?"

"I'm going," Ivor said. "I meant to check again before our meeting. Things got busy."

"That's okay," Natasha said, proud of her calmness. "It's hard to keep track of things right now."

"All the more reason to do so." Ori took his cigar from his pocket and ran it under his nose despite Natasha's watchful glare. "I want to talk about the Dantes. After what they did to Gabe Leoni, we have to take action." Ori's eyes glittered. "Brutal action."

"Please excuse me, Uncle." Ivor smoothed his cuffs. "As you know, I seem to be the only one of us who isn't in need of extra blood."

"The virus," Ori said. "I hope that delivery truck is on time tonight," Ori said. "That damned virus."

"I think I know what may be causing it," Natasha began.

"We know the answer to that already."

"Yes, Uncle, but hear me out. I think that Julian is in a mating cycle and that is the reason we're reacting. We're picking up on his pheromones or something, you get the drift. I don't think it's a malady that has to run its course. I think it's caused by his being here." Natasha paused. "He probably came here knowing full well that we would react to him. But he doesn't care. All he wants to do is take everything for himself and find the Woman from the myth." She went on about the Treasure tale, feeling foolish, but no one laughed.

"You know," Ori said thoughtfully. "That makes perfect sense. It fits with what he's told us. I'll talk to him. If the hunger and emotions will cease with his leaving here, I will request that he go immediately. And if the Treasure actually is resurrecting, he should know what to do about it. I'll have to be careful about what I say. I can't send him away and ask for help simultaneously."

"Before you do that, Uncle," Ivor said. "I have a theory of my own. It's very obvious once you think of it."

"Tell us," Natasha said.

"The elixir," Ivor said, "may be the cause of your problems. Julian may be lying for his own gain, though I don't know what that gain might be."

"What makes you say that?" Ori said.

"Do you all use your supply almost every night?" They all nodded.

"I don't." Ivor looked at them all. "I prefer to take my meals from bottled sources. I rarely drink from the guests, therefore I have no need to use it to close wounds. When I do drink from them, I wear latex gloves. Therefore, I don't come into physical contact with the potion."

No one spoke a word.

"You make a good point, Ivor. Anything that's too good to be true usually is." Ori settled back in his chair.

"Shit!" Natasha looked around at her family. "Why didn't we think of this before?"

"I should have," said Ivor, "but until the last few days there were no obvious symptoms."

"I've been edgy for months," Stephen said. "But I've noticed a pleasant effect after touching the potion." He hesitated, then added. "A drop on the tongue is distinctly pleasing."

"He's right," Natasha admitted. "I've tried that as well."

"All of us have," said Ori. "But that doesn't prove a thing."

"I have not been edgy," Ivor said. "I sleep the sleep of the dead all day. None of you do."

"I look forward to the buzz the elixir gives me," Ori said.

"It's a drug," Ivor said. "It's as simple as that. Drugs are frequently addictive and they all have side effects." He looked at Ori. "I could very well be wrong, Uncle. Perhaps it is as Julian says and I am immune, but I suggest that all the vampires at the hotel stop using the elixir immediately and see what happens."

"We already ordered them not to drink from the guests, so they should have stopped already."

"You've stopped partaking of the guests as well, Natasha," Ivor said. "Have you put away your bottle?"

"No." She looked from face to face, her eyes coming to rest on Ivor. "We'll collect all the vials and give them to you. Lock them up."

Ivor nodded.

Ori's shoulders slumped a little. "If you're right, then Julian has betrayed me."

Natasha resisted the urge to remind him that had been her theory all along and turned the conversation back to security issues, particularly concerning the blood delivery. A moment later, they were interrupted by Nipper's frantic request to enter.

"What is it?" she asked as he came through the door. More Dante trouble, she expected.

"There's a tunnel opening in the men's room," he said.

Wondering how he knew, she said, "And?"

"And it's open."

"Did you see anyone in there?"

Nipper shook his head. "A person would have to be out of their mind to go inside. Something bad is in there. I think it's starting to contaminate the entire hotel. You've noticed it, haven't you? The atmosphere?"

"Yes," she said, standing up. "What else can go wrong?"

Amanda took her time wandering down the boardwalk in the direction of Coastal Eddie and the carousel. It wasn't crowded, but there were plenty of people to dispel the spookiness of the fog. She was still a little pissed at Carol Anne and her raging hormones, and thoughts of Stephen kept trying to wriggle to the surface, but she stubbornly refused to allow either to interfere with her good time.

She liked being alone, though guys—lots of military boys were around—came sidling up to proposition her every time she stopped moving. *What do you do with a drunken airman?* Hooking up with one wasn't on her list of fun things to do. *Let Carol Anne service her country.* When she rode the double-decker Ferris wheel, the ride guy tried to stick a soldier-type in with her. "He says he's with you," Ride Guy explained. Amanda saltily disagreed and had her ride alone. Near the top, the ground was nearly invisible in the deepening fog. Ghostly orbs of colored lights broke through, but little else.

The Ferris wheel incident had annoyed her most so far tonight. Well, not counting trying to eat the chocolate-coated frozen banana while she walked. Every group (and they were always in groups of at least two) of short-haired, clean-shaven penis mongers she encountered suggested their bananas were tastier. Ignoring them all, she resolutely finished the banana even though she was stuffed and didn't really want all of it.

An unflinching connoisseur of cheap horror rides, she rode into the Tunnel of Terror in a creaky little car, enjoying it until the car rolled into a section called The Vampire's Castle. She actually flinched when she rounded the bend to find the first one leering in her face, fangs dripping with blood. It was tacky and stupid, which she usually loved, but tonight it just made her think of Stephen's bloody Bloody Mary.

Her mood improved after some time well spent at the duck-shooting gallery, where she easily won a cheap stuffed toy that was probably a dog, but maybe a pig. Moving on, she gave it to a toddler. It pleased her to see the little boy's face light up, but it also made her smile because it was pink and plush, and Carol Anne would have killed for it. *Tough titties, Carol Anne. You already chose your pink toys for the night.* She felt disgusted with herself for being so petty, but she enjoyed it anyway. What the hell.

She passed the long cut-off between buildings that led to the modest arena where Plastic Taffy would soon play. The walkway was narrow and dark, oozing fog, but people traversed it anyway. Whoops, giggles, and pot smoke pleasantly assaulted her senses, bringing back college memories, and she considered seeing the band, but nixed it. She was here to check out Coastal Eddie. Picking up her pace as the calliope music became louder, she soon saw the merry-go-round. It was antique, partially restored from the looks of it. As she watched the animals go round, horses, tigers,

a seahorse, the classic cat with his tail high—he
had always been Amanda's first choice—*The Man
on the Flying Trapeze* gave way to *Daisy, Daisy* again
She would never get the song out of her head
now. Not that she really minded. At least it wasn't
It's a Small World After All. Disney's anthem sucked
you in like a hungry monster, devouring your
mind . . . *God, don't even think about it!* She began
humming *Daisy* to protect her from possession by
the evil melody.

After watching the carousel and indulging in a
few childhood memories, she moved on to the big
KNDL van. It was white but covered with brightly
colored slogans and call letters so fluorescent that
you'd probably be able to see them in thick fog.
The side door was open and a striped awning above
a door-wide table covered with a long cloth extended from it. There were piles of KNDL bumper
stickers for the taking, sheets of ads for local busi-
nesses, and smack dab in the middle was Coastal
Eddie himself. As she watched him patter away, she
felt like an idiot standing there as if she were in
awe. *You'll be okay as long as you don't tell him you're
his biggest fan.* A pair of economy-sized teen girls,
their pimples all aglow, giggled at one end of the
table while they plastered bumper stickers to each
others' jackets. Otherwise, no one was around. She
guessed most of his listeners were in line at the
arena already.

Clandestinely, she checked out the deejay. He was
exactly what she had envisioned, which was surprising because she was almost always wrong. Long
loose hair, slender, probably about fifty, judging by
the silver streaking his light brown hair and the
crinkles at his eyes, which were, of course, behind

wire-rimmed glasses. No beard or mustache and definitely not wasted, despite his sleepy deep voice.

He saw her and waved. She tried to smile and managed to nod. *Why did I come here? The guy's a deejay, he'll say anything. He'll know you're a dweeb if you ask about those warnings he's always giving. It's just shtick.* He turned and talked to the techy guy in the van, then turned back and said, "Hi," before she could run off. "Talk to me," he invited. "I'm on a set of songs. *The Doors.* Do you like them?"

"Yes. 'Roadhouse Blues' is one of my all-time favorites." She moved closer, lured by a laid-back but genuine smile. "I love to play it while I'm driving."

"Then I bet you get lots of speeding tickets."

She found herself smiling. "A few."

"Will you sign our stomachs, Eddie?" The chunkies had moved in and the one that spoke proffered a Magic Marker.

"If I use that, you'll have a hard time getting it off."

"We know," said the other chunkette. "That's why we want you to use it."

"Excuse me a minute?"

"Amanda."

"Excuse me a minute, Amanda. Don't go away." He stood and took the marking pen. He signed one tummy, then went to do the other. "Sign mine bigger." The other girl raised her T-shirt higher than necessary, giving him a quick look at a pair of pendulous plump breasts with a couple of black hairs on the nipples. *Gross!* Eddie ignored the goods and did as instructed, capped the pen and handed it back. "You'd better hurry if you want to make the concert."

They looked at him, then at each other. The giggling started again and they twittered away toward the arena. Eddie and Amanda watched them go, then Eddie said, "You don't look like the type who wants anything signed."

She laughed. "Only my paychecks."

"Where do you work?"

"At the Candle Bay Hotel."

His eyes widened and he stood and passed a folding chair over the table to Amanda. "Have a seat."

They sat and he said, "What do you think of the place?" Eddie's eyes were riveted on hers.

"The boardwalk? Oh, you mean the hotel."

He nodded.

"I've only been there about a week," she confessed. "It's a beautiful place."

"It's a place full of secrets."

"I've heard the stories about the monks' tunnels and the hidden treasure."

"Those aren't secrets. The real secrets are much more interesting."

She wondered if he knew the tale Stephen had told her. How could he know? And was he nuts enough to actually believe an old myth like that? She didn't dare ask, lest she give away what Stephen had told her to keep secret. Instead, she said, "What are the real secrets?"

"I don't think you'd believe me."

"I hear your warnings about things lurking in the night and I almost believe those. Try me."

"You should believe them. And you shouldn't be out alone at night."

"My friend ditched me for flyboys." She paused. "Steph—my boss tells me the same thing."

"You started to say Stephen, didn't you? Stephen Darling?"

"You know him?"

"I've met him. He had me removed from the hotel one night when I'd gone in to do some snooping. He found me in the kitchen checking out the freezer."

"For what? Ice cream?"

His mouth smiled, but not his eyes. "Dead bodies."

"I see. Well, you can't blame him for kicking you out."

"No. And he was perfectly polite."

"So tell me a secret."

"I'll tell you a minor one, one that's true of most hotels. The Candle Bay is haunted."

"I know. Cool, huh?"

He grinned for real. "You *know?* You sound like you mean that literally."

"I do." She told him about the ghost that opened and closed her door.

"And you think that's cool? It doesn't scare you?"

"It was great. I hope it happens again."

"In that place, it probably will. Listen, take my advice and curb your enthusiasm a little. I wouldn't say that ordinarily, but things aren't what they seem at the hotel."

She smiled, thinking he was paranoid. "Ghosts aren't anything to be afraid of."

"It might not have been a ghost."

"What then? What could it possibly be that I should worry about?"

"You won't believe me."

"Try me."

"Okay." He looked her square in the eye. "Vampires."

"Vampires?" She couldn't believe her ears, but she felt a chill.

"The place is run by vampires. Stephen is one of them."

She fought the urge to run off. It sounded ludi-
crous, but that Bloody Mary crept into her brain.
"Do you mean they're kinky? You know, they drink
each other's blood, or get their teeth sharpened?"

"No. If any of them are kinky, that has nothing
to do with it. They drink blood, but not each
other's. They drink human blood. And they don't
need to get their teeth sharpened. They come that
way."

"Come on. Ghosts I can buy. They're just tape
loops—"

"Not always. And vampires exist, even if you don't
believe in them."

"Tell me something else." She knew the vampire
stuff was bullshit, but it was an interesting coincidence.

"But you don't believe me," Eddie said with a
Mona Lisa look. "Why would you want to hear
more?"

"I don't believe in making quick judgments."

"Good. Here's something else; there's more to
those treasure tales than monks and pirates."

Excited, not daring to talk, Amanda waited for
him to speak again.

"I've been trying to find out the real myth since
I was ten years old. That's when I really started getting into the paranormal."

"How did you know it existed?"

"Oh, I didn't know. I suspected, maybe just because I liked the idea of a mystery, or maybe because I was picking up on something without
knowing it. A few years later, I met some Chumash
native Americans who told me some very old stories
about the place where the hotel stands now being
cursed by a white god and his minions, who
sounded vampiric in nature. I haunted the hotel

when it was in operation, but found nothing until it was abandoned, prior to the Darlings moving in.

"I liked to explore, you know, looking for the tunnels full of treasure. One night I saw a vampire. It attacked a homeless guy who had crashed for the night in the pool room. It was classic neck-biting like you'd see in the movies." Eddie shook his head. "Have I lost you yet?"

"Go on."

"He left the guy alive but a little droopy. The vampire walked right past me. It was the guy who's at the gatehouse at night."

"Eliot? Tall and dirty?"

"So that's his name. Then you know him?"

"I've met him. He gives me the creeps."

Eddie looked excited. "Do you know all the Darlings?"

"I've met them all. They seem fine. The uncle is kind of eccentric but nice, Natasha is intense. The twin teens are horrors."

"They were teens when the family took up residence. What about Stephen?"

"He's nice."

"You're blushing. How well do you know him?"

"Not well." She started to rise. "I've got to get back before the fog gets worse."

"Wait, please."

Amanda reluctantly sat back down. "What about the story you heard from the Chumash. What does that have to do with them?"

Eddie knew enough to lay off the Stephen questions. "The white god is buried under the ground of the hotel. He and his followers had vampiric qualities. Now there are vampires living there. There's probably nothing to it, but it appears to add up. Maybe it's time for the white god to return." He smiled a little.

Amanda studied him, thinking he didn't seem to take his own stories too seriously, and knowing he had never heard the story as Stephen had told it. Part of her wanted to spill it to him. She refrained. "So when you warn about 'things' lurking in the dark and all that, you mean vampires?"

"For the most part."

She wished she could tell him about the pick-pockets and assaults on hotel grounds, to show him that his vampires weren't vampires but merely lowlife scum. But no. As a deejay, he couldn't be trusted to keep that off the air. "Eddie?"

"Yes?"

"Trust me, they're not vampires."

"Okay. What about the tunnels? Have you heard anything resembling what I've told you?"

She didn't answer for a long time. "Yes. I heard something like that."

"Exactly what?"

"The Chumash myth about the white god being reborn."

"Who told you?"

"It doesn't matter, Eddie. It was the same myth, no doubt from the same source you got your story from. Look," she added. "I've got to get back, but you can come by if you want to talk a little more. I'm at the concierge desk after five o'clock."

"Wish I could. But I don't dare show my face there again, not after getting caught last time. They'll remember me. They know who I am."

"Then why don't they come after you because of what you say on the radio?"

"Have you ever heard me say 'vampire'? No. I like it here, and I like my gig. If I used the v-word,

I would have to get out of town, just in case." He spoke lightly, not wanting to sound too weird. "So, what's the weather like at the hotel?"

"Foggy."

"You know what I mean."

"Okay, I can tell you one thing."

"And that is?"

"It's kind of spooky up there right now. It's just gotten that way in the last couple days and I don't think many people have noticed it, but something feels wrong. It could be my imagination, but I kind of doubt it. I'm pretty good at picking up—I don't know what to call it—feelings."

"The way the atmosphere feels?"

"Sounds stupid."

He shook his head. "Not at all. There's plenty of science to back it up. It's probably physiological. Like animals sensing earthquakes, know what I mean?"

"Yes. Now I have to get back to the hotel of the vampires."

"I know you don't believe me, but be careful anyway," he said, handing her his business card after writing on it. "Your own senses are picking up on a wrongness. Trust them if you don't trust me. Here's my card—I put my home number on it. Please call me when you want to talk more. We can meet in town for coffee."

She took it and slipped it in her jeans pocket. "Okay. It's been, uh, interesting talking with you."

"Ditto. Don't be a stranger. And don't mention to your employers that we met."

She eyed him. *What a paranoid!* "Okay. See you later."

She walked into the night, heading for the parking lot. There were fewer lights and now she was nervous about being alone because of rapists and murderers, not vampires. With a sigh of relief, she found her car and climbed in, locking the doors against what might lurk in the drifting fog. Eddie was entertaining, she thought, but absolutely nuts. She started the engine.

44

Come to me. It was a litany in Aardvark's mind, one that grew stronger as he moved deeper into the catacombs. It had begun to conquer the feeling that wasn't fear, but maybe something like it. The voice, hypnotic, drew him forward.

"Shit!" Startled by his own cry, he scrambled to grab onto a rocky wall to stop himself from falling down an unexpected stairwell. Adrenaline pumped, dissolving the calm of the voice. Breath rasping, he sat on the cool stone step, shivering. He had to find his way back, to get out of here as quickly as he could. He was suffocating, closed in by close walls and old bones, crushed by the countless tons of cemetery dirt above. He clutched his throat, unable to breath. Everything started to spin, he felt queasy and weightless. About to pass out, he had to admit that something had finally scared him.

Come to me.

The voice broke through and pulled him slowly up from impending unconsciousness. It caressed his mind, covering up the fear, if not completely, well enough, a soothing warm blanket to keep him safe.

He stood and started slowly down the stairs. The voice became stronger and the ceiling lower until, when he reached the bottom, there was only a narrow passage just wide enough to walk in. He had to stoop to keep from hitting his head. Panic started to take hold, but the voice, all-encompassing now, soothed him and called him by name. Aardvark continued forward a few more yards and came up against a wall of upright wooden timbers.

You must come to me, Aardvark. Come through the door. The latch is hidden on the right. Touch it and I can help you open it.

"Okay." In a pleasant haze, fear forgotten, Aardvark bathed in the voice as it came from within and without. He ran his fingers up and down the edge of the door twice without luck, but like they said, the third time was the charm. He hit the wooden latch just right and felt it start to release. But something was stopping it. "It's warped," he said.

You must continue. I will aid you.

Aardvark did and all of a sudden the latch pushed up and released as if it had never been stuck.

The seal is broken. Enter.

Aardvark barely pushed the door. It glided inward. He stood on the threshold, sniffing at the faint, intriguingly exotic scents. Mixed among them he recognized a ghost of cinnamon and a hint of myrrh. He knew what myrrh smelled like because he'd tried snorting it once. He was on mushrooms and figured that if it was good enough for the baby Jesus, it was probably something special. He figured wrong, and it put him off the 'shrooms for good.

Come in. Come closer. You have a light source.

The lighter. He'd forgotten all about it. Good thing too, or it'd be used up by now. He took it from his pocket and flicked it on.

Light glinted off colors. He neared one wall and

spotted something red. Nearer, he saw that it was a vase of some sort set on a crude shelf carved into the wall. More were spaced around it, no dust on any of them. There were also some small but beautiful brass boxes and bottles. He reached out to take one. The voice boomed *Come to me.*

Aardvark whirled and saw the big box against the other wall. It was sort of like a coffin and kind of reminded him of an Egyptian mummy holder because the polished wood was painted with symbols that didn't mean anything to him. There were several Egyptian-style eyes decorating the case and golden latches ran the length of it.

Turn them. Release me and I will reward you with riches you cannot imagine.

Unquestioning, Aardvark turned the latches then stood back and waited for the voice to tell him what to do.

Raise the cover.

He felt a surge of excitement as he pocketed his lighter, grasped the wooden lip with both hands and pushed it up. He heard hinges move and smelled the spices more strongly. "Where are you?" he whispered as the lid locked open.

"Here."

A cold bony hand snaked around his neck, pulling him off his feet, right into the coffin. *Slish slash.*

"Julian, a word, please?"

Julian silently cursed Ori as he turned and smiled serenely at him. He had gathered everything he needed to stop the Father from rising and renew the seal on his tomb. The twins were, hopefully, at Eliot's awaiting him, but he didn't trust them not to do something stupid before he arrived. "Yes, what is it, Orion?"

"Business?" Ori asked, looking at the briefcase Julian carried. They stood by the elevators.

Julian led the human vampire a few yards down, to a deserted area. They stopped by a large feathery fern. "Real estate matters for the San Francisco estate. I should have delivered the papers to my lawyer before now. He has to have them first thing in the morning."

"I won't keep you more than a moment, then."

Ori's gaze was stern and steady and flint-cold. He suspected something. "How may I help you?"

"Something is happening, Julian. I think you might have some answers."

"Ask."

Ori hesitated, looking uncomfortable. His gaze wavered then returned. "You must be aware of the change in the atmosphere."

Julian considered. "I've noticed tension among you. I expect it's due to the virus."

"No. It's something else. It's the Treasure, isn't it? The resurrection has begun."

"Your family believes the stories?"

"We didn't. Now we're not so sure. You must know the truth."

"The oldest trueborns said that there had been a trueborn who claimed to be the first ever created. He served as Euloa's king for many years, and then he began to claim he was a god and demanded worship. He was driven from the island. That's all I can tell you. The stories of tunnels and resurrections I've heard from various human vampires for several hundred years. I don't think there's an ounce of truth to it."

"There is. One of our tunnel entrances has been

opened and the sensations emanating from it are poisoning the hotel. When we first came here, the family of course, explored the tunnels. We found the catacombs and none of us were comfortable in them. We explored, and the deeper we went the more dread we felt and we eventually turned back. The dread—the fear—has spread. Guests are sensing it. We had a large number of abrupt checkouts this afternoon and earlier tonight. Now there's too much fog to safely leave, but I expect more checkouts in the morning. The hotel is already half empty. We were nearly full earlier. So it's not just your alleged virus." Ori's stern look returned. "Or your elixir."

He was upset about the Treasure, but it was his deductions concerning the elixir that angered him. But he could only suspect, he couldn't *know*. Julian gave Ori a questioning look. "I'll be happy to further discuss the Treasure stories when I get back from my attorney's. He's staying late."

Ori didn't look quite as sure of himself. "Very well. Please hurry."

"I will."

"You can see well enough in this fog to drive?"

"Yes. My senses are more powerful than yours. I will return soon." So saying, he turned and headed for a side exit that logically would lead to the parking lot. Hopefully Ori wouldn't follow because, by now, it would be impossible to leave the hotel, assuming the Dantes hadn't bungled their hijacking of the Slater Brothers delivery van.

"The truck still hasn't arrived," Ivor told Stephen and Natasha.

"Damn it." Natasha pushed away from her desk

and stood. "The fog. An accident? Maybe the idiot driver turned around?"

"Let's find out." Stephen picked up the phone, punched in Slater's number, and asked about the delivery. He hung up and left his chair. "The van should have been here an hour ago. They haven't heard from the driver."

"Shit," said Natasha. "Shit, shit, shit. He probably rolled in the fog and broke all the bottles." She picked up her glass and slugged down the last swallow. "Damn, I'm thirsty."

"We'll have to check the road," Stephen said. "I'll do it." Amanda still hadn't returned from her trip to the boardwalk and he was worried about her.

It didn't help any when Ivor told him, "I'd better go with you. It might not be an accident. It might be the Dantes."

"Shit," Natasha said again. "They hijacked it."

"They may have," Ivor said. "We don't want to take any chances."

Stephen shook his head, hiding his alarm. The notion had been in the back of his head, but he'd refused to acknowledge it until now. "No sign of them on the property?"

"Not yet. Everyone is on duty. They'll spot them if they come."

"I hope so," Natasha said, pulling a bottle out of her desk drawer. "We have to conserve, but if we don't drink enough . . ."

"There's no winning," Stephen replied, holding out his own glass. "We have to retain control. How's the rest of the vampiric staff doing, Ivor?"

"They're on edge. I've told them to conserve, but not ordered them to refrain from drinking. Except from the guests, of course."

"I hope they obey," Stephen said. "I'd like nothing more than a nice, juicy human right now."

"Come, Stephen," Ivor said. He looked at Natasha. "Perhaps you and Ori can supervise security while we're gone."

"Certainly. Let's go."

The Father cast aside the empty carcass that had completed his regeneration then climbed from his tomb. He could not see in utter darkness, and though his sense of location would easily guide him out, he wanted to look at the room Keliu had imprisoned him in. He found the fire light in the carcass's pocket and quickly figured out how to use it.

The small amount of light it threw was plenty for his catlike eyes. The room was as he remembered, Euloan in nature, though the spice and oil holders were obvious copies Keliu must have created here. His son was never an artisan and the quality was poor. The brass receptacles, however, were finely crafted, though not Euloan but for a very vague resemblance that was no doubt coincidental.

The symbols on the sarcophagus had helped to bind him and were the reason he could not leave it until he drank physically of an actual human. Then leaving was simple.

Satisfied, he moved to the door and met some resistance when he tried to exit. But after a moment, he was through and all bindings were undone. And so, the Father began a brisk walk toward freedom. Soon he passed the drained carcass of the human vampire. He tipped it with the toe of his boot and watched it crumble down the steps, hating the half-breed scum.

He smiled. The tunnels were lit with glass balls

of fire. Though still weak and in need of more blood, he was invincible already to the half-breeds. It wouldn't be long before he regained his kingdom and his godhood.

45

"I can hear Plastic Taffy playing, and they sound good, even through the fog. Speaking of fog, here's a report for all you weather hounds out there." Coastal Eddie paused and Amanda turned the car radio's volume up a notch. "The weather gremlins at the Caledonia weather station say the fog's going to stick around until about noon tomorrow, then it will burn off and we'll see the sun. Low tonight is supposed to be forty-eight degrees. High tomorrow in the low seventies. A special message for the young woman I met tonight. You know who you are, don't you?"

It couldn't be me. Amanda kept her eyes on the road but listened carefully. *It can't be me.*

"In case you don't, you're the one who didn't want me to sign anything."

Oh, shit! It's me!

"Be careful driving in the fog. Remember there are more than ghosts hiding in the mist, and remember to trust your instincts. I want to hear from you again. Tell me your fears and I'll tell you mine."

Amanda approached the hotel turn-off, intrigued and embarrassed at the same time. Was this guy serious? Was he? *Maybe*. She made the turn and slammed on the brakes.

Amanda was lucky to spot Carol Anne hitching at the roadside, instead of running her down in the steadily thickening fog. Fortunately, the girl appeared in a clear spot, almost as if she were in a bubble. Gratefully, she hopped into the car and flopped down in the seat. "Christ, what a night. My hair's just wrecked."

"Put your seat belt on and don't say 'wrecked.'" Amanda turned off the radio, then pulled cautiously back onto the main road, and followed it to the turnoff that would take them to the hotel. Her shoulders ached from the tension, and the narrow road that wound and curled up the hills to the hotel didn't help any. It was no more than a mile or two, but it seemed like hundreds when you couldn't see five feet in front of you. She glanced at Carol Anne. "This isn't going to be any fun."

The girl shrugged, totally trusting in Amanda's ability to drive blind. She should have appreciated the blonde's confidence in her, but felt slightly annoyed instead. She could use a little sympathy. But then, what should she expect of Carol Anne, secret slut? She looked so innocent, with that schoolgirl blond hair and perky pink attire. Even her shoes were pink. Weren't skanks supposed to wear butt-cheek-length skirts? *You should have known she'd go for the military types. You saw her with Tyler.* She probably slept with any guy who smiled at her. Amanda felt a streak of self-righteousness rising, and decided to indulge it even though, on principle, she disapproved of it. "So what were you doing out here? Why were you hitching?"

"Tom and Joey wanted to do a three-way."

"What?" Amanda taunted. "You've never done a three-way?"

Carol Anne emitted a disgusted huff. "Of course I have! Don't be ridiculous. Three and a half times, including once with Joey and Tom. That's why I wouldn't do it again tonight. The other time, I spent so much time on my hands and knees. It was like being a toilet paper spindle, you know, plugged in at both ends? And did either one of them chow down on me? I'll tell you, Amanda, all I got was a sore throat and hemorrhoids. Another time, though, I did it with this guy and girl. It was great. They had this swing—"

"Too much information, Carol Anne." Amanda kept her eyes on the road, hands clenched on the wheel. This was a real white-knuckler. She wished she knew the road better. And that she'd never started this conversation.

"Have you done it with Stephen yet?"

She yanked the wheel left as she felt gravel under the right-hand tires. "No. We're not together. Can you talk about something besides sex?"

"But you spend so much time with him. You've got to do it with him!"

"Carol Anne, let me drive. I can't talk and concentrate."

"You don't have to talk, I will."

"No. Don't speak. I need to hear the tires and feel the road."

"Wow. You sound like a professional."

"Be quiet," Amanda snapped. Amazingly, it worked. Carol Anne pouted a little, then took a compact and lipstick from her purse and got busy.

It took twenty minutes to crawl up the road. "Start watching for the gate," Amanda ordered.

Carol Anne yawned. "Okay. I think it's still a little ways—Christ! What's that? Stop!"

Amanda was already swerving the Honda onto the shoulder, barely missing the big dark mass blocking the road. Breathing hard, she stared into the shifting fog, squinting to see better.

"What is it?" Carol Anne asked in a tiny voice.

"It's a van, a big one like UPS uses. We'd better see if the driver's okay."

"You think?" Carol Anne's voice trembled. "We could just walk past it to the hotel. We're almost there. We could send help."

"We have to check. What if he's bleeding to death? Checking might mean the difference between life and death."

"I hate blood! It makes me faint."

"I'll go first. Stay behind me."

She opened her door, and heard Carol Anne do the same.

Trailing her hand along the cold, dewy metal, Amanda approached the passenger side of the van. The door was closed and locked. She couldn't see in, so she pounded on it. "Is anyone in there?" When she received no reply, she moved across the front, listening carefully for oncoming traffic. It would be so easy to get smashed into right now, but so far so good. Trying to peer into the windshield was useless; it was too high up and all she could see were shadows.

But the driver's door was wide open. Strapped into the seat was a uniformed man, neck broken. His head had fallen over onto his shoulder and his glazed eyes seemed to peer toward the rear of the van. There was a small patch of blood coagulated on his neck. "Oh, shit!" Amanda turned away, trying not to gag. At least Carol Anne hadn't seen him. "Where are you? Carol Anne?"

A gull cried in the distance.

"Answer me. Where are you?" Amanda edged along the side of the truck to the rear. Lying in the dirt was one of Carol Anne's pink sneakers.

She had disappeared into the dark and Amanda hadn't heard a thing.

Suddenly afraid, she returned to the car, turned off the headlights, opened the trunk, and took out a flashlight and her crowbar. Finally, she knew why she always carried it. A girl needed to protect herself.

Fearful of calling for Carol Anne again—whoever got her might still be close by—Amanda started walking. She kept the dim glow of the flashlight trained on the ground and hoped it wouldn't be seen by anyone else through the fog. *This is when people are supposed to pray.* The thought amused her and made her think of Coastal Eddie, then of Stephen's Treasure tale, and she wondered if there was a new god in Candle Bay. *If there is, he'll kill you.* That she knew with utter certainty. *Turn around, walk back to town. Go tell Coastal Eddie.* That was ridiculous, of course. *Go to the hotel and get help.* That was the logical thing to do. Once inside, she'd be safe. She told herself that over and over.

After leaving Ori, Julian realized how much time had passed and veered from his original path to Eliot's cottage. He left his briefcase of sorcery items beneath a live oak—no one would see it nestled into the fog-shrouded trunk—where it would safely await his return, and made a side trip down to the gatehouse, where Nicholas Dante would most likely be waiting. Julian's last-minute phone call had worked and Dante was there as promised, feeding from a swooning girl, the blonde from the lobby. Carol Anne.

"Julian." Nicholas wiped his mouth. "Would you care for some?"

"Thank you." His appetite was tremendous as he took the girl in his arms and drained her in the time it would take a human vampire to take a pint. The blood renewed his strength and resolve. He let the dead girl drop to the floor. "Has the delivery truck been plundered?"

"Yeah. It went off with no hitches. The bottles are currently on their way to San Luis Obispo."

"Good. I will make arrangements to pick up my portion later." He nodded at the corpse. "Where did you find this one?"

"One of the boys grabbed her off the road. I don't know any details. We were in a hurry."

"Was anyone with her? Another young woman?"

"When I see Bleeder, I'll ask."

"Where is he?"

"Up there with the others, surrounding the hotel as you requested in our telephone conversation."

"Excellent." Julian described Amanda. "I don't want her killed. If you find her and she dies, you die as well. Your entire clan will die," he promised. "Bring her to me with subtlety. You can do that, can't you?"

"Yeah. I'll get the word out."

"And don't let your people start killing guests. I don't need a massacre to clean up, and I want the hotel's reputation to remain intact, as if the Darlings never left."

"I warned them, but I'll do it again. We only kill other vampires."

Julian stopped listening. His senses picked up the great change in the atmosphere, and he knew the seals were broken. The Father was reborn.

For the first time in a thousand years, he felt pure fear.

"God, where *is* he?" Ivy moaned.

"He's taking his fucking good time, I'll tell you that," Lucy whispered. The pair, unable to take the horrible dread flowing from the tunnel entrance anymore, stood huddled together just outside the cottage. Lucy took her elixir from her pocket and had a drop before passing it to her sister. "This'll help."

There was a peculiar sensation, like guitar strings tightened around them, wires pulled taut. A peculiar warmth was inside her. Lucy clutched her sister, overwhelmed as the voice came again. *Come to me.* Something had changed; it frightened her, but there was a pleasure within it, an invitation.

"That's weird," Ivy said.

Lucy turned, Ivy with her, to stare at the closed cottage door, a revelation dawning. "Do you think it's . . ."

"The Treasure," Ivy whispered.

"He's coming."

"What should we do?"

"Get the hell out of here, that's what."

"But it doesn't seem so bad now."

Lucy grabbed Ivy's wrist and dragged her away from the cottage. "No. That's a good reason to leave. This is big shit. Let Julian worry about it." She paused. "We can go back to the hotel now.

When we tell them about the Treasure, they won't be mad anymore."

"Natasha will kiss our feet, I bet."

"Maybe. Let's go."

Stephen and Ivor gave up on driving when they arrived outside and saw how thick the fog had become. The gauzy stuff rolling over the ocean would probably soon follow. They started walking cautiously down the road toward the gate. "Ivor," Stephen said very softly. "I couldn't speak in front of Natasha, but I'm concerned about the safety of our concierge, Amanda. You know her?"

"Yes, of course."

"She went to the boardwalk tonight with Carol Anne. She hasn't returned. Would you ask your people to watch for her and protect her as necessary?"

Ivor glanced quizzically at him. "I will."

"I believe Julian is after her," Stephen explained.

"Oh? Why?"

"Because he thinks she's the Woman in the Treasure myth."

"Do you think so as well?"

Yes. "I don't know. Perhaps. Ivor, I care for her like no one else. Natasha must not find out."

"There *is* something compelling about her. If she is the Woman, then perhaps Julian is Keliu. The notion has crossed my mind several times."

"And mine. Keliu. Here to stop the Treasure's resurrection." Stephen stopped walking. "Of course. He believes he is Keliu, just as Uncle Ori thinks he's the Godfather."

"No." Ivor scanned the fog. "Ori plays at being the Godfather. He knows he's not. I think Julian really believes, perhaps with good reason. If the story is true, he probably is Keliu. It makes sense that the trueborn returning in the prophesies would be him. If so, he intends to take Amanda. To change her. She is Talai, at least in his eyes."

"Yes. But why wouldn't he tell us his true identity?" Stephen paused. "That means Keliu is the one to stop."

"Not necessarily. I think he's used the elixir in hopes of destroying our family. He would want the hotel for himself, the land, if he's Keliu. He would want it no matter what his other intentions are."

"True." They began walking, moving slowly, scanning ineffectively in the fog. "It still seems to me that if he's trying to get rid of us, then he is the one we should destroy."

"I doubt that has much to do with it. Good or evil, Keliu would do this. It is what I would do in his situation."

Stephen realized Ivor was right, assuming their theories held any substance.

Halfway down the drive, a vampire jumped out in front of them, baring his fangs. It was a Dante cousin, stake in hand. He grinned. "You're dead, boys," he growled and rushed them. But Ivor stepped forward, surprising both Stephen and the Dante cousin. He yanked the stake from the Dante's hands as he tripped him, and ran it through his heart as he hit the ground. It all happened in the bat of an eye.

"You're good," Stephen said.

"Yes." Ivor, not a hair out of place, withdrew the stake and wiped both it and his hands on the dead Dante's clothing before rising. He turned his head, listening. "There is more activity out here, I think. It's very quiet, but I can feel them."

"More Dantes."

"Yes. And something else." He handed Stephen the stake. "Take this." He reached under his jacket. "I have my own."

As they began walking once more, Stephen noticed a change in the atmosphere.

"He's calling again," Ivor said quietly.

"Yes, he is."

Something felt different about the night now, and as she gingerly found her way to the hotel parkway, Amanda suddenly hallucinated a face hanging in the air before her, a gauntly regal visage similar to Julian's. She blinked and it was gone, replaced by a voice that seemed to be calling her. She ignored it. *Christ! Get it together, girl!* She arrived at the hotel entrance, and paused, listening for any small sounds in the night. There was a scuttling noise in the hedgerow, a mouse-sized rustle. That was all.

She started up the parkway and quickly saw the guardhouse through the mist. Resisting an urge to run to it—*you don't know what's in there*—she instead crept up slowly staying below the window. She peeked in. At first she thought no one was there, and then she saw Carol Anne sprawled on the floor. "Oh, God," she whispered, and let herself in the door. Kneeling, she felt for a pulse, but there was none. *Could it be?* Feeling a little stupid for letting Coastal Eddie plant vampires in her head, she started to reach down to move Carol Anne's long hair from her neck. *What if there are bite marks? I guess then you'll know for sure you've lost your mind.*

Abruptly, powerful hands grabbed her from behind, pulling her up and back as if she weighed nothing.

"Don't be alarmed," Julian murmured. "I just found her a moment ago. We must get you safely to the hotel." He put his arm around her and propelled her out of the building.

Where did you come from? She wanted to ask, but couldn't make her mouth work. She felt paralyzed. She still had the crowbar; should she use it? Her arm didn't want to raise it. She couldn't let go of it anyway; her fingers had turned to stone. Thoughts that seemed to come from a separate Amanda ran through her mind. *You're in shock. Give it a minute. Get it together, you'll be okay.*

Julian guided her up the walkway to a small copse of trees that hyphenated the hedgerow. "Come," he said, his voice eerie and familiar. "We'll walk on the other side of the bushes. We're less likely to be seen."

Meekly, unable to do anything else, she let him take her into the miniature grove. There he stopped, turned her to him, and stared at her with eyes even more intense than Stephen's. *He's trying to hypnotize me.* He reached down and removed the crowbar from her numb grip. It thudded on the ground. She wasn't hypnotized, but she couldn't look away either as he held her against his bony body and stared into her eyes. "You already know that we are meant to be together," he murmured. "You already know who you are. Who I am."

"No," she managed. She raised her voice. "No!"

"You are Talai, my eternal love. And the Father hates you and will kill you if he can. But he'll not have the chance. I promise you that." He broke their gaze, bending down, pushing back her hair, and put his mouth to her neck.

She felt the briefest instant of pain as he sank his fangs into her flesh. Wonderful, warm feelings, orgasmic feelings, suddenly suffused her. She didn't want him to stop. "No!" She yanked herself away as her body sprang back to life and her head cleared. She began kicking. "No!"

Julian gripped her elbows and held her at arm's length. He appeared stunned. It was almost funny when he said, "You would fight me?"

"Let me go!" It came out as a scream.

"Amanda!" Stephen's voice, close by.

"Stephen!"

He crashed through the bushes, into the copse. "Get away from her!"

Amanda fell back as Julian let go. Stephen, holding a stake, lunged at him and knocked him down. Julian's long-fingered hand shot out and gripped Stephen's neck. He squeezed, nails puncturing flesh. Stephen struggled and tried to pull free, rising up like a wolf ready to howl.

Turning his head the little he could, he locked his eyes on hers for a millisecond. Then he opened his mouth and yelled, roared. She saw his fangs emerge. Immediately, with vampiric strength, he yanked Julian's hand away and renewed his own attack. Fury fueled him. Amanda could feel it. And hear it. They fought like beasts, growling and grunting, fangs flashing as they tried to tear into each other.

She just stared, unable to believe her eyes. *Coastal Eddie was right? How could he be right? I'm dreaming. Or in an insane asylum. Vampires?* The stake rolled away from the thrashing pair, and Amanda got to her knees to try to return it to Stephen. Then déjà vu—large hands—gently, this time—pulled her away, to the edge of the trees, and Ivor stalked into the fray, looking like Frankenstein from behind.

Together, the brothers finally got the upper hand, though it was obvious just hanging on to Julian was difficult to do. "You bastard!" Stephen growled. She saw his fangs again. "You son of a bitch!" He grabbed the stake and raised it, but Ivor took it at the top of its arc.

"We need him, Stephen," Ivor said. "Control yourself. And you'll only make him angry with that."

Ivor looked at Amanda. She saw his fangs. *If you're ever going to faint, now's the time.* But she didn't.

"Come with us, and stay close," he said. "It is dangerous tonight."

That didn't sound too promising until Stephen added softly, "It's all right. You'll be fine." He barely looked at her.

He's embarrassed.

"I'm sorry," he said, fangs glinting. "But we have to be this way for now."

"When we are in the vampiric state, we possess much more strength," Ivor explained. "We will not hurt you."

"We'll protect you."

I've heard that one before. But that was okay. She believed it from Stephen. Well, eighty percent believed, and that was good enough. She looked at Stephen, who met her eyes and nodded.

46

This was not going as planned. Julian allowed himself to be led toward the hotel by the Darling brothers for fear of further frightening Amanda. As they approached the hotel, he could hear Dante's people stalking them, but it was unlikely that Stephen and Ivor could pick up such minute sounds.

He had to get away before the Father emerged from the tunnels. He would have to find the tree he'd left his briefcase under when he'd decided to go to the gatehouse, and he would have to get to the cottage—or would he? There was the mysteriously opened passage within the hotel. Would the Father emerge there? It seemed likely.

"Have you locked your tunnel entrance in the men's room?" Julian asked.

"Yes," Ivor said.

"Why?" Stephen's grip tightened on his arm.

"I suggest you double-check it."

"Why?" Stephen squeezed harder.

"You're full of questions."

"You bastard—"

"Stephen." Ivor spoke sternly. "Now is not the time. Julian, why should we recheck the locks?"

"Because it is a portent—and a portal. The Father is coming. If I don't stop him, he'll kill you all. He despises human vampires."

"And you don't?"

"No. Why should I? My love was a human vampire. And will be again."

"You motherfu—"

"But she will leave this world altogether if the Father finds her, the same as you. He hates her. He believes she took me from him."

"That's bullshit," Amanda hissed from Stephen's side.

"Yes, it is. But you know how parents are. They tend to blame interlopers rather than submit to the notion that their children may not agree with them on all things."

"The Treasure—the Father—he's your actual father?" Stephen asked.

"Yes. That gives me the dubious honor of being, in his eyes, the son of God."

"Hail Mary," Stephen muttered.

"He believed she seduced me. In a way, she did, but she couldn't help it. Simply being Talai was enough." He paused, a spark of anger lighting within. "She was the purest creature I had ever known, yet he said she corrupted me."

"Why do you call him 'the Father' instead of 'Father'?" Ivor asked.

"Everyone called him the Father. I stopped calling him Father when he rejected Talai. I rejected him entirely."

"What was his name?" Amanda asked softly.

"Jupiter? Zeus? Peter Pan?" Anger simmered as memories stirred. "I don't know. No one knew. He claimed he had no name because he was the first and no one existed to name him."

"The old virgin-birth routine?" Stephen asked snidely.

"Something like that." Julian waited a beat, then spoke again. "If you value your lives, you'll let me go."

"Don't bullshit us, Julian," Ivor said. "We already killed one of the Dantes tonight. We know you're using them to help destroy our family."

The look on Stephen's face said, *We do?*

"We can negotiate—"

Ululating cries. He heard them an instant before the attack. Two of Dante's vampires leapt at them. The Darlings let go of him and fought back. Julian watched the fierce punching and kicking, the flying stakes, the flashing fangs. It looked like the Darlings were going to win, when a third devil, a gross chunk of a vampire, appeared and lunged at Amanda. Julian moved so fast he appeared to the human eye as a shadow, his hands on the vampire's head, yanking him away from Amanda before he could tear her throat out. Julian held the head and twisted it until he heard the satisfying sound of vertebrae crunching. He let the body drop, and saw that Amanda, as well as the Darling brothers, were staring at him, and the Dantes were all staked at their feet.

"I thought *you* moved fast," Stephen said to his brother.

"I would like to know that trick," Ivor replied.

"Stephen, Ivor," Julian said. "I have shown you what is possible. If you will help me now, I will destroy the rest of the Dantes and leave you in peace as long as I am free to return to check on the wards on the Father's tomb when I please. And when you wish this land no longer, that you will sell it to me. I will pay handsomely. And, Ivor, I will teach you that trick. And others."

"Are you serious?" Stephen asked. "How can we possibly trust you after all the lies you've told?"

Neither brother made a move to restrain him. Both stared hard, trying to see into his spirit, but they could not. "The only thing you can do is trust me. I can give you only my word."

"His word is good," Amanda murmured.

He gazed at her in a sudden haze of love. She remembered something of him then. "Thank you, Talai."

"I don't love you," she said softly. She looked at the Darlings. "His word is good, though." She moved to Stephen's side.

He could not give her up. "Let us speak of these things later. We must act now, before the Father is free. He will attract you with his charisma, then he will kill you all."

"Charisma?" Stephen asked. "It is dread that's in the air."

"My spell. A repellent to keep both vampires and humans away from him. He has nearly overcome it now. He has fed on someone—Jinxy, perhaps Eliot as well—and is walking under the earth. Can you not feel the change here? The air throbs with it. When he steps out of the tunnel and into the world, there will be nothing to stop him from attracting anyone he pleases."

Ivor nodded. Stephen asked, "Can you do that? Cast a charismatic spell?"

He glanced sadly at Amanda, then back at Stephen. "If I could, would she be standing by your side?"

Stephen nodded, and Julian knew that was the perfect thing to say. He'd given his word about not destroying the family, not about giving up Amanda. "What is your answer?"

Stephen and Ivor looked at each other. Then Stephen said, "If Natasha and Ori agree, we will."

"We don't have time."

"We will make our point quickly," Ivor told them. "We operate as a family, never apart."

"Very well." Julian glanced around. "Leave Nicholas and the others—there are only two or three more, I believe—to your people. Let's go."

They moved through the fog in a cluster, hurrying to a rear door. Ivor unlocked it and they walked into the light. A guard appeared, saw who they were, and disappeared again.

"Goddamn it! Wait up, Ivy!"

"What? You hurry up!"

"I fell on something. Oh, gross. It's a body."

"Whose?" Ivy's voice was closer. Finally, her face appeared through the fog. "Oh, it's a vampire," she said. "A Dante goon?"

"What else?" Lucy brushed herself off and checked the guy out. "I've seen him before. Down at the boardwalk, he was hanging out under the pier wagging his wiener at the chickens. God, he even grossed me out! If he wasn't dead already, I'd kill him."

"I wonder who staked him." Ivy looked around nervously. "Something bad's going to happen. I know it. I just know it."

"Suck it up," Lucy ordered. "Something's already happened. Okay?" She took Ivy's hand and they began walking together. "We've found the parkway. We're almost there."

"Hey," Ivy whispered, stopping in her tracks. "Look." She pointed up, at the lower branches of a live oak.

The fog was thinner here, seemingly webbed in the leaves and twigs of the tree like angel hair, and Lucy quickly focused on the figure crouching on a thick branch. It was facing away from them, watching and waiting. "Let's get him."

Fear forgotten, Ivy picked up a stone, a baseball of a rock, and aimed. Licking her lips, she concentrated hard, then let fly. The rock hit the person in the head and he fell to the ground, limp for a moment, then moaning and moving.

"Come on!" Lucy ran forward, kicked the guy onto his back as he attempted to sit up, then giggled. "Ivy! We've got a real prize."

The prize growled something and tried to grab her leg. She kicked him under the chin, rocking his head back.

Ivy joined her. "Wow! It's Christopher Dante." She kicked him in the ribs and grinned. "Natasha is going to love us for this!"

"She sure is."

"Should we tie him up and take him to her?"

"I want to stake him, don't you? If we give him to Natasha, she'll hog him." Dante started to move, so she kicked him again.

"We don't have a stake."

"Climb up the tree and break off a branch, nice and sharp."

Ivy nodded and moved to the trunk. She bent and picked something up. "Look. It's a briefcase!"

Something happened. She didn't know what, but Lucy saw Ivy stop dead in her tracks at the same instant she felt it. At her feet, Christopher Dante was silent.

"Lucy?" whispered Ivy. "Do you feel all warm and nice inside?"

"Uh-huh." The feeling was wonderful. Too wonderful. "Come on, Ivy. Let's get inside the hotel *right now!*"

"What the hell is *she* doing here?" Natasha demanded when she found Ori, her brothers, Julian, and Amanda gathered in the inner office lobby. They had called her out of the men's lavatory, where she'd been attempting to get the tunnel entrance to stay closed. It resisted every effort, as if it had a mind of its own.

Ori opened his office door and they all filed in. Natasha wheeled on Stephen. "I said what the hell is *she* doing here? Is this some kind of joke? And what happened to you?"

"You owe me, Natasha." Stephen, ragged and filthy, spattered with blood, just like his brother, stared grimly at her. "You said so just a little while ago, remember? I'm calling in the favor."

"I remember." *Damn him!* "What does she know?"

"She's the Woman from the myth," Stephen said. "She knows just about everything. And Julian? Tell her who you are."

"I am Keliu."

"And I'm Marie Antoinette." Natasha crossed her arms.

"Shut up and listen," Stephen commanded.

He meant it, so she did.

A few minutes later, the story told, she shook her head. "Okay. I take it you buy the story, Uncle?"

Ori nodded.

"Okay, Julian. What do you want us to do?"

"Do you feel it?" he asked.

"Feel what?" Natasha knew the answer. There was

a peculiarly pleasant sensation bombarding her, and it didn't belong there.

"The Father. He is out of the tunnel. There is no time. I need all of you to help me capture him. I need someone to fetch my briefcase from beneath the big oak. And I need you to remember that the nice feeling you're experiencing is an invitation to die."

"Excuse me," Ori said. "Lucy and Ivy just entered the lobby."

"Let them in," Stephen said.

As soon as the office door opened, the twins rushed in, gasping, almost as dirty as Stephen and Ivor. "We caught Christopher Dante!" Ivy said breathlessly.

"And we found this." Lucy brought the briefcase forth.

Julian scooped it up and held it against his breast. "This is what I need."

"Where's Dante?"

"We left him."

"Dead?"

"No. We couldn't stay out there. We came to tell you. It's too fucking weird outside. And downstairs, it's worse. It's like, I don't know. Like honey, warm honey."

"It's weird up here too," Ivy added.

"He's coming." Julian walked to the door. "Follow me. We'll try to lure him out of the public eye before anything happens."

The Father emerged from the darkness and stepped into a toilet bowl.

* * *

Amanda felt like Alice down the rabbit hole. The family kept her with them when they went downstairs because Julian had told them it was the best thing to do. The Treasure would seek her out wherever they hid her. It was better to protect her.

To Amanda it made no sense and total sense. Part of her, her spirit, she guessed, understood exactly what was going on. The rest of her was baffled but curious. And there was Stephen. He wasn't a freak. *Not a freak, just a vampire. Welcome to the monkey house, Amanda. You've lost your mind for sure.*

The lobby was virtually empty at this time of night, and no one noticed the motley little band as they entered the men's lavatory. Amanda stayed close to Stephen and Ivor. The huge rest room felt really nice, and she wasn't frightened at all.

They walked past the urinal fountain and turned into the toilet area, then faced the long row of stalls. At the end of the row stood a man.

Not just any man, but one who looked like Julian with dark hair. He was just as pale and somewhat more mature, and he radiated love. Dressed in an age-stained white robe, he held his arms out, low to the sides, like a Christ figure. *You don't believe in a christ, so stop feeling like you do.* In spite of herself, she stepped forward.

Stephen pulled her back, and Julian said, "He will kill you if he has the chance. He will make it long and ugly for us to watch." He had his eyes on his father, who seemed to have moved closer without moving. If that made any sense.

"Amanda, stay back here," Julian said. "If you think he might get past us, run."

"And keep running until dawn," Stephen added solemnly. "Get as far away as you can from this place and don't come back."

She nodded, ignoring the dirty look Natasha sent over her shoulder. Stephen gave her a hint of a smile and mouthed the words "I love you." He turned before there was time for her to respond, and despite the strange curdling atmosphere, despite what she'd seen tonight, she . . . *No, don't even think it.*

The Darlings had fought together before, in many times and many places and now they moved as one, each of them knowing instinctively what to do. They had never lost a battle, not even when outnumbered. Their pure intent, unspoken, was always to win. They had taught themselves to *know* they would win, and so they always did. They accepted nothing less. But Stephen felt a twinge of doubt as he stared at the Treasure. This was no ordinary foe.

Now they formed an arrowhead, letting Julian stand point in Ivor's place. Stephen, Natasha and Ivor stood behind him, and the final column was composed of Ori with the twins flanking him.

Stephen watched the Treasure. Julian's father could get into your mind, and make you believe him to be a god. Stephen could feel his influence working in his brain and hoped the twins could stand firm against the powerful creature. The Father made you want to believe in him through the charismatic force he exuded, like a stranger with candy captivating children. Stephen glanced at Natasha and Ivor. Both had their eyes on the Treasure; both looked grim. He wished he could see Ori, Lucy, and Ivy, but he knew enough not to take his eyes off the Treasure.

"My son." The Father spoke in a soft melodious voice.

Julian said nothing.

"You have found your human bitch again."

Anger at the Father's insult to Amanda shot through Stephen. He saw Julian square his shoulders. For now, at least, they were fighting on the same side. Julian spoke in a voice nearly as melodious and powerful as the Treasure's. "You will never change, will you?"

"Nor will you. You still do not address me properly. You can do that at least, after all these centuries. I am your father. Acknowledge it."

"I cannot, for you are nothing to me. Nothing but a bag of hot, foul wind."

Problems with your parents never end. Stephen suddenly saw Julian, the great and ancient trueborn, as a rebellious teenager, not unlike the twins. It softened his view of him; it made him more human. He almost smiled at the thought.

"My son, if you want, you may rule the world with me. You know what you have to do. Just one little thing."

"I will not kill her!" Julian raged. "And I will not let you touch her!"

For the first time, the Treasure cast his gaze beyond Julian. "Who are these creatures?"

He said "creatures" with such scorn that Stephen knew beyond doubt that the Treasure was the true evil. As much as he hated Julian, he was not the real enemy.

"Why do you hate us?" Natasha's voice was strong.

"You will address me as 'Father.' "

"Why? Your own son won't do it."

"I don't blame him." That was Ivor.

Stephen echoed the words, as did the twins and Ori. And from far in the rear, came Amanda's disdainful voice. "Why don't you just give him a break? Times change, you old bastard."

Good for you!

The Treasure seemed to physically grow larger as he stepped forward, fury in his eyes. "Bitch. Whore who broke up a family, who ruined my son. For speaking to me in such a manner, you will suffer greatly before your death."

The air around Julian—and the Treasure—spiked with their anger. Julian spoke, his voice stiff with finality. "You will never understand."

Of course not. You're his father. Stephen knew he was enjoying this too much.

"I understand completely. You are under *her* spell."

"The spell of a simple human?" Julian roared. "I'm surprised you would say such a thing. Humans have powers that human vampires do not?"

"Humans are useful and some can tap into the elemental power of this world. But human vampires are half-breeds, atrocities neither human nor trueborn. I taught you this as a child. *She* has corrupted you." He took a sudden stride toward Julian, whose hand shot up, giving the signal to act.

Stephen's blood boiled over with lust for the kill. He lunged, along with the rest of his family.

They piled on the Treasure, burying him with their weight as they ripped into his veins and arteries and began draining him of what blood he had already collected. It was difficult—if the Treasure were any stronger, it would be impossible—but gradually, his strength ebbed enough for Julian to apply physical restraints. After he did, Amanda approached and watched the Darlings as the trueborn performed a binding spell that would paralyze the Treasure long enough to get him back into his tomb.

Julian stood over the Treasure, his hair wild as a lion's mane. His nostrils flared and his eyes flashed, but there was a serenity about him as well. "Will one of you help me take him back to the tomb?"

Stephen opened his mouth to volunteer, but Ivor stepped forward and said, "I will do it."

"I'll get flashlights," Lucy said, and trotted out of the corridor. When she returned and handed them over Julian thanked her and said, "I will return eventually. This will take some time."

Ivor climbed into the tunnel and dragged Julian's father down after him. He stuck his head back into the lavatory. "And I will be back in a few hours," he promised. "As soon as I can." He glanced at Julian. "Unless you need me for your ritual."

"No. It is too dangerous for a human vampire. I must do the sorcery alone, as I did the first time."

"We will be watching for you." Natasha folded her arms over her chest.

"Good luck, Julian." Amanda pushed forward, politely ignoring Natasha. "I admire you."

Sadness flashed in Julian's eyes. "Talai," he murmured. And then he was gone.

47

Two nights had passed since Julian had taken the Treasure into the tunnels and he had yet to reappear. Amanda wondered if he ever would. She hoped he would be successful in his quest, and leave her alone forever. *It's too much to hope for.* She looked up at Stephen, standing next to her on the balcony.

He smiled. "It's a beautiful night."

Amanda gazed at the sky. There was little fog. Stars twinkled between wisps of mist. "Yes, it is."

"I didn't think you would accept my invitation." Stephen spoke lightly, but she knew there was much more to what he said. It wasn't just an invitation to his suite that he spoke of.

"I've done a lot of thinking, Stephen."

"About what?"

"You. Us. What you are, what I am."

"And?" He turned to her, one hand resting lightly on the small of her back.

She tingled from the touch. Amanda took his hand, and raised her face to brush his lips with hers. "I want you to kiss me."

His arms encircled her, she basked in his scent, his taste. Their lips came together.

Bliss.

48

"The stars and moon are brilliant tonight, my friends. They stand out in the darkness, beacons to lead you to safety. The fog is expected to return tomorrow night, dear listeners, so follow the beacons while you can. And if you're listening, my special friend, give me a call. I need to know that you made it through Saturday night without meeting the lurking monsters.

"It's nearing the hour of dawn now, and soon the first rays of sunlight will fade away the moon and stars. Take another look at the darkness, listeners, then enjoy the warmth of the sun and coming of the new day . . . That is, if you can.

"This is KNDL radio and I'm Coastal Eddie, signing off for now. But remember, I'll be back tonight when the clock strikes midnight. In the meanwhile, remember: Stay safe. Close your windows and lock your doors. And don't go out at night. In the fog."

ABOUT THE AUTHOR

Tamara enjoys hearing from her readers. Write to her c/o Kensington Publishing, and if you want a reply, make sure to include a self-addressed, stamped envelope. You may also write to her at tamarathorne@gmail.com.

More Mischief, Murder, & Mayhem in These
Kensington Mysteries

Get Hooked on the
Mysteries of
Carola Dunn

Romantic Suspense from
Lisa Jackson

Thrilling Suspense from
Beverly Barton

Available Wherever Books Are Sold!

Visit our website at **www.kensingtonbooks.com**

Nail-Biting Romantic Suspense
from Your Favorite Authors

Thrilling Suspense From
Wendy Corsi Staub

__All the Way Home	0-7860-1092-4	$6.99US/$8.99CAN
__The Last to Know	0-7860-1196-3	$6.99US/$8.99CAN
__Fade to Black	0-7860-1488-1	$6.99US/$9.99CAN
__In the Blink of an Eye	0-7860-1423-7	$6.99US/$9.99CAN
__She Loves Me Not	0-7860-1768-6	$4.99US/$6.99CAN
__Dearly Beloved	0-7860-1489-X	$6.99US/$9.99CAN
__Kiss Her Goodbye	0-7860-1641-8	$6.99US/$9.99CAN
__Lullaby and Goodnight	0-7860-1642-6	$6.99US/$9.99CAN
__The Final Victim	0-8217-7971-0	$6.99US/$9.99CAN

Available Wherever Books Are Sold!

Visit our website at **www.kensingtonbooks.com**